BOUDICCA

MORE BY P. C. CAST

THE HOUSE OF NIGHT SERIES

Marked

Betrayed

Chosen

Untamed

Hunted

Tempted

Burned

Awakened

Dragon's Oath

Destined

Lenobia's Vow

Hidden

Neferet's Curse

Revealed

Kalona's Fall

Redeemed

THE SISTERS OF SALEM SERIES

Sisters of Salem

Omens Bite

THE HOUSE OF NIGHT OTHER WORLD

Loved

Lost

Forgotten

Found

THE TALES OF A NEW WORLD SERIES

Moon Chosen

Sun Warrior

Wind Rider

THE PARTHOLON SERIES

Divine Beginning

Divine by Mistake

Divine by Choice

Divine by Blood

Elphame's Choice

Brighid's Quest

THE GODDESS SUMMONING SERIES

Goddess of the Sea

Goddess of Spring

Goddess of Light

Goddess of the Rose

Goddess of Love

Warrior Rising

THE MYSTERIA SERIES

Mysteria

Mysteria Lane

Mysteria Nights

BOUDICCA

A NOVEL

P. C. CAST

WM

WILLIAM MORROW
An Imprint of HarperCollins*Publishers*

BOUDICCA. Copyright © 2025 by Cast LLC. All rights reserved. Printed in the United States of America. No part of this book may be used or reproduced in any manner whatsoever without written permission except in the case of brief quotations embodied in critical articles and reviews. For information, address HarperCollins Publishers, 195 Broadway, New York, NY 10007.

HarperCollins books may be purchased for educational, business, or sales promotional use. For information, please email the Special Markets Department at SPsales@harpercollins.com.

FIRST EDITION

Designed by Elina Cohen
Map courtesy of Alexis Seabrook
Title art courtesy of Shutterstock/ Marek Hlavac
Part art courtesy of Shutterstock/ Eroshka

Library of Congress Cataloging-in-Publication Data has been applied for.

ISBN 978-0-06-329497-4 (hardcover edition)
ISBN 978-0-06-343039-6 (international edition)

24 25 26 27 28 LBC 5 4 3 2 1

To my agent, Rebecca Scherer,
for believing in *Boudicca* as much as you believe in me.

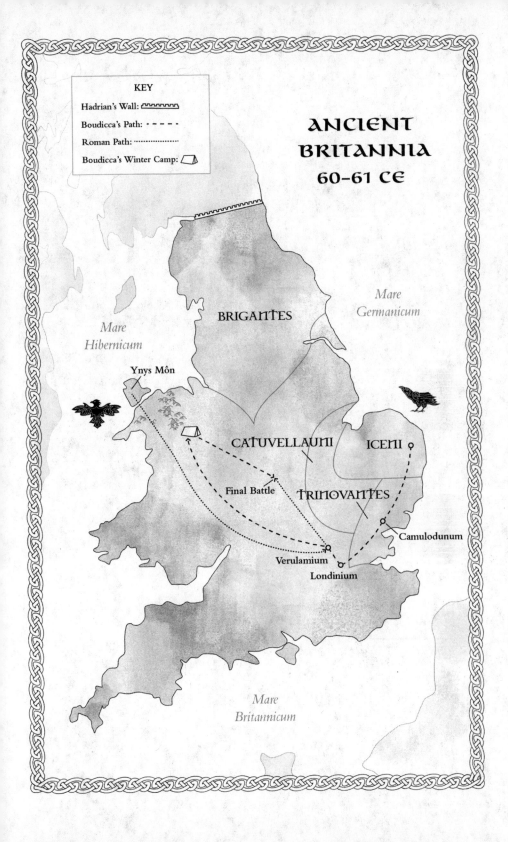

KEY

Hadrian's Wall:
Boudicca's Path: - - - - -
Roman Path: ··········
Boudicca's Winter Camp:

ANCIENT BRITANNIA 60–61 CE

Mare
Germanicum

Mare
Hibernicum

BRIGANTES

Ynys Môn

CATUVELLAUNI

ICENI

Final Battle

TRINOVANTES

Verulamium

Camulodunum

Londinium

Mare
Britannicum

PART I

SPRING 60 CE, ANCIENT BRITANNIA

CHAPTER 1

For the rest of my life, when fog swirled in with the dawn, my stomach would tighten, and the small hairs on my forearms would lift. I would remember that day and what came with the fog: the scent of fertile earth and baking bread and danger—a danger so thick and cloying that my palm called my blade and my spirit cried out to my goddess for courage and strength and cunning.

Boudicca! Awake! Come to the forest!

I jolted from a deep sleep, sat up, and flung the pelt blanket from my body. With one hand I brushed back heavy hair from my face, while the other searched the bed beside me.

My husband wasn't there. Instead of warming my bed, Prasutagus, chief of the Iceni tribe, rested entombed in the Chief's Barrow.

Do not be foolish, I told myself. *Prasutagus has been dead for three full cycles of the moon. You are Queen Boudicca, and Iceni queens do not grasp at ghosts.*

I shook myself, chasing away the last of the sleep from my mind, which sharpened instantly. From the first moment I drew conscious breath that morning I had felt a sense of anticipation. I knew *something* beckoned. I'd dreamed of it—of the ominous thing—but when I woke, the dream had dissipated like morning dew. *Is it the arrival of the Druids that calls me awake? Derwyn has not visited in months.* I rubbed the sleep from my eyes and tried to understand the compulsion that had awakened me.

On most mornings I would rise from my bed when the sun lifted above the verdant forest that surrounded my tribe's sturdy huts, lodges, and animal pens. The many fields were lush with crops growing toward harvest. As queen, I had the luxury of waking slowly. My personal servant, Phaedra—who had been with me since that happy day fifteen years before when I married Prasutagus—would help me dress and plait my hair while she whispered the latest gossip.

Not that day.

That day the compulsion that woke me came with a premonition so urgent that it usurped the dawn and the lazy light it brought.

Phaedra, who had taken to sleeping on a thick pallet near the foot of my bed since my husband's death, yawned and groggily started to rise.

"Sleep, Phaedra." I spoke softly, careful not to disturb my two young daughters, who slumbered behind the woven-bough walls that separated their bedroom chamber and mine. "I do not need you this morning." With a sigh my servant curled up on her side again and was instantly asleep.

As the words escaped my mouth, I wondered at them. I could have used Phaedra's help to tame the wildness of the copper mane that fell past my waist—its unruliness was in constant contrast to my calm, well-organized demeanor.

But the need to go to the forest was too great for niceties like combing through my hair. I quickly plaited the thick length into a single braid that hung to my waist and pulled on the simple brown overtunic I wore when my women and I hunted truffles in the woods that surrounded Tasceni, Tribe Iceni's largest settlement and home to their royal family. I shook out a moss-colored cloak and fastened it around my shoulders, clasping it in place with my favorite brooch— a mighty boar whose silver tusks were decorated with elaborate knot work. The only two outward signs that I was not just an ordinary Iceni tribeswoman were the brooch and the delicate gold torque that encircled my neck like a cuff.

From an oak chest, I took a small dagger that fit perfectly into the leather sheath attached to my belt and the large leather satchel I preferred for foraging, and added a water bladder to it before I hastily slung it over my shoulder. Then, on swift but silent cat's feet, I parted the heavy fur drape that served as the door to my opulent bedchamber and headed for the center of the lodge and its ever-burning hearthfire, where I hoped to find some bread and cheese to take with me.

"I wondered if you would awaken with me."

Arianell's voice surprised me. I spun around to see my mother, sitting beside the central hearthfire of the roomy lodge as she sipped her morning tea from a wooden mug. Behind her, perched on a small stool, her ancient servant, Dafina, slowly combed through Arianell's long silver hair.

"You startled me," I said as I made my way to my mother. I bent and kissed her cheek affectionately. "Mother, why are you awake so early?"

"A question I have been asking your mother since she woke me with a shrill scream some time ago." Dafina's voice cracked with age, but her hands did not waver in their work and her vision was still as sharp as her mind—though the servant was older than Arianell by at least a decade.

"And as I told Dafina, that interesting question must wait for my daughter to answer," said Arianell.

Dafina made a show of looking behind me. "Phaedra is not fluttering about you like a busy little wren. Are you as somber as this one today?" Dafina asked.

"Old woman, get our queen a mug of herbs to break her fast. I should question her, not you!" snapped Arianell.

I hid my smile. Dafina was more like a grandmother than a servant, and I had long enjoyed her prickly personality almost as much as I appreciated the old woman's expertise with braids and knot work.

Mumbling to herself, ancient Dafina put down the wide-toothed wooden comb and hobbled to the cauldron that simmered over the hearthfire. As she ladled hot water into another wood mug, I could feel Arianell studying me. My mother's gaze went to my haphazard braid and she sucked her teeth contemplatively before saying, "My daughter, my queen, it is unlike you to appear so disheveled, no matter the hour." She gestured at the satchel slung over my back. "What is it you seek in the first light of the day?"

Dafina handed me a mug that steamed with aromatic herbs. She bowed quickly before she returned to combing through Arianell's hair.

"Here, Boudicca." Mother pointed to a comfortable woven rush chair much like her own. "Sit beside me. Let us talk."

I blew across the tea before I sipped it but was too restless to sit. Instead I stood beside my mother and stared into the hearthfire, though what I really wanted to do was to rush from the lodge out into the predawn forest.

"The Druids will be here tomorrow and I remember how much Derwyn enjoys the taste of truffles. I thought to forage for them. It has been months since the leader of the Druids visited us and I want him to feel most welcome."

Arianell nodded slowly. Unlike mine, my mother's hair was always tamed—and even this early hour it flowed neatly down her back as Dafina's long strokes made it crackle and glisten in the wan firelight. "Truffles would please Derwyn, but the predawn light makes digging for truffles"—she paused and smiled knowingly at me—"impossible."

I blew out a long, frustrated breath. "I woke thinking of the forest and the imminent arrival of the Druids, which brought to mind truffles. I decided I must go in search of them for him."

"We have women aplenty who would be honored to forage for Derwyn," croaked Dafina.

"Yes, I know, and yet I was compelled to go into the forest. Today. Now."

Arianell's expression shifted instantly. She lifted her hand and Dafina stopped combing her hair. My mother leaned forward, staring through the predawn gloom of the lodge. "A compulsion to enter the forest awakened you?"

I recognized the sharpness in my mother's voice and my stomach tightened. "It did. Actually, all I remember of my dream is how it ended. That I was commanded to go into the forest."

"Perhaps . . . perhaps . . ." The wan light of the hearthfire reflected in Arianell's distinctive sky-colored eyes so that they seemed bottomless, as if they contained secrets from many lifetimes. Holding my gaze, she raised her voice only a little. "Dafina, bring me the hart pendant. The one with the emerald eye."

The old servant stood stiffly and then disappeared behind the heavy pelt curtain that was the entrance to Arianell's bedchamber. She returned in moments to give the piece of jewelry to her mistress.

"Come, bend down to me, daughter."

I approached my mother, who lifted a delicate chain. From it dangled a hart that had been exquisitely crafted from silver swirls and interlocking knots. The stag's head was in profile, so only one eye showed—and that eye was a perfect shining emerald, the exact color of my own eyes.

Arianell spoke formally. "I give this to you freely, my daughter, my queen, and my heart, to keep as your own, or to leave as an offering in Annwn, the Otherworld."

Wordless, I bowed my head. Mother slipped the silver chain on me so that it slid, cold and heavy, just beneath the torque that was a symbol of my rank as queen of the Iceni. The beautiful hart fell between my breasts, where the single emerald played with the firelight.

I touched it gently, reverently. "But Father gave it to you. I could not leave it as an offering."

"Its worth is exactly why it makes the perfect offering. Though as I said, that is your choice to make, should you be fortunate enough to step beyond the veil that parts the worlds."

My fingers stroked the smooth pendant and I blew out a long breath. "I am not sure I want to visit Annwn. What if it's like the legends and I return to find the world has gone on without me and everyone beloved by me has left this life?"

Arianell's smile turned into a savage baring of her white teeth. "The queen of the Iceni should not fear her destiny."

Mother's words sent a shiver down my spine as foreboding as real as the silver chain around my neck lifted the small, fair hairs on my forearms. "I will always do my best to make my people proud."

Arianell's expression softened. "I know that as surely as Prasutagus did when he named you his heir. The Iceni and the Druids knew that when they chose their queen three months ago. Though I do wish your father could have lived to see you wear the torque of a queen."

My fingers found the precious pendant again. "Mother, if you believe I should take an offering with me, let me choose something else—something valuable but not as precious as this."

Arianell patted my hand. "There are other gifts your father gave me that I treasure more than that pendant. You, my dearest, are the greatest of those gifts. He also gave us the gift of choosing your husband wisely. I freely admit I disagreed with him at first. Prasutagus was a mighty chief, but he seemed far too old for you."

I'd heard this tale many times and still it made me smile. "Because I was eighteen, and Prasutagus was already showing gray in his beard."

"Indeed." Arianell nodded. "But then I saw the way the Iceni chief looked at you—as if you held his world in your green eyes. That warmed my heart, but when Prasutagus made it clear that he valued your mind and respected your opinions—*that* was when I knew you and he would be well matched."

My stomach tightened again, this time in grief, and my voice was barely above a whisper. "He loved me and I him."

Arianell nodded. "Prasutagus won my motherly love when he sent for me after your father was entombed."

"He knew I would need you for the birth of our first child. I was so heavy with Enfys that I could not even travel to see Father's pyre lit."

Arianell nodded. "Indeed, I traveled here for the birthing of my beloved first grandchild and never left." My mother paused and her expression darkened. "I still believe your father had a premonition about what would befall his beloved Brigantes. That woman Cartimandua. That horrible woman who betrayed the tribe to ally with the Romans . . ." Her words faded and her shoulders bowed with grief.

This time I patted my mother's hand reassuringly. "Do not let your thoughts dwell on Cartimandua."

"That bitch. May her teats dry and her womb fail," Dafina muttered.

The ancient servant's words caused Arianell to share a smile with me, and I hastily returned the conversation to our topic. "Prasutagus cherished me from the moment we met. He saw how very much his wife needed you. That is why he made a place of honor for you here."

"Dearest, you were doing well without me."

"Ha! You granddaughters would be lost without their precious Nain," cackled Dafina.

"Hush, you! Our queen is an excellent mother!"

"Never said she wasn't . . . ," Dafina mumbled as she continued brushing her mistress's hair.

"My granddaughters are a great joy to me—as are the Iceni." Arianell's expression changed. She stared into the fire and spoke slowly, as if weighing each word carefully. "I did not believe I would find such joy and purpose after your father's death, but I have had a second life here with the Iceni. I want you to know that, my daughter, my queen. I have been more than content these many years."

The hearthfire seemed to stop radiating heat, and I shivered. "You are the beloved matriarch of the Iceni. How many Iceni babes have you helped to bring into the world?"

Still staring into the fire, Arianell said, "Many, with the aid of my patron goddess, Brigantia."

"Yes," I said firmly. "And with the goddess's aid you will bring many more Iceni into the world."

"Indeed," Arianell said softly. "Should it be the goddess's will."

"Should it be the goddess's will," Dafina echoed eerily.

I shivered again. "Mother, you have not told me why you woke so early."

"I was compelled awake by Brigantia. The goddess whispered that I must give counsel to Victory."

The breath rushed from me in a gasp. Father had often told the story about how he had known the moment he'd looked into his firstborn and only child's eyes that he must name me after the ancient word *buaidh*, which meant "victory." My voice broke as I asked, "A-and what counsel would you give me, Mother?"

"I have already given it you in the form of a precious offering, but in addition I simply remind you of something you already know. Listen to the forest."

"Yes, Mother. I will remember."

Arianell's smile lit the shadowy room as she turned her gaze from the fire to look fully at me. "You should be on your way. It is never wise to keep destiny waiting." Arianell turned and spoke over her shoulder. "Dafina, make ready a measure of the bannock cake and some of that excellent cheese the queen likes so much." Dafina quickly wrapped a generous portion of the still-warm wheat, barley, oat, and hazelnut cake, along with a hunk of goat cheese, in a skin and gave it to me with a fond smile and another bow.

Arianell stood. Though she was not as stiff and hobbling as her servant, I noted that Mother was slowing. She straightened with a grimace and rubbed her left hip. Arianell was not petite, but I stood more than a head taller. The wise woman I loved so well reached up and cupped my cheek gently with her hand.

"It has been difficult for you these months since Prasutagus's death."

"It was too sudden. Too soon." My shoulders sagged with sadness. His last day rushed back to me as it had over and over. I watched my virile husband, seemingly so strong—almost godlike in my eyes— stand abruptly from his place of honor at the Imbolc feast just three months before. His ruddy face abruptly drained of color. He clutched his left arm, spoke my name, and, with an expression of wide-eyed surprise, the chief of the Iceni fell and did not rise again.

Arianell patted my cheek gently. "Time eases grief. And, remember, none of us are ever truly gone. We are all connected, and will be eternally." She kissed me softly—first on my forehead, then each cheek, and finally my lips. "May the joy of the day be with you, my precious daughter, my precious queen."

My response was automatic. "And may the blessings of the earth be on you, beloved Mother."

"Now go! You are like a colt who needs to run."

With a sigh of relief I rushed from the lodge and stepped out into a world turned gray.

CHAPTER II

The Druids called it the breath of the dragon. When fog rolled in with the dawn, thick and swirling with a life of its own, it made the mundane seem mysterious and the extraordinary seem mundane. That morning it blanketed the village.

The two Queen's Guards snapped to attention when I joined them on the wide, raised wooden entrance to my roundhouse lodge. They were part of the twelve elite warriors, men and women of the Iceni, whose honor it was to protect their queen.

"Be at ease, Bryn and Briallen." As my warriors relaxed I studied the thick fog that swirled throughout the village. "It is late in the year for the dragon's breath, isn't it?"

"Aye, it's a strange one this morn," said Bryn. He gestured with his long spear out at the fog.

Briallen, a tall, slender woman who was Bryn's twin sister, teasingly used the blunt end of her spear to tap my shoulder. "Worried that it be Stoorworm coming to get you, my queen?"

I acted instantly, brushing aside the spear with one hand and stepping inside the reach of Briallen's weapon. I pulled her short sword free of the scabbard at her waist and pressed the blade of it against the warrior's throat.

Like all Iceni women, I have been trained in close combat as well as with the blade and spear and bow. Ironically, it was Briallen who had drilled me over and over again so that I was strong, confident, and accurate with all three.

"It does not worry me at all. How about you?" I said nonchalantly.

Briallen's brother threw back his head and his laughter boomed across the quiet settlement, causing a chicken to squawk irritably. That made him slap his thick thigh and laugh again.

A smile spread across Briallen's broad, intelligent face. She spoke slowly, careful not to move her throat. "No, my queen. It does not worry me overmuch."

Not long after I married Prasutagus, Briallen and Bryn had come to Tasceni. They'd been barely older than me but had left their northern Caledonia tribe already well-respected warriors looking for adventure. They had been so skilled that they had quickly been absorbed into my personal guard, and they were fiercely loyal to me. I had always loved their guttural Northern accent, which got more pronounced when either was stressed. I sheathed Briallen's dagger back in her waist scabbard and grinned at her.

"Well, may the joy of the day be with both of you. I must be off."

"Did you change your mind and decide to join the warriors?" Briallen's voice lifted with excitement. "If we ride hard we should catch them before they enter Trinovantes territory."

"Aye! They left just before the fog began," Bryn added, grinning in anticipation of being allowed to join the rest of the Iceni warriors at the annual spring games with their neighbors, Tribe Trinovantes. At the spring games they traded horses, sought and found mates, and competed in tests of strength.

"No, I just go to forage truffles for Derwyn. You must remain with your queen as I must be here to greet the leader of the Druids," I said, then added, "I am sorry you two are missing out on the spring games, though."

"It is an honor to do our duty." Briallen bowed, the familiar tone she usually took with me shifting to one that was far more formal.

"We prefer to remain with our queen," added her brother, his tone also turned formal. "The rest of the warriors will only be gone one night and back in time for Beltane. We choose Herself over revelry." Bryn bowed with a flourish, which made me smile. I had been fond of these twins for many years. They had been the first of my personal guard to take a knee before me when I became queen.

"Your queen appreciates you." My legs would not stay still any longer and I strode toward the forest.

When Briallen and Bryn moved to accompany me, the words

staying them came from deep within. "No. Remain here. Watch over my daughters and my mother."

There was a slight pause, and then the response I expected came to me on the cool morning fog. "Aye, it shall be as you say, my queen," Bryn said.

"And may the blessings of the earth be on you." Briallen's voice echoed eerily as the gray mist closed behind me.

My steps were sure as I moved through my village. Even though that morning it was like walking in a cloud, the fog did not slow my steps. I knew my home so well that I could have found my way through Tasceni blindfolded. The village was the heart of the Iceni tribe, usually home to up to four thousand souls, though that day we were considerably fewer with so many warriors absent. At Beltane, when they returned, the village numbers would swell to close to ten thousand as many Iceni made the trek to the home of their royal family to feast and celebrate the spring festival.

Tasceni was more than the heart of the Iceni. It was my home, my joy, my beloved domain. I knew and appreciated every part of it—from the grand lodge in which my daughters had been born, to the swine wallows and the herb gardens that were the pride of the Iceni cooks. It had been such since I'd first arrived, just turned eighteen and the new bride of their chief. I loved Tasceni as I had loved Prasutagus, at first sight, and the tribe had returned my affection in kind.

I paused and breathed deeply, tasting the air. As the sluggish breeze teased from the east, smelling of mud and fish, I oriented myself. The village was west of the mighty river Tas, just beyond the fen and spring floodplain—though this spring the season had been especially wet, which was the reason the redolent odor of fish and mud seemed so close.

Beyond the eastern bank of the Tas stretched fertile fields that were already green with thriving crops that carpeted the land all the way to the coast, which was a half day's ride from the river. North of the fen and fields, near the joining of the river Tas and river Yare, was the Chief's Barrow. On a clear day, if I climbed the tallest of the ancient oaks in the forest outside Tasceni I could see the large, rocky hillock, surrounded by half a dozen smaller barrows. Inside the Chief's Barrow, my husband, his favorite stallion, and a generous offering of goods, weapons, and ornaments had been entombed on a rainy day three months ago. With him was his wide chief's torque of braided gold, unique in how the jeweler had stamped it with charging boars and ended it with two circles of their golden tusks.

In the weeks since his death I had often wished I were still a girl so that I might climb an ancient oak and seek the comfort of the sight of the barrow. But I was not a girl. I was a queen who had left her tree climbing behind in Brigantes when she'd married Prasutagus.

I had not visited the barrow since the day they'd walled his body within the tomb. Others, including my mother, went often, leaving offerings tucked into the rocks and crags of the large hillock. But not me. I could not.

I was surprised that my feet immediately led me to the west, away from the scents of mud and fish. A sow, one of the many pigs that wandered the village like ill-tempered dogs, snorted unenthusiastically at me. I smiled as she gave me a view of her fat rear end and a small, curled tail wagging before she disappeared back into the gray.

Within just a few strides, the delicious aromas of bread and the fish stew the tribe baked in rounded stone bowls swirled to me with the mist. I knew to turn right and then left again, winding my way through the kitchens and the clay pits that cooked much of the tribe's food. I heard the musical sound of women's voices and caught glimpses of fires, like flickering specters in the mist, as the cooks were already hard at work preparing for tomorrow's Beltane feast and today's soon-to-be-waking tribe.

The scent of goat overpowered the baking, and I slowed to pick my way around pens filled with sleepy animals. Gossiping chickens added their music to the occasional lazy bleat as I moved quietly past them.

In the distance the low of a cow sounded eerily from the mist. The cattle were kept north of the tribe, at the edge of the forest. Again, I used sound to alter my course.

Familiar smells of sweet mash and warm flesh told me I neared the group of sturdy log buildings where I'd spent countless days—the tribe's elaborate stables, which were currently more than half empty. A favorite aspect of the brief spring games with Tribe Trinovantes was the trading and breeding of horses. I felt a pang of regret that I wouldn't be there with them, but the regret passed quickly. The Druids were deeply woven into the lives of the Iceni and all of the Briton tribes, and it was a special honor to host the high Druid, Derwyn. It would insult him if Iceni's queen was not here to greet him, especially as this was the first time he had visited Tasceni since the entombing of Prasutagus. Regret gone, I breathed deeply the homey scent of horses. In my mind's eye I could clearly see the lovingly carved doorposts dedicated to Epona that stood guardian before the stables. Automatically, I whispered a brief prayer to the horse goddess to keep the herd safe while it traveled with the warriors.

I shifted to a jog. The well-worn path that led from the stables and into the beginnings of the forest was immaculately tended and free of rocks and ruts. My nose wrinkled when the pungent odor of horse piss seemed to drip out of the mist, marking the area of the road that split, with one fork turning toward the grounds where the warriors held daily practice and drills. The woad fields and dyeing stations used urine collected in huge wooden steeping vats to extract the blue pigment the tribe used to dye their clothing.

Then the earth beneath my leather-clad feet became hard packed and the spring scent of growing wheat told me that I was crossing the warriors' practice grounds. I jogged through the familiar area until, abruptly, the earthy scent of the fields was supplanted by the sweetness of the tall, budding lime trees that were harbingers of the oak forest just beyond.

The first of the ancient trees came into view as dawn finally split the fog, turning the day from gray to pale mauve and violet. I paused for just a moment in front of the massive tree and placed my palm against the rough bark. "Good morning, Grandmother Oak." Looking up at the ancient tree, I greeted the familiar sentinel. She was fully in bloom, so that the yellowish flowers that dangled from her new growth made the tree appear as if she wore a maid's Beltane headdress.

"May the blessed sun shine upon you and warm you, old friend, and may the rain nurture you," I whispered to the tree and as always, I was rewarded with the sense of feeling the ancient one inhale and exhale beneath my hand. I stroked the tree in parting, as if it were my favorite mare.

In the oak grove not far from the grandmother tree was an altar dedicated to Andraste, patron goddess of the Iceni. I went to the carved wooden image that rested atop a circular slab of sandstone held waist-high off the ground by miniature columns. The image of the goddess had softened with weather and the touch of adoring hands, but the strength in her face was clearly visible. The goddess's features were powerful—she was strong jawed and broad shouldered. On one shoulder sat a somber-eyed raven. Andraste held a spear in one hand and a shield in the other. Around her feet shells and beads, wooden bowls filled with honey and goat's milk, and a collection of other offerings filled the top of the flat stone. I bowed my head, kissed my fingers, and then touched her feet, which were wet with morning mist. "May the joy of the day be with you, mighty goddess," I murmured before I bowed again and jogged away, heading deeper into the forest.

As the fog continued to disperse and the light filtered through the boughs of the oak grove, I stopped long enough to tie my skirt up so that I was free to run. I increased my pace and at the same time heard my mother's voice drifting like the lifting mist: *Listen to the forest.*

I relaxed my upper body, allowing my arms to move smoothly, rhythmically, with my legs, and let the forest guide me.

At a full run, I felt flush with energy. It seemed as if the matriarch oak had breathed power into my body. I was the swiftest of the Iceni women and was faster than most of the men. My legs were long and strong. My body was fit. Though I had never been in battle, I loved the way training and pushing myself to physical exhaustion made me feel. Warriors move with grace and confidence because they continually ask more and more of themselves. I was a peacetime queen of a prosperous tribe, but that did not mean I was weak or a coward. I fiercely shouted the Iceni war cry when I practiced hand-to-hand fighting with my guard. I stood taller than most men, something Prasutagus took great pride in—almost as great as the pride I took in myself.

I was queen of the Iceni, and the Iceni were not meek. Nor was their queen.

Like a creature of the forest, I leaped over fallen boughs and ferns that curled with new growth, dodged around the gnarled trunks of the trees that grew increasingly close together, and sprinted through the clearings that became farther and farther apart. My thick braid lifted whenever I leaped, allowing the back of my neck to briefly cool.

I didn't slow until the distant music of a stream passing over stones came to me on the morning breeze. Though I was not winded, my stride shortened and I changed direction so that I headed directly toward the sound, as if the murmuring water called to me.

The oaks thinned and gave way to white willows. Surprise made me stumble to a walk. White willows were sacred and only grew on the banks of rivers. They needed more water than a small forest stream provided.

My well-trained eyes searched for landmarks—trees, rocks, deer paths—that should have been familiar.

Nothing was familiar.

I shook myself. It felt as if I had just awakened from yet another dream. I had raced through the forest without noticing that the mauve and violet of dawn had burned through the fog but never matured to morning-sunlight yellow. I peered overhead, and though the day was clear I could see no cornflower sky, but only more layers of pink and purple. Still, I was not afraid. The forest was as much my home as Tasceni. It had always fed, clothed, and comforted the Iceni. It was a good friend, though one that often kept secrets. I walked on more cautiously.

Through the willows, the reflection of the unusual light off a small but quickly moving stream caused specks of brightness to obscure my vision. I blinked to clear my eyes and then my breath caught in my throat.

A mighty hart stood before me, just outside the willow wall. His back was to me as he drank from the stream. His coat was as

white as goat's milk and glistened with colors like the inside of an
oyster's shell. His beauty stopped my breath. I made no sound, but the
stag lifted his head and looked directly at me. I stared back at him in
wonder. He was crowned by horns so massive I wondered how even
his thick neck could carry them. The creature showed no fear but met
my gaze steadily.

The hart's eyes were as emerald green as my own and glistened as
brilliantly as the pendant that lay between my breasts.

There was no birdsong in the trees, and even the music of the
stream was muted. The stag turned and slowly began walking along
the edge of the water. He'd only moved a few paces when he paused
and glanced back at me.

I followed, though I did not try to move closer to the stag; instead,
I walked beside him, parallel, but kept the willows between us. If I
lagged he would pause and look back until I caught up with him.

I lost all sense of time. The strange light remained the same, so I
had no way to judge whether a moment or a day had passed, but it
seemed soon that the stream took an abrupt curve to the right. The
hart stopped and then turned to face the stream. I halted as well.
The willows had thinned, so I could clearly see that the stag was
standing in front of two rowan trees. They were covered with white
flowers the same color as the hart's miraculous coat and grew so
close together that their uppermost branches intertwined to form
a living arch.

Once more the deer turned his head to look back at me. I saw
a question in his eyes before he walked between the two trees and
plunged into the crystal stream. On the far side of the stream he
followed a slim path that led up and over what had become a steep
bank and disappeared.

Face hot and flushed with anticipation, I followed the stag and
stepped between the rowan trees, striding confidently to the stream,
planning to cross it and climb the bank after the hart. At the edge of
the water I paused to glance down to pick my way carefully over the
slick, smooth stones.

"Are you lost, child?"

The creaking voice startled me. My gaze darted up to see an old woman on the opposite side of the stream—exactly in the middle of the path the stag had just taken. The crone sat on a stump beside an elaborately carved cauldron suspended over the remains of a cold fire by a rough tripod made of boughs. Around her feet, wild hares nibbled tender grasses, tame as puppies, and in the willow behind her dozens of ravens stared silently.

I blinked rapidly and cleared my throat to find my voice. "No, Grandmother," I said respectfully. "This is my forest. I could not be lost here, but you do not look familiar to me. Could it be *you* who is lost?"

The old woman cackled and the ravens croaked delightedly, echoing her. "I am never lost but rarely found—and always exactly where I should be."

I shifted from foot to foot. I knew the crone was more than what she appeared to be, though how much more I was not yet sure.

"Well, Grandmother, do you need aid?" I reached into the folds of my hunting cloak and took out the carefully wrapped food. "I would gladly share my lunch with you. The village of my tribe is not far from here, and we welcome visitors. Might I guide you there?"

The old woman sat up straighter, her dark eyes alight with intelligence. "I do not need your aid, nor require your guidance, and I am well fed—but if freely given, I would accept an offering."

An offering . . . an offering . . . an offering . . .

The crone's words took form around me, swirling like fog, thick as the breath of the dragon.

As if Mother stood before me again, I heard her voice mix with the crone's. *I give this to you freely . . . to leave as an offering . . .*

Realization shivered through me. The creature most closely associated with Arianell's patron goddess, Brigantia, was the white hart. My body moved before I could form another thought. I splashed hastily through the stream, paying no heed to the icy water.

"I have an offering to give, and I do so freely." I took the silver chain from around my neck and held it out to the old woman. The lovely silver hart was suspended, swaying gently.

"I accept your offering with gratitude. Please help me on with it, child. These old hands are not as nimble as they once were."

"Of course, Grandmother." The crone bowed so that I could slip it over her head.

There was an enormous inrushing of air, and fog blanketed us, obscuring my sight. When it cleared, the crone was gone. In her place stood a tall woman in the prime of her life. Her beauty was as wild and untamed as the mass of her thick hair that hung past her waist. It was the black of a raven's wing and its ends were dyed the blue of the darkest, richest Iceni woad. Her body was tattooed in the same sapphire color in impossibly intricate knots and swirls that covered her bare, muscular arms and shoulders, and even decorated one side of her neck. Within the knots there were circles of hares and ravens in flight. In one hand the woman held a spear. The other rested on the generous curve of her waist. Her cloak was the scarlet of new blood, held in place by a thick golden chain. The cloak was stitched with gold and lifted in a breeze that touched nothing else, so that I could see the embroidery created a massive shield decorated with a charging boar that covered the entire garment and glittered with a life of its own.

I knew then in whose presence I stood. This wasn't one of the fey. It also wasn't my mother's patroness, Brigantia. And with that realization my body went hot and then cold. I dropped quickly to my knees, bowed my head, and pressed my hands together to stop their trembling.

"Ah, Queen Boudicca, so you do recognize me!"

CHAPTER III

Yes, mighty Andraste, I do." I was amazed that my voice was so steady but kept my head bowed and continued to clutch my numb hands together.

The goddess used the spear to tap my shoulder gently, exactly where Briallen's spear had so recently touched me. "Rise. I am pleased that you answered my call."

I stood as the goddess sat on an oaken throne, carved in the shape of an enormous boar. "I did not have a choice!" I blurted. "Forgive me, goddess. I mean no disrespect."

Andraste's laughter made the willow boughs flutter. "You always have a choice, Boudicca, and you need not ask forgiveness for speaking your mind to me. It is a good mind. A strong one, though sometimes rather stubborn, much like your husband."

I lifted my head and met her gaze but could not speak at all.

The goddess's expression softened. "Ah, you still mourn. You loved him well."

I nodded and blinked hard, determined not to weep before the fierce patroness of Tribe Iceni.

"As did I—flaws and all." Like the ravens filling the tree behind her, the goddess cocked her head and studied me. "I wonder, will you repeat his mistakes?"

"Mistakes? Prasutagus was a great chief."

"He was," Andraste agreed. "But even great leaders make mistakes. Our Prasutagus made one when he chose *not* to heed my warnings. It is a mistake he will pay for in many lifetimes to come."

Her harsh words made me feel dizzy with shock. "Mighty goddess, I do not understand."

"You will. You, too, will have a choice to make. Just as you did today."

"But you *compelled* me into the forest."

Andraste reached out and a golden goblet appeared in her hand. The heady smell of honeyed mead filled the space between us. The goddess drank deeply before replying.

"I did compel you, but you could have closed yourself to my call. Had you pulled your furs up around your ears and gone back to sleep, your destiny would be a vastly different one, and so would your people's present and future." Andraste drank again and then continued. "Or you could have answered my call but turned away from the crone."

I shook my head. "No, I would not do that. It is not the way of the Iceni."

"You might be surprised what people will do when they put their own desires first. I sent your husband omens, one and then another. Still, he chose not to hear me and instead allied himself with the enemy and gave away half of his land."

Another jolt of shock sliced me. The goddess spoke of the treaty Prasutagus had signed with Rome, making the distant emperor, Nero, co-regent of the Iceni along with me should Prasutagus die before our eldest daughter knew eighteen years.

"But he did see your omens! The hare he loosed to show him the way ran in circles before it collapsed and died."

Andraste nodded. "It did. And the raven?"

"It was killed by a golden eagle directly over my husband's head after he invoked your name!"

"Indeed."

I brushed back a lock of thick hair that had pulled free of my braid. "Prasutagus said the omens were clear. That is why he gave his oath to Rome, making the emperor co-regent with me should he die early. *Which is exactly what happened!*"

"Yes, Prasutagus's heart was the weakest thing about him. But my omens did not foretell his death. And his question to me had nothing to do with his mortality. His question was *whether he should bow to Rome.* Look at the omens again and tell me what you see, Queen Boudicca."

The goddess went to the cauldron. She beckoned me to come closer. Beside Andraste, I gazed down into the cauldron, which was completely empty. "Look with more than your eyes." Andraste passed her spear over the cauldron. Immediately, it filled with black water that began to spiral, like a mini-whirlpool. "Stare into the center of the maelstrom."

I peered down . . . down . . . down into the liquid. I lost all sense of my body. The goddess, the stream, even the rabbits and ravens disappeared as my spirit was transported to the rainy morning many months ago when the high Druid, Derwyn, had blessed and then presided over the ritualistic loosing of a white hare—a creature sacred to Andraste. My spirit hovered above the gathering as I looked down upon my powerful husband. He was so full of life that I wanted to weep, but I was there to serve as witness to something the goddess wanted me to see.

Prasutagus took the small hare from Derwyn and whispered to it the question he had for his goddess Andraste, patroness of the Iceni. Then, as the tribe looked on, Prasutagus released the hare.

I had been there, standing beside our young daughters on the grounds where Iceni warriors daily practiced their skills. I remembered that I had been close enough to the hare that I'd heard its terrible last shriek and saw the blood that had gushed from the little creature's mouth after it collapsed. But as the goddess had commanded, I watched again, this time knowing that my husband's question had not been about his own death, but about whether or not the Iceni should sign the treaty with Rome.

The hare had rushed from the Iceni chief's hands. It did not sprint into the nearby forest, or even return to the hutch where she and the rest of the sacred hares had been born and lovingly raised. The creature ran hysterically in one, two, three circles around Prasutagus before dying.

From above the scene my gaze went to my husband. That day no one, including me, had been watching him. Even the Druid was focused on the strange sight of the dead hare. But the goddess had not sent my spirit there to study the doomed hare; I watched Prasutagus.

His wide shoulders slumped and he sighed. But then he lifted his chin and shook his head, as if in disagreement with someone close by.

The scene changed abruptly and the whirling cauldron water took me forward in time a fortnight. This familiar day was clear. I had joined Prasutagus and the other warriors on the practice grounds near the edge of the forest. I watched myself trade blows with Bryn and Briallen, and had just knocked Bryn off his feet when the croaking of a raven drew everyone's attention upward. The huge black bird had perched in the top branch of the giant oak, the same tree I had greeted just that morning. Prasutagus's spear had been raised to throw at the straw target erected in the center of the grounds. The chief had paused, and instead of hurling the weapon, he'd bowed deeply with a flourish and shouted.

"Goddess Andraste! May my actions always bring glory to your divine name!"

The warriors joined Prasutagus as he raised his spear to the sky and shrieked the fearsome Iceni war cry.

I remembered well what happened next, so, as with the previous vision, I did not turn my gaze up with the rest of the Iceni when the raven took wing with the chief's cry. I did not need to see the golden eagle that had seemed to materialize from the cloudless sky. I did not watch it dive and strike the raven, killing it and then dropping it at my husband's feet.

I observed Prasutagus instead. This time his shoulders did not slump, but his chin did lift again and his jaw set. I recognized the look well. I'd seen it whenever anyone pressed the chief too far and stubborn defiance filled my husband. I'd seen it when I'd spoken to him about my hesitation to ally with the Romans. I'd reminded him Cartimandua of the Brigantes had done so and had since been shunned by the other tribes. He'd said he would give the issue to Andraste, which I thought he'd done. Now I knew otherwise.

A few days after the two omens sent from Andraste, Prasutagus had signed the treaty with Rome.

I felt a dizzying wrench as I returned to my body and blinked away a rush of vertigo, trying desperately not to be ill.

"Drink." The goddess held the goblet for me and I swallowed the rich mead. But the liquor didn't fog my head—instead it steadied my resolve.

"Prasutagus lied about his question to you," I said.

"Yes," said the goddess.

"He did not heed your warnings." The words slipped past my cold lips.

"He did not."

"You did not mean for him to pledge his oath to Rome."

"I did not."

I met the goddess's gaze. Her eyes were as black as the inside of a tomb. "Did you kill him because of that?"

"No. His heart stopped beating. That is what killed him."

The relief I felt made my skin tingle. "Now what?"

"That is up to you, Queen Boudicca. Today the mistake your husband sowed when he pledged the Iceni to Rome will be harvested."

Ice filled my veins and I staggered back a step. "I—I must leave! I must return home!"

"Must you? You have a choice to make that will shape your future as well as your tribe's. Your destiny, my beloved Boudicca, and your people's are irrevocably woven together."

My breath was coming fast and I could not hide the trembling in my limbs, though I fisted my hands. "I do not understand my choice! I must return to Tasceni and warn them about Rome."

Andraste's eyes were filled with sadness. "I already warned their chief. Your husband did not heed me—just as he would not have heeded you had I compelled you to come to me while he lived. It is too late. You cannot stop the consequence of his choice. You must avoid it, survive it, or die with it."

"How? Make sense!" I shouted at the goddess, and then pressed my trembling hands against my mouth, terrified I had finally offended Andraste. But the goddess was unperturbed.

"You have three choices. Remain here, unharmed, with me, until I tell you it is safe for you to return to Tasceni. Leave now and join today's grim harvest. Or decide to survive the harvest, grow stronger because of it, and use it to sow new seeds that will mature into a crop of vengeance like this land has never before known."

I wanted to ask what the harvest was that I would need vengeance for, but I couldn't form the words. I feared I already knew the answer.

"Can't I stop it? Won't you help me?"

The goddess sighed heavily. "Your husband's choice has been made. It cannot be unmade. And I *am* helping you. That is why you are here. But I will answer you truly, specifically—you may choose to remain here, in Annwn with me. You will be safe. You will return to Tasceni tomorrow, after the Romans have gone. If you make that choice I cannot see your path clearly, except that you will no longer be Iceni queen, though you will survive."

"The Romans threaten my people. I will *not* remain here!" I almost spit the words.

"Ah, then you have two choices. You may choose to face the Romans and not submit to them."

"I am an Iceni queen. I will not submit to Rome!" My body went hot as anger roiled through my veins.

Andraste remained serene. She nodded. "Yes, that would be momentarily fulfilling, though if you fail to submit, the Romans will kill you."

My mouth went so dry that I had to swallow several times before I spoke again. "I did not imagine that death in battle would be mine, but it is an honorable death."

"It is. And I shall welcome you to Annwn and my Summerlands if that is your choice. Though if you heed my words and let today fuel your anger instead of your demise, a great blue tide of vengeance will sweep across your world and you will ride its crest, leading the charge."

"Me? But I am the wrong queen for that! I rule in peace and prosperity. I—I am not a warrior."

The goddess grew in size. Her hair whipped around her as her cloak lifted like she was in the middle of a raging windstorm. Her eyes flashed dark fire and her voice became terrible. "Not a warrior? I whispered your name to your father the night you were born.

Victory! I compelled you here to be my vengeance! Do you doubt my wisdom?"

I dropped to my knees, though I did not bow my head. I could not look away from the fierce beauty of Andraste. "Never!" I pressed my fist over my heart. "Not even with my last breath will I doubt you."

"Then make your choice!"

With three words I changed the course of the world. *"I choose vengeance."*

The goddess did not alter her terrible war visage. She pointed her mighty spear at the cauldron and in a voice that shook the trees around us said, "Then rise and take from the cauldron my gift, though you must not wear it yet. You will know the time and the place. Listen with your heart and see with your mind."

On unsteady legs I stood and went to the cauldron. The swirling water had disappeared to reveal a golden chief's torque resting against the iron bottom, where it glistened with an otherworldly light. I reached down and took the torque. It was thick, twisted gold—open ended, as are all torques, so that it could be fitted around a chief or queen's neck—and it was stamped with charging boars completed by circled, golden tusks. I gasped with recognition and my gaze met the goddess's.

"This is my husband's torque." I would eternally recognize the sign of my husband's rank. I had never seen him without it. He had even worn it when we entombed him in the Chief's Barrow three months earlier.

"And now it is yours—a gift from the goddess of war to Victory. Keep it close until the time is right to reveal it to all."

My hand was steady as I slipped the torque inside the satchel still slung over my shoulder.

Andraste raised her spear and brought the butt of it down, striking the ground thrice with such blows that the earth trembled. Immediately the white hart returned, standing on the bank behind us. The goddess inclined her head slightly to him.

"Deliver my gratitude to my sister Brigantia for allowing me to borrow you today. To show my appreciation I return this offering to your goddess, whose beloved Arianell has treasured it for many years." Around the hart's neck the silver pendant appeared, with his likeness glinting against the moonlight white of his chest. Then she placed her hands on my face and cupped my cheeks as gently as a mother would her newborn.

"For the pain you will feel today, I am truly sorry. Know that I grieve with you and that with you I shall also blaze with vengeance. Do not forget that I will be beside you every moment. You will be a queen of my forging, and the fire from which you shall be birthed will be lit today. From this day forth I will hear your voice, my Victory—on that I give you my oath." Then the goddess kissed me gently, first on the forehead, then on both cheeks, and finally on my lips, exactly as my mother had earlier that day, saying, "May the blessing of light be upon you. May the blessing of rain be upon you. May the blessings of earth be upon you, and—someday in the not-too-distant future—may the joy of the day be with you again." Andraste stepped back and lifted her spear. She struck it against the earth thrice again and her voice rang in my ears. "Now, my Victory, *run!*"

The stag rushed past us and leaped across the stream. On the far bank he paused and gazed questioningly at me as he had before.

I turned to say goodbye to Andraste, but the goddess, the cauldron, the hares, the ravens, and the throne were all gone. All that was left was the heaviness of the torque in my satchel and the despair that had already begun to live in my heart.

Run!

Andraste's voice filled my mind and I did as my goddess commanded. I ran through the stream to join the stag. Together the hart and I raced through the mauve-and-violet-tinted forest that was as silent as the barrow in which my husband's body rested.

CHAPTER IV

I could not tell how much time had passed. None of the forest I raced through was familiar and the strange light did not give way to the sun. I only knew that I did not tire and had no trouble keeping up with the stag.

Eventually, he began to slow from run to trot, and then the stag broke stride completely and walked, picking through a grove of oaks so ancient that their bottommost limbs brushed the fern-covered ground.

I did not gaze around the forest. I felt no inquisitiveness about the Otherworld we call Annwn. Dread and purpose filled me and left no room for peaceful curiosity. I did find comfort in the solid presence of the hart. He walked so close beside me that I could feel the warmth of his body and smell the sweetness of his breath. It made me feel close to my mother, especially when the odd light caused the emerald eye of the pendant he wore around his muscular neck to flash.

Finally the creature halted. He lifted his muzzle, gesturing ahead of us, and I recognized something. Even in the mauve and violet light there was no doubt that we were standing before the ancient grandmother oak that grew just beyond Andraste's altar and marked the edge of Tasceni.

The stag took a step back and, again, gestured with his muzzle.

Before I turned from my companion I reached out slowly, allowing him time to move away should he so desire. He held very still as I pressed my palm against his forehead and stroked him gently. His coat was soft as water and through my hand I could feel the power that radiated from him.

"Thank you. I do not fully know what is to come today, but if you could, please be close to my mother. She has faithfully served your goddess, Brigantia, her whole life."

The stag lifted his muzzle and blew his warm breath gently against my cheek before whirling and, with his tail up, fleeing back into the Otherworld forest of Annwn.

I drew a deep, steadying breath before I stepped from Annwn to the mortal realm.

Tasceni was still fogbound, though the pastels of morning were beginning to filter down from above. I ran. As I did I marveled at how little time had passed since I'd left the village. It had seemed as if I'd spent the day in Annwn in the presence of the goddess, but in the mortal realm it was as if I'd just left the village and entered the forest, changed my mind, and returned.

I was glad of the fog. It hid my bloodless face and stricken, terrified expression. *Faster! Move faster!* I gulped air, felt as if my legs would fail, and wished for the mighty hart in whose presence I had the stamina of an immortal.

Finally! My lodge materialized through the fog and I stumbled to a halt. Bent at the waist, I pressed a hand to my side to stop the pain there as I panted and struggled to regain my breath.

"Herself?" Bryn's deep voice called the question from the raised entrance to the royal lodge.

"Queen Boudicca!" Briallen leaped down the wooden stairs to me. "Are you injured?"

I shook my head and sucked in air. "No! I—I was in Annwn." I spoke between gasps. "With Andraste." Briallen paused at my pronouncement, clearly not sure what to do. I wiped my sleeve across my sweating face and straightened. "The goddess warns that the Romans—"

An ominous, metallic clanking cut off my words. Frowning and confused, I peered past the lodge in the direction of the sounds, which came from the narrow path that snaked from the boggy fens to the rear entrance to the village. The dirt road was mostly used by the tribe's fishermen, and the echoing sound was so foreign, so out of place, that even the two faithful members of my guard were, at first, more curious than alarmed. Then shapes emerged from the shrouding fog; the foremost of them was on horseback. Behind him more men appeared. They marched in a neat two-column formation. Above them they carried a standard displaying an eagle made of gold. On its breast was carved *IX*.

Briallen stepped in front of me as her brother took a defensive stance before the closed oak doors of the lodge.

"Ninth Legion! Halt!"

I recognized the man riding at the head of the soldiers as soon as he spoke. His nasal voice was unmistakable. I remembered all too well how Prasutagus and I had made fun of Nero's tax collector, the diminutive procurator Catus Decianus. He had been a full head shorter than me and his arrogance had been fodder for our humor. He had represented the Roman emperor the day the chief of the Iceni mistakenly signed half of our tribe away to the Romans.

Decianus glanced at Briallen. "You there! Servant! Wake your chief! Tell him Rome is at his door." As with most Roman officials who spent time with the tribes, he spoke our language, though his accent was heavy, turning the fluidity of our words cumbersome and stilted.

I lifted my chin, stepped around Briallen, and answered him in the Latin all born to the royal houses of the tribes had learned as more and more Romans infested our country. "I am Boudicca, wife to the Iceni chief, Prasutagus."

The Roman looked down his straight nose at me. "You?" He barked a quick laugh and shrugged. "Each man has his own tastes, to be sure, but I shall never understand the desires of barbarians. No matter. Wake your husband. Rome has business with him."

"Prasutagus has been dead three full cycles of the moon," I said. "He cannot be waked."

Decianus cocked his head as he studied me. One short, thick finger pointed at my delicate golden torque. "I remember when last I saw your husband he wore something much like that cuff about your neck. It has been explained to me that it is the symbol of rank by you *Brittani.*" He pronounced the word as if it tasted foul. "Perhaps you might explain why a woman would wear such a symbol."

I straightened my spine so that I stood tall and proud as I met his gaze. "I wear the symbol of chief because my husband named me his heir. Our people supported his naming. The Druids consecrated my coronation. I am Boudicca, queen of the Iceni. This torque reflects my rank."

Decianus said nothing for several long moments. When he finally spoke, his voice was scornful. "And I thought Paulinus jested when he told me Prasutagus had been replaced by a woman. I should have known better than to bet against that wily bastard. Now I owe him a purse full of golden denarii." The tax collector's gaze slowly traveled from my mud-splattered skirts up to my disheveled hair. Then he threw back his head and laughed so long and so heartily that several of the soldiers nearest laughed as well. When he was able to control his mirth, he continued. "Well then, *Queen* Boudicca. It is to you I shall speak."

I maintained my calm and replied as if he had not just mocked and insulted me. "Very well. I require you remain here so that I might ready myself and my lodge for such an"—I paused, but not long enough for Decianus to take offense—"honor as your visit."

"Of course. Of course. Take your time. We did come unannounced. The centuria and I shall await your pleasure, *Your Majesty.*" The tax collector chuckled.

With Briallen on my heels, I nodded briefly in acknowledgment of Decianus's response before I swept past the Romans and hurried up the wide wooden stairway to the lodge. "A centuria," I whispered urgently to Briallen. "How many is that?"

"No more than two hundred soldiers. No less than thirty," Briallen said as she followed me inside. Her warrior brother remained firmly planted before the door.

"And how many of our warriors remained here instead of going to the spring games?"

"Countin' my brother and me—mayhap two dozen. Likely less," Briallen said.

My stomach heaved. We were defenseless. "Get our people out of here and into the forest. Now."

Arianell had dressed and was at her usual place before the hearthfire. My two daughters looked up as I entered, grinning sleepily at me.

"Mama! Enfys said I cannot have strawberries with my cream today. Tell her I can!" Ceri, who had known ten namedays, fisted her small hands at her waist and glared at her sister, who was three years her senior—and never let her forget it.

"I was just kidding! Don't be a baby who runs to—"

"The Romans are in the village." I cut off my daughters' bickering as soon as Briallen closed the thick wooden doors behind us. Quickly I slid the satchel that held Andraste's precious gift over my head and hid it behind one of the tapestries that covered the wall from floor to ceiling.

"Oh, goddess! What do they want?" Arianell stood so abruptly that she stumbled into Dafina, who had moved to stand beside her mistress.

"Nothing good. Andraste warned me they were here. Mother, Dafina—get the girls out through the rear door." As I spoke, I hurried toward my bedchamber. Phaedra was standing just outside the thick deer-pelt curtain that served as the door, eyes wide, wringing her hands. "I've stalled them, but they will not wait long. Get out now. Warn every villager you can. Tell them to leave immediately—fade into the forest—meet at the Chief's Barrow. The Romans are loath to trespass there." Romans did not desecrate graves. They knew the barrows were where we buried our dead, a place specially protected by our gods and goddesses, and thus they avoided them.

I turned at the entrance to my chamber. "Briallen, go with my daughters. Protect them. Phaedra, help me change and put out our second-best mead. Then follow the girls to the forest."

Briallen frowned but nodded in acknowledgment of my command. "Come, Arianell, bairns, let us go with haste as Herself—"

The double wooden doors to the lodge burst open. Skewered by a Roman pilum, Bryn's still-twitching body fell inside. Decianus stepped over him and spoke with a sneer. "I have waited long enough. This discourtesy is what happens when a woman thinks she can lead men." Then he replaced his sneer with a wide, feral smile as he studied Enfys and Ceri. "The daughters of Prasutagus. How fortuitous that you are here to take part in this valuable lesson."

CHAPTER V

Briallen moved with the speed of a viper. She placed herself between the Roman and the two girls. She unsheathed her sword and stood at ready.

Decianus's look hardened and he commanded, "Drive the girls and the queen from the lodge. Kill anyone who gets in the way." A mean smile slid across his florid face. "Except for this fierce woman." He pointed at Briallen. "Let us toy with her. I find females who masquerade as soldiers fascinating."

Decianus stepped aside to allow two Roman soldiers to rush within, and the lodge exploded into movement. Briallen slid the point of her sword up between the leather strips of the first soldier's tunic, slicing his groin. He dropped with a terrible scream. Briallen spun around and her sword cut neatly through the second soldier's throat, causing him to fall backward out onto the raised wooden stairs as blood geysered in an arc around him.

"Mother! Take the girls! Go!" I shouted as I pulled the dagger from the leather sheath at my waist. I didn't think. I reacted. I met Phaedra's shocked gaze and commanded, "Go! Now!" My servant sprinted to the rear of the lodge and the shadowy back door. Then I rushed past my screaming daughters and lunged at Decianus. My knife almost found his throat, but the tax collector shrieked and staggered back as another soldier burst into the lodge. Set on killing Decianus, I tried to follow through with a deadly lunge but the soldier was there, blocking my way. "No!" I sobbed brokenly, bowed my head, and dropped my shoulders in pretended defeat. When the soldier momentarily relaxed I jabbed the hilt of my blade into his thigh.

"Get in here, you fools!" Decianus commanded.

And then there was no more respite. The well-trained soldiers of Rome's Ninth Legion poured into my home.

"Do not touch her!" Arianell shouted, and pulled Ceri from a soldier's grasp. And then my mother gasped and her eyes went wide when the blade of his pugio—a short sword—plunged into her belly.

"Nain!" Ceri sobbed.

"Nooooo!" Ancient Dafina howled her rage. The gray-haired woman, who had spent her life serving and loving Arianell, hurled herself at the soldier.

In more of a twitch of reflex than a true strike, the soldier met her hysterical onslaught with his iron-tipped pilum. He speared her through the chest as easily as if the old woman had been a lamb rushing to its own slaughter. She crumpled to the ground beside Arianell's motionless body. The Roman soldier pressed his foot to her soft belly as he pulled his spear from her body.

I watched Mother and Dafina fall but had no time for tears. I rushed to my daughters and shoved them behind me. Briallen took up a position with her back to me, my two frightened daughters between us.

"Do not kill them!" Decianus shouted. "Drive them from the lodge as I commanded!"

The attack paused. The soldiers reevaluated, regrouped. When next the soldiers entered the lodge it was with the practiced control for which Rome's legions were renowned. They entered in pairs with their body-covering shields raised and locked. Though Briallen and I thrust at them, they did not break ranks but surrounded us with an impenetrable wall. Then slowly, methodically, they closed their circle of shields and forced us from the lodge.

The world was death and confusion. Screams echoed through the fog around us. I knew my people were being slaughtered but could only catch glimpses of the village between brief breaks in the wall of shields surrounding and herding the four of us through the settlement.

"Mama! Mama!" Little Ceri fearfully panted my name.

I brandished my dagger before me as I tried to keep the soldiers from getting any nearer. With my other hand I reached back to touch my youngest daughter. "Stay between Briallen and me! And when we tell you—*run for the woods!*"

"Yes, Mama! We will! We will!" Enfys said between sobs.

I'd spoken automatically, trying to soothe Ceri, but I knew my girls and I could not escape the Romans. Smoke lifted in dark tails above the shields, obscuring my view. Tasceni was burning.

And then I heard a sound that momentarily had my heart swelling with joy—voices raised in the Iceni battle cry followed by the crash of steel on steel. The soldiers who were herding us forward paused as other Romans met the few Iceni warriors who had chosen to remain in the village as well as the sick, the feeble, the elderly, and those heavy with child. No matter the age, each Iceni was a warrior who bravely charged at the Romans. And each Iceni warrior fell nobly as they attempted to protect their queen, her heirs, and their village.

An officer called out a sharp command and the marauding soldiers fell into formation, making a column with their shoulders pressed against one another so that their large, curved shields extended the impenetrable, confining wall. They held their pilums—long, deadly spears—at the ready as the circle of soldiers herding us continued to move forward, inside the Roman column. I realized we were being forced to the Iceni practice field.

My tribe, the brave Iceni, continued to resist. They tried to get to me, but the Roman formation never broke—never even wavered. They threw themselves at the soldiers as they shrieked the Iceni battle cry. Over and over, grandmothers and grandfathers attacked the Romans—and each of them fell. Suddenly I understood what my people were doing. The tribal elders were keeping the attention of the centuria on them so that the next generation of our people— brave children and their young mothers—were able to flee into the safety of the forest.

The Roman soldiers easily cut down all challengers. I felt each of the blows as if they had sliced through my own body.

Impotently, I tried to pull the attention of the soldiers from my people. I struck, thrusting my dagger over and over at them.

The Romans ignored my attempts to break through their shields. The most they did was to parry my thrusts—careful never to strike me—and continue to crowd us toward the Iceni practice field.

But they toyed mercilessly with Briallen.

From the edge of my vision I could see that Briallen's tunic was soaked scarlet from stab wounds to her breasts. Every time she had to swivel even a little to parry a blow from one man, another soldier from the column would dart forward and slash at her buttocks—and then the soldiers would laugh uproariously.

My hands were slick with sweat, and the metallic scent of Briallen's blood thickened the air by the time our little group reached the practice field.

From his horse, Decianus watched everything. He called the order. "Make an end of it! I tire of the goat-shit smell of this place."

The circle of shields suddenly tightened, separating Briallen from my daughters and me. Briallen shrieked like a banshee, whirling and slicing so that it took five Romans to subdue her. They knocked her to the ground and dragged her behind a goat shed—and then she stopped shrieking.

Everything went silent. The Iceni warriors were dead. The elderly Iceni had all fallen. There was no one left to worry the soldiers.

I straightened my spine as Andraste's words echoed in my mind: *Your husband did not heed me . . . You cannot stop the consequence of his choice. You must avoid it, survive it, or die with it.*

I stood tall and proud as I tried to shield my daughters. But I had no chance against the mass of soldiers, so I lifted my chin and leveled my gaze on the tax collector.

"I demand a queen's right to speak with your governor Gaius Suetonius Paulinus!"

Decianus made show of looking around before he shrugged. "My good friend Paulinus does not appear to be here. Pity. You will have to speak with me instead."

I shook my head and sneered at the little fat man. "I have spoken with you, *tax collector*, and I am done speaking with you. You overreach your station with borrowed soldiers. What you have done today breaks our treaty—one approved by your emperor and signed by Paulinus. You have no authority over the Iceni!"

"Again, I see no one here except me, which makes my authority absolute. And to be clear, Rome does not acknowledge a woman's right to rule; therefore, you may demand nothing!" His nasal voice mocked me as he turned away. "Take them to the stake!"

The soldiers closed on us. I circled my daughters, lunging forward with my dagger as I tried to find a weakness in their wall of shields. One soldier parried my jab. Using the pommel of his pugio, he struck me hard across the cheek. My world grayed and I staggered, gasping for breath. He easily slapped away my dagger, and then he and two of his comrades used their long pilums to herd the three of us through the rest of the column of Romans to the center of the training field.

Decianus had gotten there first. He dismounted, and as my daughters and I spilled out of the column of soldiers to the open ground before him, he commanded, "Tie Boudicca to the post."

We were doomed. I knew it as surely as I drew breath. We could not escape a centuria of Romans, but I would not break before these usurpers. I would not break before my daughters. Let them witness the strength of will of an Iceni queen. I blinked away the last of my dizziness and wiped my sweaty, bruised face with my sleeve. Then I put myself between my girls and the procurator. I looked down my nose at Decianus and spit in his face.

Laughing, the procurator pretended to turn away, but then he spun around and punched me in the stomach. Air rushed from me as I doubled over and fell to my knees. While I retched onto the hard-packed dirt of the training grounds, Enfys and Ceri shrieked and tried to reach me, but Decianus grabbed them by their slim wrists and threw them at the soldiers closest to him.

"You may have sport with them, but do not kill them."

"No!" I screamed, and staggered to my feet to lunge after my girls.

Decianus caught my braid as I tried to rush past him and jerked me off my feet.

"You see what happens when you aren't polite?"

From the ground I looked up at him and pleaded. "Please! Do as you will with me, but they are *children*. They are no threat to you."

"Ah, but they will grow up, and because you insist on arming your women, they will become my enemies. Think of this as a lesson in propriety. I am actually doing them a favor. Perhaps, when they are adults, this will teach them not to bear arms against their betters."

"Mama!" Ceri sobbed.

"Help us!" Enfys screamed.

Rage filled me to overflowing. I surged to my feet again. Shrieking the Iceni war cry, I ran directly at Decianus. I bared my teeth to use them as weapons and made my hands claws as I went for his eyes. The procurator staggered back. Off balance, he fell against the soldiers who were struggling to contain the two hysterical girls.

For an instant I thought Ceri and Enfys might escape—might dart between the wall of soldiers and shields and flee into the misty, concealing forest. But the men only laughed, made the mocking sounds of clucking hens at the girls as they closed their wall of shields. Ceri and Enfys ran in the other direction. Again, the wall closed and the soldiers taunted. Hand in hand, the sisters raced from the column and ran into the only building on the field, the hut in which straw targets and wooden practice swords were stored. They closed the door. My heart ached with the futility of it. The hut was no barricade against the lust of Rome. Still laughing and clucking like hens, soldiers broke down the door and entered the hut.

As my children's screams lifted to the boughs of the great, watching oak, Decianus backhanded me before he wrapped my long, thick braid around his hand and dragged me to the center post.

"Tie her!"

The waiting soldiers did as he commanded, binding my hands above my head so tightly that my face pressed into the thick wooden post.

"Stop your men!" I pleaded with the tax collector as I hung from the post. "I will not arm my daughters. If you release them unharmed I give you my oath as queen that they will never take arms against you!"

Decianus took his pugio from a sheath strapped to his side and approached the post. With ironic gentleness, he lifted my thick braid and brushed it aside so that it no longer covered my back. Then the procurator leaned into me so that his hot, foul breath brushed my cheek. His body pressed against me and I could feel his erection, hard and insistent. "But what good is the oath of a queen who is so weak she cannot even protect her children?" A cold blade touched the patch of skin that was visible at the base of my neck. "Your daughters must learn what happens when women are not ready to serve their men."

With a swift stroke that left a line of warm blood dewing my skin, Decianus cut through the back of my tunic. He pulled and ripped the garment until I was naked from the waist up. Then he went to his horse and unwrapped a long, braided whip from his saddle. It ended in several strips of leather that were knotted. Decianus shook it out and cracked it over his head as he approached me again.

"And now, *your* lesson begins, Iceni *queen*. But let it not be said that I am without mercy. All you need do to stop your flogging is cry out and ask me to do so, and I will know you have learned your place. I shall put away my whip then."

I said nothing as he marched away. I could not think past the screams of my daughters. I had no time to prepare. The first lash struck like a hot knife fileting my skin. I opened my mouth to scream, but the whip snaked out immediately again. My gasp of pain cut off my scream as it struck my back, leaving a hot ribbon of agony. The pain was so all-encompassing that it took my breath, my voice—it felt as if it took my soul. I had no control over my body; it jerked spasmodically with each blow. My bound hands grasped the wooden stake. My fingernails broke and bled as I clawed the post, but I did not cry out. I could not cry out. I had no breath. It had fled and taken my words. Decianus struck again—and again I could not scream, could not gasp, could not cry out. Instead I struggled to hold to consciousness as my sight tunneled and blood washed down my back with every lash.

The only sounds in the field were the murmur of soldiers, my daughters' fading screams, and the crack of the whip.

"Cry out, woman! Beg me to stop!" Decianus commanded.

My cheek pressed against the wooden post. I did not close my eyes but stared up into the mighty oak before me and said nothing.

"I said, *cry out!*" Decianus's voice was shrill. Nero's tax collector struck me over and over until blood ran down my hips and thighs and calves to pool around my feet.

And still I did not cry out. Instead I continued to stare into the tree. The watching soldiers had gone silent. My beloved daughters had stopped screaming. The day held its breath.

My mind became very clear. Gone were dizziness, confusion, anger, and fear. I realized that Andraste had known I would not choose to remain in Annwn while my people were attacked. The goddess had also known that her Victory, though not a queen who had led Iceni warriors into battle, would not bow to the will of Rome. With that icy clarity that often preludes the end of life, I understood that I had come to the real choice the goddess had foreseen and asked me to make. Die or survive. I could feel the seductive allure of death as surely as I felt the white-hot lash of the coward who flogged me.

A raven lit on a bough of the oak. Its gaze caught mine. I stared into its dark depths. I could easily remain silent. I could already feel Arbred, the mortal world, slipping away. The pull of Annwn was great. Prasutagus was there. My mother was there. So, so many beloved Iceni elders were there. My daughters quite probably were there. If I just let go, my spirit would follow my loved ones. Andraste had given me this choice; she said she would welcome me to her Summerlands. This day I could feast with those most dear to me—free of pain and of the oppressive fist of Rome.

But with every lash a new raven landed in the oak. Each great black bird stared at me in silence until one raven opened its obsidian beak and I heard the goddess's voice inside my mind. *Look around you, Victory.*

My vision, like my mind, was preternaturally sharp. I turned my head to gaze around the training field and the path my children and I had so recently been forced to walk. The bodies of the elders of Tribe Iceni were strewn everywhere. Ancient limbs had been severed.

Skulls had been broken. Bellies that had carried children who now had children of their own had been opened, spilling entrails across the hard-packed ground.

If I chose death, what would the Iceni do? In a span of a few short months they would have lost their chief, their queen, their royal family, and their elders.

My gaze returned to the tree. The raven's dark eye caught mine again. *If you choose death, the Iceni will be no more. They will be absorbed by other tribes who will bow to Rome. With the extinction of Tribe Iceni, so too will life as you know it end—and Rome will go unpunished for its crimes.*

With those words—*Rome will go unpunished for its crimes*—anger began to build within me. With each stoke of the whip, that anger grew into a rage that burned away the lethargy that had begun to lull me into death.

"Submit to me!" Decianus shrieked, and the whip snaked against my blood-slick back again as yet another raven landed to perch in the great oak and bear witness to the flogging of a goddess-anointed queen.

The memory of Andraste's promise filled my mind. *If you heed my words and let today fuel your anger instead of your demise, a great blue tide of vengeance will sweep across your world and you will ride its crest, leading the charge.*

Vengeance.

It was then that I spoke. My voice filled the field with such authority that the leaves on the oak trembled and the ravens croaked eerily.

"Stop!"

"Ah! Good!" Decianus's words released in bursts as he gulped air and tried to catch his breath. "Good! You are strong. I acknowledge that." His panting voice drew closer to me as he continued. "Your strength makes it more gratifying that you finally learned the lesson I came to teach you. You see, *Queen* Boudicca, I knew Prasutagus was dead. I came for you—not him. To teach you a lesson, which it seems you may finally have learned." He halted beside me. From the edge of my vision I could see that sweat dripped like tears from his fat, florid face. "One last thing." Nero's tax collector wrapped his thick fingers around my delicate golden torque and ripped it from my neck. With a self-satisfied smile he hefted it, testing its weight, before he slid it around his meaty bicep and pinched it closed. "There, lesson over." Still smiling, he used his pugio to cut the ropes that trapped my wrists over my head.

My legs would not hold me. I dropped to the ground, which was wet with my blood. My head lolled uncontrollably and as I fought off the graying of my vision, Andraste's voice lifted from my memory once again. *Do not forget that I will be beside you every moment . . . I will hear your voice, my Victory—to that I pledge my oath.*

Righteous indignation filled me. It cleared my vision and sent a wave of strength through my battered body. I gripped the post and stood. My chin lifted and I looked down to meet the diminutive tax collector's hot gaze. Then my rage spilled from me. I spoke with the fury and force of a tribal carnyx, the war horn that struck fear into the heart of anyone who stood against Iceni warriors.

"Catus Decianus, procurator of the emperor Nero, I curse you and every man here. For taking my mother's life and violating my daughters, you will know the fire of Brigantia. For what you have done to the Iceni, you will know the vengeance of Andraste."

Decianus's self-satisfied smile faltered. His sweaty face blanched the color of a dead fish's belly. "Shut up, woman!" His voice was a shrill obscenity—and utterly impotent compared to the power of my curse.

I was not a defeated queen. I was the instrument of a warrior goddess who blazed with the fierceness of a mother calling down vengeance on the abusers of her children. As I finished the curse, my voice echoed throughout the silent field.

"Your homes will burn. Your women will burn. Your children will burn. You will all—every one of you—suffer more than my daughters and my tribe. You will cry out for mercy and you will be shown none, because, Caius Decianus, through my blood and with my goddess-blessed breath, I have cursed you unto death!"

As I pronounced the last two words of the curse, *unto death,* every raven took wing from the oak and circled so low over me that Decianus cringed away from them, before they flew into the fog and disappeared.

"I said shut up!" The procurator struck me across the face, knocking me onto the ground.

Through vision blurred by sweat and blood, I watched him turn his back to me and walk hastily to his horse. He gestured wildly at the gaping soldiers.

"Well, what are you waiting for? Move out! We have more of these Brittani to attend to, and this rabble has cost us far too much time. Thankfully, I need not return to this pathetic village until after harvest to collect that which is owed us." But the soldiers around him were staring at my torn body and made no move to obey his command. Decianus picked up the bloody whip and cracked it over his head, drawing every man's attention to him. "Shall I inform Paulinus his soldiers disobeyed my order? I said we return now! I need a bath and a drink."

Silent and subdued, the Romans withdrew. The men who emerged from the hut were laughing. As they observed the somber expressions on the faces of their comrades, they, too, went silent, so that, soundlessly, the Roman centuria disappeared into the fen like wraiths returning to their graves.

CHAPTER VI

The rage that roiled within me was second only to my need to get to my daughters. I tried to stand. My legs would not hold me. "Enfys! Ceri! Girls!" I called, but the hut remained as silent as the rest of Tasceni. Fear began to replace my rage as I crawled toward the little structure. My back was on fire. My mouth was so dry I couldn't swallow, but I did not stop. I did not think. I gripped the ground with my hands, digging my broken fingernails into the hard-packed dirt, and dragged myself to the soundless hut.

When I reached it I only paused long enough to put my arms through the ragged sleeves of my tunic, which I rearranged so that from the front, at least, my girls, should they be alive—*Oh, Andraste, please let them be alive*—would not easily realize the extent of my wounds. I gritted my teeth against the pain and drew several deep breaths. Using the side of the hut, I pulled myself up so that I stood on unsteady legs. I drew another deep breath and then pushed open the rickety door.

My children were naked. Curled together, they lay still and silent in each other's arms. When my shadow darkened the doorway, Enfys looked up. Her eyes, green as my own, were open and glassy with shock. Enfys's scream echoed off the interwoven branches that made up the curved walls of the hut. Ceri whimpered and held tighter to her sister, but she did not open her eyes.

"Enfys! Ceri! Oh, my little loves! It is me—your mama!" I staggered to my two girls and dropped to my knees beside them.

"Mama!" Enfys cried my name. "M-mama! Th-they hurt us! They h-hurt us over and over!" Through teeth that chattered, words and sobs flowed from my eldest daughter, thick as the dark blood that coated her thighs.

"I know, sweet girl," I said soothingly as I brushed back Enfys's sweat-matted hair. "I am here now. All will be well." I scooted closer so that I could stroke Ceri's bruised cheek. "Little dove, can you open your eyes for Mama?"

Ceri only whimpered and trembled as if in the grip of a terrible fever.

I wanted to curl myself around them, hold them close, and will their pain away, and for a moment I was paralyzed with grief. *No! I do not have the luxury of grief. Not now. Not yet. They need me.*

My gaze searched the hut until I found the wooden trough that captured rainwater. The water was kept fresh for Iceni warriors after they practiced their skills. I made my body stand and staggered to the trough to lift the ladle. I drank quickly, greedily, several ladles full and felt stronger and less dizzy. I filled the ladle yet again and returned to my girls. I helped Enfys drink and then went back to the trough for another ladle full of water.

"Ceri, let me help you drink."

The little girl whimpered again and did not open her eyes, but I was able to hold the ladle to her lips so that she choked down some water.

"Mama, we tried to fight them. I promise we did!" Enfys cried softly as she spoke.

"Shh, shh, sweet girl. Of course you did. You were so brave. Both of you *are* so brave."

"B-but we could not stop them!" Enfys said between sobs as soundless tears leaked from Ceri's closed eyes and washed down her cheeks.

Then I did put my arms around them. I held them close and stroked their damp hair gently. "Listen to me. Both of you did the bravest, most courageous thing you could ever do—you *survived*."

Another shadow fell across the doorway. Enfys shrieked again. I ignored the agony in my back, grabbed a wooden practice sword from those piled in the hut, and whirled to face the intruder.

"Och, goddess! What have they done?"

I did not recognize Briallen until she spoke. The warrior's face was purple and black. One eye was completely swollen shut and pink-tinged tears leaked down her dirty cheek. The woad-colored short tunic worn by all of the queen's guard was tattered ribbons. Briallen's blood had soaked what was left of it, changing the blue to the purple of her bruises. Like the two children, her legs were painted crimson down to her ankles.

"Girls, little loves, it is only Briallen!" I moved to help the warrior get water, but Enfys clutched my tunic and would not loose me. "Drink." I gestured at the trough. "Then sit here, beside me."

Briallen took the ladle from me, went to the trough, and drank deeply. Then she returned to the three of us.

"Sit. Rest."

Briallen shook her head and grimaced at the pain the motion caused. "My queen, we cannot rest here. We must get the girls to the lodge so that their wounds and yours can be cleaned and packed."

"But you're wounded, too! You're bleeding everywhere. You cannot—"

"I can because I must! We both *will* because we must." Briallen cut off my words. She went to her knees beside me and beseeched, "Forgive me for speaking so to you, my queen." Then Briallen lowered her voice and added, "How badly wounded are you? I cannot tell through the blood that covers your back."

"I do not know."

"Can you walk?"

I met my warrior's gaze. "I can because I must."

Briallen nodded quickly. "Aye, my queen." Her one-eyed gaze flicked to the children. "I can carry Enfys if you can carry Ceri."

I nodded. "It will be so." Then I spoke softly as I gently pried my eldest daughter's hands from my torn tunic. "Enfys, Briallen is going to carry you and I shall carry Ceri. We must return to the lodge, where we can care for your wounds. Do you understand?"

Enfys's eyes were glazed with shock, but she nodded and allowed the warrior to lift her. Then I turned to my youngest daughter, little Ceri. The child was curled on her side, knees to her chest, eyes tightly closed as she shivered violently.

Rage roiled within me again and I used it to fuel the fire that kept me moving. I drew a deep breath and caressed Ceri's sweaty hair. "Little dove, I am going to carry you home." Eyes still tightly closed, Ceri said nothing but allowed me to lift her into my arms.

I stood still for a moment until the world stopped rolling and pitching around me while I cradled Ceri's body against my chest, as I had when she'd been a sweet infant—and was shocked by how light and boneless she felt.

Side by side, the only Iceni warrior left alive in Tasceni and I carried the girls to the lodge. The trek was like moving through a waking nightmare. Bodies of men and women I had known for fifteen years littered the path. I paused at the first of them and pressed Ceri's face against my shoulder as I bent beside Heulyn, a mother of ten and grandmother of six, revered as an expert baker. I touched her face gently to see if there was any sign of life in the old woman. Heulyn was gone.

Briallen turned away so that Enfys was shielded from seeing the elder's body. "None will be alive. The brave old ones who remained in the village to protect their queen and give the bairns and mothers time to flee into the forest were slaughtered—every one of them— along with the few warriors who were not at the spring games."

I met Briallen's gaze. "I am sorry. Bryn was a fierce warrior."

"He died protectin' his queen." Briallen's voice broke. She paused, collected herself, and continued. "He will join your mother in Annwn, as is right. Except for the four of us, 'tis a village of the dead."

"It will live again. *We* will live again."

I continued the trek to the lodge. As we approached the open wooden doors, the knowledge that my beloved mother was within— dead and cold—had me staggering.

"Steady!" Briallen caught my elbow and lent me her strength. "We will because we must."

I drew a deep breath, nodded, then spoke gently to my girls. "Enfys, Ceri, you must do something for me. You must close your eyes and keep them closed until we are in my bedchamber."

Ceri cried and pressed her face into my shoulder, soaking it with her sweat and tears, but Enfys turned her head so that she could meet my gaze. "Nain is in there with Dafina. I will look. I will remember."

I thought my heart would break, though I was filled with pride at her fierceness. I badly wanted to command my daughter to close her eyes—to remain a child—but what had happened to her, to us all, had changed everything. And I understood intimately that in this new, terrible world of ours, anger fueled action. I met my oldest daughter's gaze and saw the reflection of the fury that boiled within me, that kept me on my feet, that would keep me moving forward from this day on. "Then look. Remember. And know we will get vengeance."

"Aye, bonny lamb. 'Tis as Herself says. We will get vengeance," said Briallen.

"We will get vengeance," echoed Enfys.

We entered the lodge. The scent of blood and loosed bowels permeated the air. There were only three bodies. Bryn's body slumped just inside the door with the long pilum spear still embedded in his chest. My eyes were drawn to the middle of the spacious lodge, where my mother rested beside her beloved servant. In their final moments of life they had curled toward one another, and the two old women's hands were joined—holding as tightly in death as in life.

I tore my gaze from the two women I had loved the longest in this lifetime and moved woodenly past them, pushed aside the hide that was the door to my private chamber, and laid Ceri carefully on my wide bed. Briallen placed Enfys beside her sister. The older child instantly took Ceri into her arms.

Enfys looked up at me through eyes a century older than thirteen namedays. "Go ahead, Mama. Do what you must. I will stay with Ceri."

The pride I felt for her took my breath. I touched her cheek. "See how brave you are. I have never been prouder to be your mother than at this moment." I pulled a blanket up over my beautiful, violated daughters. "We will not be long."

I left my bedchamber with Briallen beside me and closed the pelt door. Then the warrior and I paused. Except for the three bodies, the lodge looked remarkably normal. The hearthfire was still burning, though the iron pot of water that had been boiling there was knocked over. It soaked the rushes along with the blood of Arianell and Dafina.

"We need to tend to our wounds, but first we must move them." My hand shook as I wiped sweat from my face. My back had become so tight that every movement was agony, but I'd felt no new warmth of blood and my dizziness had passed, so I ignored the pain. My daughters must come first.

"Aye. We can take them outside and care for their bodies properly after we tend the living," said Briallen.

We worked together silently. Bryn was the most difficult to move. In life, he'd been a massive but graceful man, like one of Tribe Demetae's oceangoing war vessels. Now, in death, he was battered and beached. It took both of us, a human tide pulling and heaving, to remove him from the lodge.

I carried my mother myself. I cradled Arianell much like I'd so recently held my youngest daughter—tightly against my chest. I breathed in the familiar scent of the rosemary that Mother had liked to rinse her hair with and fought back tears by embracing rage instead.

The Romans will pay for this. I cursed them. Andraste heard. The goddess and I will make certain the curse comes true.

Gently, I placed my mother's body on a pile of clean rushes just outside the great lodge. Briallen had already taken armfuls of the rushes into the lodge to replace the blood-soaked ones. Lastly, Briallen placed Dafina beside her mistress, where she had been for more years than I had lived.

Then we reentered the lodge. I could feel my strength waning. If I moved too quickly, my vision narrowed and spots of light obscured my sight. I spoke hastily to Briallen, knowing that I must get the next part done quickly, before I could no longer force my body to do anything. "I'll draw and heat the water for the bath and add healing herbs. We need to get the girls warm, bathe the remnants of those beasts off them, and then dress and pack their wounds. You need your wounds tended as well."

Stiffly and carefully, I moved to right the cooking tripod over the fire and then hooked onto it the cauldron my servants used to heat bathwater. Behind elaborately embroidered tapestries that decorated the lodge's curved walls were shadowy recesses that held pots, buckets, and dishware of all sizes. I grabbed two of the largest wooden pails and turned to shuffle to the rear door of the lodge, just outside of which was the deep, cold well my attendants used to draw water for their royal family—and almost ran into Briallen.

The warrior swayed precariously and looked as if she might fall over at any moment, but her voice was firm. "I'll be takin' one of those buckets. We can fill it faster if we work together. And you must be tended, too, my queen."

I opened my mouth to tell Briallen not to be ridiculous—that she was barely standing—and then I saw the iron in the warrior's gaze and recognized the anger there that was almost as deep as was her need to do something, *anything*.

I nodded shortly. "Get clean linens from Mother's sewing chest. There should be a covered wooden pot beside the baskets of yarrow and goldenrod. We'll need the herbs to add to the girls' bathwater, and the salve in the pot is numbing and healing."

Briallen nodded. "Aye. Arianell is a great healer."

"She is. She was." I corrected myself, blinking hard to keep the tears that welled from falling. "Get enough herbs to steep in the cauldron, as well as in the bathwater. There is a pitcher of water and a basin on the table near my bed. Fill it with the herbed water from the cauldron. You can clean the girls' wounds with that while I draw from the well and fill the bath."

Briallen nodded and began gathering the items. I did not think. I moved. I went to and from the well until the cauldron was filled, and then repeated the filling as I poured the hot water into the huge copper tub Prasutagus had given me fifteen years before as a betrothal gift. I stoked the fire and hung a fresh cauldron of water. Then I went to my mother's medicinal chest and carefully chose herbs that induced sleep, placed generous portions in two wooden mugs, and poured boiling water over the mixture to steep for tea before I joined Briallen with my daughters.

Briallen had cleaned Enfys's face and was carefully wiping the blood from the girl's body. Ceri had curled into a tight fetal position with her back pressed against her sister.

"Ceri will not allow me to touch her," Briallen said softly.

I nodded, wetted a strip of linen in the already pinkening water, and sat close to Ceri. "Little dove, will you let me clean you?" The child whimpered and burrowed her face into the goose-down-filled mattress. I stroked her matted hair gently. "Ceri, look at me."

Ceri's body trembled and her voice sounded even younger than her ten years. "If I open my eyes I will know it is not a dream."

Her sister's words made Enfys sob, and Briallen wiped away her tears, speaking softly to her, as if she were a wild hare that had been wounded and needed to be soothed so that it would not attempt to run away and further injure itself.

I thought my heart would break but forced my voice to be steady.

"Yes, little dove, my little love, I know. I wish we were dreaming, but I will not lie to you as if you are still a baby. You must be strong. We all must be—you, Enfys, and me. For Nain. For our people."

Ceri's eyes fluttered open. She whispered three words. "Nain is dead."

It was not a question, but I answered. "She is. Death is the only thing that could keep her from our side right now."

"She died because of me." Tears leaked slowly down Ceri's smooth cheeks.

"No, little dove. She did not. She died because Romans attacked us."

"C-could you not have s-stopped them? You are a queen," Ceri sobbed.

I felt my daughter's words like a gut punch. "I tried, little dove. I—" My words broke off and I bit a bloody hole in my cheek to keep from screaming or sobbing or both.

Briallen spoke solemnly into the silence. "Your mother our queen was brave and fierce. Her words saved us all."

Ceri turned her head to stare at the warrior, but it was Enfys who asked, "Did Mama truly save us?"

"Aye, she did. She cursed the Romans. 'Twas the power of Herself's curse that affrighted the soldiers so bad that they crawled off me. One of them had raised his spear to strike me with a killing blow at the moment our queen said, 'Through my blood and with my goddess-blessed breath, I have cursed you unto death!' It seemed to turn the soldier to stone. He stood there—spear raised—as if entranced and stared at Herself. While he and the rest of the Romans gaped at the sight of our mighty queen, I fled so that I could live to serve her." Briallen's gaze met mine. "Had she not cursed them, the Romans would have burned the village and made sure we burned with it." Briallen bowed her head deeply, respectfully.

I tried to speak, but my daughter was quicker.

Ceri sat, grimacing painfully. "Wash me now, Mama. I will be brave like you."

Silently, the warrior and I wiped the blood and dirt and fluids from my children, and then we carried them to the steaming tub. We added several more buckets from the well to make the water bearable before gently placing the girls within. Enfys and Ceri were so small that they both fit in the tub together. The children gasped and cried out as their wounds met the water, but they bore it like the daughters of a queen. As Briallen washed the girls, I gave each of them a mug of tea, adding dollops of golden honey. My pride in them was so fierce it lifted my spirit.

"Drink, my little loves."

The girls did as they were told. The tea and the warmth of the herbed water worked on them. Their eyes began to close and their breathing deepened as they rested more comfortably in the tub.

While the girls soaked in the healing warmth, Briallen spoke softly but urgently. "The Romans set fire to the stables. I'll go see if any of the horses escaped. If so, I'll catch one and ride for our warriors."

Before I responded, I took a bucket already filled with the herb-steeped bathwater and got another fresh cloth from Mother's sewing chest. I gestured for Briallen to join me in Arianell's bedchamber.

"Take that ruined tunic off and sit so that I can see to your wounds."

"I should clean your back first, my queen," said Briallen.

"My bleeding has stopped. Yours has not. Sit," I commanded.

Briallen sighed but shrugged out of her tattered tunic. "It shall be as you command, but I cannot sit." She turned so that I could see the bloody sword slashes that covered her buttocks.

Kneeling beside the warrior, I began to clean her wounds. "They aren't men. They aren't animals. Those who did this to you—to me—to my daughters—are monsters."

Briallen's voice sounded ancient and incredibly tired. "They aren't monsters. They're just men from a people who do not value women. It could happen to any men, even our own."

"Do you excuse them?"

Briallen snorted. "Och, no. I only explain. The Romans are rabid animals and should be culled from our land."

I stood and gently, carefully, cleaned the lacerations that covered Briallen's breasts and ribs. And as I tended the warrior, it was like a dam loosened within me. Words flowed, horrible and thick, almost drowning me.

"They came from the fen, but I don't understand how. How could they have made their way through the fen in the fog? Why didn't the sucking mud swallow them?"

Briallen moved her shoulders. "I do not know. But had they come by the main road we would have heard them and not been taken by surprise."

"Heard them, yes. But still not been able to defend ourselves with almost all of our warriors at the spring games." My rage—which was now always there, just waiting to boil over again—felt good. It warmed me. It burned away grief and pain and fear. "They knew the warriors would be gone. They had to have known."

"How? Tribe Trinovantes are our allies and not in league with Rome."

"I do not know, but I will find out." I spread healing salve over Briallen's wounds. "Some of these need to be sewn."

"We don't have time for such things, my queen. Wrap the wounds tightly. They will heal."

"They will scar terribly," I said.

Briallen's feral smile showed missing teeth from where the last Roman had struck her with the hilt of his pugio. "Aye, that they will. It will be my honor to wear them."

I nodded and wrapped the worst of her wounds tightly before taking a plain tunic from Arianell's clothing chest and carefully helping the warrior into it.

"Now you, my queen."

Gratefully, I slid the filthy, torn clothes from my body and kicked them into a pile with the warrior's bloody rags. Then I stood still, breathing in small, shallow gasps as Briallen cleaned the long lacerations the whip had carved into the soft flesh of my back, and then sighed in relief as she smeared salve into them. Moving quietly and carefully, I went to my chamber and dressed in a soft linen tunic as Briallen added hot water to the girls' bath and took the empty mugs from them.

When I rejoined Briallen, I checked on my daughters, who were drowsy and pink faced from the steamy bath. While I was dressing, the warrior had brewed us herbal tea, rich with honey, which we drank quickly. It gave me the strength to go to where I'd hidden the satchel just before the Romans had attacked. I breathed a sigh of relief when I lifted it and felt the reassuring outline of my husband's heavy torque. I grimaced as I slid the satchel over my shoulder and its leather strap pressed against my wounded back, but I needed to keep the goddess's gift close.

Briallen went to me and bowed stiffly. "My queen, allow me to ride to our warriors. If I leave now our warriors may catch Decianus before the river reaches the sea. We will cut him down like the rabid dog he is and send him to be judged in their Underworld."

I spoke firmly to my warrior. "Brave Briallen, I want vengeance, too, but our people will begin returning, and some of them will be wounded. Today we need healers more than soldiers. The Druids must be within a day's ride; they always travel with healers. My injuries are not as grave as yours. You remain here and see to my daughters. I shall go meet the Druids and ask that they send a rider south to fetch our warriors."

Briallen began to protest, but my hand on her arm stopped her words. "You cannot help my daughters if you die on the road to the Trinovantes. I must think of our people. What is best for all of us at this moment is not to ride after a mere centuria and a tax collector *who are already dead*."

Briallen nodded. "Aye, your curse."

"Andraste heard me. I know it as sure as I know my own name. We will kill every one of them. First we heal. Then we will have our vengeance."

Briallen's shoulders slumped. "I will do as you command, my queen."

A keening lifted from the practice field and drifted to the lodge like smoke from a hearthfire. Ceri's scream pierced the peace of the lodge.

"The Romans return!" Enfys cried.

The water from the tub sloshed over the sides as the girls tried to scramble from its depths.

"No!" I spoke sharply. My tone caused the girls to stop flailing in the water and stare at me with wide, panicked eyes. "Think! Romans would not keen over our dead."

"'Tis too soon for the tribe to have returned. They should still be in hiding at the barrows."

I nodded. Like Briallen, I knew where we would find the Iceni who had managed to escape into the woods. As soon as an Iceni child could walk and talk, he or she was taught the way to the Chief's Barrow and memorized which of the hillocks that surround it were burial mounds and which were hollowed sanctuaries that waited to succor the tribe in a time of need.

I met Briallen's gaze. "I will whistle if they are friends. If I do not, get the girls out the back door and into the forest. I will meet you at the barrow. Guard them."

"With my life," said my warrior.

As quietly as possible, I moved through my ravaged village toward the practice grounds and the keening of the many voices that lifted and fell from there. As I passed a goatherd's hut that still smoldered,

I got my first glimpse of the grounds. My breath whooshed from me in a wave of release as I whistled the distinctive song of the whip-poorwill, signaling to Briallen that the visitors were friends. From the lodge came the answering birdcall. Satisfied that the girls knew they were safe, I hurried through the village.

The practice field was filled with people moving from one fallen Iceni elder to another. The people swayed side to side as they keened in grief. They were cloaked in the blue, green, and brown colors of the three Druid orders.

Dizzy with relief, I staggered the rest of the way to the practice grounds. As the Druids caught sight of me, the keening silenced and the cluster of people shifted. From the center of the group a tall man strode toward me, dressed in the white robes that marked him as the revered high Druid. His voluminous garb was decorated with deep blue painted knots that appeared to shift and change shape as he drew closer. His long, thick hair was as white as his robes. His face was clean-shaven, as was the Druids' custom, and tattooed with Ogham letters. I had known him my entire life, and though he had to be older than Prasutagus at his death, his face was almost unlined. His familiar eyes were the gray of a stormy sea and ineffably sad as he strode to me.

I bowed my head respectfully as he grasped my hands in greeting. "Queen Boudicca! Blessed Andraste has kept you safe! Do your royal daughters live?"

"They do, though they have been gravely injured." I lifted my head and spoke in a clear, strong voice that carried to each of the raptly listening Druids. "They were violated by Roman soldiers while Catus Decianus did this to me." I turned and shrugged out of the linen tunic so that it fell down around my waist, exposing my ravaged back to the Druids. I heard their gasps of shock as I stood still and proud, allowing each of them to stare at my wounds.

"But you did not leave the procurator unharmed." A woman's voice came from somewhere behind me. I did not need to see her to know who spoke, and the wave of gladness that came with that recognition felt foreign in my grief-numbed body.

Gingerly I put my arms back through the tunic and turned. "No, I did not."

She stepped out from the group of ovates, who wore robes of green. I had not seen her for sixteen years, but her hair was still as pale as a full moon, which was startling because her eyes were dark as a fecund field. Her features had not seemed to age and were as delicate as I remembered—though even as a child, Rhan, daughter of Addedomaros, chief of Tribe Trinovantes, had commanded a strength that went far beyond the physical, just as her ability to see went far beyond the boundaries of this world.

As Rhan approached me, I said, "I cursed Decianus and the monsters the Romans call soldiers with the vengeance of Andraste and Brigantia."

"And you, Boudicca, will fulfill that vengeance."

"Yes, Rhan. I shall."

Rhan's expression softened with a hint of the impish smile I remembered so well. "It is good to see you again, though I wish it was under different circumstances."

"So do I, old friend. So do I."

Rhan opened her arms and we embraced. For just a moment I allowed myself to take comfort from my childhood friend.

CHAPTER VII

The gods were good for guiding you here early," I said to Derwyn. "The goddess Andraste spoke through Rhan. Her compulsion to arrive early was so great she would not let us rest."

Compulsion . . . The resonance of the word reverberated through my mind as I watched the Druids of the highest rank begin to gently tend to the bodies of the Iceni. They wore plaited mistletoe belts and robes of all three colors, blue, green, and brown, woven together in a muted plaid.

Derwyn followed my gaze. His deep voice was thick with sadness. "I fear you have many bodies that will need preparation for the pyre."

I nodded. "The elders tried to protect me and hold off the Romans so the young mothers and children could escape. There are bodies throughout the village."

Derwyn's eyes caught my gaze. "Where are your warriors?"

"They are at the spring games. There they sport and trade with the Trinovantes. There were only a little over a score of warriors remaining in Tasceni. All of them except one member of my guard perished."

"This slaughter happened because your warriors were absent," Rhan said.

"That is only part of why," I said darkly. "But there will be time for that explanation later."

"I will send a bard south along the Trade Road to bring the Iceni home," Derwyn began, and then his gaze sharpened as he searched the forest around them. "You said it was the procurator who led the Romans? Why did they not meet the Iceni and Tribe Trinovantes on the Trade Road? Camulodunum is the Roman capital, and it is south of the spring games in Catuvellauni lands. They should have crossed paths with your warriors on the way here."

"The Romans did not come by land. They came by water from the river through the fen, arriving with a thick fog," I explained.

Derwyn's brow creased. "Something feels wrong about this attack. The Romans usually travel by the roads they so meticulously lay, not by water."

Rhan spoke abruptly. "Send someone to the fen."

"You won't find the Romans anywhere near. Decianus spoke clearly of his eagerness to leave, and his intent to return at harvest," I said.

"It is not a Roman you should seek," said Rhan.

Derwyn motioned to a blue-robed Druid, who hurried to him and bowed respectfully.

"Take our fleetest horse and go south down the Trade Road to the grounds of the spring games. Tell the Iceni of this tragedy and bring them home."

"As you ask, so will I do." The bard hurried back to the horses and wagons that were grouped at the edge of the tree line.

"Gar!" Derwyn called.

A brown-robed Druid approached. I recognized him instantly as an Iceni tribesman who had left our tribe to train with the Druids at the isle of Ynys Môn just before Ceri's birth. He was just one of many familiar faces among the Druids. All of the tribes sent those who showed aptitude for communing with nwyfre, the life force that runs through every living thing, to Ynys Môn. If accepted, they entered the lengthy training that marks the life of a Druid. They no longer held allegiance to a single tribe and instead were allied with the gods and goddesses, but that didn't mean they lost their memory of their first home. Gar's cheeks were wet with tears he did nothing to hide. He bowed to Derwyn and then inclined his head to me respectfully as well.

"Queen Boudicca, this day fills me with sorrow," he said.

I nodded, finding it difficult to speak.

"Gar, you recall how to get safely through the fen, do you not?" Derwyn asked.

"I do. I was raised here in Tasceni."

"Go then, and bring to me anyone you find there," commanded Derwyn.

"As you ask, so will I do." Gar turned to head off through the field to the east and the river Tas.

A shiver of premonition made my body go cold and I allowed my intuition to form words. "Gar, blend with the fen and the bogs. Do not let yourself be seen. The person you seek must be surprised if he is to be captured."

Gar nodded. "Easily done, Queen Boudicca."

I stared after Gar, wondering silently what the Druid would find in the swampy grounds that flanked Tasceni, until Derwyn's voice pulled my attention back.

"Where are your daughters?"

"The lodge, with the only Queen's Guard who survived, though she was gravely wounded. I will show you there. I must return to them. My daughters are not—" I paused as my voice began to break. I drew a deep breath, cleared my throat, and continued. "I am afraid if I am not there when you and the healers enter the lodge they will—" My voice cracked again. I pressed my lips together as grief strangled my words.

Rhan gently touched my arm. "We understand, as will the healers."

"Indeed we do," said Derwyn. He raised his voice, calling out to two women and a man who immediately joined them. "Glain, Adara, Conway—come with us and bring your baskets. The queen's daughters are in the lodge."

"There will be more wounded hiding at the barrows, and along the way if they were too badly injured to make it there," I said.

Derwyn nodded and added, "Glain, take the wagon and several of the horses. Choose a few of the other healers to join you. Make your way to the Chief's Barrow to tend to the wounded and bring the Iceni home."

"As you ask, so will I do."

Relief washed through me. The Druids would gather my people and bring them back to me.

"We will attend your daughters and the warrior at the lodge," Derwyn continued. "And my seers will see to the washing and preparation of the dead, as well as begin building the funeral pyre." Several Druids nodded. More spirit than flesh, they melted off into the village to collect and care for the dead.

"Thank you." Anger rekindled within me. "Build the pyre here, in the middle of the practice field around the stake where the Roman tied me. Tear apart the hut. Use it for kindling." I made a cutting gesture at it. "It was there that my daughters were brutalized. It should burn."

"It will be as you say," said the high Druid.

"Derwyn, may I have permission to remain with Boudicca?" Rhan asked.

The high Druid studied her carefully before nodding. Then the four Druids walked the macabre path through the village with me. This time I forced myself to look at every corpse that lay still and cold—and as I did I repeated each name silently, memorizing the dead. *You will be avenged*, I promised each of them.

I had closed the huge double wooden doors as I'd left the lodge, and when I opened them I called within, "Enfys, Ceri, healers and old friends have come to aid us."

The hearthfire was blazing, and in the short time I had been with the Druids, Briallen had lit the thick pillar candles spun from beeswax and scented with lavender that Arianell had loved so much. Light and fragrance combined, and for a moment I almost expected to hear Mother greet us warmly.

Instead Ceri's hysterical shriek echoed from the curved walls.

"No! Make the men leave! Make them leave! Make them leave!"

She and Enfys were wrapped in thick woolen blankets. They had been seated before the hearthfire drying their hair, but the moment Derwyn and the male healer, Conway, entered the lodge, they stood so abruptly that the bench on which they sat toppled over. They darted behind Briallen, clutching the warrior's tunic. Enfys whimpered and Ceri cried with terror. The sound of their fear almost broke me.

Derwyn's voice was ineffably sad as he backed slowly out of the door, taking the male healer with him. "Conway and I shall wait outside."

I nodded, already hurrying to my daughters. Rhan and Adara followed more slowly.

"Little loves, it is only Derwyn and one of his healers. You remember Derwyn. He has been here often," I said soothingly as I coaxed the girls out from behind Briallen.

"No men, no men, no men, no men." Ceri refused to move as she repeated the two words over and over.

The healer, Adara, crouched before the girls. Her auburn hair was streaked with gray and her eyes matched the dark green of her ovate robes. "The Romans have gone, fawns. No man here will harm you. I am a healer. I attended your mother for each of your births, and what a blessing those days were. The queen was so happy and your father so proud."

Enfys spoke solemnly. "We do not remember that."

"No, of course you do not. It is my job to remember, just as it is my job to help you heal. Will you let me help you?"

Enfys nodded, and after only a brief hesitation Ceri did so as well.

"Take them into Mother's chamber and close the curtain," I said.

Adara stood and held out her hands for the girls to take, but as she began leading them to Arianell's chamber, Ceri dug her heels into the rushes and pulled her to stop. She turned to face me.

"I want you to come with us."

I steeled myself. More than anything I wanted to retreat into my mother's bedchamber with my girls, crawl into the bed, which still smelled of rosemary, hold them close, and never, ever let anyone harm them again.

But I was not just their mother. I was also their queen.

"I want that as well, but I must see to the rest of our tribe," I said solemnly.

"Then I will stay with you," said Ceri stubbornly.

"You cannot, little dove," I said. "You must let the healer tend you, and I must get on with the business of leading our tribe."

Enfys spoke up. "If you cannot be with us, then Briallen must come."

"The warrior has been wounded as well." The healer spoke up. "Perhaps she should join us so that I might tend to her." Then she met my gaze steadily. "The girls will sleep soon."

"Yes, Mama. Briallen must stay with us while we sleep," Ceri insisted. "She will protect us."

I nodded my permission and Briallen went to the girls. She took Ceri's hand in hers. "Always, bonny lassies. I will always protect you."

The children, walking as stiffly as the battered warrior, went through the heavy pelt curtain to the queen mother's chamber with the healer, who closed it securely behind them.

I thought my heart might shatter.

"They will heal." Rhan's voice was almost inaudible, but I could hear the tears in it.

"Their bodies will. It is the damage to their minds I most fear."

"If you allow it, I will meditate on how to help them heal completely," said Rhan.

I nodded as my childhood friend and I made our way back to the entrance to the lodge. "Thank you. I will gladly accept your help." Derwyn was there, alone, waiting just outside the wide wooden doors. He stared at the darkening sky as if the answers of the universe could be found there.

"Are the girls calmer now?"

"They're with Adara. Briallen, the warrior from my guard, won't leave them. It gives them comfort. Please, you are welcome in my lodge."

Derwyn did not enter. Instead he spoke solemnly. His next words shook me to my soul. "I understand it has been too much too fast—losing husband and mother and the elders of your tribe within three short months."

He put a heavy hand on my shoulder, and I suddenly felt small and weak as his sorrow and compassion cooled my anger.

Derwyn continued. "But you must put aside your grief. The Iceni need you desperately. You are their stability."

"And only you can fulfill the curse," Rhan added.

The screams of my daughters lifted easily from my memory. I thought they would always be there, waiting so close to the surface of my mind that they would shadow the rest of my life. I heard their screams anew and let rage burn through my grief. "I will make Decianus and his soldiers pay."

"Your curse shall be fulfilled. Decianus will be punished," Derwyn said slowly. "But do not be blinded by lust for vengeance. The men who violated your daughters and killed your people were not Decianus's men. Like the procurator's power, they were only borrowed from your true enemy, Gaius Suetonius Paulinus, named governor by the Romans."

"I remember Paulinus from the signing of the treaty," I said. "I told Prasutagus he had eyes that looked dead."

Derwyn nodded. "An apt description. It is that dead-eyed governor who commands the Romans who infest our country." His voice deepened with anger. "Our people have begun living in constant fear. Romans tax us beyond reason so that we, *the people who tend this land*, starve while our invaders grow fat. They desecrate our shrines and build temples to their foreign gods." His gaze met mine. "They must be stopped. Paulinus must be defeated. It is to him the new Iceni queen must look for true vengeance."

"Derwyn, I have no experience leading warriors into battle!" As I blurted the words I felt the weight of the golden symbol of leadership that rested unseen within the pouch still slung across my body, as if it were made of sorrow and not gold.

"The gods care nothing for your battle experience. They care for your heart, for your spirit, and for the bravery and wisdom that fill both," said Rhan.

"If the warriors acknowledge you as their queen, it matters not at all whether you have led them into battle once, a hundred times, or never," Derwyn said. "As your husband already taught you, gain the support of the warriors and you have gained the tribe."

"But how do I do that? I could not stop the Romans. Decianus flogged me, and he is a weak little man. I watched them slaughter grandmothers and grandfathers and could do nothing." Though the words disgusted me, I felt a great sense of relief in spitting them out.

"No single warrior could have stood alone against Roman soldiers—not even the most experienced of them," Derwyn said.

"You could have thrown your life away fighting the Romans. Instead you chose to live. You chose to survive. You made the right choice." Rhan eerily echoed the words of Andraste.

"Rhan speaks wisdom. Your survival will give your people hope," said Derwyn.

"It will give them more than hope," said Rhan. "It will give them a focus for their anger, and the power of that anger is what will fulfill your curse." The ovate reached out and tapped me once on the center of my forehead. "Speak it, Queen Boudicca!"

Heat blossomed through my head, permanently etching into my memory the curse that had lifted from my soul to Andraste's ravens and to the goddess herself.

"*Catus Decianus, procurator of the emperor Nero, I curse you and every man here. For taking my mother's life and violating my daughters, you will know the fire of Brigantia. For what you have done to the Iceni, you will know the vengeance of Andraste. Your homes will burn. Your women will burn. Your children will burn. You will all—every one of you—suffer more than my daughters and my tribe. You will cry out for mercy and you will be shown none, because, Caius Decianus, through my blood and with my goddess-blessed breath, I have cursed you unto death!*"

I blinked and scrubbed a hand across my face when I finished. I felt strange, as if I had just surfaced after a deep dive into cold waters. "Andraste was listening. Of that I have no doubt."

"Then do not doubt your goddess! She found you worthy to lead the Iceni *now*, not at some future date when you are a more experienced warrior," said Rhan.

Derwyn nodded. "Remember that when you face your people. And now I will leave you to ready yourself."

"Ready myself? The warriors are more than half a day away. Even riding hard, they will not be here before dawn."

"Derwyn means to ready yourself to face your people. The mothers and young ones will return soon, and they will need you to look and act like a queen."

I glanced down at my simple tunic. It was not the right time to wear my husband's torque, but the Druids were correct. Discovering that their elders had been killed and their royal family attacked would be devastating. My people would need comfort, and I must give them that.

I lifted my chin. "I will wash and change my clothes."

"I will help see to the dead," said the high Druid.

"Derwyn, I would ask a favor." As I spoke, the words lifted through my veins and pounded through my heart. "Let us not wait the traditional three days before lighting the funeral pyre. Let us light the pyre tomorrow on Beltane."

Derwyn nodded in approval. "On Beltane the veil between Arbred and Annwn will be thin."

"The Iceni dead can join Andraste in Annwn for the Beltane feast. It will be joyous for them," said Rhan.

"My mother's patron goddess is fiery Brigantia. We must build a pyre so great that Brigantia herself will see it in the Otherworld," I added.

"The Druids will make it so," said Derwyn.

"I, too, will leave you to prepare for your people." Rhan turned to Derwyn. "Do I have your permission to anoint Arianell's body?"

Derwyn paused, and I knew why. The consecration of the body of the mother of a queen would normally be left to the senior-most Druid—Derwyn himself.

Derwyn's gaze shifted to me. "I leave that decision to the queen."

Instead of answering Derwyn, I spoke directly to Rhan. "When I returned to the Iceni after the five years I fostered with your family, Mother often said how grateful she was that I had found a sister with the Trinovantes. I believe she would also be grateful that you were the one preparing her for the pyre."

"As you ask, so will she do," said Derwyn.

Rhan wiped away a tear, and then she followed the tall, white-robed man from the lodge and into the encroaching dusk.

chapter VIII

Feeling centuries older than my thirty-three years, I returned to the well to draw fresh water. As I carried the bucket to my bedchamber, Adara emerged from my mother's room.

"How are they?" I asked the healer.

Before answering, Adara said, "Please show me where I can find a pot in which I can brew tea. I gave the girls the juice of the poppy and they are sleeping soundly. The warrior refused it, so I would prepare her a strengthening tea instead."

I showed the healer to the hidden alcove that held the cooking pots, cauldrons, and buckets, and the wooden cabinet that stored dishware, then the healer began brewing a fragrant pot of tea.

"Your daughters are gravely wounded," Adara said as she stared into the warming pot, adding sprinkles of herbs she drew from the basket she'd carried into the lodge. "What those men did to them—" She shook her head in disgust. "Enfys's injuries are the worst. She may never bear children. But it is Ceri's mind for which I am most worried."

Adara's words sickened me and I struggled to speak through the mixture of guilt, grief, and rage they invoked. "How can I help them?"

"They need rest and they must feel safe. I will continue to give them sleeping potions over the next day, but they will eventually have to rejoin the world. Your presence will help, as will Briallen's. Give them time and encouragement. Surround them with the women of the tribe. Petition Andraste to grant them courage. Be patient with them."

It was so new, this world where my daughters were no longer laughing, playful children. A wave of loss washed through me. Too overwhelmed to speak, I could only nod.

"Might I brew some tea for you as well?"

I cleared my throat and forced myself to speak, to think, to continue. "Yes, thank you, Adara. Though nothing that will make me sleep."

"You will share Briallen's strengthening brew—as you also share her fierceness of spirit, Queen Boudicca."

I sighed and whispered, "I do not feel very fierce right now."

The Druid's gaze was gentle with compassion. "The warrior rests within you. She will awaken when she is needed. Do not doubt her. Your mother never did."

Surprise warmed my face. "Truly? Mother never spoke to me of fierceness. When I was granted the torque three months ago, she only talked of being compassionate and just."

"A fierce queen can also show compassion and rule justly. Your mother knew that. Arianell was so proud of you. She said you reminded her of Brigantia's flame, and she loved you well for it." With a caress that had me longing for my mother, the healer stroked my cheek. "In these awful days our leaders must be fierce or our people will be completely wiped out by Rome."

"I will do my best."

"Of course you will. That is all anyone, even the gods, can ask of you." Adara patted my arm.

"I must dress. My people will return soon." I shook off crushing weariness. "Please bring the tea to my bedchamber."

"I shall, Queen Boudicca."

Slowly, I poured warm water from the cauldron into a bucket, then I went to my bedchamber. The first thing that caught my eye as I entered was the neatly made-up pallet that belonged to my servant, Phaedra. Hastily, I scanned my memory for the girl's face among the dead.

"No, I did not see you," I said aloud, and hoped that gentle Phaedra would not be added to that list as the Druids collected the bodies.

I slid off the wide leather strap of the travel satchel that held the torque of Prasutagus. I did not take the golden symbol of leadership out of the bag but did run my hand across the rough leather to caress the outline of the thick torque.

It was still there—tangible proof that I had spent the day in Annwn and had received it as a sacred gift from Andraste. I would reveal my husband's torque when the time was right. I vowed then that until that time made itself known, I would keep the torque close.

Carefully, painfully, I stripped off the simple linen tunic. It had adhered to my back, and as I pulled it from my wounds they began to weep anew. Grimacing, I used a cloth to clean them as best I could before I dunked my hair in the bucket, washing away blood and sweat and dirt. Then I dried the thick scarlet mass with a woolen blanket and went to my clothing chest. Placed on the top of the clothes, neatly folded, was the dress Mother had embroidered for me as my Beltane gift.

My fingers trembled as they stroked the precious garment. Arianell must have put it in my chamber before the Romans attacked. She had refused to let me see it, saying that it was a gift and meant to be a surprise, so I had not so much as glimpsed it until that moment.

The fine linen gown had been dyed the lightest of blue, the color of the sky when frothy clouds obscured it. Arianell had been a gifted artist. She had used thread that had been dyed a much darker blue—the blue of Iceni woad—to create a tree that began at the hemline of the dress and grew up. I shook out the dress and studied it.

The tree was obviously the grandmother oak, which almost made me smile. I remembered how Mother used to worry when I was a girl and refused to stay out of the uppermost limbs of the mighty oak trees that surrounded Isurium, the royal village of Tribe Brigantes. As my mother's expert stitches re-created those boughs, they turned into intricate knots and swirls that danced their way up the fabric to form Andraste's raven, wings spread over the bodice. When the intricate pattern reached the shoulders, the embroidery shifted form again to become the heads of two mighty boars, each capping one of the shoulders. Their tusks met to create the rounded neckline. It was beyond beautiful. What my mother had created was a powerful dress for a warrior queen.

I shivered, remembering that my mother had been awake that morning, which seemed so very long ago, because she had been compelled by her goddess to advise her daughter. I wondered what else Brigantia had compelled my mother to do.

I'd watched my mother stitch the girls' Beltane dresses. They had been covered with flowers and delicate plants and playful baby animals that reflected Enfys and Ceri's sweet dispositions. My dress was completely different—completely what my people needed to see their queen wear.

"Thank you, Mother." I wiped tears from my eyes and attempted to put on the dress, but my newly exposed back would not allow me to lace it up, so I smoothed the soft cloth carefully, leaving it unlaced.

Then I sat before the precious mirror my father had traded for and gifted me with when I'd returned from fostering with the chief of the Trinovantes on my seventeenth birthday. As always, there was a wooden pot of woad paste on the table and a small horsehair brush. I dipped the brush into the sticky paint and drew the symbol all tribes knew as distinctly Iceni across my forehead—sickled moons with star points at each of their ends and small, rounded dots clustered in threes. The symbol evoked Andraste's moons, crescent and full, as well as the curve of the tusk of a boar. Then I lifted a wide-toothed wooden comb and began to work my way through my matted hair.

The pelt curtain moved and Adara's voice drifted through it. "Queen Boudicca, may I bring the tea to you?"

"Yes, thank you."

The healer approached. She put the cup of fragrant tea on the table and studied me. "Might I help you dress?"

"Yes. My back . . . I tried, but I could not . . ." I breathed a long, frustrated sigh. "I do need help. Thank you."

Adara said, "Just a moment, Queen Boudicca."

She disappeared through the pelt curtain and returned quickly with a woven basket of healing supplies. First, she applied a salve that stung. I sucked in air at the sharp pain, but within moments my shoulders relaxed and I was filled with relief as the salve worked its herbal magick and my back went completely numb. Then the healer carefully wrapped clean strips of cloth around me and tied the bandages securely in place so that the deepest of the lacerations were covered. Finally, Adara laced up the dress, though not tightly.

The healer breathed a long, appreciative sigh as she studied the garment. "Oh, I would know your mother's hand anywhere. This is magnificent."

My fingers reverently stroked the design. "It is perfect."

Adara gestured at the comb in my hand. "Allow me. I have given the warrior her own tea and your daughters sleep soundly. Some say I am rather skilled at the braiding of hair."

"I would appreciate your help combing through it, but do not braid it. My mother used to call it my flame, and I would honor Brigantia by allowing it to blaze."

"As you ask, so will I do," Adara murmured.

She sectioned off my thick mane and gently worked the comb through it. Neither of us spoke. I gratefully sipped the tea. Its warmth and the magick of the healing herbs soothed me, and for the first time since that terrible dawn, I relaxed. Adara's ministrations brought to mind the grooming ritual the Iceni women loved so well. Once a week they gathered in the houses of friends and family—and the lodge of their queen—and the women would bathe their hair in herb-scented water. Then, as they shared food and drink and talk, they would brush out each other's hair and create elaborate braids, woven with beads and feathers and strips of ribbon and brightly dyed cloth.

I closed my eyes and could hear the musical laughter of content, joy-filled women echo from my memory. For a moment it comforted me, but too soon grief spoke louder than the memory and I wondered if I would ever again feel the peace and comfort of simple rituals surrounded by happy, prosperous people.

"Time. Give yourself time, Queen Boudicca." Adara seemed to read my mind. "You are stronger than you know, and soon you will prove that strength to everyone—including yourself."

I studied Adara in the reflection of the mirror, noting her green robe, which showed that she was an ovate, a healer who was also often a seer.

"Did one of the gods give you a sign?" I asked.

Adara's reflection smiled. "The gods speak to me through intuition, not signs." The healer stepped back and her sharp gaze swept over me. "Your people will be comforted by their strong queen. Go to them and you will find they comfort you in return."

I stood and slid the leather strap of the satchel that held my husband's torque over my head and shoulder so that it rested securely against my right hip. "Thank you, Adara."

The healer's voice followed me from the lodge. "It is my great pleasure to serve the Iceni queen."

CHAPTER IX

At first the people returned slowly, trickling from the forest in a weak stream. They were the ones who had been too desperately wounded to make their way to the safety of the barrows. Many of them collapsed as they reached the field—some from their injuries and some from the despair of discovering their queen's mother and so many of their elders dead. I supervised the arrangement of pallets in the main room of the lodge. It was there that they were brought, tended, and comforted.

As night darkened the village, cook fires were lit as well as campfires all around the field. The stables were the only building that had been burned to the ground. Its location was far enough away from the farmers' huts that the fire had not spread to Tasceni. The procurator's haste to leave hadn't allowed the Romans time to pillage the village properly, and the damage they'd done was minor, though they had needlessly killed many of the pigs and several of the goats. The tribe's herd of cattle had been grazing in a forest meadow off the northern side of the village and had been left completely untouched. Soon the homey scents of roasting pork and goat cut through the despair that hung heavy over Tasceni. And then from the forest spilled the rest of the tribe. Some rode in the Druids' wagon, but the majority of the Iceni, silent and somber, walked back to their village.

The Druids had been hard at work building an enormous funeral pyre in the place of the wooden stake to which I had been bound before I was whipped. They had quickly erected simple shelters with roofs of ferns and sides draped in strips of braided hemp cloth. It was inside those shelters that they bathed and prepared the bodies for the pyre.

"Queen Boudicca!"

I turned at the sound of the familiar voice, and Phaedra rushed into my arms, weeping with relief.

"We were so afraid the Romans had killed you too!" Phaedra clung to me and sobbed.

"Andraste kept me safe. My mother died honorably protecting her granddaughters." I held the girl at arm's length. "Are you wounded?"

Phaedra shook her head. "No, when you commanded I flee, I slipped out the back of the lodge and into the forest. The Romans did not care about us. They did not seem to care about anything except you and the girls." Phaedra pressed her hand to her throat and gasped. "The girls! Are they—"

"Alive," I interrupted. "Though they were brutalized by the Romans."

"Oh, goddess!" Phaedra spat on the ground. "May their cocks shrivel and their balls turn black with rot."

"I have much worse planned for them. But now my daughters need rest and stability. Find my other attendants and have them go to the lodge. Enfys and Ceri sleep, but they will need tending, and it would best be done by familiar faces."

"Of course." Phaedra hugged me again and then bowed quickly before hurrying off.

I continued to move through the village, stopping at each hut to speak to my devastated people. Tasceni was awash with tears and sorrow, but I made myself a bright brand of hope and strength and comfort to the Iceni. I missed my mother with every step and in every moment. Arianell should have been there beside me, lending her healing arts and compassion to the tribe she had loved so very much.

I will not weep for Arianell. Not until I am alone. My people need a queen, not a grieving daughter.

As the deep of night settled over the village, I made my way once again to the warriors' practice grounds and the largest, grandest of the preparation structures. The Druids had hung cloth dyed in Iceni blue to create walls. Sacred mistletoe was draped along the roofline. The front of the structure was open and the fire that burned before it lent a somber golden light within.

I hesitated outside the tent and could not force my feet forward. I could see that there was a body on a crude table in the center of the hut, and a dark silhouette worked over it. I knew it was foolish. My mother was dead. I had closed her clouding eyes. But it suddenly felt as if it would be too real, too permanent, if I entered the preparation chamber.

"Come in, Boudicca. You are welcome here."

Rhan's voice made me jump, but it also compelled me to enter the hut.

Arianell was covered almost to her shoulders with a piece of cloth much like the woad-colored strips that hung from the sides of the structure. Her eyes were closed, and two smooth, round river stones had been placed over them. The killing stroke from the Roman's blade was covered by the shroud, and Mother appeared to be sleeping. Her long silver hair hung down over the edge of the table. Rhan stood there, at her head. She was braiding Arianell's hair into an elaborate crown.

Rhan's sad smile did not reach her eyes. "After I finish with your mother's hair I planned on painting her body, but as you are here now it is appropriate that you do it."

I ignored the horrible, empty feeling in my stomach. "I would like that. Very much."

"The pot is there, by her feet."

Wordlessly, I took the pot, noting that beside it was a fine painting brush made with clipped horsehair bristles, much like the one I had used to decorate my own face. I dipped the brush in the pot of indigo dye made from simmering bilberries, black beans, and purple cabbage, which had been cooled and thickened. It was the exact color of our woad-dyed clothes. Then I joined Rhan at my mother's head. Rhan paused in the braiding of Arianell's hair to fold down the cloth, baring Arianell's chest and arms.

I hesitated. "I—I am not sure what to paint."

"Think of what was dear to your mother. Brigantia will guide your hand."

Rhan spoke with such certainty that my hesitation evaporated, and I began painting symbols of the Iceni on Arianell's forehead, like those on my own, which had brought my tribe comfort as I greeted their sad homecoming that night.

From her forehead I moved to Arianell's chest, where I painted Brigantia's symbol, the head of a stag, in the center between her breasts, with massive antlers that covered each of her shoulders, the tips of which would decorate her pale neck.

As I painted the elaborate image, a great sense of peace came over me. Anointing my mother's body was an intimate thing, a beautiful thing—a thing that I did with love and care and the bittersweet understanding that this was the last time I was going to touch her, care for her, be a daughter to her. I worked slowly, patiently. I was not the artist my mother had been, but I did have some skill in creating the symbols that were such an important part of our lives, and as they took form I felt as if Arianell was close by, watching with approval.

"She is, you know." Rhan had returned to braiding my mother's hair.

"Can you hear everyone's thoughts now, or still just mine?"

"I remember telling you many times that I could not truly hear your thoughts; I could only guess them as I studied your face. But, yes, my skill has improved over the past years."

"She is really here?" I asked the question with a voice that was soft with seeking.

"Your mother is close. I can feel her presence. As we get nearer to Beltane the veil between the Otherworld, Annwn, and our world, Arbred, becomes thinner and thinner—and Arianell is of the newly dead. She will remain close until her pyre is lit, and perhaps even after, be it the will of her goddess."

"I want to make her proud."

"If you do what is best for your people, you will make her proud."

"But how do I know what is best for us? My husband thought he knew, and he gave us away to the Romans. He was older, wiser, and had led us for decades—yet still he chose poorly."

"Prasutagus did not heed the signs sent to him by Andraste."

I looked up from my work to see Derwyn standing just inside the open front of the preparation room. I met his gray gaze and spoke the truth.

"The hare was the first omen. Its death was meant to show Prasutagus what would happen if he made Rome co-regent with me."

"Indeed." Derwyn nodded slightly. "You see the proof of that before you."

I turned my gaze back to the symbols I was drawing on my dead mother's body but continued to speak to the high Druid.

"Andraste sent Prasutagus another sign. Just before he made the treaty with Rome, an eagle slew a raven and dropped it at his feet in this very field, almost exactly where the procurator tied me to the post and flogged me. Mere paces from where our girls were brutalized."

"Prasutagus did not tell me of this second sign, but I observed the first one."

"I remember. I was there that day. Could you not have warned him?"

"I interpreted the omen accurately!" The Druid's voice filled the hut, raising the hairs on my forearms with its power. "It was Prasutagus who would not listen, who refused to see and only believed a truth he had already chosen!"

I lifted my head and met the Druid's gaze again. It took all of my will not to flinch and allow my eyes to dart away. *I am queen of the mighty Iceni, consecrated by the Druids, chosen by my people, blessed by our goddess. I will not be cowed by any mortal man.* But Derwyn was not a normal mortal, and it was all I could do to meet his gaze. I could not form the words to defend a husband who had been so purposefully blind, no matter how much I had loved him.

The Druid sighed and the small structure returned to normal. Derwyn was, once again, familiar and kind. "You forget yourself in your grief or you would know that I have always spoken truth to the chiefs and queens of the great tribes."

"Andraste showed it to me. My husband ignored the goddess's signs."

"So you did visit Annwn today," Rhan said.

I glanced up at her. "I did. I was compelled there by Andraste and led by Brigantia's stag."

"The queen of the Iceni was named Victory by the goddess of war at her birth." Derwyn nodded slowly. "I have known you were to be queen since that day. And now I know that you will also lead us against the Romans."

"I will right the wrong my husband did," I said.

"The goddess will send sign to show the people you are her choice to lead them into battle," said Derwyn.

Silently, I returned to painting my mother's body, but the weight of my husband's torque hidden in the bag that rested against my hip reminded me that Andraste already had sent sign.

"It is late. The village has settled for the night," Derwyn said. "The Druids and I will keep watch over the dead and finish the preparation of the pyre. Rest tonight, Boudicca. Tomorrow the warriors will arrive."

I almost said that I wasn't sure I could ever sleep again, but Rhan's question interrupted my thoughts.

"Derwyn, has Gar returned from the fen yet?"

"I do not believe so," Derwyn said. He cocked his head and studied Rhan. "What have you seen?"

"It is more a feeling than a vision, but he will return with news that could change everything."

"What do you mean *could* change everything?" I asked my friend.

Rhan moved her shoulders restlessly. "That is all the goddess has allowed me—and the knowledge that the rest will be up to you."

And suddenly I felt unimaginably weary, so much so that my hand trembled as I painted the last line on my mother.

Gently, Rhan took the brush from me. "I will finish the queen's preparation. As Derwyn said, you must rest."

"Rhan, there was a servant whose body lay beside Mother's when you found her. I would ask that she be anointed by you as well." I wiped a shaky hand across my brow.

"Ancient Dafina? I remember her well. She was ever at your mother's side," said Rhan.

I nodded. "She died at her side."

"Then she shall be anointed as I would another queen mother, and she will be close beside Arianell on the pyre. Now, my friend, go. Rest. You must ready yourself for tomorrow," insisted Rhan.

"But you need a dress for Mother and . . ." My mind was a muddle and my words faded.

Derwyn's voice took up the thread of my weary thoughts. "I shall walk with you to the lodge. You may give me your mother's robes. I will return them here."

"Yes. Thank you." I turned to Rhan. "She looks beautiful. Your preparation of my mother has been perfect."

"*Our* preparation," Rhan said, and bowed her head to me respectfully as Derwyn escorted me from the silent tent.

"How many are dead?" I asked the Druid as we walked through the quiet village.

"Seventy elders, three children, one mother, and twenty-five warriors in their prime. The healers say that three more mothers are likely to enter Annwn before dawn."

"They will be good company for my mother and the others." I tried to sound strong and sure, but my voice shook with grief and exhaustion. So many daughters and sons had been made motherless today.

"They will, indeed. There will be feasting and merriment in the Otherworld tomorrow." Derwyn rested his hand lightly on my shoulder as we walked. "Do not despair, Queen Boudicca. They fought well and died protecting their queen and their people. Their welcome to Annwn is assured and eventually they will be reborn new again, with the pain of their violent departure from this lifetime left behind."

"I know all of that. It is just so much loss . . . so soon after . . ." My words faltered and then trailed away as grief usurped my voice.

"Focus on the living. You have much left to do." Derwyn stopped, and his pressure on my shoulder halted me as well. "I found this not far from the stake in the practice field. I thought that you should have it as I believe you will make good use of it."

From inside his white robes Derwyn brought forth the procurator's pugio. The blade gleamed in the dim light. I stared at it and for a moment was unable to move. And then I took it from the Druid and gripped it with enough strength to whiten my knuckles.

"I believe I will, too." I opened the flap of my leather satchel and slid it within, where it rested next to the heavy golden torque.

Silently we continued our trek through the village. Soon we'd come to the doors of the lodge, which had been closed against the night. I was surprised to see Briallen, dressed in a fresh Queen's Guard tunic, holding a spear and shield and standing at her post beside the doors.

"Briallen! You should be resting with the girls."

"The bairns sleep. Adara said they will not stir until after dawn. I will stand here until the rest of your guard relieves me."

I opened my mouth to protest, and then thought better of it and replied like a queen worthy of such loyalty. "I will sleep well knowing that you watch over us."

Briallen's one good eye shimmered with tears, but they did not fall. The warrior only bowed stiffly and then returned to her watchful stance.

"I'll have my servant, Phaedra, bring Mother's robes to you. Thank you—for all of this," I said to Derwyn.

Derwyn inclined his head but said nothing. My body felt leaden and I had to move slowly through the lodge so as not to stumble. The main room was littered with pallets that held the most gravely wounded. I stopped and spoke to each person who was conscious, and touched the foreheads of those who were slipping toward Annwn. The Druids in their forest-colored cloaks were night birds, flitting silently from person to person.

In my bedchamber, Phaedra rose from her pallet instantly, rushing to me. "It is so late! I was afraid you would never rest. Let me undress you and comb out your hair. I brought cheese and bread and smoked meat for you. Have you eaten at all?"

"Go to Mother's room—quietly, so that the girls do not wake. Gather the green plaid dress woven with the blue that matched her eyes and also the cloak of green with the stag stitched in gold on it. Do you remember?"

"I do."

"Take her favorite cuffs, the ones decorated with Brigantia's flames, and the necklace with the largest emeralds set in gold. Give them to the lead Druid, who waits outside the lodge."

"I will do as you command. Then I will return to help you."

"Thank you, Phaedra." On impulse, I hugged the girl who had served me for more than a decade, and Phaedra clung to me as she sobbed quietly. "Go now." I gently unwrapped myself from the young woman's embrace and wiped the tears from her cheeks. "Arianell is waiting to be dressed."

"Yes, my queen." Phaedra bowed deeply to me before she hurried from the queen's chamber.

Adara's salve still numbed my back enough that I was able to unlace the dress without help and slip on a soft tunic to sleep in. I meant to eat and to wait for Phaedra to return to brush out my hair but instead sank onto my bed. Unable to keep my eyes open a moment longer, I finally was able to allow sleep to take me away.

CHAPTER X

It was a dream, but it was also a memory—so clear and real that to my sleeping mind it seemed I gazed into a mirror that reflected the past.

The scene my dream conjured was one from my youth. I was almost seventeen, near to the end of the time I fostered with the Trinovantes. Children of royal families often fostered with neighboring chiefs or queens as a way to solidify alliances and strengthen the ties of trust and friendship among tribes. A friendship between the daughters of Tribe Trinovantes and Tribe Brigantes, future tribal leaders, was an important relationship to forge, and Rhan and I happily did become close.

In the dream she and I were at our favorite spot in the woods outside Camulodunum, which was then a village still in Trinovantes territory and as yet not usurped by Rome. We had woven vines and twisted them into torques, which each of us wore proudly around our neck. I brandished a wooden sword and Rhan held a long branch she'd carved to look like a spear. We stood side by side on a high bank above a stream that had been dammed by a family of industrious beavers. As my dream began, we were speaking to the hawthorns that lined the stream as if they were an elder council.

I remembered the day clearly, though I hadn't thought of it in over a decade. The dream was so vibrant that I could smell the fragrant hawthorn flowers that crowned the trees. Rhan and I were the eldest children of our fathers, though Rhan did have a brother, younger by two years. He would not automatically succeed her father; succession was always the choice of the gods and the tribe, and never as simple as blood or gender or birth order. Unlike Romans, we value our daughters equally to our sons and give little thought to birth order, which allows us to choose the best person to lead each tribe instead of being mired in the nonsense of patriarchy and birth order. So, Rhan and I were being raised to be queens, and our play was more practice than a child's game.

My sleeping mind followed the events that lifted sharply from my memory. Rhan and I had finished addressing the "council" behind us, and we had turned to face the new set of boughed and flowered "elders" before us, across the clear pool the beavers had created. I had just raised my sword and declared that there would be more generous portions of pork haunches in everyone's stew henceforth when something in the pool below caught Rhan's attention.

"What is th—" Rhan began.

But her words were cut off as she leaned forward and stared down into the quiet crystal pool. Rhan's body had gone rigid at the same time the birdsong in the trees silenced. I stared down into the water too, trying to see what had so captured my friend's attention, but saw nothing except water, river rock, and fallen branches. I turned to ask Rhan what I was missing and felt a shock of understanding when I realized her face had lost all of its color and her dark eyes had rolled to show only their whites.

Then Rhan's body seemed to turn boneless and she began to fall. Had I not moved quickly—and not been taller and physically stronger than my friend—Rhan would have toppled headfirst into the pool and drowned.

I carried her to the hawthorns and laid her on the carpet of moss under their fragrant boughs. I held her tightly, cradling my best friend—the friend who had made my five-year separation from my beloved family bearable—and murmured softly to her, beseeching her to come back to me.

Soon, Rhan's eyelids fluttered, and though her face was still white as milk, her eyes had returned to normal.

"What is it? What happened? What did you see, Rhan?"

Rhan stared up at me, and when she spoke her voice sounded decades older than sixteen short years.

"I saw you. You were queen. You wore a golden torque."

I smiled and hugged her tightly, feeling great relief that Rhan seemed herself again. I was pleased by her vision. When I was seventeen, becoming a queen was a fantasy that brought with it daydreams of rich clothes and loyal attendants, and the childish belief that a queen answered only to herself.

"Well, of course I will be a queen. You will be, too. We'll commission our torques from the finest jewelers. I want mine to be delicate and beautiful and decorated with—"

Rhan touched my cheek with fingers that were bloodless and cold. "No."

"But do not tell me what you saw; not now. You can tell me when I become queen so I choose the right decoration for my torque."

In my dream memory I watched my seventeen-year-old self chatter as Rhan and I collected our things and returned to the Trinovantes village. But this time I focused on Rhan and noticed now what I hadn't had the wisdom to see then.

My friend had remained somber and pale. Rhan only spoke enough to keep the young version of me from asking her more questions about the vision. Then, I had believed Rhan had been shaken because the vision was proof that she must leave to train with the Druids, which meant that she would never be queen of the Trinovantes. Not long after that day, I returned to the Iceni and Rhan began the journey to the Druid stronghold on the isle of Ynys Môn. Until the dream, I had forgotten about Rhan's first true vision.

Rhan was so quiet, so pale, because she had seen the truth. She spoke literally. She saw me wearing a golden torque. But which torque? And what else did she see that day?

"Boudicca, you must wake."

Like a memory swimming up from the past to surface in the present, Rhan's voice intruded on my dream. I opened my eyes to see my friend, no longer a girl, leaning over my bed and shaking my shoulder.

"What? What is it?" I sat up abruptly and then winced at the pain in my back.

Phaedra was suddenly awake as well. "Oh! I did not know the Druid had entered! I am so sorry, I was—"

"Ssh, Phaedra. All is well. This is my friend Rhan the seer. She has long had the ability to move unseen and unheard." I ignored the pain and stiffness in my back and swung my legs off the side of the bed as I smoothed the hair from my face. "It is dawn?"

Rhan nodded. "Just so. The warriors have returned, and so has Gar."

"Gar? He is just now returning from the fen?"

"He is, and he did not come alone. He brings with him a captive, the reason the Romans found their way through the fog and the sinking sand."

I felt a flush of anger, and as it receded, it left clarity and calm in its wake. I knew exactly what I must do. "I will dress quickly. Tell Derwyn to assemble the warriors and the tribe at the practice grounds around the pyre. Have Gar bring the intruder to me there."

"As you ask, so will I do." As silently as she had arrived, Rhan slipped from the chamber.

"I will get you fresh food and ale. Then I can—"

"There is no time," I interrupted. "Help me dress. There is still bread and cheese from last night here. I shall eat while you comb out my hair." Phaedra helped me into the beautiful gown that had been my mother's last gift.

"Should I triple-plait your hair in the style your mother preferred?"

"No," I said around bites of unleavened bread and thick goat cheese. "Brush it out and leave it unbound—as all Iceni should be."

chapter xi

The morning was completely clear, the sky so blue it seemed an ocean above us. No clouds. No fog. There was only the beauty of a spring day that heralded the newness of life. It was an innocent day that knew nothing of funeral pyres and the tragedies that swam just below its surface.

The Iceni spread around the practice grounds in a great, living circle. I paused on the path that led down to them, taking in the sight of the mighty tribe and the people I loved so dearly. Purposefully, I was unescorted. My hair was thick and free. The warm morning wind lifted it, revealing a restlessness I otherwise hid. I wore the dress my mother had created, embellished with no jewels, no golden cuffs or ornate silver brooch. Over my shoulder rested the leather satchel that held a gift from the goddess of war. From the woven leather belt at my waist peeked the iron hilt of a Roman pugio.

My back was stiff and sore, but a full night's sleep and food had restored my strength. I walked with my chin lifted and held my body straight and proud.

As I began the trek down to the field, Briallen was suddenly there, at my right. She wore the short woad-dyed tunic of my Queen's Guard, but today she had added leather greaves tied to her shins and vambraces to her forearms, and she'd painted her battered face with Iceni symbols as if she were going into battle.

A few steps farther and Rhan joined me on my left. She was dressed in her finest—a moss-green dress and an embroidered green cloak. Her face was painted with Ogham symbols that told everyone present she was a seer, trained on the isle of Ynys Môn, and respected as an oracle of Annwn.

I did not speak to either woman but drew strength from their presence and support. Heads held high, we approached the tribe.

The circle parted before me as the people shifted to allow our entrance. Druids and the newly returned warriors made up the heart of the circle. They packed the area in front of and around the massive mound that would be the funeral pyre. Derwyn stood in the center with his gleaming alder staff, which ended in the sickle of the crescent moon, held in his left hand. His snow-white robes were bright in the morning sunlight. To his right and left were the leaders of the Iceni warriors—the men and women I must convince to support me should I wish to continue to reign as their queen.

I did wish it—very much.

Directly to Derwyn's right stood a grizzled veteran named Cadoc, the man whom Prasutagus had chosen more than two decades ago as his shield. That title made him his chief's, then his queen's, most trusted warrior and advisor. It also made him a viable choice to become chief himself should the people fail to support me.

Cadoc towered above Derwyn. His thick, silver-gray mustache framed his lips, dropped below his chin line, and was braided with his long hair, which had turned completely white years ago but was still as thick and vibrant as the aged warrior's scarred body. That oak-strong body was covered with a bold knot work of tattoos that encircled his massive biceps and forearms. On his knees were the faces of twin boars—their huge tusks wrapped up his thick thighs.

Beside Cadoc was a leanly muscled woman, the ends of whose blond hair, shorn short, were woad colored and arranged in spikes. Her forehead bore our inked tribal symbol of crescent moons back to back, star points, and clusters of triple full moons. Abertha had been the spear master of the Iceni for almost a decade. She was the warrior responsible for my ability to hurl a spear accurately, as well as protect myself with a short sword in close combat.

To Derwyn's left was the youngest of the Iceni lead warriors, Maldwyn the horse master, whom I had elevated to the position just weeks ago. He was even taller than Cadoc, though his body was lithe and graceful instead of thick like the much older shield. His hair was wavy and rested on his shoulders. He, like all of our cavalry and charioteers, used a lime paste to bleach his hair shocking white, which contrasted brilliantly with the intricately tattooed images of rearing horses that decorated his broad shoulders and neck. His cornflower-blue eyes were rimmed in red, and he unashamedly let tears flow down his cheeks.

I wished with all my heart that they had been at my side the day before, as I could not imagine even a centuria of Rome cutting them down.

I felt more than heard Rhan's sharp intake of startled breath. I glanced at my friend and followed her gaze around the circle to see a small group of warriors clustered together who wore the distinctive red cloaks of Trinovantes royalty. I instantly recognized Rhan's father, Addedomaros, chief of our longtime allies.

Good. I stilled my nerves by reasoning. *With Addedomaros here it will save me the need to spread the word that I remain queen of the Iceni. Because I shall continue to rule. I must continue to rule. I have a curse to fulfill.*

I spoke directly to the grizzled shield of the Iceni.

"Cadoc, I greet you with great sadness, though I am pleased to have our warriors home again."

Cadoc inclined his head slightly, showing respect to me as queen but not the deference my warrior husband would have commanded from him. "Boudicca, our hearts broke when the Druid came to us with such tragic news. Our queen's mother is dead. And so many of our grandmothers and grandfathers have joined her that our tears could coax the Tas from her bank and change the course of that mighty river. We are heartened to find you alive and unharmed. Derwyn has greeted us, but he has not explained to us how this horror came to be."

I faced his underlying question without flinching. *Let me get this over with and still the wagging tongues before they can ruin me and our people.*

"How this horror came to be I cannot answer, though I may know one who can. I can answer the question you leave unasked, which is how I am alive when so many of our elders died and my daughters were brutalized so badly that they cannot leave their mother's lodge." Restless murmurs rustled through the tribe. I continued speaking while my gaze traveled around the tribe, lighting on familiar faces with a confidence and ease the Iceni would later boast of—how their mighty queen was a master at holding an audience rapt. "The goddess Andraste compelled me to enter Annwn yesterday at dawn. She appeared to me before the Romans invaded our village. She gave me a choice. Die fighting the Romans with my mother and our elders, or live and correct the grave mistake made by Prasutagus."

The murmurs around me grew to angry words so numerous that they were like the tall stalks of wheat in the surrounding field rustling in a great wind.

Derwyn's staff rang against the hardened ground, silencing the tribe. "Your queen speaks! She will be heard before you judge her."

I fisted my hands at my sides. My fingernails dug into my palms, drawing blood. But I did not flinch, nor did I waver.

"I was given the same choice my husband had been given before he signed away our freedom to the Romans—listen to the goddess or to my own ego. I chose to listen to Andraste. He did not."

Cadoc's eyes narrowed on me. "You insult your husband, our chief?"

"Never. I will never insult my husband, our chief, whom I loved well. But I will not hide the truth Andraste showed me." My gaze held Cadoc's. "Derwyn, tell them."

The high Druid stepped forward. "Iceni, you wonder why I have been absent these many months, before and after the death of your chief? The reason is simple. I interpreted the omen Andraste sent when Prasutagus asked whether he should sign the treaty with Rome. The goddess's answer was clear. The hare died suddenly, here, on the spot where months later your queen was flogged almost unto death by the procurator." Derwyn's gaze met Cadoc's. "You misspoke, Iceni shield. Your queen is not unharmed. Her back was flayed to the bone." Then his gaze continued around the circle. "Boudicca speaks truth. Your chief did not heed Andraste's omen, though I spoke her response to his question honestly and truly."

Shocked whispers passed through the tribe. At my lifted hand, they went silent.

"I witnessed the goddess's second warning sign," I told them, "the day it happened and again yesterday, in the cauldron of Andraste. You witnessed it too, Cadoc. Our goddess's raven was killed by a golden eagle and dropped at my husband's feet. It happened here—almost exactly where a man who carried the talisman of an eagle on his golden armor bound me to a stake.

"But, once again, Prasutagus ignored the sign. He refused to listen to the goddess. Yesterday I chose to listen and to follow Andraste, our goddess of war, until every Roman is washed from our land in a river of their own blood."

The people remained silent. I saw Cadoc's internal struggle on his well-lined face. He had loved Prasutagus dearly. I understood how difficult the truth was for him to process; it had been difficult for me as well. But I also knew that Cadoc was a wise warrior. He could be reasoned with, should I gain his support.

"I hear you, Queen Boudicca," said Cadoc. "I look at the signs sent by Andraste with new eyes. I hated the Romans before today. Now my loathing takes on a new life. Our queen mother is dead. My beloved mother is dead. I have seen her old, frail body, impaled by a Roman pilum. I want vengeance with my every breath. But you have only ruled for three full cycles of the moon, and you have never led warriors into battle."

Derwyn spoke up. "When did the Iceni begin measuring courage strictly by experience on the battlefield?"

Cadoc shrugged. "Derwyn, I do not question Boudicca's courage. It is her experience, or lack thereof, that gives me cause to question her." The warrior turned back to me and continued. "In normal times, when we are at peace, I would gladly continue to bend my knee to you. But what happened yesterday changed that. The days have turned red as the river you boast about drowning the Romans in. Tell me, Boudicca, how a queen who is not a warrior survives such a flood—especially a queen who seems to have misplaced her torque."

My face blazed with heat and I had to force myself not to reach up to touch the empty place around my neck.

"The symbol of my leadership is missing because a cowardly Roman stole it from me while I was bound and beaten. But in answer to the rest of your insolent question, I will repeat to you—*to all of you*," I shouted, "the words I cursed the Romans with—the words I know Andraste heard because I chose to follow her will and not my own."

As I repeated the curse, a wind swept through the field. It swirled around me, lifting my fire-colored hair as if I rode a war chariot against our enemies. It amplified my voice and carried it to each tribe member as if I spoke to him or her individually.

When I finished I waited a moment, and then, as the echo faded, I repeated, "*Through my blood and with my goddess-blessed breath, I have cursed you unto death!* I will not rest until every Roman who was here yesterday—every one who slaughtered our elders, violated my daughters, and flogged your queen—has been sent to their underworld for judgment." I strode forward. Briallen and Rhan moved with me as if we three were one, until I stood directly before Cadoc. "Andraste set me on this path. She did not speak of my inexperience. *Instead the goddess reminded me that she named me Victory!* Do you claim to be wiser than a goddess?"

The field was hushed. Even the wind had gone still.

Cadoc ignored my question and repeated stubbornly, "I would follow you in peace, but you have never been in a battle. Never led a tribe into war."

I turned my back to Cadoc. Before he could respond, I commanded. "Gar! Bring forth your captive!"

Gar pushed his way forward, his hand gripping the arm of a man whose wrists were tied behind him. Over dirty leather pants the hostage wore a tunic that was the brown of the fens. Its only embellishment was a design painted with the black dye of walnuts that formed moons and hidden faces—the unmistakable symbols of the Catuvellauni tribe, a tribe that had exchanged their freedom to ally with Rome.

I heard the mutters of the tribe as they, too, recognized the symbols on the man's tunic.

Derwyn moved to stand at my side. As leader of the Druids, it was his responsibility to dispense tribal justice.

"Gar, how did you come to capture this man?" Derwyn asked his Druid.

"You bid me search the fen for someone who did not belong there. Queen Boudicca asked that I search with stealth because the person I sought must be surprised were he to be captured." Gar jerked his chin in the direction of the captive at his side. "The queen's words were wise. I knew by his tunic this Catuvellauni did not belong so close to the heart of the Iceni people. Had I not come upon him secretly, he would have escaped into the river, as he surely tried to escape me several times on the way here."

I met the silent captive's gaze. He was an older man, probably one who had seen at least forty years. His long hair was a unique shade of bright blond that shined gold. His face was pale and a spot of red burned over each of his cheeks.

"My mother is dead," I said to the captive without preamble. "My daughters were raped. Our elders were killed by a Roman centuria that surprised us by stealing into our village from the fen with a fog so thick it hid them perfectly."

Derwyn cocked his head, studying the captive. "How did the Romans, weighted down by armor and weapons, without any knowledge of Iceni lands, find their way through the fen? Why did the sinking sands and sucking mud not swallow them? Why would they even attempt such a thing unless they had a guide to lead them— a guide who knew the Iceni warriors would be at the spring games? Explain that."

The tribesman remained silent as he stared at a place behind Derwyn.

"I know this man." Cadoc moved closer, peering at the captive. "Hefeydd, it is you!"

The captive reluctantly met the old warrior's gaze. "I see you, Cadoc."

"Shield of the Iceni, how do you know this man?" Derwyn asked.

"Several of us know him, though he was a youth when last we saw him. I only recognize him from the color of his hair and the symbols on his tunic. Hefeydd was the last of the Catuvellauni royalty to foster with us before they whored themselves out to Rome. He is Chief Togodumnus's nephew. Prasutagus treated him like a son for the years he spent with us."

Derwyn's voice was filled with disappointment. "You played in the fen as a youth. That is how you were able to guide the Romans through it. And you knew the Iceni warriors would be visiting the Trinovantes just before Beltane, because that is their tradition."

Around them the Iceni moved restlessly, like warhorses aching to charge the enemy.

My anger burned hotter. I moved closer to Hefeydd, forcing Cadoc to step aside. I was taller than the Catuvellauni tribesman and looked down my long nose in disgust as I spoke. "So you repaid my husband's kindness by leading Romans to his door."

"Prasutagus died three months ago," Hefeydd said. He looked around me at the high Druid. "Derwyn, I ask that you ransom me to Togodumnus. My uncle will pay to see me safely returned to him."

Derwyn surprised everyone by ignoring Hefeydd and speaking to me instead. "This man repaid your husband's hospitality with betrayal. Your back will, for the rest of your life, bear the scars of Rome. It was your daughters who were brutalized, your mother killed, and your elders slaughtered because this man led the Romans through the fen when he knew your warriors would not be here to protect the tribe; therefore, I grant the judgment of Hefeydd, nephew to Togodumnus, chief of the Catuvellauni, to you, Boudicca, queen of the Iceni."

I watched Hefeydd's eyes widen in shock and his face lose all color. But he stood straight and met my gaze.

"Boudicca, I say again—ransom me to my uncle. Catuvellauni will pay the Iceni richly," pleaded Hefeydd.

"Ransom you? As if you were caught stealing cattle? No, Hefeydd.

You will *not* be ransomed." I appeared to turn away from him. Then, with the speed of a well-trained Iceni warrior, I pulled the Roman dagger from my belt and whirled around, slicing through the traitor's neck. "My judgment is death!"

"Judgment has been meted out!" Derwyn cried, spreading his arms ceremoniously.

Hefeydd gurgled in shock. His blood sprayed strong and thick for one, two, three heartbeats before he fell to his knees and then collapsed.

The Iceni went completely still.

The moment the blood began to pump from his death wound, the full realization of what I had done hit me. My strike had been graceful, lethal, swift, and accurate—everything the master warriors had drilled me to be for the fifteen years I had been married to their chief.

But I hadn't practiced the emotions that came with taking a life—watching a man's eyes go dim as his blood soaked the ground.

Killing a man was not like slicing into a straw target. Killing a man, even one who richly deserved it, was a terrible, dark thing that I felt settle heavy and sick in the depths of my spirit.

A wave of nausea crashed over me. My hands and feet went cold. I swayed and might have stumbled, even fallen, but a firm hand took my elbow and lent me strength.

"Courage. You did the right thing," Rhan whispered. Then she swept her arm dramatically up to point at Derwyn, and in a voice filled with power, she cried, "Behold, Tribe Iceni! Andraste has given sign!"

Silently the tribe stared at the high Druid, whose white robes were spattered with Catuvellauni blood spray—which clearly formed the outline of a scarlet raven in flight.

Derwyn took several strides to stand in the center of the raptly watching tribe. He turned slowly as he held out his arms, giving the Iceni plain view of the bloody omen sent from our patron goddess as he announced, "Andraste approves of Boudicca's judgment!" When he had come full circle he stopped, facing me. "But this is not the only sign the goddess has sent to show she has blessed your leadership, is it, *Queen* Boudicca?"

My heart hammered so hard that in the eerie silence of the waiting tribe I thought they should all be able to hear it. Still, I strode to stand beside Derwyn to address my people.

"I already told you I spent much of yesterday in Annwn, in the presence of Andraste. The goddess gave me knowledge of the past, revealing my husband's terrible mistake, as well as asking me to choose to either survive the Roman attack or join my people in the tragedy. When I let Andraste and not my ego guide me, the goddess showed her approval by giving me a gift."

It was time.

I reached into the satchel and grasped the thick gold torque that had been my husband's sign of leadership, buried with him three months earlier. I raised the torque above my head so that it caught the morning light and glittered as if it had been lit from within.

"Behold, the torque of Prasutagus!" Derwyn shouted.

The Iceni gasped. Echoed whispers of "'*Tis the chief's torque!*" rustled through the tribe.

Rhan lifted her arms. "Now, who among you will tell the chosen of Andraste that she is not fierce enough to lead?"

I looked only at Cadoc as the shield of the Iceni approached. He stopped in front of me and then dropped to one knee and bowed, deeply and respectfully.

"I give you my pledge to follow you into battle, Queen Boudicca," he said.

Briallen was next. She quickly took one knee and bowed to me. Tears washed freely down her face and with a voice filled with strength she said, "My pledge is yours, my queen!"

Each of the leaders of the warriors followed her and then, like ripples from a stone thrown into a still pool, the Iceni knelt in waves around me, and as they knelt I finally put the heavy golden torque around my neck and bent it into place.

The Druids did not kneel—they knelt only to the gods and goddesses—but Derwyn, Rhan, and the others bowed deeply to me.

Even the Trinovantes royalty and their warriors bowed, acknowledging the queen of the Iceni.

"Hail our warrior queen Boudicca!" Cadoc shouted as he stood, and then he stomped his leather-clad foot against the packed ground of the practice field as he began the chant: "Bou-dic-ca! Bou-dic-ca!"

The Iceni took up the chant, stomping against the ground until Tasceni reverberated with my name.

Amidst the tribe's shouts of acceptance, Briallen approached me and bowed deeply. "My queen, should I tie the body of the Catuvellauni traitor to a horse and return him to his uncle?"

I forced myself to look at the man I had killed where he lay in the middle of a wide pool of scarlet. I swallowed back the bile that rose in my throat and studied him with a queen's gaze, considering my options as I bent and wiped the bloody dagger on the ground before sliding it back into my leather belt. I straightened and shook my head. "No. Let his body be the first of the traitors we offer to Andraste. Sink him into the mud of the fen. Pour libations of ale and honey over him to make him more palatable to our goddess. Togodumnus will not know that we have found him out. But we have been warned of the depth of Catuvellauni treachery." I paused and looked at the tall warrior who stood not far from me. "Unless the shield of the Iceni has a wiser, more experienced idea."

Cadoc smiled at me then. "I do not, my queen. I am in agreement with your wisdom. I, too, would have slit his throat and offered his blood to Andraste with my own hand had Derwyn granted me judgment. You are correct. The Catuvellauni chief knew of this plot. Had he not, Hefeydd would not have been so eager to be ransomed. It is good that now we know of their treachery."

"Briallen, have two warriors bring libations to the goddess with you and sink the traitor in the fen."

"As you ask, so will I do, Queen Boudicca."

Cadoc nodded. "And what is your command for me, my queen?"

"Help the Druids finish preparing the funeral pyre. We will care for our dead. And then you and I will prepare to serve vengeance to the living."

CHAPTER XII

With Derwyn's approval, I ordered everything prepared and the funeral pyre to be lit at dusk, the beginning of Beltane, when the veil between Annwn, the realm of the gods, and Arbred, the world of mortals, is so thin that it is often such an easy thing to slip between the two. On Beltane the Iceni lit many bonfires throughout Tasceni and kept them burning all night long—beacons to guide the spirits of our ancestors home.

In total, ninety-eight people, including my mother, died at the hands of the Romans. Twenty sows, two boars, and ten goats were needlessly butchered by the soldiers. Five horses were trapped and perished in the burning barn. Two more died of their wounds the following day.

I ordered the tenderest flanks of the sows to be divided among the dead and offered on their mass pyre. The bodies of the two horses, as well as the charred bones of the other five, were added to the pyre, too.

I decreed the tribe would continue our tradition of Beltane feasting and revelry—dedicating the night to my mother, who had a special love for that particular festival as it was a favorite of her fiery patron goddess, Brigantia.

Preparation of the pyre and tending of the wounded had to take precedence, so I was unable to hold a formal meeting with Chief Addedomaros, my husband's old friend, ally, and neighbor. I knew I must not avoid that meeting long, so I invited him and the Chief's Guard who had accompanied him to stay for Beltane, which he graciously accepted.

Then, as dusk turned the clear spring day to a cool night, all that was left for me to do was to stand witness to the funeral rite Derwyn would lead and then open the feast by lighting the pyre and sending the Iceni dead to Annwn.

Phaedra carefully cleaned my wounds and Adara reapplied the numbing salve. To my fierce Beltane dress I added a green cloak Arianell had embroidered years before with black thread in spirals and knots that formed charging boars. I hadn't often worn the cloak. She had asked me once, several years ago, why I rarely wore it. I explained to my mother that it was a glorious cloak, perfect for a warrior queen of the Iceni but not the gentle, peaceful wife of a prosperous chief. I remembered how Arianell had smiled knowingly at me that day and said nothing.

I fingered the cloak and whispered, "You knew, didn't you? You always knew someday I would have to be fierce enough to wear it."

Phaedra stepped back, admiring me. "You look magnificent. I know it is tradition to braid and dress your hair, but I like that you decided to leave it unbound. It is somehow fitting."

I responded with the simple truth. "It is free; that is why it is fitting."

The pelt door rustled and Rhan stepped within. A smile lit her entire face, as it used to when we were youths. I thought she looked like a girl again, impishly mischievous and eager for adventure. But it was the mature seer who spoke, though the smile remained in her dark eyes.

"The Iceni are ready. They await their queen."

"What of my daughters?"

Rhan's expression sobered. "They dressed and allowed the attendants to braid their hair, but they are still in much pain—in their minds as well as their bodies. I have heard Ceri say that she cannot bear to go to the warriors' practice grounds again."

I nodded slowly. The weight of my daughters' distress pressed down upon me. "I will speak with Adara and with them. Perhaps I should not force them to do anything that frightens them until their bodies are stronger. Please, come with me, my friend." Rhan followed as I headed to my mother's spacious rooms, which my daughters had claimed as their own.

The wounded had been moved to neighboring huts and the lodge transformed from a place of death and sadness to something much more familiar—the site of an upcoming feast. Long trestle tables laden with clay pitchers of beer and ale, as well as great plates filled with bread and others with wheels of rich cheese, stretched from wall to wall. On every table were bouquets of spring lavender and lilac, as well as sprigs of fragrant apple and lime blossoms. All around the lodge, those tending the cooking fires had been busy grilling spitted pork and goat, and the succulent aromas permeated the daub-and-wattle walls and the elaborate tapestries that decorated them.

I nodded approval to the cooks and servers, who paused in their last-minute touches to bow to me.

Briallen intercepted me halfway to Mother's chamber. The warrior's face was purple and yellow with bruises, but a sliver of blue peeked through her swollen lid and I was relieved to see that there were no bloody spots on her tunic from wounds breaking open or seeping.

Briallen cleared her throat and said, "My queen, I've been speaking with your daughters."

"Yes, I know they're frightened. I was just going to check with the healer before I went to them."

The warrior clasped her hands behind her back and looked down at her leather sandals. "I have done something. Forgive me if I over-reached."

Curiosity piqued, I asked, "What have you done?"

"I hope I've made your bairns feel safe again."

"I don't understand," I said.

"'Tis easier to show than tell. Will you trust me, my queen?"

I answered with no hesitation. "With my life."

"Aye, well then. With your permission I will get the girls."

I glanced at Rhan, who caught my eye and gave a slight nod. "All right."

Briallen led the way to Arianell's chamber. She swept aside the thick tapestry door. Enfys and Ceri sat on the edge of their grandmother's large bed pallet. They stood as I entered, holding hands and looking pale and nervous.

The Druid nodded respectfully to me. "Queen Boudicca, your daughters are healing well."

I smiled at my girls. "And they look lovely in the dresses Mother stitched for them." Arianell had decorated the matching green dresses with blue stitching that had spirals of baby animals, flowers, and birds frolicking all along their hems and bodices. I remembered watching Mother bend over the clothes as she lovingly embroidered them. The memory caused my breath to hitch. *Will I ever be able to think of my mother without it causing such sharp, terrible grief?*

Enfys's chin shook as she spoke, but she did not cry. "Mama, I do not want to see Nain's pyre."

"I know, love, but your nain is dead and we must witness her funeral rites and then send her off to Annwn with our people. This is what she would want."

"It is very hard," said my eldest child.

"It is," I agreed. "But it is also something we must do for her because of how much we love her."

Ceri spoke suddenly. Her voice trembled and sounded as wan and fragile as she looked. "Mama, I-I do not think I can go there. B-back to that p-place."

Before I could formulate a reply Briallen stepped forward and knelt in front of the girls. She repeated the question she had so recently asked me. "Do you trust me?"

They, too, did not hesitate in their answer. Both girls nodded.

"Will you believe—if I give you my word—that I have found a way to make you feel safe, even there, on that field?"

Again, they nodded, though more slowly than before.

"Then let us go and show everyone the courage of the daughters of Queen Boudicca." Briallen straightened and held out her hands, so that each girl took one. Then she bowed to me. "We follow you, my queen."

"Rhan, please walk with us," I said.

My friend bowed her head slightly. "As you ask, so will I do."

I walked from my mother's chamber through the lodge, which was now completely empty. At the closed doors, I fisted my hand

and rapped three times against the thick wood. Two Queen's Guards flung the doors wide open, and what I saw made me gasp in awe and appreciation and pride.

Before us, stretching all the way through the village and down to the massive pyre, were the women of the Iceni tribe. Dressed in their finest to honor their fallen loved ones, as well as their queen's mother, they faced one another. Each woman held a long strip of blue-dyed cloth over her head, connecting her to the woman across from her so that it seemed they had built a tunnel of women and Iceni woad, surrounding my daughters and me with the maternal strength of our tribe.

Humbled by the love of my people, I bowed my head and whispered a prayer. *Mighty Andraste, help me to be worthy of them.* Then I looked back at my daughters. Their eyes were wide and round with wonder. Ceri was smiling. My gaze lifted from them to the silent warrior standing at my side.

"This is what you did?"

"Aye, my queen."

I went to the warrior, and as Briallen bowed before me I lifted her by placing my hands on her bruised cheeks, and—just as my mother would have—kissed her gently, there in front of the watching tribe, before I spoke in a voice that carried with the breeze, floating to the women like the blue banners over their heads.

"Briallen, let it be known that for this kindness I name you leader of the Queen's Guard. You have my eternal gratitude." Then I turned to face the tunnel of woad. My gaze scanned the Iceni women. "You have my eternal gratitude as well."

As one, the women shouted the Iceni war cry, which lifted and fell with the wind. Then the drummers began and the pounding of the tribe's bodhráns, handheld drums that were beaten by carved wooden sticks called tippers, pulsed around us. Using powerful flicks of the wrist, the drummers beat out the untamed music of the Iceni.

Head held high, followed by a seer, a battered warrior, and my two brave daughters, I strode through the tunnel of women and woad as the pulse of the Iceni filled the night.

At the practice grounds, the tribe, once again, surrounded the pyre in a living circle. Arianell's body was the center point. Her section of the pyre had been elevated. At her head were the antlers of a stag, and around her wrapped body on the flat wooden litter were hunks of meat, mounds of herbs, pots filled with dye, precious spices, and her favorite perfumed oils—as well as the body of her beloved servant and friend.

The queen mother was joined by a full circle, wheel-like, of shrouded bodies. They lay side by side, with items of value and importance to each of them at their feet and head: more choice hunks of meat, favorite pieces of jewelry, shields, and spears, as well as carved images of patron gods or goddesses. Completing the circle were the bodies of our beloved horses and woven baskets filled with grain.

Derwyn waited at the end of the tunnel of women with a burning brand held in his hand. He had not changed his robes, and the outline of Andraste's raven had turned a dark, rusted color that was even more pronounced against the otherwise spotless white. He turned to greet me and the tribe went silent.

"Are you ready, queen of the Iceni?" the Druid asked.

"I am."

He faced the east, lifting his arms. With him the tribe turned to face east as well. Derwyn's voice filled the darkening night with the power of nwyfre, the life force that runs through the earth, sky, and water around us and fills each of the Iceni with a spark of immortal spirit.

"Bright Brigantia, I call on you first as patron goddess of Arianell, mother of the queen of the Iceni. Let your fire cleanse her of the pain of leaving this world!"

Derwyn and the tribe turned to face south. "Gracious Brigantia, I ask that your snow-white hart guide Arianell to your side, where she may feast the night away!"

The Druid and the tribe continued to turn, now facing west. "Next, I beseech the god of youth, Mabon ap Modron, to touch Arianell and those who perished with her and breathe youthful joy into them. Lead Arianell and her people in revelry tonight and many nights hence with dance and drink and feasting befitting a beloved Iceni matriarch!"

Finally Derwyn turned to the north, facing the pyre. "Lastly, I call forth Andraste! Patron goddess of the Iceni, triple-faced goddess of fertility, the hearth, home, and war. Many of your children died with the Iceni's queen mother, so many that I know this night your feast table will be long and filled with familiar faces. You will sacrifice the fattest sow and open the golden casks of ale for all—*all died the death of warriors and all are worthy!*"

He nodded to the other Druids who stood beside him, and as he finished the prayer, they stepped forward to lay woven sprigs of sacred mistletoe at the feet of the dead atop the mound of dried boughs. Then he finished the funeral rite, speaking the final prayer.

Arrayed in some new flesh disguise
Another mother gives birth.
With sturdy limbs and bright new brain.
The old soul will someday take the well-traveled road to Arbred
    again, again, again.

The Druids disappeared silently into the circles surrounding the pyre as Derwyn turned and called to the shield of the Iceni.

"Cadoc, it is now!"

"Bows!" Cadoc shouted.

From all around the circle, Iceni warriors, dressed in their finest clothes and jewels, took a step forward. They each held a longbow and one arrow, notched and ready to fire. Their flint tips were wrapped in lard-soaked cloth.

Then the aged warrior went to me. Cadoc bowed deeply, respectfully, before handing me a longbow and another prepared arrow.

"They await you, Queen Boudicca."

I fitted the arrow and then nodded at Derwyn, who touched his torch to the arrowhead, igniting it. All around the circle, Iceni holding torches stepped forward to light the arrows of the warriors.

I steeled myself against the pain in my back and drew the bow along with a deep breath. I aimed up into the charcoal sky, sighted, and held my breath. I released my breath and the arrow together. All around me the twangs of many arrows sizzled through the night as flaming brands lifted to the sky after mine, hesitated, and then, as if called back by their fallen tribesmen and -women, they rushed to earth, embedding in the tinderbox that was the pyre.

I stood there as long as I could bear it. Heat eddies lifted my mass of hair and curled my cloak. Later the tribe whispered that their queen had seemed to be Andraste herself standing fierce and immortal before the roaring pyre, but that night I did not feel fierce or immortal. I was an orphan who longed for something I would not know again in this lifetime—my mother's touch. I would never hear her voice again. I would never see her smile again. She would never comfort me or share her wisdom with me again. I stood there, as close to her as possible, as her pyre dried the tears that washed my face.

I did not want to look away from Arianell, who was illuminated by the licking flames. I wished so badly for one last touch, one last word.

And as I wept and squinted against the brightness of the fire, I was rewarded. The smoke that curled up from the center of the pyre, thick and grayish white, danced and flowed over and around itself until it took the shape of a mighty hart, whose face was as familiar to me as my mother's.

My tears did little to protect me from the heat. Just as Rhan took my arm and whispered, "Boudicca, you must come away now," the sky above us opened and a gentle rain began to fall as the night wept with the Iceni.

CHAPTER XIII

P ride in my people carried me through the rest of that long night. The eve of May is usually filled with feasting and passion and remembrance. Young women dress their hair with wreaths of ivy and flowers. It is a celebration of the fertility of the growing season— a magickal night from which many handfasts and babies result.

I had always loved the lighting of the tribal bonfires that illuminated Tasceni in jewellike gold and orange so that it seemed otherworldly. It was easy to imagine the spirits of our ancestors dancing among the flickering shadows as they rejoined their living tribe for a night of revels.

Not this Beltane.

As I sat in the center of the raised queen's table in my lodge and presided over our subdued feast, I felt the absence of my husband and mother as a constant ache deep in my bones. To my right, in the place of honor, was Derwyn. To my left sat Addedomaros, chief of Tribe Trinovantes. Stretched along the queen's table were my lead warriors, as well as Addedomaros's shield, Mailcun, who I had long thought resembled a large brown bear.

As if my thoughts drew his gaze, Mailcun's eyes met mine. I glimpsed a deep sadness there and remembered that he and Arianell had been friends. They had carried on a flirtation over the many years since my father's death; he had often brought her gifts when our two tribes met, small animals carved from wood that made my mother smile. He dipped his head respectfully to me and returned to pushing the food around his plate. It was then that I noticed the little wooden owl he'd placed beside his goblet of untouched ale. The owl, like the white stag, was beloved of my mother's goddess, Brigantia. The sight of that ungiven gift pulled me from my fog of grief so that my gaze traveled around my lodge and I saw my people through clearer eyes.

My daughters had retreated to bed. Briallen stood unmoving just outside their pelt door. Every table was filled, though at each was at least one plate that had been piled high with choice cuts of meat sprinkled generously with salt and spice and left untouched. Each Beltane, plates were offered to our ancestors while living Iceni feasted and drank, laughed and loved. Tonight there was no laughter. The tribe's voices were muffled, their eyes dull, their shoulders slumped.

I turned to Derwyn. "They mourn," I said softly.

"You must help them." His voice, like mine, was pitched not to carry.

I felt the weight of his words press down on me as my gaze swept across the lodge. "How can I? I mourn, too."

"Queens do not have the luxury of mourning. If the Iceni fall into despair, your curse will not be fulfilled. Your tribe will splinter and, like tinder, quickly burn out."

My gaze snapped to his as my rage, which had cooled after the lighting of the pyre, sparked and took flame again. Under my breath, I almost spit the words at the Druid. "I am not just a queen. I am a widow. I am an orphan. I am—"

Derwyn lifted his hand and touched the golden torque that encircled my neck. As his fingers met the twisted gold, heat spread from it through my body, cutting off my words.

Slowly, distinctly, Derwyn said, "You are Victory, named by Andraste. That is, indeed, more than just a queen."

Victory . . .

The goddess's voice lifted from my veins and echoed through my marrow. *You have a choice to make that will shape your future as well as your tribe's.*

I made my choice. I survived. I will not let it be all for naught.

"Mailcun, shield of the Trinovantes, I see you brought a gift for my mother." I raised my voice, making sure that it carried throughout the somber lodge.

Mailcun's surprised gaze lifted to mine. "I did, Queen Boudicca."

"Might I see it?" I held out my hand.

"Of course." The old warrior handed the little owl to his chief, who passed it to me.

The lodge watched me study the figure, and as I did I heard my mother's ancient servant's voice so clearly that she could have been standing behind me, as she had always stood close to Arianell. My lips lifted, and when I looked up and spoke I knew my smile had reached my eyes. "You know what Dafina would say?" I didn't wait for an answer but continued, doing my best to mimic the old woman's voice. "'Could you not have made it bigger for my lady?'" I raised one brow and looked at Mailcun.

Caught off guard, Mailcun barked a laugh, which he quickly stifled. I shook my head and spoke warmly to him. "No, do not silence your laughter. Arianell loved the sound of it, and my mother most certainly would be teasing you along with her Dafina." I turned my gaze to my people, allowing it to linger here and there as one and then another and another met my eyes. "We cannot be bowed by the deaths of our elders. That does not honor them." I looked down my table to Cadoc. "Iceni shield, what would *your* wise mother say of this somber feast?"

Cadoc had been slumped over his mostly uneaten plate. He straightened, and a hint of a smile played across his wide, expressive mouth. "She would cuff the back of my head and remind me that Beltane is a night of joy and revels. She would say wasted happiness is wasted life." He nodded, and his thick silver beard bobbed up and down on his chest. "Aye, and were she here she would be cackling happily with the queen mother about the diminutive size of Mailcun's . . ." He paused, and his clear gaze went to the Trinovantes shield, looking his bearlike body up and down, before he finished suggestively, "*Owl.*"

This time several people laughed, and I felt the grief in the lodge begin to ease. It did not release its hold on my people—that would not happen so easily or quickly—but it was suddenly not so difficult to breathe.

I stood and raised my untouched mug of ale. "To Arianell!"

Mailcun raised his mug so quickly ale sloshed onto the table. Though his eyes were bright with unshed tears, his deep voice boomed. "To Arianell!"

The lodge joined him, raising their mugs and drinking deeply. When I sat, Cadoc stood. He bowed to me and then began recounting a story of how early this spring his mother, who had been a surprisingly tiny woman, had discovered an eagle diving on her beloved hens. The raptor's wingspan had been wider than the old woman was tall, but she hadn't hesitated. She'd grabbed a broom and begun beating the huge creature until it squawked in fear and took to the sky, leaving her hens in peace ever after.

Laughter replaced silence. Servants refilled mugs and others stood to share stories of their loved ones. Soon the lodge echoed with laughter and remembrance and life—and I felt just a little of the weight that had been pressing down on me lift.

"Well done, Queen Boudicca," Derwyn said, bowing his head ever so slightly to me. "Well done."

After the ale and tales of our lost loved ones began to flow, it was a simple thing for me to slip from my lodge. It was still raining, though gently—more mist than drops. The fires that burned brightly throughout Tasceni created halos of light, within which I was pleased to see couples dancing to the rhythmic music of drums and flutes and lyres. It was not, of course, as exuberant and passionate as Beltanes past, but once the gloom had been lifted from my lodge, the rest of the village seemed to breathe a long sigh of relief, as if they had been given permission to live again.

I skirted the edge of the many rings of light as I made my way through Tasceni, my feet carrying me toward the still-burning pyre. I was grateful that the damp breeze blew steadily across the fens inland, taking with it the smoke and stench from the pyre. I'm not sure what I meant to do. Perhaps see if my mother or her goddess would send me another sign. Or maybe I simply meant to be as near to her mortal remains as I could be until her ashes, and that of the other fallen Iceni, were gathered and taken to the Chief's Barrow, where they would be entombed with Prasutagus. But as I drew close to the field that held the glowing pyre and the Druids who stood watch around it, my steps faltered, and the heaviness in my soul that had briefly lifted pressed upon me again.

I changed direction and made for what was left of our stables. They still smoldered, but our herd, strong and proud and so recently returned from the spring games with the Trinovantes, were corralled a safe distance from the ruins. Three fires had been lit in a triangle before the corral, and the leaping flames drew me as surely as the comforting scent of horseflesh.

Two young stable hands fed the flames. When they noticed me they immediately stood, bowed, and shuffled their feet nervously. "Queen Boudicca!"

"Be at ease," I said, smiling at the boys. "Have you feasted?"

"Not yet, my queen," said the taller of the two. As he spoke I recognized him and the other boy as my horse master Maldwyn's younger brothers. "Maldwyn said we should tend the fires until he sent someone to take our place."

Even in the misty rain and flickering light of the bonfires, I could see that both boys' faces were grim and tearstained. From the list within my mind of those elders lost, I found the name Gwladus, Maldwyn's gregarious and ancient grandmother.

"You are relieved," I said. "Go to my lodge, where you will find your brother, with whom you may feast and share stories of your beloved grandmother."

"Thank you, my queen," the boys said together as they bowed again, and then disappeared into the gloom.

I breathed out a long sigh and made my way the short distance to the corral. As I came to the wooden fence, my favorite mare, Tân, named for her fiery red coat, greeted me with a low nicker. I stroked her sleek neck and whispered a prayer of thanks to Epona that she had been safely with the warriors in the Trinovantes camp instead of Tasceni. Tân lipped my cheek, which made me smile.

"I knew I would find you here."

I did not turn, though my smile remained. "Mind reading again?"

Rhan moved into the space beside me. "More remembrance than mind reading. Horses have comforted you since you were a girl, and I knew you would need comfort tonight."

I felt a little jolt of surprise as a long-buried memory surfaced. It had been the first night of my fostering with Tribe Trinovantes. At just twelve years old, I had used up all of my bravery as I watched my father and mother ride away with the rest of my escort, leaving me with strangers. Five years had seemed a lifetime, and by dark I was homesick and unable to hide my tears, so I escaped to the stables and found solace sobbing in the warm neck of a friendly mare.

Rhan had found me there. She'd brought a mug of beer, which we'd shared, and hadn't mentioned my tears but instead had talked of her excitement at having me as a sister and of the adventures she'd planned for us. Our friendship had begun that night.

"I remember," I said, still stroking Tân's neck. "You were very kind to me that night."

"You would have done the same for me had I fostered with your family." She moved up beside me and smoothed Tân's mane.

Tân blew against my cheek and then went back to drowsing. I turned to face my childhood friend and leaned against the fence. The firelight touched Rhan's large, dark eyes, making them look like deep pools with a depth of secrets just below their surface.

"It was a wise thing you did back there in the lodge," she said. "It loosened grief's chokehold on your people."

"I am not as good at lightening a mood as Arianell. Had my mother been here tonight, beside me where she belongs, even after our losses, this Beltane would be less somber, less heartbreaking."

Rhan cocked her head in that particular way she used to when we were girls and she had something important to say. "As you are now a queen and not simply my foster sister, I probably should not say this, but you are wrong."

I snorted. "I will always be your friend and I value your truth telling. Speak as freely as you did when we were girls."

"Well then, the truth is, had Arianell witnessed what the Romans did, she would have fallen into a despair so dark she would have never truly recovered." When I was unable to speak, she continued. "Boudicca, did you not know that you were your mother's strength?"

"I—no. She always seemed so wise. So steadfast."

Rhan nodded. "Yes, because she had you and the Iceni from which to draw strength. Oh, I do not mean to disparage Arianell. Indeed, she was wise and loving, but you were the fire that warmed her, the victory she followed after she lost your father and her tribe. Does it help to know that she would not have wanted to survive today?"

I felt the truth of her words settle within me and I had a sudden flash of the day my mother had come to Tasceni after the death of my father. She had looked frail and old and defeated, but I had put that out of my mind because her vitality returned as she cared for me and her first granddaughter, born shortly after her arrival.

"Yes, it does help." As I spoke I felt the shackles of grief loosen. "I hope Mother is not despairing now. I hope being in the presence of Brigantia has filled her with joy instead."

"It is Beltane. Look, Queen Boudicca." Rhan made a sweeping gesture with the blade of her hand. It parted the mist so that as I peered past the triple fires at Tasceni, I clearly saw that the figures illuminated by the other Beltane blazes had multiplied. In their glow were many, many more Iceni, jubilant as they twirled and laughed, danced, and loved.

Two of the dancers, a tall flame-haired man and a slender young woman who moved with the grace of youth, turned their faces to me. My breath caught. I knew them from my youth. I knew their smiles and the love that radiated from them to me, and to each other, as they danced their way around the fire.

"Rhan! Do you see them?" My voice shook with excitement but was hushed lest I break the spell she'd cast and the veil to Annwn close.

"I see them," Rhan said, linking her arm through mine. "I see their happiness and their love. Remember, Boudicca, love is as eternal as are we."

"I'll remember . . ." I stared through the unveiled mist at my ethereal loved ones, who reveled, young and strong again, until the gauzy curtain between worlds was drawn once again.

"Do not mourn for them," Rhan said softly. "Your grief does not honor them. They want you to think of them with happiness."

"Thank you. I shall remember." Then I wiped the tears from my cheeks, turned to meet her gaze, and spoke formally. "Seer, that day at the pool when you had your first vision, the torque you saw me wearing wasn't a queen's but this one, wasn't it?" My fingers touched the thickness of twisted gold around my neck.

Rhan's gaze dropped from my eyes to the torque before they lifted to look into mine again. "Yes."

"Why did you not tell me?"

"You were not ready to hear that truth," said Rhan.

"And since then? You did not think I was ready to hear the truth that would be my future during those long years?" I hadn't realized that I was angry at Rhan until that moment.

"Do I answer the queen or my friend?"

I blew out a long breath. "I am queen *and* friend."

"Are you?" Rhan paused and shook her head briefly. "No matter, Queen Boudicca and friend, I will answer you honestly. You were not ready to hear the truth until Andraste spoke it to you yesterday. You were not ready to believe your beloved husband's arrogance would be the impetus that caused the Romans to target you and Tasceni."

My face flushed with anger and shame. Anger at Prasutagus and shame that she was right. I hadn't wanted to believe Andraste. I would not have believed Rhan.

Rhan reached out hesitantly with the hand that had so recently parted the curtain between Arbred and Annwn. She grasped my wrist and heat shot through me as our shared girlhood returned to me in a rush—a carefree time when we raced, hand in hand, through the forests of Tribe Trinovantes weaving stories of what our lives would be. At her touch, the anger and shame drained from me. Her soft words held the echo of those days, as well as the wisdom of the seer she had become. "It would not have changed anything had you known. Prasutagus was set on his course. The fact that I saw you wearing his torque would not have swayed him. It would only have brought conflict and worry to your life, which was full and happy."

I sighed and nodded before she loosed my wrist. My skin felt cold after the warmth of her touch. "Can you give me your oath that you will keep no future visions from me?"

Rhan's gaze snapped to mine. I tried to read the depths there, but all I saw was her sharp intelligence. Something else flickered within her eyes, but it faded quickly.

"I can give you my oath that I will share all future visions with you, Queen Boudicca," said Rhan formally.

As she spoke, a wave of relief crested over me, but before I could acknowledge her newly given oath, movement on the ground caught my attention. Silently, Rhan and I watched as a wild hare hopped from the center of the pyramid of fires before us. The little creature came to Rhan and circled her three times before it fearlessly curled between her leather-clad feet.

My gaze rose to meet Rhan's. "Stay with me. Be the seer of the Iceni, blessed by Andraste, as well as my advisor. Derwyn will return to Ynys Môn when the pyre is cold and the ashes have been entombed, but I have need of your Sight and your wisdom for what is to come. I give you an oath of my own. I will always be ready to hear the truth you speak."

The three fires suddenly crackled as one, sending sparks into the misty night sky. Like fireflies, they reflected in Rhan's eyes as she said, "As you ask, so will I do."

When we looked back down at her feet, the little hare had disappeared.

CHAPTER XIV

I woke early the next morning, and for an instant the familiar sounds and scents of my lodge being readied for the day lulled me into the belief that nothing had changed—that my mother and Dafina were just on the other side of the reed wall that sectioned off my bedchamber, readying the lodge for another busy day.

Then a small, warm body stirred beside me while from my other side soft snores made sleepy, rhythmic music. I jolted fully awake and remembered everything.

Gently, I disentangled myself from my girls. I had to step over Briallen, who was sleeping on what had been Dafina's pallet at the foot of Arianell's bed. As I did, the warrior woke. I pressed my finger against my lips and motioned for her to stay where she was. I could see she wanted to argue, but I shook my head and made a firm staying gesture with my hand as I whispered, "Sleep. The girls will want you close when they wake." Unspoken was the fact that Briallen's injuries also needed sleep to heal, and I wanted her whole and at my side as soon as possible.

Reluctantly, Briallen nodded. Her eyes were already closing as I crept from what had been my mother's bedchamber out into the main part of the lodge, which was quietly buzzing with activity.

Phaedra saw me and told one of the other servants, "Begin pouring the queen's bath. Remember to scent it with the lavender and goat's milk she prefers." As the servant hurried to the already steaming cauldron that hung over one of the several cooking fires, Phaedra came to me and bowed. "Good morn, my queen. It is not quite dawn. You have time to bathe and break your fast before Addedomaros comes to take his leave of you. I have put out your blue and green plaid tunic, the one decorated with silver thread. Is that to your liking?"

"Yes, Phaedra." Then, before my servant rushed away to gather brushes and sponges, as well as salve for my back, I touched her arm, halting her. "You have done well this morning, Phaedra."

Her ivory cheeks flushed pink and she dropped her head in another bow as she averted her gaze. "Dafina usually directs the readying of the lodge for the day. I—I did not mean to overstep, but there are so few of us left, and . . ." Her voice faded as she wiped tears from her cheeks.

I lifted her chin gently. "Dafina would be proud of you, as would Arianell. As am I." I raised my voice so that the other servants heard. There were so few of them—only six, four women and two young men. From the list of those killed by the Romans I picked out the names of the other six servants, those who hadn't escaped into the forest. They had been decades older than Phaedra.

"They will be missed," I said softly as I slid into the copper bath. I made a mental note to put out the word that the queen's lodge needed servants.

"They will be, my queen." Phaedra's voice was laced with anger. "But the Romans will not dishearten us. We want you to know that. We will survive and thrive once again."

I met her gaze. "And get vengeance."

"Yes, my queen."

"While I bathe, send messages to Cadoc, Abertha, and Maldwyn, as well as Derwyn and Rhan. I call them to a war council. Make ready the lodge. I would have the Trinovantes know the Iceni have not been broken."

Her eyes glittered. "As you ask, so will I do."

I ate hastily as Phaedra smeared salve over my healing wounds, helped me dress, and then brushed out my hair. I made the decision to leave the bulk of it unbraided, though I did have her plait raven feathers throughout it. Using the woad-colored paste, I painted my face, touched the thick torque that rested heavily around my neck, and spoke a quick prayer to Andraste. "Goddess, let me continue to do your will. I am your Victory." Then I parted the pelt curtain to my chamber and strode out into my lodge.

Phaedra had relayed my orders to make ready for a war council. Before the center fire of the lodge was a large square dais made of gleaming oak carved with Andraste's familiars—ravens, hares, and boars—in intricate knot work around the base. On the dais was the massive chair Prasutagus had commanded be carved from the same oak and also decorated with symbols of our goddess. As I took my seat in the chair I was glad for my height and the broadness of my shoulders so that I wouldn't appear a child usurping the throne of her elders. To my right on the dais were three smaller chairs, one for each of my lead warriors. To my left I'd had Phaedra add two additional chairs so that Derwyn and Rhan could join me.

"Open the doors to the lodge," I commanded.

Cadoc was the first to enter. I met his gaze and motioned surreptitiously to the chairs to my right. The seasoned shield led Abertha and Maldwyn up to the dais. He sat in the chair nearest me as the other two lead warriors took the remaining seats.

"Derwyn, Rhan, it would please me if you would lend your wisdom to my war council," I said as I gestured to the chairs on my left.

Derwyn's brows rose, but he and Rhan joined me on the dais. Many Iceni warriors followed the Druids into the lodge as word that I had called a war council spread throughout Tasceni. I'd known it would, and I'd known my people would come, curious to see how their peaceable queen would, or would not, lead. Lastly, Addedomaros; his shield, Mailcun; and the half dozen warriors the Trinovantes chief had brought with him to Tasceni entered. The Iceni parted, letting them approach the dais.

Addedomaros had come to be chief of Tribe Trinovantes before his sixteenth nameday, immediately after his father had been killed in a hunting accident. He was older than Prasutagus, but not by much. He was not as tall as me, but what he lacked in height he made up for with thick cords of muscles that had always reminded me of a bull. His hair was the same color as Rhan's, moonlight blond, but instead of her dark eyes, his were faded blue green, as if they couldn't decide between the two colors and chose instead to be a tepid mix of both. He held himself like a chief—shoulders back, chin high, gaze steady. It was rumored that he was still virile and had several lovers, though after Rhan's mother died birthing their only son he had not remarried. To me Addedomaros would always be a father figure, as he had stood in for my beloved father during the five years I fostered in his household. His voice was a deep, pleasing rumble.

Addedomaros nodded respectfully to me. "Good dawning to you, Queen Boudicca," he said formally.

"And to you as well, Chief Addedomaros."

"We thank you for your Beltane hospitality and wish our visit had been in happier times," said the chief. "Now we must return to our own lodge and our own people."

"The sadness here was not of your making, old friend." Had Prasutagus been there, he would have talked of crops and horses, trade goods and the spring games. But my husband was dead and I had no patience for pleasantries. I met the chief's gaze steadily. "Tribe Trinovantes has long been allied with the Iceni, longer even than you were allied with the Brigantes, from whom I came to you as a child and fostered as a second daughter."

Addedomaros nodded. "I remember your fostering well." His gaze went to his daughter and his eyes softened. "You and my daughter were inseparable."

"I assume you do not welcome fosterlings from Tribe Brigantes now," I said.

His gaze snapped back to me and he scowled. "Not since Cartimandua whored her tribe out to the Romans."

"And, with the traitorous Catuvellauni, helped them steal Camulodunum from you," I added.

His scowl deepened at the reminder of what the queen of the Brigantes had taken from his tribe.

"All here know of the Catuvellauni's hand in the tragedy that has befallen Tasceni, as well as Cartimandua's treachery," said Addedomaros. "Most especially you, Queen Boudicca, as you grew up in the heart of Tribe Brigantes and are kinswoman to their royal house."

I didn't take his bait. The Iceni had witnessed my mother's heart-break when news had come that the queen of her beloved Brigantes had allied herself with Rome. With the aid of the Roman legions and other, weaker tribes like the Catuvellauni, the Brigantes had begun stealing land from their neighbors. They also remembered, as did I, that Prasutagus had declined to join with Addedomaros to beat back the traitorous queen. He and I had had one of our very few disagree-ments over his decision. I'd believed he was wrong not to ally with Addedomaros against Cartimandua. He'd believed it was too dangerous to openly attack an ally of Rome and said I did not see the situation clearly because of the love I had for my parents and for the tribe that had fostered me.

I lifted my chin. "Cartimandua is, indeed, my father's kinswoman—though only by a marriage that is no more. I wish you to know had the decision been mine those many years ago, Iceni spears would have joined with Trinovantes blades to drink her blood."

The old chief's body stiffened in surprise, and then his eyes nar-rowed. "Tell me, Queen Boudicca, do you mention the past because you need the aid of Tribe Trinovantes in the present?"

"Yes!" I spoke the word fiercely as I leaned forward. "I ask that Tribe Trinovantes be the first to pledge to join the Iceni to rid Britain of the infestation of the Romans—to serve vengeance for the deaths of our elders, the rape of my children, and the flesh they scourged from my back. In doing so you may reclaim Camulodunum as your rightful land. Will you join me, mighty Addedomaros? Will you aid me in the fulfillment of Andraste's curse?"

Addedomaros paused, and when he spoke he did so slowly, choosing his words carefully. "Queen Boudicca, I feel your rage. I understand it. I even agree with it. I have felt the Roman boot on my neck for many years, and I sicken of it. But open war against Rome is something I must not choose rashly on a tide of passion."

His response was more positive than I had hoped, and as he spoke

I could see his shield, Mailcun, move his wide shoulders restlessly, as if he chafed under a binding yoke.

Still holding the chief's gaze, I asked, "Derwyn, do you believe it is a rash thing to war against the Romans?"

"My belief is of no consequence," said the Druid. "It is the goddess Andraste who has opened the dam and calls the tide of war and promised revenge for the Iceni. I only interpret the signs she sends, and on that, the goddess of war is clear. She thirsts for the blood of Rome and has chosen Queen Boudicca, her Victory, to lead the Iceni into battle."

Addedomaros nodded. "But, High Druid, what of the omens of war? Are they auspicious or will a revolt be futile?"

Derwyn used his staff to gesture at Rhan, and I felt the tiny hairs on the nape of my neck lift as he addressed my childhood friend. "Iceni seer, what say you of the portents for war?"

From her raised place of honor, Rhan stared down at her father. Her voice was strong and carried throughout the lodge. "Andraste has been clear! She named Boudicca Victory at her birth and reinforced that naming the day the Romans invaded Tasceni by gifting her with the chief's torque. You witnessed Andraste's sign yesterday, chief of the Trinovantes." While Rhan spoke, the lodge was so silent it was as if the room held its breath. I had forgotten about the singular ability she'd had since childhood to hold rapt an audience. When she was a girl, the power had been nascent. As a fully trained Druid seer, Rhan was mesmerizing. "The goddess of war has chosen. She thirsts for Roman blood."

"Ah, but will Andraste lead Boudicca to the victory her name promises?" asked Addedomaros, seemingly unmoved by his daughter's words.

I spoke before Rhan could answer and felt the thrumming of Andraste's power vibrate through my body as my words echoed preternaturally around me. "The goddess has not promised that we will defeat the Romans, though she has promised that the curse I placed upon the centuria who attacked Tasceni will be fulfilled. But consider, chief of the Trinovantes, is an assurance of victory the best reason to go to war? We *must* war against the Romans because we cannot continue to stand idly by and do nothing while Rome preys upon us, enslaves our people, and wipes away our tribes and our gods. If we do not try, are we not already gone? Are we not doomed to become like them, a people who have so little honor that they violate children and subjugate their women to appear powerful?" I paused as the warriors before me growled their agreement. Emboldened, I stood, threw wide my arms. "I will not become Roman! Will you?"

Cadoc surged to his feet as he shouted, "No!"

Abertha and Maldwyn stood and cried, "No!"

"No!" My people echoed their roar.

I raised my hand and the lodge went silent. "The Iceni have decided. We war against Rome. What say Tribe Trinovantes?"

Addedomaros drew himself up to his full height. He looked from his daughter to me and then bowed his head slightly. "I say that I will return to my tribe and call my own war council. I give you my oath that I shall consider your words carefully before I make a response. Will that satisfy you, Queen Boudicca?"

"The only answer that would truly satisfy me is to hear the Trinovantes war cry join with the Iceni," I said.

I saw the surprise in his eyes and read there that he had not expected me to be so decisive. Addedomaros would not be the last man to underestimate me.

"I take my leave of you," said the chief. "You have given me much to think on."

"Then fare thee well, Chief Addedomaros. May the joy of the day be with you," I said.

"And may the blessings of the earth be on you." He turned, and my Iceni parted to let the chief and his warriors through the tightly packed lodge.

I breathed out a long breath and sat. As Cadoc and my other lead warriors took their seats again, the old shield caught my eye and spoke quietly. "Well done, my queen."

I felt a wave of relief at his praise. I was not weak. I did not lack in confidence. I was accustomed to leading my people, but readying my tribe for battle was not the same as readying them for the spring planting or the fall harvest. My hands curled on the smooth wooden arms of the throne that today finally felt truly mine. I lifted my chin and continued.

"Let us proceed as if Tribe Trinovantes will not ally with us. The Iceni are strong. Even alone we will fulfill Andraste's curse, but to do so we must be subtle. The procurator explained his plans clearly as he invaded Tasceni. He will not return to our lands until harvest, when he intends to collect Rome's taxes." I turned my head so that I could meet Cadoc's sharp gaze. "If we do not call his attention to us, we have time to ready ourselves and bring our vengeance to him at Camulodunum. We will burn that Roman city to the ground with him in it. Catus Decianus will never defile Tasceni again."

The warriors who filled the lodge murmured agreement, and Cadoc nodded. "If we gather the Iceni, we can destroy Camulodunum, though the Romans will surely respond by bringing their legions against us. We will not easily hold the city, my queen."

I sneered. "I have no need to hold Roman ashes and ruins."

Cadoc bared his teeth in a feral grin. "Again, I agree with your wisdom. I advise alerting all Iceni blacksmiths so that quietly, in each of our villages, they immediately begin forging spears and swords, arrows and shields."

Maldwyn spoke up. "My queen, it would be wise to command the making of new chariots."

Abertha leaned forward so that she could meet my gaze. "The weapons could be stockpiled within the barrows. The Romans do not go there."

"The new chariots can be hidden in the forest surrounding the barrows," added Maldwyn. "Romans rarely stray far from their roads."

"Send runners to every village commanding it." I shifted my attention to the two Druids beside me. "Derwyn, I planned to ask your permission to allow Rhan to remain here to serve as seer to the Iceni when you leave." I paused and smiled into his wise eyes. "But it seems you answered my request before I could make it of you."

He tilted his head in acknowledgment. "Last night Andraste sent a raven to my dreams. The bird spoke Rhan's name before it flew to perch upon the roof of your lodge. It seems the goddess agreed with your request, and as I am here to serve the gods, I must also agree."

My gaze returned to my people. "Then let it be known henceforth Rhan is seer to Tribe Iceni."

"Let it be known!" the warriors shouted.

I turned to Rhan, and even though it had been many years since we had been inseparable, I read her face as if we had only parted yesterday. "Has Andraste sent you an omen to interpret, Seer Rhan?" I asked.

"She has, Queen Boudicca," she replied formally. "At dawn, as I walked from the tents of the Druids through Tasceni to the lodge, every hen in the village suddenly ran past me, toward the fields." Rhan did not raise her voice and the lodge went absolutely still as the Iceni listened, spellbound, to their newly appointed seer. "Their behavior was so odd that I followed. They appeared to be in a trancelike state, though when they reached the fields they ravenously attacked the young crops as if they were starving. When I drew near they turned as one to look at me and then they were released from their frenzy, ruffled their feathers, and trotted sedately past me to return to their roosts."

"How do you interpret this omen, Seer Rhan?" asked Derwyn.

"Andraste used the hens to send sign that the Iceni must prepare now to feed an army this winter," said Rhan firmly.

I shivered at her words. For a moment my confidence faltered. Feeding my army—I should have thought of it! Then I stopped that mental admonishment. *I am but one person. I cannot possibly know everything. I will not be a queen driven by pride rather than wisdom. There is no shame in seeking and taking advice from my seer, my council, my goddess.* I nodded respectfully to Rhan. "Then we will make it so. Pick every orchard bare. Harvest our crops early. Send word to all Iceni hunters to smoke venison and boar now, as if winter and not summer were upon us. Fatten our goats and cows. Cast our nets into our bountiful rivers and fill barrels with salted fish. The Iceni will be strong and ready for war."

"Let it be known!" my people shouted.

"I will send out riders on our swiftest horses," said Maldwyn.

"As you do so, tell them to also speak this command from their queen," I said. "'Come to me, mighty warriors of the Iceni. Come to me and together we will serve the vengeance of Andraste to the Romans.'"

"As you ask, so will I do," said Maldwyn, his eyes glittering with excitement.

CHAPTER XV

The change that came over Tasceni began that day. Grief and defeat were replaced by determination and action. I ate the midday meal outside the lodge on tables I'd ordered placed along the main thoroughfare of the village so that the people could be fed quickly as they took short breaks from repairing the damage left by the Romans. There was a sense of excited anticipation that permeated Tasceni. Pens were rebuilt. The blackened thatched roofs of huts were replaced. The ruins of the stable were demolished and a new, simple structure was begun closer to the corrals. Throughout it all, the sounds of our blacksmith and his apprentices forging weapons rang like the knell of victory bells.

I ate with my people and then visited the huts where our wounded had been housed to recover and was gratified to learn that the Druid healers believed they would all survive.

The only dark spot on the day was that my daughters did not leave the lodge. Adara remained with them as they soaked their battered bodies in healing herbs while Briallen stood guard—and then, drugged by the healer's tea, they returned to my mother's bedchamber to sleep.

Adara found me as I emerged from the last of the huts housing our wounded. "Queen Boudicca, Derwyn has announced that we leave on the morrow. With your permission I will ask to remain so that I may continue to oversee the recovery of your daughters and the rest of the wounded Iceni."

I nodded. "Yes, you have my permission and my gratitude."

Adara easily read my expression. She patted my arm in a maternal gesture that had my stomach clenching with longing for my mother.

"Your children will recover." Her voice was as gentle as her touch. "Be patient. Give them time."

"I will, and I—" My words were interrupted as my attention was drawn to the main road that fed into Tasceni from the forest. Along with me, villagers turned toward the sound of approaching carts. Warriors pushed forward toward me, and within several heartbeats I was surrounded by my guard.

My body went very still. Terror speared through me as I had a visceral memory of the Romans descending upon Tasceni. Panic narrowed my vision. I would have swayed and perhaps even stumbled and fallen had Rhan's warm hand not gripped my elbow, steadying me.

"Breathe," she whispered.

I forced myself to draw one breath, another, and then my mind overcame my body's fear. There was no clanking of Roman armor—no rhythmic stomping of marching feet. My vision cleared in time to see three wooden carts filled with women entering Tasceni.

Rhan dropped my arm immediately, though she remained close beside me. I fisted my hands and pressed them against my tunic, so that no one would see that they trembled, and strode forward to meet the carts. As I got closer to our visitors, I saw that they were wearing Iceni blue. Each woman's face was painted the same blue with our tribal symbols as well as the bold war strokes Iceni men and women wore into battle. They looked so fierce that it took a moment for me to realize that most of them were matrons—mothers and grandmothers whose wild white hair hung as loose as mine.

From the first cart a woman climbed to the ground with a nimbleness that belied her age-lined body. She approached me and bowed low.

"Queen Boudicca, I greet you and wish you the joy of the day." Her voice was strong and her eyes were sharp with intelligence.

It was her voice I recognized before I saw through the battle paint that decorated her face, shoulders, and bare, sinewy arms. "And may the blessings of the earth be on you, Wulffaed," I answered.

Her face split into a smile. "I am honored you remember me, my queen."

I dipped my head slightly. "I cannot easily forget the most renowned weaver of the Iceni and the Mother of Twenty." Wulffaed was the matriarch of an Iceni farming village half a day's ride northwest of the Chief's Barrow. Her wisdom and weaving ability were almost as legendary as the fact that she had given birth to twenty daughters—and each had survived childhood and become as fertile and as gifted a weaver as her mother. She had been a favorite of Arianell, who often traded with her for the finely dyed and woven fabrics Wulffaed created. I suspected the fabric of the dress I wore that day had come from her.

The old woman put her hands on her hips and cackled a laugh. "Our goddess has, indeed, greatly blessed me. It is Andraste who brings me here." Wulffaed met my gaze, and the lines that crossed her brow deepened with sorrow. "Our queen mother is dead."

"She is," I said.

Wulffaed sighed as her gaze left mine and searched the faces of the villagers who surrounded us. "And I see many elders have joined her in Annwn."

"They have."

Wulffaed met my gaze again and nodded. "Last night Andraste came to me in a dream. She said you have need of me and mine. I cannot replace the queen mother, but my daughters and granddaughters and I can be sure your lodge is in order, your bread is baked, and your clothes are woven so that you, my queen, may focus on readying us for war."

I blinked in surprise, knowing that my riders could not have reached her settlement with the news calling the Iceni to arms yet. Andraste had, indeed, sent this matron to me. I stepped forward and took her gnarled hands within mine.

"Thank you," I said simply. "You are most welcome, Wulffaed, Mother of Twenty."

Wulffaed squeezed my hands. "As the goddess asks, so will I do."

The Mother of Twenty was right. I hadn't realized how much

it had weighed on me that my lodge was in disorder. Arianell and Dafina had long directed the tedious details of the daily running of the lodge, which served as the heart of the Iceni, leaving me the freedom to rule beside my husband, who had from the beginning of our marriage valued my judgment.

After Prasutagus's death three moons before, it had fallen to me as Iceni queen to keep the administration of the Iceni running smooth. With my lodge in order, I was able to decide disputes, answer requests for aid or sanctuary, and direct the planting of crops, breeding of livestock, and trading with neighboring tribes. Things I'd had time to do because my mother directed the daily running of my lodge. With Arianell gone and Phaedra overwhelmed, I'd only just begun to understand the chaos that awaited me.

But by the evening meal, Wulffaed and her troop of daughters and granddaughters had filled my lodge with the sounds of contented, busy tribeswomen and set out trays of sizzling meat, onions and potatoes drenched in fat, and sweet, seedy cakes. But what I appreciated most was seeing my daughters sitting around the central hearthfire of the lodge with Wulffaed, who had them combing through flax threads to make them ready for the loom. The girls did not eat outside at the long tables with the majority of the tribe, but they also did not hide in their bedchamber. I took it as a small victory.

After the evening meal I asked Rhan to walk with me to the warriors' practice grounds, where Derwyn was overseeing the collection of the bones and other remains of our dead that would be interred in the Chief's Barrow so that in death, as in life, the Iceni followed their chiefs and queens.

The day had been warm, but as the sun sank closer to the western horizon, the breeze from the river Tas cooled, softening the night. The enticing, homey scents of baking bread and smoking meat wafted with the breeze, but Tasceni didn't feel sleepy, as it used to most evenings. Tasceni felt energized and poised for a future that held change.

"Can you feel it?" I asked Rhan softly. "It is almost as if my people hold their breath as they wait to see if the warriors will come to my call."

Rhan looked up at me and gave a little snort so reminiscent of how she'd responded as a girl when I made outlandish predictions about our futures that I laughed. "What? You do not think they wait?"

"Oh, they wait, but not to see if the warriors will come. They *know* they will come. The waiting you feel is their impatient need for vengeance. Now that you have declared war on Rome, they are like horses, champing at the bit with their need to bolt into battle."

As I thought about Rhan's words, I looked at my people. Each Iceni I passed paused to bow to me, which was new. Neither Prasutagus nor I required our proud people to bow or cower before us. We did not hold ourselves aloof or apart, as did some chiefs and queens of Britain's tribes. We held our people's respect and maintained our right to rule through our actions, our honor, and the unyielding truth that the Iceni royal family always put the tribe first. So the obeisance they showed to me was a reflection of not just their faith in me but their agreement with the path I'd set them upon.

"Let me be worthy of them," I murmured.

"You are." Rhan spoke without looking at me.

Her words warmed me immeasurably. "I'm so glad you are here and that you will stay with me."

"I will remain with you as long as you have need of me," said Rhan.

There was a strange tone to her voice and I looked sharply at her, but we'd come to the edge of the practice field and Derwyn approached, pulling my attention from Rhan.

Behind him, Druids in forest-colored tunics used long, hooked tools to poke the ash and remove bones and other fragments from the remnants of the pyre.

"Queen Boudicca, we will have the Iceni remains gathered by midday tomorrow and ready to rest in the barrow," said Derwyn. The bottom of his white tunic was gray from ash. Dark circles bruised his eyes. With a jolt of shock I realized that he looked old and tired.

"Are you well, Derwyn?" I asked.

He sighed and ran a hand through his thick white hair. "Ynys Môn calls to me. Last night in my dreams the oaks keened."

Beside me I felt Rhan stiffen.

Ynys Môn was more than just the island where the Druids trained and lived. It was their spiritual center. Their hearts were tethered there by the sacred oaks that grew thick and strong on Ynys Môn. Prasutagus and I had visited the island several times. From the first moment I'd stepped on the isle, I'd felt the love with which the Druids tended their oaks—much like they were beloved children. "Do the oaks keen because I have declared war on Rome?" I did not want to hear Derwyn answer yes, though I had to ask.

He shook his head. "No. Andraste has been clear. She supports you; your vengeance is hers. The oaks grieve, but I do not know why. I planned to remain here, with the Tasceni, until much closer to Samhain and harvest, but I cannot. I must leave tomorrow, and I must take all of my people with me except Rhan and Adara."

"Of course you must," I said quickly as dread fingered up my spine. "Derwyn, have the oaks keened before?"

"Never in all of my days have I heard such a sound."

"We should make offerings to Andraste," said Rhan. "And ask her to comfort the grove and hasten your return to the isle."

"Yes," said Derwyn, though he stared to the west, toward the distant place that was his home.

I looked around us and motioned for a young villager to approach.

"My queen," the boy said after he bowed to me.

"Go to the lodge. Tell Wulffaed I need libation bowls for Andraste—honey and milk. Bring them to the altar by the oak."

"Yes, my queen." He sprinted off.

"Come," I said to Rhan. "Let us go to Andraste."

Wordlessly the seer and I moved through the practice field, skirting the huge ash pile and the Druids who pecked through it. I wanted to avert my eyes. I did not want to see my mother's bones, but the ash drew me as surely as Andraste had compelled me to the forest. The evening clouds parted and the setting sun caught the remnants of treasures burned with our dead so that the field sparkled, and my dread quieted. I had no reason to turn my face from the remains of my mother or my people. They had been precious, the living jewels of the Iceni. I changed direction so that I walked through the ash and stopped, bent, and scooped up a handful of it. Resolutely, I spit into my hand and swirled my finger through the hastily made gray paste before I drew a line down my nose and two down either side of my cheeks from the corners of my eyes to the strong edges of my jaw.

"You will not be forgotten," I promised the dead.

Rhan nodded, and silently we continued to the altar. It was darker under the boughs of the massive oak, though the waning sunlight glinted through the thick canopy of leaves. Before I approached the altar I rested my palm on her skin. "I greet you, Grandmother Oak."

"Can you still feel their breath?" Rhan asked.

I nodded, surprised that she remembered.

My friend smiled. "I remember everything."

"Or you really can read minds," I quipped as I joined her at Andraste's altar.

Rhan didn't respond. Instead she gazed up at Andraste. "I love the fierceness of this likeness of the goddess."

I kissed my fingers and pressed them to the goddess's feet. "I have thought that since the first day I glimpsed this altar when I was little more than a girl, and a very nervous new bride. When Prasutagus and I rode past her, I felt her welcome me—not with the gentle touch of a mother or matron, but with an intensity and a strange kind of joy. I thought her beautiful then and think her even more so now that I have seen her in person. Her fierceness is blinding in its magnificence."

"That is because Andraste was not welcoming a young bride to Tasceni," said Rhan as she continued to stare at the statue. "She welcomed Victory."

I continued to press my hand to her feet. "Let it be so."

We moved the tribe's offerings so that we could clean the leaves and forest debris from the altar. I lifted my skirt and used it to wipe clean the statue. We were replacing the offerings around the feet of Andraste when the boy hurried to us. He clutched two large wooden bowls close to his narrow chest and placed them carefully on the flat sandstone on which the goddess's image stood.

"Now return to Wulffaed and tell her that I said you are to be given an extra seed cake and your own bowl of honey to drizzle over it," I told the boy.

His smile lit the clearing. "Yes, Queen Boudicca!"

With the altar cleaned and tended, Rhan faced me. "Andraste has chosen you, so it is you who should invoke her aid while I pour libations and call nwyfre, the life force that fills the world, to carry your prayer to her."

I nodded, and as Rhan took off her leather shoes and chose the bowl filled with rich, amber honey, I breathed deeply, grounding myself. Slowly at first, the seer began dancing a circle around the raised altar and me. Her feet followed the music of her soul; her movements were so graceful she appeared to flow. She sang a wordless tune, increasing the tempo of her spirit song. Her voice was high and true. She swayed and twirled with a sensuality that was beautiful and alluring. Her bare feet traced an intricate pattern as she circled, drizzling honey around the base of the altar. The pleasing scent of sweetness lifted from the loamy forest floor and I felt a rush of pleasure at the rich offering—a feeling that I knew did not come from me. Andraste loved sweets and rich foods, and it was those things she craved as tribute from her suppliants—that and the blood of her enemies.

The words came easily to me, and I spoke them in a singsong rhythm that wove with Rhan's dance.

Andraste, you are the word of knowledge;
the power of the point of the spear;
the lure that calls us beyond the ends of the earth when our lives are over.
You have been raven and boar and hare.
You are the wind and earth, our fire and water.
I am yours, Andraste. Always yours.
Your Victory, who comes to you today to ask that you hasten home
Derwyn, who has long been beloved of Annwn.
The oaks of Ynys Môn keen for him, but he is here tending to the Iceni.

I paused, and when I spoke again words spilled from my mouth as Rhan continued in her dance and poured the fatty goat's milk over the honey.

Soothe the oaks as Derwyn hastens to them.
Ready him for what is to come.
Strengthen him. Be near him. Give him courage.
He has well and truly served the gods his long life.

As I ended my prayer, Rhan poured the last of the libations and then dropped into a deep, fluid bow to the goddess. Then a mighty gust of wind sluiced through the boughs of the ancient oak so that her leaves whispered and moaned and sighed. The flesh on my forearms and neck prickled as my hair lifted and the evening clouds that had so recently parted closed, casting the grove deep into shadow.

We left the bowls at Andraste's feet, knowing that the tribe would fill them with sweets and treats for our goddess. Rhan and I walked slowly back through the trees. We paused at the remnants of the pyre, where the Druids had been joined by those of our people most experienced with plowing our fertile fields. Somberly the Iceni tilled the ashes of our elders into the soil. In the days to come the warriors would return to the field and their feet would hard-pack the ashes into the earth. Every day after this one, we would know that the ashes of our people who had died defending their village and their queen were just below the surface, giving us strength for battles to come.

Then Rhan and I took the main road that would lead us to my lodge, where the voices of women would be filling it with life again. My steps were lighter. My girls would recover. My people would answer my call—I felt sure of it. We would fulfill Andraste's curse. Vengeance would be ours.

We'd reached the area just outside the lodge that had been lined with trestle tables. It wasn't full dark yet, but fires had been lit around the tables and the Iceni shared ale as they relaxed after a long, productive day. Beside me I felt Rhan stiffen, and then I heard horses approaching, but this time fear didn't smother me. Even before I turned to see them I knew by the way their hooves beat out the sound of freedom that we had nothing to fear.

The faces of the Tasceni villagers reflected my joy as ten horses and a chariot drawn by two galloped to me and slid to a dramatic halt. The Iceni warriors who rode and drove them were dressed in full battle regalia. Bronze helmets decorated with plumes of horsehair caught the last light of the sun and gleamed. Short shields and quivers filled with arrows were slung across their painted shoulders. They wore leather breeches dyed Iceni woad blue. Their faces, as well as their horses, were painted with Iceni signs and symbols of Andraste. They were small in number but they were magnificent.

The tall blond man who was their leader was unfamiliar to me, but he dismounted gracefully and dropped to one knee before me. He, like the horses and the other warriors, was covered in sweat and breathing heavily, but when he spoke, his deep voice did not falter.

"Queen Boudicca, I am Ealhhere, horse master of Durobrav."

"Rise, Ealhhere. You are most welcome to Tasceni."

He stood. "More of our warriors follow, though slower as they come with carts filled with weapons."

"You say you are from Durobrav?" I asked.

"We are, my queen."

"But Durobrav is a hard day's ride from here," I said. "My riders could not have reached your village."

Ealhhere stood even taller as he replied, "We met two of your riders half a day from here."

I shook my head as if to clear it. "But how could you have known to come?"

"We came as soon as we heard the Romans had attacked Tasceni," said Ealhhere.

From behind Ealhhere the driver of the chariot shouted, "We did not wait for your call, my queen. We came!"

"Aye!" shouted the other warriors together. And then they spoke the words that would become our war song.

"We heard what the Romans did," another warrior said.

"And we came!" shouted the rider on the horse beside him.

"Aye, we came!" repeated Ealhhere.

My heart thrilled at their cries. I stepped forward and put a hand on Ealhhere's shoulder. "May Andraste bless you."

Ealhhere's smile blazed. "Is it true then? Have you declared war on the Romans?"

"I have," I said.

The warriors behind him loosed the Iceni war cry, which my village answered. Cadoc strode up to us. Eyes sparkling, the old warrior greeted Ealhhere fondly. "I should have known you would be the first to come." Then he tilted his head and studied the sweat-lathered horses. "But our riders have just reached Durobrav. How do you know Queen Boudicca called for you?"

I took up the words to the song that would sustain us. "They did not wait for our riders to relay my call. They came."

Cadoc clapped the tall horseman on the back as his gaze found mine. "Aye, well, the call of Victory is impossible to ignore."

Wulffaed was suddenly there at my side. "Shall I bring the warriors food, my queen?"

"Yes, and prepare more. A great deal more food." My voice was filled with pride. "These warriors are only the first of many."

chapter xvi

As would become habit for me, I woke the next morning at first light. Phaedra dressed me in my best riding leathers. Derwyn and his Druids would inter the remains of my mother and our people today. When I painted my face that morning I did so with white paste to honor the Iceni who had so recently crossed over to Annwn. That morning I had Phaedra wrap my hair back loosely in long hemp yarn that had been dyed white by the same lime paste our cavalry and charioteers used to dye their hair. My first order of business was to have Briallen alert my guard that they would be escorting the remains of our people to the Chief's Barrow and that I commanded they dress and paint themselves as if for battle. I would do this one last thing to honor my mother and those who had died so bravely with her.

Wulffaed had mugs of steaming tea and plates of fresh bannock ready, as well as strips of pork sizzling with newly gathered eggs. She ran my lodge with an ease and efficiency that was solace to my battered home and heart. Ashlynn and Ravenna, two of Wulffaed's granddaughters, gregarious girls in their late teens, had attached themselves to my daughters. They'd taken to sleeping on pallets at the foot of their bed, and they coaxed the girls with smiles and a lightness of spirit that spoke to Enfys and Ceri. The girls left their bedchamber to join me near the hearth. They still moved stiffly, but they cast fewer furtive looks around the lodge, and when my guard opened the wide front doors to allow Cadoc, Abertha, and Maldwyn to enter, my daughters did not bolt at the sight of the two male warriors, though Briallen did move from the doorway to stand close to the girls.

"My queen," Cadoc said. "More warriors arrived with the rising of the sun."

"From Durobrav?" I asked.

"There and from several other villages between here and Duro-brav," said Cadoc.

"We counted almost one hundred warriors—all cavalry," said Maldwyn, my young horse master, with a smile.

"We should discuss how we will house them," said Abertha as she snagged some bannock from the mound Wulffaed had placed on the long table beside the main hearth of the lodge.

I motioned for the other two warriors to join Abertha in breaking their fast, which they eagerly did as I thought about the dilemma of housing warriors.

"Aye," said Cadoc around a mouthful of pork and egg. "And there will be many more than this hundred. These came without being called. In the next fortnight we will be flooded by Iceni eager for Roman blood." He swallowed, and his gaze met mine. "When do you plan to attack Camulodunum?"

"Not until we are fully armed and my three lead warriors say we are ready," I answered with no hesitation.

"To prepare fully will take months. The gathered warriors will get restless," said Abertha.

"Then the three of you will keep them so busy training that they will be too exhausted to be restless," I said. "I will not rush this attack. Our numbers must swell so high that there will be no question that we can overpower the Roman stronghold. We have one opportunity to strike while Rome is still congratulating itself for having taught the barbarian queen a lesson."

Cadoc nodded. "After Camulodunum they will know all too well that the barbarians have come for them."

"How do we keep them from knowing until then?" Maldwyn asked.

The words came to me so easily that I knew Andraste had placed them there years before. It was her preparation of me in those years when Prasutagus valued his Victory enough to keep me close to his side. My voice was calm and sure from listening and learning at the side of a warrior chief blessed by a warrior goddess.

"The Romans are loath to leave their cities, and when they do they follow the roads with which they scar our lands. We will house the warriors who come to us in the thick forests surrounding Tasceni, well away from Roman roads. We'll send Iceni to close our borders to the Catuvellauni and Brigantes, and not allow so much as one wagon from either tribe to trade with us, as both have whored themselves to Rome."

Cadoc grunted in agreement and said, "If either Catuvellauni or Brigantes knew we are arming ourselves against the Romans, they would surely sell that knowledge to Decianus."

"Agreed," said Abertha. "And should they try to cross into our territory, they will feed our fens as sacrifices to Andraste, every one of them. None will be allowed to run, tail tucked, to Camulodunum to tell tales to their masters."

"Yes," I said.

The lodge doors opened again, admitting Derwyn and Rhan. Both wore white funeral robes. Their faces were painted with Ogham symbols in white paste. Derwyn wore the horns of a stag strapped to an elaborate headdress, and Rhan's head was crowned in sacred mistletoe.

"Queen Boudicca, we have the baskets of remains loaded onto carts and we are ready to take them for interment in the barrow," said Derwyn.

Even magnificently dressed to lead the interment rite, the high Druid looked as weary as he had the night before, and I saw that Rhan's expressive eyes were shadowed, too. I was worried about him—about all the Druids—but the best thing I could do for them was to be sure he and his people began their return journey to Ynys Môn this very day.

"Thank you, Derwyn, I am ready to oversee the interment. Briallen, gather my guard," I said, and then turned to the three lead warriors of the Iceni. "Cadoc, Abertha, begin setting up campsites in the forests starting at the edges of our fields. Stay to the west and north, well away from Roman roads. Busy the warriors with building shelters, and when that is done put them on a training schedule as if they go to war." I bared my teeth in a fierce smile. "Because we shall go to war."

"As you ask, so will I do," said Cadoc.

"And I, Queen Boudicca," said Abertha. Both warriors bowed to me before leaving the lodge.

"Maldwyn, have my mare readied for me and then continue to oversee the new shelters for our horses," I said.

Maldwyn stood and bowed. "As you ask, so will I do."

I turned my attention then to the two weary Druids. "Come, sit, break your fast while my horse is readied." Derwyn and Rhan took the bench seats my lead warriors had just vacated. As Derwyn picked at bannock, I said, "Thank you for allowing Adara to remain with me. My daughters do well under her healing touch."

"Queen Boudicca, I read sign this morn at dawn that clearly showed me Adara and Rhan must remain with you as long as you have need of them." The old Druid met my gaze. "I believe you will have need of the skills of a healer and a seer as you bring vengeance to the Romans."

"Have you seen it?" I sat forward in the big throne that felt more my own every day. "Have you seen my victory?"

Derwyn nodded somberly. "As the sun lifted I came upon the remains of a golden eagle on the warriors' practice field—not far from the center of where the pyre had been. Iceni boars had trampled it so that its bones and feathers were crushed and broken and mixed with ash and dirt. Andraste will ensure that your curse is fulfilled."

It was a somber but beautiful procession to the Chief's Barrow. My Queen's Guard stretched out along the forest path so that the Druids' wagons moved forward framed by Iceni in full battle regalia. The contrast was striking between the Druids, all in white robes with their faces painted white, and my guard, who wore Iceni-blue tunics, had covered themselves with fierce tribal paint and dressed their hair with beads and shells that clanked ominously as they marched, and held shields and spears at ready.

I couldn't help thinking back to the last time I'd traveled this path, face painted white, body and spirit numb with grief, as my people and I escorted my husband to his resting place. The echo of that day's shock and sadness lingered along the path. I felt it in every shadow and heard it in the muted birdsong. But today my body wasn't numb. The anger that simmered in my spirit left me clear minded and determined instead of grief-stricken and insensible.

The Iceni barrows were located an easy ride north of Tasceni near the joining of the rivers Yar and Tas. Though graceful white willows lined the riversides, the barrows were bare of trees. Knee-deep grasses the rich green of emeralds decorated their overturned bowl-like design. The smaller barrows were covered only by grass. The larger were littered with stones, as if one of the immortals had been casting Ogham and after reading them had abandoned them where they lay. The area was sacred. Even the Romans felt the power of the place and stayed well away. The Chief's Barrow was the largest hillock. Around it were lesser mounds, several of which were empty and served as sanctuaries for our tribe. They were where the Iceni had fled when the Romans attacked. Our procession went directly to the central barrow and halted in front of the large entrance.

The doorway faced the east, as was customary. Two wooden pillars stood on either side of the entrance, with a wooden lintel over the stone door. Ogham symbols of protection, the Iceni sickle moons with stars, and Andraste's ravens had been carved into the pillars and across the lintel. A large round sandstone slab had been placed on the ground before the door. Into its flat surface more Ogham symbols had been carved. To gain entrance to the tomb, the slab had to be crossed. Should anyone except the Druids and the newly dead enter the barrow, the symbols would activate and the desecrator would carry from the barrow much more than stolen treasure. A Druid's curse would cling to them like lice, eventually infesting their spirit and their life with the darkness of their deed. Few people dared to awaken such a curse.

All around the entrance tucked into the deeply carved pillars and the rocky face of the barrow were gifts and offerings, many of them fresh, as the Iceni did not easily forget their chiefs and queens.

When we had interred Prasutagus, I had followed his body, with my mother by my side, to the entrance of the tomb and watched from there while Derwyn led the Druids in the procession that placed my husband and his riches within. I remembered well the darkness inside, relieved only by the smoking mullein torches the Druids had carried. The barrow within had been lovingly lined with more wooden pillars that, tunnellike, opened to the large round inner tomb. The walls and ceiling of it, too, were fortified by wood.

Derwyn used his staff to break the clay seal he had so recently placed around the stone door. Then, with iron bars, the strongest of the Druids pried open the thick door. When it opened I caught the scent of decay that escaped from within. It was laced with the lavender and rosemary that had been mounded around my husband's body, and that is what I focused on as Rhan opened a bronze tinderbox, from which she lit a thick funeral torch of dried mullein stalk that had been dipped over and over in tallow and then encrusted with fragrant herbs. As the first funeral torch was lit, the Druids began to sing. Like Rhan's song at Andraste's altar the day before, their tune was wordless and beautiful. The Druids who remained in the carts set the rhythm of the song with drums of stretched hides and rattles made from gourds grown on Ynys Môn.

Then Rhan approached the line of Druids, who, two by two, carried between them the large woven baskets filled with Iceni bones, ashes, and finery not destroyed by the heat of the pyre. As the Iceni seer ceremonially lit the torches each Druid held, their feet began to follow the rhythm of the music and the undulating song. Rhan's grace was mesmerizing as she moved like water between them, leaving light and herbed smoke in her wake.

When the last torch was lit, Rhan went to Derwyn, bowed low, and gave him the blazing brand she held. Moving in time with the heartbeat of the music, Derwyn led the funeral procession into the mouth of the tomb.

I could see the Druids, illuminated by the flickering torches, spread out around the ornately carved wagon in the center of the tomb on which rested my husband's body. They encircled Prasutagus with the baskets as if he were their moon and they were his stars. And then the Druids followed Rhan in her dance and they wove around the circle they'd made of our dead while Derwyn went to each basket and traced protective symbols in the air over them. Their dance was primal and raw and passionate. It was a release of life, of pain, of being tethered to Arbred. Its magic brushed against my skin—a caress that was a question. Would I allow grief to rule my life?

As the old Druid finished at the last of the baskets, he turned to Prasutagus and raised his staff to the fallen chief. The Druids' dance and their music went silent. Derwyn's voice echoed from the center of the barrow, sounding as far away as if he had entered Annwn.

"Rest well, mighty Iceni chief. Be at peace as your people join you. Feast, dance, make merry—and save a place at the long table for those yet to make the journey to Annwn."

His words released a great pressure from my breast. The sorrow of losing my mother and so many elders was not so overwhelming when I imagined them together again with Prasutagus. And I realized I'd answered the question asked by nwyfre, the life force that flowed through us all. I chose not to allow grief to rule my life. Anger replaced grief, but deep within me I hoped that someday I would not need to hold to anger so tightly, though for now it served me well.

As Derwyn led the Druids from the barrow, a raven called from above us. The great black bird circled the hillock the entire time it took for the Druids to close the stone door and Derwyn to reseal it with the wet clay he had prepared and brought with the procession. As one, the Druids extinguished their funeral torches in the remnants of the clay, which my guard would carry back to Tasceni to be burned as the sun set that night.

Slowly, Derwyn approached me. He still looked uncharacteristically weary, though his eyes were no longer shadowed. With his clay-caked finger, he traced the Iceni symbols painted on my forehead as he gave me a final blessing.

"May Andraste's strength sustain you. May you borrow the cunning of her ravens, the strength of her boars, and the fleetness of her hares—and may you fulfill her naming, Victory of the Iceni."

Warmth sizzled from my forehead down my body. Rhan moved to my side, leading the extra horse my guard had brought for her.

"Remember that Rhan remains with you as more than your childhood companion. She is your seer, Andraste's voice. Be wise, queen of the Iceni. Do not make the same mistake the mighty Prasutagus made. Do not allow ego to drive your decisions."

I bowed my head. "I will remember, Derwyn, high Druid and friend," I said formally. "Until we meet again, may the joy of the day be with you." I raised my head to see that his smile was fatherly.

He touched my cheek gently, fleetingly, and replied with, "And may the blessings of the earth be on you."

Then he turned and the Druids helped him into the lead cart. The rest of his people filled the other carts or walked along with them as they turned to the west and the distant isle that waited for them. The raven that had circled over the barrow followed above, calling with a voice that sounded like a woman screaming in rage.

Though Derwyn did not look back, I remained there watching until he, the Druids, and the accompanying raven were out of sight.

CHAPTER XVII

"I f I have your leave, I will supervise your guard in how to make a
bonfire with what is left of the funeral torches, so that at dusk they
can be lit and the smoke offered to Andraste." Rhan spoke softly to
me as we reached the outskirts of Tasceni and headed to the corrals
and shelters being built to replace the grand stables the Romans had
burned.

"Yes, of course," I said. "Do you need me to join you?"

Rhan smiled knowingly. "No. You are free to remain here, with
your Tân, who soothes your spirit."

I stroked Tân's smooth neck. "You know me well." Then I turned
in my saddle and spoke to the warrior who marched closest to me.
"Dreda, Rhan will give you instructions on how to make ready the
funeral torches to burn at dusk. Mind what she says carefully."

The tall, chestnut-haired woman bowed. "As you ask, so will I do."

The funeral column broke off from me then as they followed the
main road into the heart of Tasceni. I didn't have to guide Tân the
rest of the way to the corrals. The intelligent mare took over for me,
which allowed me the luxury of a little pocket of temporary solitude.

Tasceni hummed with activity. It was just after midday, but in
the time I'd been at the barrow even more warriors had joined us.
Warriors, strangers and those familiar, greeted me when I rode past.
I nodded and smiled but did not stop. The Druids' entombing ritual
had eased my grief, but I needed time to break the lingering tendrils
of loss that were now more like delicate spiderwebs instead of the
chains that had been weighing me down.

Tân followed her head and I was pleased that she chose a corral
that was not currently surrounded by warriors, but instead was quiet

and had tufts of early alfalfa heaped in a pile beside a clean trough brimming with fresh water.

From her back I opened the corral gate and then dismounted, took off her bridle, and unbuckled the thick pelt and leather riding pad before I made my way quickly to a nearby newly erected shelter that held storage space for tack and grain. I chose a wide-toothed wooden comb for her mane and tail, a soft horsehair brush, and an oiled cloth to keep her coat gleaming and repel insects.

When I returned to the corral, Tân had her muzzle buried in the mound of alfalfa and she stood contentedly while I groomed her. Each stroke brought me peace. As Tân sighed, cocked a back leg, and dozed, I sorted through the threads that still bound me with grief. They were lighter and easier to bear, but they clung to me, sticky and insistent.

I ignored what was left of them and cleared my mind, allowing the mare's peacefulness to flow through me. The cloth moved easily over her smooth, warm coat and smelled sweetly of horse and the oils of lavender, mint, and basil that repelled insects. The scents worked to bring back my childhood, and remembrance lifted my lips in a nostalgic smile. I could almost hear my father proudly telling my mother how steady my seat was and predicting I would make a fine horsewoman.

I rested my head against the mare's neck, allowing the remembrance to bring me joy rather than loneliness and longing for that which I would never hear again in this lifetime—the voices of my parents.

Behind me someone cleared his throat. I sighed and schooled the annoyance from my face. I was queen of the Iceni, and queens are granted many things, but privacy is not often one of them. I turned to see my horse master, Maldwyn, standing just outside the corral. He was holding two squirming bundles of fur. I frowned in confusion as the wriggling little creatures whined weakly.

"Wolf pups?" I asked.

Maldwyn nodded and smiled sheepishly. "Yes, my queen."

Intrigued, I approached, slipping through the corral gate. All tribes used hounds to hunt. Prasutagus always had a favorite dog that ate scraps from our table in the lodge. At his death his current favorite, named Bran, had taken to following Cadoc around so much I'd finally told the old warrior to keep the hound in his hut. I'd meant to choose a pup from the next litter born to the tribe and gift him to my daughters. I liked dogs, though not as much as horses, but I'd never seen a wolf pup this young, nor this close.

"They're thin and look ill—and are so very young," I said as my finger touched their matted fur. They were small, clearly not old enough to be weaned.

"I—I hope I have not overstepped, my queen."

Maldwyn's voice was hesitant, and I looked up from the pups and into his eyes. He was young for a lead warrior, several years even my junior, but he'd had a special connection with horses, and all animals, since he was just a child. Horses in particular seemed to speak to him. The tribe's dogs followed him around. If he sat still long enough, even Iceni chickens would roost around his feet. His features were strong. His thick hair was white blond, dyed with lime paste, as was the hair of all Iceni cavalry. He would not have been considered handsome except for his striking blue eyes and how his smile transformed his face with warmth. At the moment, though, he appeared nervous as he met my gaze reluctantly and shifted from foot to foot.

"Overstepped? Because you did not put these pups out of their misery?" I glanced down at the little creatures and felt a tug of pity. There had been so much death recently. I thought I could understand how Maldwyn would be reluctant to end their lives.

"Yes and no." He drew in a deep breath, and as he exhaled he said in a rush, "I thought they might help your daughters."

"How so?" I asked.

"Because of how I found them. Because of what happened to their pack—their tribe."

"Tell me." As Maldwyn explained how he'd come to save the pups, I felt my gut tighten in anger.

"I know pups this young need constant care," Maldwyn was saying. "And after I found them I had a sudden thought that Enfys and Ceri might be able to give them the care they need to heal and thrive. In doing so these pups might . . ." Maldwyn's words faded as he shrugged and had a hard time meeting my gaze.

"And in healing them my daughters in turn might be healed, and also thrive again," I finished for the horse master.

"Yes, my queen." He shook his head. "Forgive me for the presumption."

"You did not presume. All Iceni know my daughters are battered in body and spirit." I paused and touched the pups again. This time they raised their heads and looked at me. I saw within their eyes a spark that I recognized and understood. They'd been broken and battered but they wanted to live. Had they not, they would have perished with their littermates. "I think you're right. These pups could be very good for my daughters. Come with me, Horse Master, and tell Enfys and Ceri how you came to find them."

The horse master and I walked through the village, and as we did so the Iceni paused in whatever they were doing and bowed to me. There were so many faces I didn't recognize that I asked Maldwyn, "Have you a count of how many warriors have newly joined us?"

"For that you will have to ask Cadoc. I was away all morning scouting the best camping spots for what I believe will soon be an army that overflows Tasceni." Maldwyn kept the pups tucked close against his chest and spoke softly, but his chin lifted proudly and his cornflower eyes swept the village and the new faces.

"I can feel them," I said. "Their excitement and their purpose. Andraste was right. We will serve our vengeance to Rome."

"Did you doubt it?" he asked so quietly that I barely heard him above the muted whines and grunts of the pups.

I stared at the lodge as we came to the front stair and the wide open doors. "Only a fool never doubts."

I led Maldwyn into the lodge, which was buzzing with busy women and fragrant with newly baked bread. Briallen was one of the guards at the doors, but when I gave her a small gesture, she followed me within. My daughters were sitting at the trestle table before the large cooking fire. They each had a piece of beautifully dyed cloth that Wulffaed's granddaughters were helping them embroider. They looked up and saw me, but their smiles of greeting dimmed as their gazes rested on the tall warrior beside me.

"Be close to the girls," I said under my breath to Briallen, who nodded slightly and moved to stand between them. I halted a few strides from my daughters and touched Maldwyn's arm so that he stopped at my side. "Enfys, Ceri, our horse master has brought you a gift." I nodded to Maldwyn, and he lifted the pups and held them high so the girls could see them. They protested, whining and wriggling with strength that surprised me and gave me hope for their survival.

"Are—are they puppies?" Enfys asked.

"Wolf pups," Maldwyn said. He did not approach the girls, though Ceri cringed as if he'd lifted his hand to strike her.

"They are very young," said the Mother of Twenty as she wiped her hands on her apron and peered at the pups. "Looks like their eyes have just barely opened. They should be at a she-wolf's teats."

"Indeed they should," said Maldwyn.

"Tell my daughters why the pups are here," I said.

"I was scouting for campsites south of Tasceni and came upon their pack, slaughtered and skinned and left for the vultures. I found an arrow painted with stars on its shaft embedded in a tree nearby," he said.

"Catuvellauni." Wulffaed's voice was filled with scorn and her mouth pursed as if she'd eaten something sour.

"Yes." I watched my daughters. "The same traitors who led the Romans to us."

"They killed the whole pack?" Wulffaed came closer and touched the pups. "Even a she-wolf who'd just whelped?"

"Yes," said Maldwyn.

I spoke to my daughters. "This winter when your father signed the treaty with Rome, I noticed that their *men*"—I almost spat the word—"seemed overly fond of wearing wolf-skin cloaks. The Catuvellauni must be determined to be sure they continue to swath themselves in the spoils of our land."

"H-how did these pups live?" Ceri's voice was hesitant, but she was looking at Maldwyn when she asked the question—and this was the first time she'd spoken to a man other than to scream in terror since the Romans had brutalized her.

Maldwyn replied with gentleness and honesty. "They survived by will. They refused to die with their pack and instead chose to keep breathing when their littermates chose death. These two little ones did not succumb. They did not give up. They reminded me of my queen's daughters with their bravery, and so I brought them home to you." He held the pups up again as they yipped complaints.

My daughters exchanged a long look, and then Enfys took Ceri's hand in hers. They stood and together approached Maldwyn. I held my breath and the horse master did not move until they stood directly in front of him. Then slowly, ever so slowly, he bent and offered the pups to the girls.

Enfys moved first. She reached up and took one pup from Maldwyn. Ceri grasped the other. She even smiled shyly at the horse master before turning all her attention to the skinny, wriggling pup.

"I can fashion teats from a bladder for the pups," said Wulffaed. "Last whelping season one of our hound bitches had not enough milk for her litter of eleven, and I found a way to help suckle the puppies. Goat's milk and a little honey mixed with the blood of a pig worked well. We did not lose one pup."

"They are very dirty." Enfys wrinkled her nose.

Ceri nodded and her sad eyes met mine. "And they smell of fear and death."

I felt a premonitory chill shudder down my spine as I remembered that Rhan used to do that—used to scent feelings. Did I want to lose Ceri to Ynys Môn? I mentally shook myself. That was not a worry for today. "They are yours," I told my daughters. "Bathe them, feed them, show them you understand their bravery, and I believe they will richly reward you."

Enfys looked up at me. "We *do* understand their bravery. They deserve to live."

"Yes," said Ceri firmly. "They do."

"Then with the queen's permission, let's get these pups bathed and fed," said Wulffaed.

"Permission granted," I said with a grateful smile.

As Wulffaed and her granddaughters began heating water to bathe the pups and gathering supplies so they could be fed, Briallen met my gaze. "That was wise of you."

"Not my wisdom." I pointed my chin at my horse master.

"Aye." Briallen smiled at Maldwyn. "All beasties come to this one."

Maldwyn's face flushed as he bowed to me. "I'm glad to serve my queen and her daughters."

"And you can continue doing so. Sit with me." I motioned to the trestle table my daughters had just vacated. I glanced around the lodge until I spotted my longtime servant. "Phaedra, bring us mead."

Maldwyn sat across the table from me. We did not speak until Phaedra placed two full mugs of spring mead before us. I drank quickly, only then realizing my thirst and hunger, which clever Phaedra had noticed as well. Soon she placed a pitcher of mead and a platter of bread and cheese and dried fish before us. I nodded for Maldwyn to join me. We ate silently while I sorted my thoughts. I heard Wulffaed's gruff voice tell one of her daughters to be sure I had privacy and was glad that Maldwyn and I had a small pocket of solitude in which to speak.

"I will lead us into battle," I said with no preamble.

Maldwyn's brows lifted. "May I make a suggestion?"

"As long as it is not that I remain behind the battle lines, yes."

"I would never think such a thing. I saw you slit the throat of our enemy. I watched you closely. For a moment the fire of the banshees blazed in your eyes. I knew then you would lead us into battle."

His words sent a thrill through my body. Banshees were Druid warrior women who became so consumed by battle lust that they brought terror and death to any man who attempted to stand against them.

"I suggest you fight from a chariot," continued my horse master. "From there you can lead our warriors into battle, and with the right driver, you can be deadly as well as protected better than you would be on horseback."

I nodded slowly. I knew he was right—our chariots were light and swift and deadly—but I had drilled more often with sword and spear from horseback.

He broke into my thoughts. "You have time. When you lead us you will be ready."

"And which driver would you choose for me?" I asked.

He bowed his head and put his fist over his heart. "None but me, my queen."

It made sense. I'd elevated him to horse master for more than his ability to communicate with horses. Maldwyn's expertise at fighting from horseback was second only to his skill with a chariot.

"I agree. Make me a warrior fit to lead our people."

Maldwyn's eyes blazed as he replied, "You are already that, my queen. I give you my oath that I will be sure your spear arm is as true as your banshee spirit when you lead us, Victory."

"Good. Then let us begin."

He blinked at me as if in surprise. "Now?"

"Now."

Chapter XVIII

An Iceni war chariot is a thing of dangerous beauty. For our first practice session Maldwyn chose his favorite. It was decorated with the Iceni sickle moons and sheets of gold pounded flat and thin and wrapped around the front of the cart so that it glittered in the sunlight.

"We have time, so you could begin with a simpler, lighter chariot," he said as we worked together to yoke two matched stallions into their harnesses. The pair was a striking gray; they seemed as if they'd been dipped in moonbeams. "But I have seen you take up the chariot reins on the practice field. You are ready for this challenge now, so why waste time?"

I looked up from threading the double reins through the dorsal yoke. "You've seen me?"

His cheeks flushed, but he replied nonchalantly, "As did most of the tribe when you and Prasutagus drilled together."

I smiled as I knotted the reins, remembering the mock fights my husband had so loved. I'd preferred to battle him from horseback using wooden practice swords, but he was more partial to the showier light chariots. We'd used spears with their wooden ends flattened so that it was almost impossible to strike maiming blows, though I'd often emerged from our sessions bruised and sore. Once I'd drawn my husband's blood when the flattened end had scraped across his bare bicep as we thundered past each other. My smile widened and I could almost hear his proud laughter again as he held up his injured arm and declared me fierce as Andraste.

I was going to work hard to prove his jesting words true.

When I met Maldwyn's gaze he was smiling, too. "Thinking of the day you bested our chief?"

"I was." My smile sobered. "I want you to teach me to best all who come against me."

"It will be my honor, my queen." He tossed a spear to me that I easily caught. It was not the blunt-ended practice spear with which I'd been accustomed. I raised one brow.

"Balance is what is most important when fighting from a chariot. Practice spears, with their blunted, wooden ends, have a different center of balance than a real spear," he explained.

I nodded and hefted the weapon. "We have time, but not time to waste."

"Yes, Queen Boudicca."

"The practice field is ready!" shouted a young warrior who galloped up to us.

My gaze went from his excited face to Maldwyn, and the horse master again understood my unspoken question. "The warriors must have spread the word that their queen is taking to the field."

I felt a shiver of nerves. I was used to drilling with the warriors, especially those of my guard, but this was something entirely different than simply practicing skills I had never believed I would use in battle. Now these warriors who flooded into Iceni did so because of me—because I had uttered a curse and proclaimed war against an enemy that seemed unstoppable. I wiped my sweaty hand on my riding leathers. I could not fail them. I would not fail them.

"I'm ready." I hoped saying it would make it so.

Maldwyn handed me a long wooden shield made of oak covered in leather with cross strips of wide iron. He turned and placed a half dozen more spears in a leather holder tied to the sideboard of the carriage. Then he climbed up into the chariot and went to his knees on the ribs of the carriage, which were made of leather thongs woven together and attached to the sideboards so that they were suspended above the wooden floor. The leather weaving added a supple platform that allowed us to move more easily with the chariot as it thundered across the land. Chariot drivers were unarmed. Their only defenses were the arched sideboards and the shieldlike front of the carriage, which Maldwyn would kneel behind as he guided our team into battle.

I stepped up beside him and took a wide-legged stance, holding my shield before me in my left hand and my spear in my right.

"Ennis, Finley, *hup!*" Maldwyn snapped the reins and the well-trained pair moved out together. Necks bowed, they were a beautiful sight as they eagerly pulled against the traces. Maldwyn clucked and murmured to them. Their sensitive ears flicked back to catch his words while they pranced and tried to contain their desire to surge forward, ready for the excitement of battle.

As we emerged onto the practice field I was surprised to see that warriors framed it, and when they caught sight of me a mighty cheer lifted from them. *"Victory! Victory!"*

It should have made me more nervous, having so many Iceni watch me with such hope bright in their eyes, and perhaps it would have had not their shouts of *Victory* been echoed by the throaty *kraa-kraa* that came from dozens of ravens who circled over my chariot and then landed in the boughs of Grandmother Oak.

Rhan stepped from the side of the field. "Andraste gives sign!" Her voice lifted above the warriors' cheers and the ravens' encouragement. "The goddess of war greets Victory!" She nodded to me, her grin more of a baring of her teeth than a smile, before she moved back to rejoin the watching Iceni.

Six chariots faced us from across the field. Each of them held a warrior-sized straw target strapped to the carriages beside kneeling drivers.

"They'll be moving?" I asked Maldwyn. The only moving target I'd ever drilled with had been Prasutagus, and then my spear had been blunted and my husband and I had used the light practice chariots that were more easily maneuvered.

Maldwyn turned his head to meet my gaze. "Yes, as will the Romans. The warriors know to begin slowly, but move they must. This is how we train for war."

This is not play or show. The rest of what he meant remained unspoken, but I heard the truth in my mind and nodded. "Yes. I understand."

"For these first runs, brace your shield against the front of the carriage, here." He guided my shield into place. As it settled in a grooved notch, I could feel my weight shifting and my balance becoming surer. "When the straw targets are replaced by living warriors, you'll practice lifting the shield to protect you against spears and swords."

"And that won't be today?" I asked, only half in jest.

The corner of his lips lifted. "Not today." He turned his attention from me back to the field. "But perhaps tomorrow. Ready yourself. You have six opponents. We will drill until you have struck each of them in one run."

I lifted the first spear, finding its balance. A glance at the others waiting in the basket that pressed against my right thigh showed me that Maldwyn had been careful to choose spears all of the same size and weight.

"When you are ready, queen of the Iceni," said Maldwyn.

I stood tall, my shoulders back, drew in a deep breath, and with my exhale I let loose the mighty war cry of the Iceni. Maldwyn cracked the reins and the moon-colored team shot forward. The watching warriors took up the cry and my adrenaline surged.

In a line, one behind another, the chariots pounded toward us. The speed was faster than when I'd sparred with Prasutagus, though I could tell Maldwyn and the teams opposing us were holding back.

My first throw struck the straw target, though it didn't embed itself. It glanced off the side of the target, much as my practice spear had that past day when I'd bested my husband. I could tell some of the watching warriors remembered that day as they whooped encouragement.

Not used to rearming myself so quickly, I missed the next target completely but steadied myself and struck the third in the chest. The fourth I missed as well, but I hit the fifth and then I got the rhythm of it and hit the sixth, my spear burying itself deeply in the center of the target's chest.

As Maldwyn pulled the pair up I shouted, "Again!" and the young warrior who had earlier proclaimed the field ready ran to us, bringing me six more spears. We began anew.

I did not hit all six targets in one run until the sun had dipped behind the raven-filled oak. By then, sweat soaked my leathers and lifting my spear arm felt as if I were attempting to heft a limb made of iron, but when I did it—when I struck all of the targets in one single run—the Iceni, my Iceni, raised such a cry that it shook the ravens from the tree and the sky echoed with shouts of *Victory! Victory!*

For the evening meal, long tables filled the main road of Tasceni from my lodge almost all the way to the practice field. Food came from throughout the village—steaming wooden trays of pork roasted with chestnuts and spices, fried cod, succulent goose, and meat pies. Loaves of freshly baked bread soaked up gravy, and deep bowls of baked apples as well as thick berry pies and honey cakes sweetened the air. Pitchers of spring mead were shared generously as fires were lit all along the village road.

I sat at the center of a raised trestle table that Wulffaed had situated at the bottom of the lodge stairs and ate with the same ravenous gusto as did the rest of the warriors. Rhan was on my right in her place of honor as Iceni seer. I had Maldwyn seated on my left where Cadoc would usually be to show my appreciation for his excellence on the field. Cadoc sat beside him and was engaged in an animated conversation with the horse master about my future training. Abertha was seated beside Rhan.

I knew this couldn't be how we ate every night, not if our numbers climbed to those that we'd need to bring vengeance to the Romans at Camulodunum, but this night it was a joy to watch my people. The Iceni seemed to shine with determination and courage and joy. I marveled at that joy and realized that neither Prasutagus nor I had understood the depth of the despair our people had fallen into under Rome's booted foot.

No more. No more would we live in fear, slaves in our own land.

I finished the last bite of a succulent mound of buttery cod and then lifted my mug of mead to drink deeply, making sure I didn't wince at the weariness in my arm muscles or the terrible stiffness from the wounds in my back, which had yet to completely heal.

"It will get better in a few days." Maldwyn's voice was low and for my ears alone.

I met his gaze with a chagrined half smile. "Is it that obvious?"

"No." He chuckled. "But I was there with you for every moment. I know how much strength it took to throw those spears over and over and over. I also know your back must still be raw and sore. Mint salve will help, as will a hot bath, but mostly it will just take time for your body to get used to the training and to heal."

"I will not falter," I said.

"Of course you will not, my queen."

Cadoc bumped his shoulder then and launched them into a discussion about whether or not the shield I carried into battle should be wood crossed with iron, or wood covered with bronze. I was glad to leave them to the minutiae of battle, trusting that they would more than likely have me drill with both to see which would protect me best. I was exhausted and sore but content. I loved listening to the easy way my tribe joked with one another and told stories of the day. Their voices were filled with hope, and that hope was contagious.

"Boudicca?" Rhan pulled me from my thoughts and I turned to her. "The sun has set and the time is right for me to light the central fire and burn the funeral torches. May I do so?"

"Of course, my friend. Of course."

Rhan made her way to a carefully stacked pile of kindling and wood several paces in front of our main table. Around the top of the triangular mound, the seer had placed the half-burned funeral torches, so that they stuck out from the rest of the wood like thick candles. Using a torch she'd kept from the pile, Rhan went to the closest burning fire and lit it. The conversation had quieted as the Iceni watched their seer. Rhan's movements were confident and held such grace that in the flickering firelight she seemed to have slid through the veil from Annwn.

She lifted the blazing torch high and spread her other arm out wide so that her ovate robes of green and brown plaid rippled around her. Rhan circled the woodpile, lighting each of the remaining funeral torches as her musical voice proclaimed,

Fire, I call you to blaze high, blaze true.
And air, I call you to carry the last of the burial smoke from Tasceni
Home to Annwn with you.

The torches lit instantly, catching the dried wood, and with a *whoosh*, fire licked the darkening sky. Smoke swirled and eddied, and as it lifted into the deep sapphire of the night it seemed that faces formed within it. They looked down upon us like eternal guardians before they floated away into the sky.

Rhan returned to her place by my side, and as the Iceni went back to their talk and stories and feasting, the seer brushed back her blond hair and said, "The signs are clear. Andraste watches. Andraste approves."

I'd known it, but Rhan's proclamation had my shoulders relaxing as I exhaled a shaky breath. I opened my mouth to ask Rhan more about the signs she'd witnessed, but Briallen's voice at my back had me turning.

"My queen, the bairns would like a word," said the warrior.

There, beside Briallen, stood Enfys and Ceri. My only sadness that night had been that they had not joined me for the meal but remained inside the lodge under Ashlynn and Ravenna's watchful eyes. I was surprised to see them there, standing still and strong as they used to. Each cradled a wolf pup in her arms. The pups were asleep and I could see that they had been washed and their bellies were full and fat. I smiled at my daughters and cleared the sudden thickness in my throat before I spoke.

"I am always happy to hear from my daughters."

"Well, Mama, it is not you we need to speak to," said Enfys. I could see the strain of being close to so many men written on her pale face and how the little hands that held her pup trembled.

"Yes, Mama, we must speak with Maldwyn." Ceri spoke with more confidence, and I noted that the darkness under her eyes had cleared and her cheeks were, once again, pink with health.

Maldwyn reacted to his name by turning to see who spoke. When he sighted the girls, his face gentled, and moving slowly, as if they were wild hares he did not wish to frighten, he clasped his hands together in his lap and then looked to me.

"Enfys and Ceri would speak with you," I said.

"How may I serve the Iceni princesses?" Maldwyn asked.

"You already have!" Ceri said with such cheer in her voice that I had to bite my cheek not to gasp in happy surprise.

"Yes." Enfys spoke with markedly less cheer and she didn't seem to be able to look directly at Maldwyn, but she did not back away. Nor did she go silent. When she continued, her voice did not tremble, though her small hands still did. "We would thank you for your gift of Mona and Sunne. We did not do so earlier today as we should have."

"Yes, thank you, Horse Master," added Ceri, nodding so enthusiastically that her whole body bobbed and her sleeping pup grunted.

Maldwyn bowed his head. "It is my pleasure to bring you such gifts. Moon and sun—you have named them well."

"Mine is Mona." Ceri lifted the pup, who continued to grunt in annoyance before she buried her muzzle in the crook of Ceri's arm.

"And this is Sunne," said Enfys. As she stroked her pup her gaze finally went to Maldwyn.

"You are doing well with Sunne," said the warrior. "He would not be resting so easily in your arms were he not full and safe."

"I will always keep him safe," said Enfys with a somberness that did not match her thirteen years.

"I believe you," said Maldwyn.

Holding their pups close to their chests, my daughters nodded to me before turning to climb the stairs to the lodge with Briallen close behind.

I breathed a long sigh of relief.

"The pups are helping them heal," said Rhan.

"Yes." My eyes met Maldwyn's gaze. "Thank you."

My horse master's cheeks flushed. "There is no need to thank me, my queen."

Cadoc's bearlike palm slapped Maldwyn on his back. "Well done."

With a bow to me, Maldwyn returned to his conversation with the old shield.

As soon as I could without its being obvious that the queen was retreating, exhausted and sore, I did exactly that—retreated to my bed-chamber and the steaming bath Phaedra had prepared for me. I sank into the tub as my servant handed me a warm mug of mead mulled with spices that I was pretty sure were going to cause me to sleep, though I didn't need herbs to do that. Before Phaedra left me to soak I asked her to send for Rhan. As Phaedra did so, I finished the mug of mead and then settled back in the hot water. The sounds of women tending to the lodge drifted to me. It was a familiar sound that lulled me so much that I startled when Phaedra returned with Rhan.

My childhood friend laughed softly. "Remember the Aqua Springs?"

I stood, and Phaedra wrapped me in a hemp cloth and then began combing through my hair as I sat beside my bed and dried. I rubbed my eyes and yawned sleepily before answering Rhan. "I do. The water was so hot there it almost scalded me."

"And yet you soaked until you turned the red of ripe strawberries—just like you are now."

My hand found the heavy torque that rested around my neck. "Do you ever wish you could return?"

"To the Aqua Springs? Of course, but now they are filled with Catuvellauni traitors and Romans," said Rhan, her expression twisting in disgust.

"I meant return to our childhood," I said.

Rhan cocked her head and studied me before she answered. "Not unless I could know then what I do now."

I met her gaze and thought how foreknowledge could have changed the events of my life, and nodded slowly. "Agreed." We didn't speak again as Phaedra plaited my hair for the night and helped me into my soft sleep shift. "Phaedra, you may go."

"Yes, my queen." She bowed and left me alone with Rhan.

I climbed stiffly onto my thick bed pallet and looked up at my old friend. "I would ask that you move into the lodge."

"As you ask, so will I do," said Rhan.

I shook my head. "No, I don't command it. I *ask* it." I patted the side of the bed. "Come. Sit."

Rhan did so, still studying me with that particular way she'd had since she was a child. I used to believe she could see through my body to my spirit. I realized then that I still believed she could see my spirit.

"Why do you ask me to move into the lodge?"

"Except for Enfys and Ceri, you are the only family I have left. You are also the only person in Tasceni who I know will always tell me what I should hear and not simply what I want to hear."

Her lips twitched up into a smile. "That I will."

"I need my family close," I said softly.

Rhan reached out and put her hand over mine. "Then I shall happily live in your lodge, my queen, my friend."

I squeezed her hand in thanks and then winced as I leaned back and my shoulder hit the thick oak headboard.

"Where is that mint paste I heard Maldwyn speak of?" Rhan asked.

I jerked my chin toward the table beside the bed. "There, but I cannot make myself get up to fetch it."

Rhan laughed as she went to the table and lifted several wooden cups, sniffing each, until she found the correct one. Then she returned to the bed, and in a voice that sounded exactly as it used to when we'd been girls pretending to be queens speaking to our beloved subjects, she said, "Roll over so I can rub this on your shoulders and arms and back."

"Yes, Queen Rhan," I muttered into my goose-down-stuffed pillow.

She began working the mint salve into my protesting muscles and my healing scars. "You know, I never really believed I'd be queen of the Trinovantes."

"No, I did not know that." I paused and then added, "Well, perhaps I did when you had the vision by the pool, but I didn't want to believe it. I wanted us to be queens together—allies of neighboring tribes who visited each other often."

"And demanded only the best cuts of meat be served to us and draped ourselves in jewels," continued Rhan. "Though I remember you used to speak of a golden sword you would wield. Even then you were Victory."

I snorted into my pillow. "If my sword was made of gold, I wouldn't be Victory. I'd be the queen whose sword was cut in half by the first iron blade that struck it."

"You know what I mean. I never wished for any weapons, even gold- or jewel-encrusted ones."

"What is it you wished for, Rhan?" I asked sleepily. Her strong hands were easing the ache in my arms and shoulders and I could feel the herbs making my eyelids heavy.

"Perhaps I will tell you one day," said Rhan softly.

"I will be happy to listen when you choose to tell me." My eyelids fluttered and I fought to keep them open. "Will I be victorious? Can the Romans truly be defeated?"

Rhan was silent so long that I thought she would not answer and was almost asleep when she whispered, "You will fulfill Andraste's curse. The Romans can be defeated."

I sighed. "That is good to know." And then, while her hands continued to soothe my aching muscles, I was pulled into a deep, dreamless sleep.

CHAPTER XIX

I woke slowly. Rhan warmed the bed beside me, and the sound of her deep, even breathing brought back the many mornings we'd woken together as girls after spinning tales of our futures so late that we'd fallen asleep without meaning to, so that those tales became dreams, and then those dreams—at least *my* dreams—had become reality.

I watched Rhan sleep and wondered what it was she had wished for and why she wouldn't tell me. Sometimes it seemed as if there had never been a gap in our friendship—that I still knew her as well as I had when we were girls—but that was impossible. This Rhan was a Druid. A trained seer. An adult who had lived more than a decade without me. Perhaps I would truly come to know this Rhan as well as my childhood friend. I hoped so.

Her eyes opened and met mine. She blinked several times and then sat up, looking around the bedchamber as if she didn't recognize it.

"It seems some childhood habits are easy to fall back into," I said with a grin as I stretched and groaned at the soreness in my muscles.

She yawned and brushed her hair back from her face. "I assume you didn't mean for me to move into your bedchamber when you asked if I would make the lodge my home."

I shrugged and sat up, groaning again. "I thought that you might choose one of the girls' rooms as they seem to have taken up permanent residence together in Mother's chamber, but if the past can predict the future, this will not be the last time we talk ourselves to sleep."

Phaedra peeked her head through the thick blanket that served as door to my chamber.

"Oh, good. There you are, Phaedra. Have one of Wulffaed's daughters send for my lead warriors. They can break their fast with me as we discuss the business of the day."

Phaedra bowed and left, and I realized that she'd not spent the night on her usual pallet at the end of my bed, where she'd slept since the day Prasutagus died.

"I must be healing," I said more to myself than Rhan, but the seer responded with a soft laugh.

"You are, and that is obvious, but I do not believe Phaedra slept outside your chamber last night because of that."

Before I could say anything more, Phaedra returned and began going through my wardrobe, readying my clothes.

"Phaedra, I will be drilling with the warriors daily, so I'll need my riding leathers." I paused and considered how filthy my clothes and I had been by the end of practice yesterday and added, "I believe I will need more leathers."

Phaedra nodded. "Yes, my queen. I thought as much and already spoke to the Mother of Twenty. You shall have more suitable clothes soon."

"Well done, Phaedra." I turned to Rhan. "From today on I would like you to break your fast with me as well."

Rhan bowed her head slightly. "As you ask, so will I do, Queen Boudicca," she said formally. "I shall retrieve my own things, choose one of the bedchambers not currently in use, and then join you— if that is agreeable."

"Of course. And thank you, Iceni seer," I added just as formally.

Our eyes met just before she left the chamber and we shared a secret grin that harkened back to our girlhood. Rhan made me feel young and filled with energy, even though my sore muscles were reminding me I was no longer a girl.

By the time I was dressed and entered the lodge's great room, Cadoc, Maldwyn, and Abertha had arrived. I could hear the voices of my daughters coming from the rear of the lodge, and as Wulffaed placed bannock, cheese, and thick slices of ham on the main table for us, she told me, "My queen, your daughters have already broken their fasts and are feeding the pups. Again. Seems they must eat often enough that your girls got very little sleep last night."

"It is good for them to be busy. As our horse master said yesterday, helping the pups to heal will also help them recover." I smiled at Maldwyn, who sat up a little straighter, though his cheeks did flush. I was beginning to understand that he would rather keep to the background, though his sharp gaze missed little. "Maldwyn, I will drill with the chariot as well as the sword and bow every morning until midday."

"You are a quick study, my queen. You shall be ready to lead us into battle," said the horse master.

Cadoc grunted and spoke around a mouthful of pork. "How long do we have before the warriors should be ready to bring vengeance to Camulodunum and the Roman scum trespassing there?"

"We must attack before harvest. That is when Decianus said he will return to steal from us—what Rome calls taxes." Rhan joined us then and sat at the place I'd left open beside me. I turned to the seer. "As harvest approaches we will ask Andraste to send sign to show us when the time is favorable to strike." I looked to Cadoc. "But all of our plans will fail if we do not have enough warriors."

The old shield snorted. "We will have enough warriors, my queen."

Abertha nodded. "It has only been but days and already our numbers swell to over twenty thousand."

I felt a thrill chase down my spine at her words. "Twenty thousand! All Iceni?"

"All Iceni," said Cadoc. "And more join every day. I estimate if only the Iceni answer your call we will have nearly one hundred thousand warriors by harvest."

"We cannot possibly keep that number hidden here," I said.

"No, we cannot," agreed Cadoc. "And without Iceni warriors to work the fields, the crops will not be harvested. We know that must be done early this year to sustain us for the winter."

"I have thought on this," said Abertha. "My queen, what say you about sending the warriors home after they have been fully armed?"

"And trained," added Maldwyn.

I considered as I chewed a bite of bannock. "It is wise. Cadoc, you, Abertha, and Maldwyn will judge their readiness. When you believe a group of warriors is prepared, they should return to their villages until they are called for in the fall."

"May I speak, my queen?" asked Rhan.

"Freely," I told her.

"Perhaps one warrior chosen from each group should remain in Tasceni. Then when it is time to take our vengeance to the Romans, those warriors will return to their villages to recall their people to us, ready for battle."

"Yes. That idea has merit. This"—I swept my hand before me, taking in each of my advisors—"is how I shall begin each day. Cadoc, I will need updates on our numbers. Abertha, you will advise me on our armament and food stocks. Maldwyn, you are in charge of my training. Rhan, keep me advised of Andraste's signs and omens." I looked from one to another as I continued. "Always speak truth to me. There must be no dissent among us if we are to gain victory against Rome. You see"—I leaned forward—"Rome believes we are so barbaric, so ignorant, that we cannot unite and become the single-minded, living weapon we must be to defeat them."

"Rome is wrong," said Cadoc.

"Aye," said Abertha.

"They do not know us," added Maldwyn.

"They believe our passion and pride are weaknesses," said Rhan.

"They are not," I said firmly. "And *that* is a lesson I look forward to teaching Catus Decianus in exchange for the failed one he attempted to teach me."

My warriors pounded the table with their fists in agreement.

That day a pattern was set that we followed like a wagon wheel in a grooved path. My warriors, my seer, and I met every morning just after dawn. As more and more Iceni flooded into the village, my lead warriors set up a training and armament system where each group of new volunteers was evaluated, drilled, and armed. When Cadoc, Abertha, and Maldwyn were in agreement that the group was ready, they were sent back to their village after choosing one warrior to remain in Tasceni—a warrior they would watch for when the call came to return.

I drilled with Maldwyn on the open field, surrounded by my people. The sounds of warriors training beside me became music for my spirit and I realized quite soon that though my anger simmered and waited to boil, I was also content, even happy. Tasceni was filled with faith—in me, in our righteous cause, and in our goddess. We were of a single mind, and within that mind the word *victory* echoed over and over.

"Good morn! Training today will be *interesting*, my queen." Cadoc had a glint in his eyes that bespoke mischief as he broke his fast.

It was the tenth morning since we'd begun my daily training ritual, and over a steaming mug of morning herbs, Maldwyn had just informed me that this was the day I finally graduated from battling unmoving straw targets to real warriors. I glanced from my horse master to Cadoc, and then from Abertha to Rhan. I looked forward to our dawn meal, where I began each day learning how the pulse of the Iceni beat. We'd grown accustomed to one another. I knew them so much better already. Cadoc loved to jest and his bawdy sense of humor often had me laughing during drills. Abertha's wits were incredibly sharp. When there was a problem on the training field, it was to her I looked for the solution. Maldwyn was quiet and rather shy, but he observed everything and seemed to remember even the slightest detail from the training field. We'd become so at ease in one another's company that they were comfortable jesting with me—and at that moment the four of them were grinning at me as if I had just missed one of their jests.

"What?" My gaze returned to the old shield. "Do you not think I'm ready to take on warriors instead of straw men?"

"Oh, that is not it at all," said Cadoc quickly, a grin still lifting his lips.

When he didn't elaborate, I looked to Maldwyn, who moved his shoulders restlessly. "There was a downpour last night."

I frowned at him. "Yes. What does that have to do with our training today? The rain ended before dawn. The sky is clear."

Cadoc chuckled as Maldwyn answered me. "The sky is clear, but the field will be soaked and slick."

"It has been unusually dry lately," said Abertha after she'd swallowed a hunk of cheese. "You haven't trained in the rain."

"Or in its aftermath," added Cadoc.

My gaze found Rhan, who was trying unsuccessfully to hide a smile. "Should I be worried?"

"Absolutely," Rhan said as my lead warriors snorted laughter.

"Mama?" Ceri asked.

I turned as my daughters approached the table with Briallen shadowing them. Their wolf pups were growing remarkably fast and were fat and gregarious. They trotted after the girls, waddling like toddlers.

"Yes, little dove?"

Ceri lifted her chin, suddenly reminding me very much of my mother. "We would like to train with you."

Surprise had me looking from her to Enfys, who nodded firmly. "Yes, Mama. We must fight, and fight well."

Enfys was right. All Iceni drilled with practice weapons from the time they were very young. Those who showed talent for the sword or spear, bow or horse and chariot, continued their training and became warriors. My daughters, as the children of a tribal chief, had practiced with wooden swords, were proficient with the bow—even little Ceri—and, of course, they rode well. But they needed more. It wouldn't have saved them from what the Romans did to them, but perhaps it could in the future. One well-aimed sword or spear thrust, especially from someone Roman soldiers would not consider a threat, could be the difference between survival and death, even on the periphery of a battle.

"Briallen and Abertha, I give you the charge of training my daughters for war," I said formally.

The two warrior women bowed.

"And Cadoc," Ceri said quickly.

"Cadoc?" Instead of looking at Ceri, my gaze focused on Enfys.

My eldest child nodded somberly. "Yes, Mama. If we can come even close to besting the shield, we will be safe."

Before I could respond, Cadoc stood and walked slowly to stand before the girls. Then he knelt on one knee and looked from Ceri to Enfys as he said, "It would be my honor to train the royal daughters."

"Thank you, Shield." Enfys sounded decades older than the thirteen namedays she'd known.

"Yes. Thank you, Cadoc." Ceri attempted to sound likewise older than her years, but she was unable to hide her dimpled, little-girl smile.

I had to swallow several times before I could speak. "Cadoc will also drill with my daughters." When the old shield stood, I met his gaze and bowed my head to him in gratitude. As he walked past me, fatherlike, he patted my shoulder.

CHAPTER XX

My lead warriors and seer had been right. I'd had reason to worry about the rain-soaked practice field. Before that day I'd been confident that I'd found my battle balance, but just watching the other chariot teams careening through mud told me today would not be the same as those before.

The horse master took position in the cart. I'd already filled the basket with spears, and as I had the days before, I hefted one and the bronze-covered shield my lead warriors had decided would best protect me as I climbed up beside Maldwyn.

"Take some deep breaths." He spoke low so that the warriors closest to us could not overhear. "It is good to be nervous. You will be nervous every time you go into battle," said Maldwyn. "To feel otherwise would be foolish."

"So this is good practice."

"Yes. Remember, your body has found its rhythm. Your balance is good. Your arm is strong and true."

I wiped my sweaty spear hand on my leathers. I was going to give Maldwyn the order to charge when I realized that Cadoc and Abertha were two of the warriors in the chariots opposing me. "Cadoc? Abertha?" I whispered incredulously.

Maldwyn smiled up at me from where he knelt, reins in his gloved hands. "They honor you, Queen Boudicca."

"A little less honoring would be good," I muttered.

Maldwyn laughed. "Let us teach them a lesson about the strong, sure arm of their queen."

I had just opened my mouth to reply when I heard a loud *kraa-kraa kraa-kraa* and looked up to see an enormous raven soar over our chariot. It circled the field three times as the Iceni watched it and called out welcome to blessed Andraste before it landed in Grand-mother Oak.

Confidence filled me and I lifted my spear. "Forward!" I told Maldwyn, and shrieked the Iceni battle cry as the chariot surged onto the field.

Hitting a moving warrior was much more difficult than hitting a straw target. I'd spent the past ten days becoming more and more accurate spearing straw targets, so muscle memory said I should be able to at least hit the shield of one of the warriors thundering past me.

On the first run I received a valuable lesson in the art of evading spears from moving chariots. Not that I evaded every spear—Cadoc in particular bellowed a laugh when his spear thumped my shield so hard that I was almost knocked from the cart.

There was mud everywhere. It flew up from our horses' hooves and sprayed us from the wheels of the opposing chariots. My shield kept me from being blinded by it, but it stung my face and arms, mixed with my sweat, and caked my hair.

We reached the opposite side of the field and Osberth, the boy who had been restocking my spears since the first day, rushed out to fill the basket and hand me another weapon. Maldwyn guided the team around and we hastily wiped muck from our faces. The stallions pranced in place, their hooves squishing in the soggy field as they waited impatiently for Maldwyn to command them forward.

I readied myself and caught sight of my daughters just off the edge of the field. They held short wooden swords and were sparring with Briallen. Both were focused only on the leader of my Queen's Guard as she demonstrated parries and thrusts. Though the field was crowded as men and women of the Iceni drilled, my girls had eyes only for Briallen. Ceri was so small that her sword appeared huge. Enfys's face was the color of pale milk, but her eyes watched only Briallen and her sister, whom she fought beside.

Ashlynn and Ravenna stood not far from the girls. They held Sunne and Mona. The pups' gazes never left my daughters. *When the wolves are grown they will fight beside Enfys and Ceri.* The thought filled my mind and I knew it as the gift it was from Andraste.

I will be Victory for them. My gaze swept the field, taking in the hundreds, thousands, of Iceni who crowded in and around it. *For all of them.*

I shrieked our war cry again and the chariot shot forward. This run my spear glanced off Abertha's shield and a cheer went up from the warriors who had paused their own drills to watch. I almost struck the shield of the next warrior in line, too, but our chariot hit a patch of particularly slick mud and standing water and slid to the side, causing me to overthrow.

This time when Cadoc's spear thumped my shield I did not lose my balance and saw the old warrior's eyes widen before he nodded his approval.

"Again!" I shouted.

On and on we drilled. I was used to the effort. Every evening my body was less stiff and sore. Every morning I moved with more grace and strength; I needed both that day.

As we rearmed before the sixth run, Maldwyn said, "Cadoc is leaning away from you and dropping his shield after he throws his spear. Anticipate that lean. Instead of hurling your spear at him this time, change your grip and strike him with it as we pass."

"With the tip?" I didn't think I could get past Cadoc's guard, but if I did, surely I could harm the old shield.

"No, flip your spear and strike him with the blunt end as if you were a girl again practicing with a wooden weapon."

I grinned. "I will never let him forget it if I do hit him."

Maldwyn laughed. "It would be a fine thing to witness."

The last chariot that charged against me held Cadoc. I was so focused on him that my showing against the other five chariots was weak. And then the old shield was racing toward us. I quickly changed my grip on the spear so that I could strike with the blunt end of it. As we neared one another Cadoc hurled his spear at me. It glanced off my shield, and then he did exactly as Maldwyn had said he would—Cadoc dropped his shield and leaned to the side.

With a movement I will forever take pride in, I shifted my stance and smacked the back of the old shield's shoulder with the blunted wooden end so hard that it made a slapping sound that carried above the pounding of our horses' hooves. The watching warriors cheered and I grinned.

But my pride was short-lived. As I tried to shift my weight back and regain my balance after the unconventional thrust, the chariot skidded awkwardly to the side and I was airborne.

Maldwyn had drilled me over and over on how to fall from a chariot, and I tucked my shoulder. Something sharp hit my forehead as I rolled across the muddy field. I'd lost my shield, but my spear was still in my hand as I came out of the roll sitting in the middle of a shallow, sticky puddle. My heart pounded in my ears and adrenaline rushed through my body. I could see Maldwyn struggling to keep the chariot upright as he wheeled the horses around to come back to me, but Cadoc was faster. He abandoned his chariot, and with a speed that belied his size and age, the shield sprinted to me, face white and grim.

"My queen!" he shouted as he reached me. "Are you—"

Fast as a viper, I struck. Using a move Cadoc himself had taught me, I hooked my leg around the back of his right ankle and flipped him off his feet so that he crashed into the mud beside me, landing flat on his broad backside.

In absolute silence I got to my feet, wiping a sleeve across my forehead, surprised to see a streak of blood come with the mud. I stood over Cadoc, looking down my nose at him, before I reached out and offered him my hand. With a booming laugh, Cadoc took it, stood, and then, with a flourish, he bowed to me.

The Iceni exploded with cheers and shouts of *Victory*. Grinning, I turned to face the side of the field nearest to me. Standing among my people was a tall man swathed in a red cloak, flanked by warriors wearing the same Trinovantes red.

Chief Addedomaros strode across the field to me, flanked by his shield, Mailcun, and a young man I recognized as his son, Adminius. Behind them red-cloaked warriors formed a blood river flowing down the road into Tasceni. Their numbers were so vast I could not see the end of them.

Addedomaros halted before me and bowed his head slightly.

His gaze swept my body and I lifted my chin, proud of the blood that ran down my face and mixed with mud and sweat. I placed the butt of my spear into the mud and returned his gaze. I did not speak first, nor did I look away. I was queen here, and he had come to me.

Addedomaros nodded, and when he spoke his deep voice carried across the newly silent field. "Queen Boudicca, Tribe Trinovantes has come. We wish to ally ourselves with the Iceni."

I was compelled to speak one word, and that word rang in the air around me. "Why?"

"The Romans were not sated by their attack on Tasceni. They have been raiding Trinovantes villages that border the sea, stealing away my people to be their slaves. I understand now that we *must* war against the Romans because we cannot continue to stand by idly and do nothing while Rome preys upon us." The chief echoed the words I'd spoken to him so many days before. "If we do not try, we are already gone. Tribe Trinovantes will not become Roman!" His people shouted in agreement. Addedomaros raised his hand and they quieted. "Will you accept us? Shall we fight the invaders at your side, mighty Victory?"

I bared my teeth in a feral grin and lifted my spear. "Yes!"

Behind me Cadoc began the chant. "Bou-dic-ca! Bou-dic-ca!"

Breathing heavily, Maldwyn and Abertha sprinted up. Lifting their spears, they joined the shield's chant. "Bou-dic-ca! Bou-dic-ca!"

And then the Iceni and the Trinovantes joined them, shouting *"Bou-dic-ca! Bou-dic-ca! Bou-dic-ca! Bou-dic-ca!"* until the leaves on Grandmother Oak shivered with the sound of my name and Andraste's raven calling *kraa-kraa* victoriously into the morning sky.

PART II

FALL/WINTER 60 CE

I believe it is time." I gazed up at Grandmother Oak. Her leaves were just beginning to turn yellow as the days became shorter and the nights longer and cooler.

Beside me Rhan nodded. "I shall petition Andraste." She didn't need to ask me to explain what I meant. In the almost six months since the Romans had attacked Tasceni and Rhan had become seer of the Iceni, she and I had grown even closer than we'd been as children. "I assume you want the petition to be public."

"Absolutely," I said. "How soon can you be ready?"

"I am ready now." Her grin flashed. "Last week when you commanded that the harvests begin, I prepared. I have been leaving offerings to the goddess every day since then. It has been seven days. Andraste will give an answer should you ask today."

"Reading my mind again?"

She laughed softly at our old joke. "It's much simpler than that. You called for the harvest to begin, and then my father followed your lead by commanding the Trinovantes to harvest as well. I expected him to come to Tasceni to announce his crops had been safely stored just as the Iceni's are now at the winter stronghold in the forest of Thetford. I knew you would want my father present for Andraste's response, so I prepared."

"And this morning Addedomaros arrived. Your seer gifts are impressive," I said as I pressed my hand to the skin of the oak's bark in greeting before Rhan and I continued walking.

Rhan snorted. "Foretelling my father's visit has far more to do with the fact that he cannot seem to stay away from Tasceni than any gift I've been given."

I glanced at Rhan. Her face was shadowed and difficult for me to read. "Have you quarreled again with him?"

She sighed. "Not directly. But I believe it will always be awkward for him to be near me. He cannot seem to reconcile the fact that I am more seer than daughter now."

"Why can't you be both?" I asked.

Rhan waited so long to answer that I was trying to think of another way I could frame the question when she finally said, "Because my father is frightened of me."

"You've not told me that before."

She shrugged. "I've only come to realize it is true these past months, but I've suspected it since just before I left for Ynys Môn those many years ago. Remember the look on Father's face that day I had my first vision at the pool?"

"I remember the day, of course," I said. "But all I recall about Addedomaros is the fear I saw in his eyes when I recounted how you almost fell into . . ." My voice faded as I realized the truth. "The fear he showed wasn't because you'd almost drowned."

"No," Rhan said softly.

"And that is why he sometimes speaks abruptly to you, or ignores you completely."

"Yes."

"I'll talk with him about it," I said.

"It won't help," Rhan said quickly. "It will only humiliate him."

I was silent as we continued to walk toward Andraste's shrine. We had taken to visiting the goddess together every day after I trained with the warriors. Sometimes Rhan and I left the goddess offerings. Sometimes, like today, we brought beeswax to rub into the wood of her statue to protect it against the rain so that Andraste would shine her welcome on all who passed this way to enter Tasceni. As the large wooden statue came into view, I said, "Rhan, if Addedomaros is frightened of you, then why does he keep returning to Tasceni? He could simply wait for me to send word when it is time to attack Camulodunum."

"It is not to me he is returning," she said.

Before I could ask Rhan what she meant, Enfys and Ceri ran up to us, both girls talking excitedly at once. They were followed closely by the two half-grown wolves who never let my daughters out of their sight.

"Mama! Mama! We did it. Sunne and Mona and Briallen helped, but we did it!" Ceri shouted.

As they reached us the scent of blood came with them, metallic and heavy. The girls' tunics and faces were blood spattered. Their braids were coming undone. Ceri's sleeve was torn almost all the way off. From the wrists down, their hands were scarlet, like they'd dipped them in a vat of blood. They carried bows slung across their backs, but their arrow quivers were empty.

My stomach went hot as my face went cold. I thought my knees would buckle and automatically reached for the short sword I strapped around my waist every morning. "Where are you injured? What has happened? Where is Briallen?"

"Oh, Mama, we are fine," Ceri said with the same innocently dismissive tone children always use with worried parents. "Briallen's back there with—"

"We killed a boar," Enfys interrupted as she placed her bloody fists on her narrow hips and beamed with pride. She even smiled, reminding me of the open, happy child she had been before the Roman attack.

Ceri frowned at her big sister. "I wanted to tell Mama!"

Enfys raised one brow. She looked and sounded so much like my mother that longing for Arianell speared through me. "It was *my* arrow that brought him down," she insisted. "Briallen even said so."

"But *my* arrow was the first to strike him." Ceri mimicked her sister's stance, refusing to back down.

I felt dizzy with relief that my girls were safe and was grateful Rhan spoke so I could breathe deeply and attempt to quiet my thundering heart.

"A boar? That is quite the accomplishment." Rhan reached down and ruffled Sunne's ears as the big male wolf's tongue lolled.

I fixed a smile on my face. "Where is this boar?"

Enfys pointed behind them into the forest. "Back there, but not very far. We gutted it, but it's so heavy that Briallen sent us to get help to drag it back to Tasceni."

"Oh, Mama!" Ceri bounced up and down on her tiptoes. "I cannot wait for Wulffaed to make us her wild boar pie."

"It is delicious, little dove," I said. "Hurry now, though. You don't want to leave Briallen alone in the forest defending your prize."

"Bears have begun gorging for the winter, and it would be a bad omen should brave Briallen be forced to kill one as it prepares for its slumber," Rhan added.

"Why would that be a bad omen?" Enfys asked, the somberness that had usurped her previously gregarious nature settling back around her like a cloak. "Bear pelts are very warm to sleep on."

"Because if it is a female bear there is a good chance she will be pregnant," explained Rhan.

"Oh, I understand," said Enfys thoughtfully. "That would offend the goddesses."

"It would," agreed Rhan. "Best do as the queen says and hurry. Cadoc is still on the training field. He will help you."

Ceri turned to Enfys. "Cadoc is big enough to carry the boar himself!" And the girls were off, running past us with their wolves keeping pace beside them.

I staggered the rest of the way to Andraste's shrine and leaned against it. Grasping her feet with hands that trembled, I bowed my head and whispered a prayer of gratitude that it had been boar blood and not human blood spattered on my daughters.

"More deep breaths," Rhan said from beside me as she gently rubbed my back. "Your girls are safe."

Breathing shakily, I lifted my head. "After they were attacked I often wondered if they would ever recover."

"I know." Rhan's hand rested on my shoulder.

"They did recover. They've even grown strong and confident again."

"But the blood took you back to that day," Rhan finished when I could not.

"Yes." I whispered the word. "I cannot let them see it, but yes. I don't think time will ever fix that. I don't think I'll ever not see their bloody, violated bodies in my nightmares."

Rhan's pressure on my shoulder forced me to face her. "This is your sign."

"My sign?"

Rhan nodded. "Andraste will give you a more public sign. She will show the Iceni when it is time to take their vengeance to the Romans at Camulodunum, but what just happened was your goddess speaking to you privately, reminding you, rekindling within you the anger that has waned these past six months."

I shook my head as I felt that anger stir. "I haven't forgotten that we were attacked."

"No, of course not." Rhan paused, and when she continued her voice was gentle with understanding. "But you have found happiness again, and happiness cools anger and stagnates vengeance."

I looked up at the face of the goddess—serene yet fierce, strong yet motherly—and I knew deep within me Rhan spoke the truth. "So Andraste reminded me of my duty."

"No! You have not forgotten your duty. The Iceni and Trinovantes know that. But what just took your breath, tightened your stomach, and drained the blood from your face is something you must remember and carry into battle with you," said Rhan. "You seek vengeance. Not just for your daughters' violation, but for the violation of all Britons."

I nodded. "I will not forget again."

"Oh, you might," said my friend. "And if you do, the goddess will remind you."

I said nothing as Rhan's words shivered through my body.

We were polishing Andraste's idol when Cadoc and Maldwyn galloped past us with Ceri and Enfys riding double with them, holding on tightly to the warriors. The young wolves ran beside the horses as the girls whooped the Iceni war cry and Cadoc and Maldwyn waved at us and grinned. I was fiercely proud of my girls. Once they'd started training with Cadoc and Briallen, their confidence had begun to return. As their bodies strengthened and their skills improved, my girls had been reborn. They'd shed childhood like a stifling chrysalis they'd been forced to battle their way through. Today they were strong and sure of themselves, but they could have easily never recovered. They could have closed down, refused to fight to heal, and rejected a future where the possibility of more brutality waited just around the next bend in the forest, unseen but lurking.

Andraste was right. It was time to bring vengeance to the Romans.

"I will tell Cadoc to gather our people at the field before we go in for the evening meal," I said.

"I will be there—as will the goddess."

My gaze went to Rhan. She and I had climbed up on the flat stone slab on which the statue of Andraste rested. We'd brought clean hemp clothes with which to rub the wax into the statue, but our hands were slippery and Rhan had a smear of wax on her cheek. She looked up at me from the goddess's shoulder.

"What? There is nothing to be nervous about. Andraste has been waiting for this day—as have the Iceni," she said.

"I'm not nervous. I trust her. I trust you. I was just thinking how grateful I am that you are here with me," I said.

Her dark eyes lit with pleasure and she flashed me the impish grin that hadn't changed since our childhood. "I am happy to serve the Iceni queen."

"No." I spoke softly and her hands stilled as she listened. I hadn't meant to say these things to her. I'd only recently come to understand the truth I was putting into words, but as I continued to speak I felt the rightness of sharing them with Rhan. "This isn't the queen of the Iceni being grateful for her seer, though she is. Rhan, before you came to Tasceni I didn't often think of friendship, if at all. I've realized that is because before his death Prasutagus had been my friend, and his presence in my life was so large, so overshadowing, that he eclipsed everyone else.

"When he died I gravitated to my mother. Arianell's dedication to

my daughters, my people, and me was enough that I did not understand that except for her I had no true friends." Rhan tried to speak
but I raised my hand. "I need to say this. Arianell filled the space left
by Prasutagus's absence. She was more than mother. She was friend
and confidant. I had my daughters, of course, and my people looked
to me for guidance and stability. But except for Arianell, I had no one.

"The day Mother was killed, it seemed something within me
died with her—something that had been wounded with the death
of Prasutagus." I reached across the statue of Andraste to take Rhan's
hand. It was smooth and slick with wax but warm and familiar, and
she wove her fingers with mine. "Having you here healed that which
I thought had died within me. You are more than friend. You forged a
path that led me to open myself to others. Today I can say that Cadoc,
Abertha, Maldwyn, Wulffaed, and Briallen are truly my friends. Because of you I am rich with those who return not just my trust but
my *friendship*, and that is a gift few chiefs or queens can boast of."
I bowed to her. "Thank you."

When I raised my head, Rhan's eyes were bright with tears that
tracked down her flushed cheeks. "I did not know until I arrived in
Tasceni how very much I had missed you. Boudicca, I will be content
if I can spend my life at your side." Then she squeezed my hand before
she let it loose to wipe at her cheeks.

Then I asked a question that had been niggling at my mind for
the past several months. Rhan was beautiful and wise and, of course,
a respected seer. During the past many months of daily training, the
warriors had become so accustomed to my presence that they spoke
freely around me, and I'd overheard several of them, men and women,
comment on Rhan's beauty and exceptional grace. Though my friend
was kind to all of the Iceni, she didn't appear to favor one over others,
and my curiosity had finally become unbearable. "Will you not choose
a mate? Will you not marry?"

Her gaze avoided mine as she returned to rubbing wax into the
goddess's shoulder. "I will not marry."

"Marriage wouldn't change your standing," I said. "Even Derwyn married." The high Druid's wife had died in childbirth many years ago. I had not known her, but Arianell had told me that he had been devoted to her.

"Yes, I know."

Then another thought came to me and I added hastily, "I've seen one of Wulffaed's daughters watching you. What's her name . . ." I hesitated, thinking.

"Lianne," Rhan said, still without looking at me.

"Yes, that's it. Lianne with the honey-colored hair. She's lovely and clearly she's interested in—"

"Boudicca, forgive me, but I do not want to talk about it."

"There is nothing to forgive. We won't speak of it until you're ready. If you are ever ready," I added hastily before I returned to polishing the statue. Rhan spoke with such finality that any further questions on the subject died in my throat.

The shadows of the watching trees were lengthening into dusk when I strode onto the training field. I'd grown to love the feel of its hard-packed soil under my feet as much as I loved the changes daily training had forged in my body. After six months, my strength and balance complemented my height and speed. The curves of my body were no longer soft, but instead long, lean, flexible muscle. My spear arm threw true. There were no chariot teams who could best Maldwyn and me on the field. After the rainy day when I'd fallen from the cart, Abertha had drilled me over and over with a short sword until even Maldwyn, who was the most overprotective of my lead warriors, agreed that he was no longer fearful that I couldn't protect myself on foot in the middle of a battle.

Just days before, I'd overheard Cadoc bragging that the queen of the Iceni moved with such graceful strength that even he envied me. I let the words of the mighty shield propel me forward to the middle of the crowded training field. The tribe packed the area. They parted eagerly, murmuring fond greetings as I passed. I'd become more than their queen or figurehead. I'd become one of them, and my pride in that would stay with me until breath no longer filled my body.

In the center of the field was a large circle that was clear of the press of people. I stopped there, gazing around at the warriors who were so familiar and so dear to me. Addedomaros and the Trinovantes shield, Mailcun, stood across from me beside Cadoc, Abertha, and Maldwyn. I noted several scarlet cloaks scattered among the woad blue of the Iceni. That pleased me.

Briallen stood between my girls, their half-grown wolves at their sides. Though the Iceni pressed around them, Enfys and Ceri appeared as calm as their pups.

I did not see Rhan but knew she had to be close.

"Iceni seer, come forth!" I shouted.

To my right the warriors rippled and parted enough to allow Rhan through. She carried an elaborately stamped bronze pitcher and a woven reed cage that held one of the sacred hares that were raised in a hut behind my lodge, bred for their color, size, and temperament. This creature was large—much bigger than a wild hare. Except for the woad-colored crescent painted on the creature's chest, its coat was white and gleamed with health.

Rhan's entrance was dramatic. She hummed a hauntingly melodic song as she circled me thrice before she stopped in front of me, put the cage at my feet, and, still holding the bronze pitcher, turned to face the raptly watching crowd.

The change that possessed Rhan when she performed the rites and rituals of a seer always amazed me. It was as if she shed mortal trappings and took up the mantle of the gods. Her blond hair washed down her slim back, and her eyes, always expressive, gleamed like deep water.

Rhan raised the pitcher so that her forest-colored robe fell back, exposing the tattooed Ogham symbols that circled her slender biceps. Her bare feet began to stomp rhythmically, *da-da, da-da, da-da*, a strong, steady heartbeat. She gestured, and the Iceni joined her until the field was one beating heart.

Then, in time with the tempo the tribe kept, Rhan began to dance a circle around the caged hare and me. As she did so she poured a libation from the pitcher. The sweet, familiar scent of strong honey mead laced with lavender perfumed the air while Rhan invoked Andraste.

"Wind, whisper Queen Boudicca's petition to the goddess of the Iceni, blessed Andraste. Fire, blaze Queen Boudicca's petition to the goddess of war, our Andraste. Water, wash Queen Boudicca's petition to Andraste, goddess of wealth and plenty. And, earth, let even the rocks sing Queen Boudicca's petition to the goddess of the harvest."

Rhan ended the invocation in front of me. She placed the empty pitcher on the ground, opened the cage, and lifted the hare so that I could whisper my petition to it, and through the little creature to Andraste. All around us my people continued to stomp a heartbeat that filled the field.

But I had decided to change tradition. I raised my hand and the people stilled. Rhan's gaze met mine. She did not look at all surprised; instead she dipped her head in agreement.

"Iceni and Trinovantes, I will not whisper my petition to Andraste. Instead, I would shout it so that *all* may witness my question as well as the goddess's answer. I refuse to repeat mistakes made before me." I would not list the faults of Prasutagus that had led us here. Everyone present knew them. But I also would not pretend as if he had been infallible. The longer I ruled alone, the more I understood what had driven my husband to ignore the signs sent from Andraste— something he could not have done had the Iceni witnessing those signs heard his whispered petition. So I did not whisper to the hare. I shouted and was glad that the creature had been bred for a calm temperament, because instead of startling and struggling to get away from me, its brown eyes watched me calmly, as if it listened closely to every word. "Andraste! Your Victory seeks sign! Is it time to serve our vengeance to the Romans? I beseech you, mighty Andraste, show me your will!"

When I'd finished speaking, the hare began to struggle against Rhan's hold. The Iceni seer placed the creature at my feet and it sprinted, circling me thrice, before it dashed south—in the direction of Camulodunum. As it darted into the watching crowd, people parted, but not just for the white hare. There were several shouts, and then a wide area was suddenly clear and five hares raced after the goddess's messenger. They were wild hares, smaller and brownish gray. Single-minded, the creatures ignored everyone except the sacred hare as they all ran southward and directly toward a large cook fire that marked the beginning of the corrals. For a moment it seemed all six hares would hurl themselves into the fire, but at the last moment they darted around it and disappeared into the south.

I looked to Rhan. "Seer of the Iceni, what say you of this sign from Andraste?"

Rhan spoke, projecting her voice throughout the field. The power of her words shivered across my skin. "Andraste's hare circled Queen Boudicca three times before racing to the south and being joined by five wild hares. The goddess's sign is clear. The queen must travel to Camulodunum and back in three days. Five days after that, the Iceni, joined by Tribe Trinovantes, will burn the city to the ground."

I blazed with Rhan's words, lifted one fist to the sky, and shrieked the Iceni war cry. The tribe took up my cry and it mixed with the whooping of the Trinovantes so that as the sun retreated into the horizon it seemed to do so in response to our voices.

CHAPTER XXII

Y ou know you cannot enter Camulodunum without being recognized by the Catuvellauni. They'll immediately report you to the Romans. At best they will be more vigilant in guarding the city. At worst Paulinus will send for the Ninth Legion to reinforce the centuria stationed there, the centuria that attacked Tasceni." I spoke quietly and firmly to Addedomaros. "You cannot join me until we ride at the front of our combined armies and burn Camulodunum to the ground."

I would always feel the affection of a foster daughter for the Trinovantes chief, but he did not rule in Tasceni and all I owed him was the courtesy of hearing his words—not following them. He sat on my right, at the place of honor at the head table within my lodge. To his right was his son, Adminius, and beside him was Mailcun, the faithful Trinovantes shield. The evening meal had a feastlike quality as Tasceni celebrated the battle sign Andraste had given. I did not want that spoiled by Addedomaros's petulant insistence that he must join me to reconnoiter in Camulodunum.

"Queen Boudicca, if I may?" Rhan, who sat on my left with Cadoc, Abertha, and Maldwyn seated beside her, leaned close to me and spoke so that her voice did not carry farther than our table.

"Of course, Rhan," I said.

"I do not see why she should speak!" Adminius snapped. Several heads turned toward us at the sound of his sharp words. Rhan's brother had visited with his father only a few times during the past several months. I had not known him well when I fostered in his home. He was two years younger and had not shown any interest in his sister or me, or really anything except himself. I'd thought him petulant and selfish, when I thought of him at all.

"Rhan speaks because I have given her leave to speak and I am queen here, Adminius." My voice was just as sharp, though considerably quieter than the Trinovantes chief's son. "You would do well to remember that she is seer of the Iceni, conduit to Andraste, appointed by Derwyn himself."

When Addedomaros looked as if he would protest, Mailcun spoke up. "My chief, it is proper that the seer speak."

Addedomaros blew out a long breath as he ran a hand through his thick hair. He nodded, turning to his son. "Mailcun is wise, as is the Iceni queen. Of course Rhan should speak." He looked around me at Rhan. "Sometimes I forget that you are a gifted seer and not simply my daughter."

And if you or your son insults my seer again, you will be very sorry. The words were on my tongue, but I pressed my lips together and held them in. It would not serve me to threaten my only ally. Instead I nodded for Rhan to continue.

Rhan leaned forward again so that she could keep her voice low. "The sign Andraste sent was clear. The hare circled Queen Boudicca thrice before the wild hares joined it. The Iceni must make the first foray into Camulodunum alone, for the very reason Boudicca gave—a reason I know the chief of the Trinovantes must agree with."

Addedomaros nodded. "Yes, yes, yes. But to remain behind is difficult for this old warrior."

"And yet you will remain behind," said Rhan. "Because you are not just an old warrior. You are a wise old warrior."

"Excellent point," said Cadoc through a mouthful of wild boar pie. "Should you join us I doubt we would be allowed to leave the city."

"Agreed," I said to stop the pointless discussion. "Cadoc, Maldwyn, and I leave for the city in the morning."

"What of Abertha?" asked Cadoc. Abertha was seated beside him and looked up from her plate as she heard her name.

Instead of answering my shield, I stood and waited for the lodge to be silent. When all heads turned to me I said, "As Andraste commanded, I leave for Camulodunum tomorrow. The Iceni who have waited here will leave at dawn to recall all of our warriors to Tasceni.

I take with me my shield and my horse master." My gaze went to Abertha. "While I am gone, my spear master, Abertha, will oversee the last of the preparations for war."

"As you ask, so will I do!" Abertha's voice rang with pride and the warriors pounded their tables in support of the well-respected warrior.

"I return in three days. Then, following the sign given by the goddess, we will wait five more and then ride to fulfill Andraste's curse. We will burn Camulodunum to the ground!"

The lodge erupted in cheers and war cries. I sat, and Wulffaed's legion of daughters and granddaughters refilled tankards of mead until they overflowed.

We left Tasceni shortly after dawn. Rhan and my daughters saw us off. For a moment I struggled against an urge to have Rhan join us, but I knew better. Rhan wasn't a warrior and we might have to fight our way out of Camulodunum. It was wisest to keep our group small and swift and ready to fight. Rhan would spend all the days leading up to the battle pouring libations and leaving offerings for Andraste.

"Did you remember to bring an offering with you to leave at the Temple of Brigantia?" she asked as I mounted Tân.

"I did. I chose one of Arianell's necklaces, the gold pendant stamped with Brigantia's fire," I assured her, patting the leather satchel I'd slung from my shoulder—the same leather satchel that had once carried the torque Andraste had gifted me, which now rested warm around my neck. "It is what Arianell would want."

"All will be well." Rhan spoke softly as she placed her palm briefly on my mare's neck. Then louder, she said, "We will rejoice at your return, Queen Boudicca."

"Yes!" said Ceri as she bounced on her toes and waved.

"We will take care of Tasceni while you are gone, Mama," said Enfys in a very grown-up voice.

I looked back at my daughters, the two faithful wolves at their sides, and nearby Briallen, who was never far from them. I did not doubt that they truly would take care of the village while I was away.

Camulodunum was a hard day's ride south, and that was for rested riders on swift, strong horses. It would take our army two days to reach the city. That worried me. The Romans would know we were coming. With the addition of Tribe Trinovantes our numbers had grown to a little over one hundred thousand, and though we had not all gathered at once, it was likely our enemies were at least somewhat aware that the tribes had been in constant movement since spring. Andraste was wise. We needed to know the strength of the legionnaires in Camulodunum. Had they, too, been quietly amassing their forces?

Addedomaros had lived in Camulodunum when it had been the home of Trinovantes royalty. He had sketched maps of the dyke-and-ditch system that had protected the city when he'd occupied it as well as the main gate, which he labeled Balkerne, through which he recommended we enter—though even he admitted that his city hadn't been well fortified. Had it been, it would not have fallen to the Catuvellauni and their Roman allies. But in the decade since the Trinovantes had called it home, what defenses had the Romans erected? I knew that Roman legions had been stationed there for many years and a large temple had been raised for Claudius by the cult who worshipped the dead emperor they had proclaimed a god. Had a wall been erected? Had the dykes and ditches been fortified with sharpened stakes to thwart a chariot attack? How well was the Balkerne Gate guarded? Soon we would know.

The fall day was crisp and clear. There was a snap of coolness in the air that turned leaves to bright but fleeting yellow and orange and scarlet, yet there was still enough warmth left in the weakening sun that the breeze did not chill us, only kept our sweat cooling as we rode hard and fast into the south.

We had chosen to pose as traders and had left behind Iceni blue and covered our easily recognized sickled-moon symbols. We did not bring a cart, as that would hinder our ability to move swiftly and stealthily. Instead each of us led a pack-laden horse specially chosen for stamina and fleetness.

I rode Tân and led a gelding who was her younger brother. I'd missed the long rides I used to take on Tân before I'd begun my daily chariot training. Even with the hard pace we set, I found myself relaxing and enjoying the freedom of horseback again.

Our pace shifted from canter to trot to walk and back to canter again, and as I settled into the travel routine, I found myself studying Maldwyn, who rode beside me on Ennis, one of the big gray stallions he loved so dearly. Off horseback he was a pleasant-faced man who smiled easily. His body was lean and lithe. We were of the same height—something I appreciated, especially when we trained together. He didn't talk a lot, but when he did speak, his observations were insightful as, unlike too many people, his silence was a listening one.

Astride a horse, Maldwyn evolved from pleasant faced to beauty in motion. He moved seamlessly with his horse. He held his reins slack; sometimes he dropped them completely so that they lay knotted on Ennis's neck. Though he would say that he guided the stallion with his legs and his balance, I had come to understand that it was much more than that. Maldwyn was one with the horse. The trust that was between him and his mount was unspoken and unfathomable.

"What is it, my queen?" We'd slowed to walk the horses, making conversation easier.

"I was just envying your connection with Ennis," I said. "If I dropped Tân's reins she would probably weave and wander."

"I think you would be surprised," he said. "Try it. It will help you connect with your Tân in a new way."

"Aren't we riding too hard for that?" Cadoc asked, though with more curiosity than censure in his voice.

"No, it is a good time to practice. Tân will naturally continue with us and it will give Boudicca the opportunity to gain confidence in her ability to guide the mare with her legs."

Cadoc grunted gruff agreement. "Won't try it myself," he grumbled. "The only implement of war I desire to become one with is my sword."

"Horses are more than war implements." Maldwyn and I spoke the words together and then laughed.

Cadoc nodded, making his beard bob up and down on his broad chest. "And that is why *you* will drive our queen's chariot into war and not me."

Maldwyn and I shared an amused look before I dropped Tân's reins and spent the next several hours communicating with her through my legs and how I adjusted my balance. I was surprised at her elegant response. I would have thought that she would pay more attention to me with the reins in my hands than without, but I was wrong. Tân's ears flitted back to catch every word I whispered to her and soon she was responding to the shifts in my body as well as to the pressure of my legs against her.

At midday we reached Catuvellauni land and the Roman road, and halted near a stream to water the horses and feed them sweet mash while we ate some of the hearty travel food Wulffaed had so carefully packed for us.

I had just washed my face in the cool stream when Cadoc approached with unusual hesitancy. I used my tunic to dry my face while he shifted from one foot to the other.

"You should just say it," I told him.

"Aye." He nodded and cleared his throat. "My queen, you must remove your torque."

My hand went automatically to touch the familiar weight of gold around my neck—the sign of my rank, my power. When I said nothing, he continued, speaking quickly.

"We know the Romans who attacked Tasceni were from Camulo-dunum. We know they returned to the city and from there made forays into Trinovantes land, taking captives and looting villages. Forgive me for saying this, but they would have boasted of what they did to Tasceni, to your daughters, and most especially to you." He paused as he shook his head and his mouth twisted in disgust. "So if the soldiers see a tall, flame-haired barbarian woman wearing the torque that announces to all that she is a queen, *they will take notice.*"

"Yes, Shield, I agree." I took off the torque and returned it to the satchel it had rested in before. My neck felt strange without its weight and warmth, but I knew Cadoc was right. It was not wise to be recognized in Camulodunum.

"I told you she would be reasonable," Maldwyn said as Cadoc and I returned to the rested horses.

"I am always reasonable," I said as I put my foot in Maldwyn's entwined hands so that he could boost me astride Tân.

Cadoc snorted and I smiled at him as I guided Tân back to the road.

"Well, almost always," I said.

Behind me my shield chuckled and we urged our horses onto the road.

The sun traced its path down the sky and the thick forest began to be interspersed with farmland. We met many more travelers as they headed to and from the city with their trade goods and tax payments. It was easy to tell which was which. The farmers whose carts were filled with payment to the Romans were somber. They kept their eyes on the road and did not greet us. Traders were gregarious. Some even offered us their wares, saying they would save us the trip to the city if we bought from them. If they offered us pelts, we said that we traded for wool and hemp cloth and so on, pleasantly declining all offers and riding on, though we always paused long enough to listen in as the little groups of travelers chatted together. Thus we began to learn how the farmers and traders felt about their foreign governor.

"They chafe under Rome's yoke of taxation. Farmers are being forced to give up food and goods their families need to survive the winter, but they know if they don't they will be met with the kind of violence our tribe has known," said Cadoc darkly after we'd passed a cart loaded with baskets of produce driven by a sour-faced man and his bitterly complaining wife.

"That is good for us," I said.

"Aye," agreed my shield.

As we got closer to Camulodunum, the farm huts changed from our wooden roundhouses to cold stone things built in squatty squares and topped by tiles.

"Have they all become Romans?" I asked Cadoc.

"No, my queen. These"—he gestured at the latest stone building we cantered past—"*are* Romans. Soldiers who have behaved valiantly in battle or who have retired are often gifted farmland by the Roman governor. I've heard the Trinovantes warriors speak of it often. It is how they were pushed off the land when the Catuvellauni allied with Rome and defeated Addedomaros. Rome gifted the Catuvellauni traitors with land that Tribe Trinovantes had farmed for generations."

"That is the doing of the Roman governor, Gaius Suetonius Paulinus," I said.

"Yes. He leads the legions here as well," continued Cadoc.

"I am aware. I remember him from the signing of the treaty with Rome. We bring vengeance to Decianus for what he did to us, but Paulinus is our ultimate enemy—he and the legions he leads."

"Indeed," agreed Cadoc.

"So the Roman governor gifts his men with lands belonging to Britons," said Maldwyn. "First taking it away from the Trinovantes and then taking it away from the Catuvellauni warriors, even after they fought beside Romans."

"Yes," said Cadoc.

"The Romans will take even from their allies. Were I Catuvellauni, that would make me very angry," said Maldwyn.

"Perhaps all is not as neat and tidy in the city as the Romans would like us to believe," I said.

"Perhaps not," agreed Cadoc.

We slowed with the flow of horses and carts and people that crowded the road as the westernmost gates of the city came into view before us, four rounded specks on the eastern horizon. I thought from this distance they looked like the backs of beetles crouched on a hedgerow.

"The Balkerne Gate," Cadoc said, keeping his voice low and

guiding his horse closer to Tân. "It's as Addedomaros described and as I remember from when I was here with Prasutagus well over a decade ago. Four arched entryways. Then this was the only gate wide enough for chariots to enter."

"Guard towers on either side of the gates," Maldwyn said. I rode between them so close that my legs often brushed theirs.

"Let us turn off before we reach the gates," I said. "Even from here I can see that the dykes and ditches stretch around either side of the city."

"They should run the circumference of the city," said Cadoc. "And meet with the two rivers on the east side."

We kneed our horses onto a dirt path that fed into the Roman road before we reached the gates and were able to increase our pace to a canter again, covering ground quickly as we traveled around the outside of the city.

The foolish Romans had built no wall to protect Camulodunum, nor had they staked the ditch-and-dyke system that served as their only defense. It was true that the expansive V-shaped ditches were chariot deterrents, but several of the banks were low enough that cavalry could ride over them. The only established lookouts were at the Balkerne Gate. Chariots would have to enter through those main gates, but the rest of the army could easily rush the others as the cavalry hurtled over the ditches. My shoulders loosened with relief and I almost laughed at the arrogance of Rome. *That arrogance will be their downfall.*

The setting sun reflected the saffron and orange of the changing leaves into the clouds over the western forests when we'd finished scouting outside the city and trotted back toward the Balkerne Gate.

"Shall we enter? Find an inn and a warm meal for the night?" Maldwyn asked me.

"Let's eat within the city, but the crawling feeling I have along my skin says we should camp outside in the woods," I said.

Cadoc grunted agreement. "I have no desire to lie with traitors."

Just before we entered through one of the four large stone arches that marked the Balkerne Gate, I turned to glance over my shoulder at the road and surrounding woodlands and farms behind us, and I had to blink spots from my eyes as the sun touched the tree line and roofs of the farmers' houses. Still blinking my vision clear, I entered the city. The soldiers standing atop the square stone lookouts that butted against the arches gave us only a glance—we were just part of the long line of traders, weary after a day's travel, glad to enter the city and dismount for the night.

I was surprised by the lax attitude of the Roman guards. Any soldier who looked sharply enough at the three of us would have seen more than farmers or traders, but their gazes were not sharp. They were dismissive and restless, as if they had somewhere else they'd rather be.

"I'd replace every one of them," Cadoc grumbled low.

"Aye," Maldwyn agreed.

I only whispered *Thank you* to Andraste. I saw the laziness of the guards and the city's meager defenses as blessings showered on us by the goddess of war.

Just inside the gates there were two large stone shrines. The one to my right was dedicated to the Roman goddess Venus, who stood graceful and naked, one hand holding a robe that was obviously Roman and the other lifted to the crown of hair ringing her head. Candles burned at her feet amidst coins left as offerings. *Venus, why are you here?* I thought. *Do you not long for home?*

I turned my attention to the second shrine and pulled Tân to an abrupt halt.

My stomach tightened. It was a large stone statue of Epona astride a horse with an arched neck. As with many of the shrines dedicated to our goddess of the horse, Epona was bare breasted, her hair cascading down her back and shoulders. But unlike *any* rendering of her I had ever seen, a bronze crown of laurel circled her head, and a Roman tunic had been draped around her stone body and fastened at her shoulder by a golden brooch in the shape of the Roman eagle. Horrified, I could not look away, could not move at all.

Then Maldwyn was there with Ennis, who gently crowded Tân to turn us from the desecrated shrine so that we were, once again, part of the ebb and flow of the busy gate.

"They've tried to make her Roman!" I whispered fiercely to Maldwyn, who remained so close to Tân that Ennis's shoulder kept nudging us forward.

"Aye, but to stop their desecration we have to survive," said Maldwyn softly. "So we must keep moving."

In front of us Cadoc kept glancing over his shoulder, sending worried looks my way, until I finally shook off my disgust and moved Tân forward myself.

As Addedomaros had explained, Camulodunum had been built on a grid, with the wide main stone streets running east-west and the smaller, hard-packed dirt streets north-south. The outer ring of the city was an awkward mixture of Britain and Rome. I found the rectangular stone buildings the Romans preferred to be cold and unattractive—soulless. Interspersed between those stone structures were our wooden roundhouses. I hated how shabby they looked.

The city was crowded with Roman soldiers. Torches were lit on the outsides of the taverns and inns that lined the main streets. Periodically large metal braziers provided light and warmth along the streets. Those braziers seemed to be meeting places for the soldiers clustered around them, throwing strange shadows as they drank and laughed and gamed.

The city was divided into three major sections. The Sheepen District was in the northeast, and it held the main Roman barracks, a theater, a basilica, and the trading center. The Gosbecks was an older section in the southeast of the city where, situated on a gentle rise in the land, a temple dedicated to Brigantia had stood for generations. We would scout both sections tomorrow, but that night we followed the main road that fed directly into the third section, the Roman colonia, which sat in the center and held the monstrosity the Romans had built to their dead emperor Claudius. The temple filled a city block. Stone arches gleamed in torchlight revealing an immaculate courtyard that held an enormous central building high up on a podium-like base. White stone stairs stretched up to tall columns.

As we passed slowly by the temple, I peered within. Multiple braziers, too many to count quickly, threw licking shadows over a bronze statue of Claudius, making it appear as if his empty eyes came alive, only to die again in darkness.

There were none of our roundhouses in the colonia and it seemed uncomfortably as if we had been transplanted to the heart of Rome. The temple was surrounded on three sides by barracks. Soldiers walked about the courtyard, calling to one another and raising mugs of wine. These were older men than the Romans who filled the city streets and pubs. They were gray haired, scarred, and grizzled. They paid little attention to travelers but laughed and joked easily with one another.

"These barracks are for retired soldiers," Cadoc said quietly. "I've heard reports that Paulinus had them built for his legionnaires, the ones not gifted land and farms. After pillaging the countryside for him, they're meant to live out the rest of their lives in luxury here, cared for by Britons who have been made slaves in their own country."

"Oh, they will live out their lives here," I said. "But their end will come much sooner than they imagine."

We kneed our horses around and returned to the outer part of the city, though I still felt as if I had crossed into a different world.

It was ironic that we finally chose to stop at an inn that blazed a brightly painted wooden image of Epona over its door and called itself the White Horse Inn. We dismounted and Maldwyn led all six horses to the rear of the building, where he would pay the stables to feed and care for them. I knew we would not see the horse master again until he had wiped each horse down and made sure they were properly watered and fed.

Cadoc and I entered the busy inn. The main room was large but had a low ceiling and a smoking fire that stung my eyes. We chose a narrow table in a corner facing the door and ordered a pitcher of beer and roasted chicken, which we paid for with Catuvellauni silver we'd brought from the Iceni treasury. While we waited for Maldwyn to join us, the shield and I sipped our beer and listened.

Cadoc had opened his mouth to speak to me when I made an

abrupt motion to silence him, then cut my eyes to the table to our right, where several farmers were deep in conversation, gesturing so wildly with their mugs that beer sloshed around them.

"Say it again. I haven't heard a word about it," said one red-nosed man whose beard was moist with drink and grease.

"And I tell you that you haven't heard a word of it because *they* don't want you to know, but it fell!" answered a farmer whose hair was braided into a single blond length that stretched down his back. "I saw it with my own eyes. Straightaway off the top of that damned arch. No wind. No storm. Just the goddess Victory breaking off to fall and shatter on their stone road as if she were made of the same glass as their wine goblets."

"Which road?" asked another man who wore a cloak of Catuvellauni brown and moss green.

"The one that leads from here to Londinium," said the man with the braid.

The first man clucked his tongue. "'Tis a bad omen. A bad omen."

"Aye. It's as if Victory meant to escape what is to come." The bearded man wiped his mouth on the back of his sleeve. "I hear the Iceni and Trinovantes have harvested early."

The other two men nodded and shared pointed looks.

The bearded man continued. "Mayhap that's where the Fourteenth and Twentieth legions are headed. Out to put the boot to the two tribes as they collect the harvest tax."

I felt a chill of fear as I listened intently.

The Catuvellauni shrugged. "Why take the legions to do that? It only took a centuria to attack Tasceni, and they returned from that missing only a handful of Romans—or so they bragged. No, Paulinus is up to something else."

"Mark my words," said the man with the braid. "Victory falling was a warning to us. I'm taking my family and heading to the inland forest. Won't return until snow bites the air, if then."

The Catuvellauni nodded slowly. "I'm going inland too, well away from any Roman road or city. I have no love for Iceni or Trinovantes, but less for Rome." He leaned forward and hatred deepened his voice.

"I fought with them against Addedomaros and they still took my farm and divided it between three Romans." He spit on the floor. "I'll never raise my sword to aid them again."

The other two men grunted and nodded before they refilled their mugs.

Maldwyn joined us as the serving woman placed three platters filled with succulent baked chicken and beets, red as blood, swimming in onions, before us. We didn't speak while we ate. We continued to listen as the conversations around us all held a similar theme—Tribe Catuvellauni strained under the yoke of their Roman overlords.

It was fully dark with only a fat yellow crescent moon to light the night after we retraced our way to the almost deserted Balkerne Gate and trotted west. We found a deer path that led away from the stone road into the forest and a grove of silver birches that clustered around a narrow stream. The ground under the trees was thick with moss. Cadoc and Maldwyn raised a crude shelter while I built a fire, and then we spread out our bedrolls and shared a bladder of Wulffaed's honey mead.

"I want to warn them," I said. "I wish I could tell every Briton to leave Camulodunum."

Cadoc raised a thick silver-gray brow at me. "Have a care, Boudicca. We are vulnerable here. If we draw too much attention to ourselves we could be discovered and killed. Then we will be of no help to anyone."

"I will not give us away, but I would not have our countrymen within those walls when we bring our vengeance to the Romans."

Maldwyn nodded. "My queen, I believe Andraste has heard you. She will find a way to warn the people who will listen. Have faith."

I met his steady gaze. "I do."

Cadoc blew out a long breath. "We could spread the story of Victory falling from the arch. Call it the warning it is. Encourage those who might be considering leaving the city to do so immediately."

"Yes," I said. "Tomorrow as we move through the city blocks among those who come to trade with the Romans, that is what we must do. It is the right thing to do."

"Remember that the Catuvellauni are not our friends," grumbled Cadoc. "Do not trust them."

"They are not friends, but they did not attack Tasceni. They did not kill our elders, rape my daughters, or flay the flesh from my back, and they cannot force us to pay taxes to them. The Catuvellauni are a familiar enemy, one that can be dealt with swiftly once the Romans are not infesting our land. We will kill them if they stand with Rome. If they do not . . ." I shrugged.

"As you ask, so will I do," Cadoc said, though with obvious reluctance.

Maldwyn's smile flashed white in the firelight. "Andraste will find a way, my queen. I am sure of it."

I do so hope you are right, I thought as I stared into the fire.

CHAPTER XXIII

In the morning the Balkerne Gate was even more crowded than it had been the evening before. I was glad we were mounted and not on foot or dragging a cart. Instead we were able to guide our horses around the slower-moving traffic. The soldiers stationed at the two lookout towers were as apathetic as the day before. Cadoc's lip curled in disdain when we passed unchecked and unnoticed through the gates again.

We turned north at the first of the side streets and followed the large square that was Camulodunum, noting each of the other gates and where the ditch was shallowest and would be easiest for our cavalry to navigate. By midday we'd made mental maps of the circumference of the city and headed to the Gosbecks, where I meant to leave my mother's pendant as an offering for Brigantia. On the way we stopped at a public house to eat, making sure that we engaged the scullery maid in a lively conversation about Victory falling and the dark omen that must be. I was gratified when several of the tables around us paused their conversations to listen, nodding along with us.

Andraste, I know I cannot save them all, but let those who will take heed save themselves. I found myself praying quietly to my goddess all that day as it seemed she listened with the wind and watched through the eyes of each raven perched on the foreign tiles that roofed the soulless stone buildings the Romans called home.

There were fewer Roman houses in the Gosbecks and instead many round huts with goat pens, chickens, and hutches filled with fat hares. In this area of the city there were also decidedly fewer Romans walking the streets and haggling with merchants. I was able to relax just a little and breathe deeply of the familiar scents. If I closed my eyes it almost seemed I was back in Tasceni.

The land lifted gently to a green clearing, in the center of which large stones carved with Ogham symbols were interspersed with oaks. The focal point of the clearing was a circle of flat stones from which blazed an ever-burning flame, similar to the fire that was never allowed to extinguish before Brigantia's shrine at Isurium, the seat of the Brigantes' royal family, where I'd been born. There were a few people present, all women and all dressed in the style of the tribes. I smiled at the absence of Romans. Brigantia would approve.

Maldwyn waited with our horses outside the clearing, but Cadoc joined me as I walked between the standing stones, finding comfort in the flame and its warmth. My attention was on the ever-burning fire, so I did not raise my gaze to the stone statue of the goddess until I was very close to her. I'd dipped my hand into the satchel slung across my body and felt around the torque that rested there to find the pendant I'd brought as an offering. As I lifted it out of the satchel, my eyes rose to the goddess and the breath left my body. Beside me I heard Cadoc curse.

Brigantia was no more. The huge slab of upright stone from which the goddess had been carved generations before had been permanently marred. No longer was she my mother's goddess, keeper of the flame of Tribe Brigantes, patroness of stags, our bright shining forest goddess. Where once her head had been haloed with rays of light, as if she stood untouched but surrounded by flames, she now wore a Roman helmet. In one hand was a long Roman pilum. In the other she cradled the head of Medusa against her breasts. Roman lettering was carved into the base of the statue.

I turned my face away and didn't realize I wept until the tears dropped from my cheeks to my tunic.

"Makes ya ill, doesn't it?"

I looked back at the statue to see an old woman with a mane of wild silver hair dressed in the deep-blue robes of a bardic Druid. She was covered with tattooed Ogham and wore a belt of mistletoe.

She nodded as if I'd spoken. "Aye, makes me ill as well, though I still tend the goddess's flame. She's in there, Brigantia, waiting . . . watching."

"They've ruined her." My voice was rough, as if I'd been screaming.

"No. They've tried to remake her in the image of their goddess Minerva, but our Brigantia, like this land and its people, is not so easily overcome." She tilted her head and studied me. "You are she."

"We should go." Cadoc pushed forward so that he stood between the Druid and me.

"Aye, go, but you will return," said the Druid. "First, did you bring something for the goddess?"

"Yes, but I brought the gift for Brigantia, not Roman Minerva." The name felt sour in my mouth.

"Brigantia knows when offerings are left for her. She knows we see her beneath what they did to her." The old woman's sharp blue-gray gaze swept around the clearing and the other women who were leaving libations of beer and offerings of cakes at the shrine. "What brings you to Brigantia?"

I lifted the chain that held the fiery symbol of my mother's goddess. "I brought my mother's pendant. She belonged to Brigantia and is now with the goddess in Annwn."

The Druid nodded and gestured at the defiled statue. "Place it there, around her neck. Whisper your prayer. Brigantia will hear. Brigantia will answer."

I met the old woman's gaze. "Do you think Minerva also listens?"

"Perhaps. Not many Romans come here, though I have some-times felt the presence of the foreign goddess." Her gaze narrowed. "Do you have a petition to bring to Minerva?"

"Perhaps," I said, echoing the Druid.

At my side Cadoc moved restlessly. I could feel his tension, but I also felt something else—something radiating from the statue. I felt anger. Moving purposefully, I walked around the flame. The heat of it brushed my skin as I unhooked the necklace, placed it around the goddess's neck, and then refastened it. The chain glinted and the sun-light reflected off the flame-stamped gold. I touched the goddess's cheek. "I ask nothing of you, beloved Brigantia. Instead I give you my oath that I will return and I will free you." Then I dropped my hand and took a step closer to the defiled statue. I lowered my voice so that it would not carry to any of the other supplicants or the watching Druid. "Minerva, it is to you I speak now. You do not belong here." I flung out my arm toward the colonia in the city center and the temple of Claudius. "Send sign to your people. Tell them to leave this land and take you home to Rome where you belong. *Where all of you belong.*

"If you stay here, Andraste and Brigantia will rain arrows of fire down upon you and yours until nothing but ash and bone remain. On that you have the oath of Boudicca, queen of the Iceni." As I spoke I took out the short sword I wore in the sheath strapped around my waist and made a shallow cut on the pad under my thumb. I reached out and wiped my blood across the cheeks of the statue. "So I have spoken, so shall it be," I whispered ferociously.

When I stepped back, the old woman was watching me closely.

"I will not see you again, Victory. I leave this place in six days and will be sure all who know Brigantia and will listen to my words leave with me," said the old Druid.

"You know me?"

"I do not, but Brigantia does, and I know her. You are Andraste's daughter, are you not?"

"We should—" Cadoc began again, and moved to take my elbow.

I shook my head and his hand dropped to his side, though he glared at the old woman and his troubled gaze kept searching the clearing as if he expected soldiers to leap out and attack us at any moment.

I knew they would not. I could feel a rightness to the Druid and understood that Brigantia had placed her here, at this moment. And for that I was so very grateful.

"Yes," I answered her. "I belong to Andraste and the Iceni."

The Druid's wide smile showed several missing teeth. "I knew you would come when the statue fell from the arch. May Andraste and Brigantia bless you richly." She nodded to me before she turned to the statue, raised her hands, and began reciting prayers of thanksgiving.

"Now we go," I said to Cadoc. Without another look at the sullied goddess, I strode away from the shrine.

Anger simmered within me as we entered the Sheepen District. The streets were crowded and we paid a stable boy to watch over our horses while we explored that area of Camulodunum.

Flanked by Roman buildings, the wide stone streets of the Sheepen District led past the temple and out of the colonia to a basilica and then farther on to a large theater. As we reached the basilica, the crowds thickened and merchants filled the courtyard in front of the round building, as well as inside its arched entryways. For reasons I could not understand, it seemed Romans had to create buildings within buildings, as if to find ways to take up as much space in our world as possible. The arches led to an internal area that was dotted with Roman statues, all grim men who didn't appear nearly as fierce as I was sure the artists intended. How could they be? Romans are so diminutive in stature.

"They look like children playing dress-up." Cadoc's deep voice rumbled low beside me and I had to choke back laughter.

Past the internal courtyard of the basilica there was a square stone building with stairs leading up to a wide entrance. Waves of men came and went through the open front doors. I caught sight of rows of seats within and a tall speaker's podium. It was a busy place, filled with men in uniform and also quite a few wearing white togas trimmed in colors from red and blue to rich royal purple. I saw not one Roman woman.

The crawling feeling that shivered across my skin told me we were running out of time and needed to leave Camulodunum. I motioned for Cadoc and Maldwyn to step with me into the shadows under a cluster of trees near the basilica. "Let us separate. Explore around this building and between here and the theater. See what we can each overhear and then meet back here."

"We should leave the city soon," said Cadoc.

"Agreed," I said. "Explore briefly. We meet back here and then we leave."

Maldwyn ran his fingers through his thick blond-white hair. "Good. This city repels me."

"This city will not exist much longer," I said quietly.

Before I moved off toward the south side of the basilica, I pulled my cloak closer around me and lifted its hood, even though I had been careful to tightly braid my mass of red hair and then drop the braid beneath my plain travel cloak. I made sure I walked close to the open archways of the basilica, listening carefully to the conversations within. The road was crowded with merchants and farmers. The thriving market held wonders—foreign spices that filled the air with scents that tickled my nose and made me sneeze. Tables and tented stalls sold hemp and wool, and many rolls of fabric were dyed colors so rich that even Wulffaed would have envied them. Roman glassware and lamps as well as urns of oil drew the attention of traders. The glassware was a marvel. Goblets and urns were carefully arranged so that they caught the sunlight and became jewels. I had never seen so many mirrors. Produce was stacked high in baskets beside crates and pens holding live chickens and geese, goats and pigs—and then there was the wine. Barrel after barrel of Roman wine was for sale.

I could acknowledge my curiosity about many of the items that surrounded me. I could appreciate their beauty and the craftsmanship it took to create them. But my curiosity and appreciation were tempered by the undeniable knowledge that the presence of these wares meant that my people were being erased.

I moved through the market with purposeful strides, careful not to meet the gazes of sellers, noting how few women were among the vendors and traders. It wasn't until I followed the curve of the building around to its rear that I found the women. They lazed in front of a block of modest Roman buildings. They all sold the same product, though in many different sizes, shapes, and proclivities. Some exposed their breasts; some lifted their tunics to show their calves and thighs as men hesitated, attempting to choose between them. As I studied them I realized that not one of the women was Roman, though many of them were dressed in the draped Roman style of clothing that the men clearly preferred. Several of the women even had their hair braided and wound around their heads in elaborate Roman crowns, with rather ridiculous-looking ringlets framing their faces. Their Roman dress was in stark contrast to the fierce tribal tattoos that decorated their arms, thighs, necks, and faces. I wondered how many of these women had been taken captive and were forced to sell themselves to Romans. The thought made me sick.

One woman in particular caught my attention. She lounged on an upholstered bench in front of a building over which hung a large eagle painted gold. She was statuesque and wore an almost transparent sheet of fabric wrapped revealingly around her voluptuous body. Her dress did nothing to hide the circular Catuvellauni moons with hidden faces tattooed in black that stretched from one bare shoulder across her chest to the other. She reclined and sipped from a clear glass goblet filled with red wine as she surveyed the crowd, often calling out to a passing man by name and leaning forward so that her breasts threatened to spill from the sheer material. She was quite beautiful, though when she wasn't smiling at a man her light hazel eyes looked hard and her expression flattened to boredom.

There was a break in the crowd in front of her building as a woman down the street had begun to dance in time to a drum. She whirled in a circle while she unwound pieces of an elaborately draped mantle from her body, revealing enough soft white skin that men clapped in time and encouraged her to continue.

"What are you looking at? Never seen a whore before?"

At first I glanced around me, thinking she was speaking to someone else. I hadn't realized that I'd stopped walking as I studied her and the dancing woman, but she had noticed and turned her hard gaze on me.

I shrugged. "I have. I do not judge how any woman feeds herself."

"Bah!" she snorted. "Your eyes say something else."

I'd started to walk on but paused at her words and turned to face her. "Yes. They say that I know you have sold something more precious than your body." My gaze lingered on her Roman hair and her Roman dress and the goblet of Roman wine she held. "Here in this Roman place you have sold your spirit."

She narrowed her eyes and sat up so suddenly the wine spilled, spattering the cushions with blood-colored drops. "I know your kind." She almost hissed the words. "You think your tribe is better than everyone else, but you have it wrong. We must join Rome or perish. I choose not to perish."

I felt her hatred as a physical thing pushing against my skin, and the anger simmering within me bubbled up and overflowed into my words. I closed the space between us and glared down my nose at her.

"Then that is your choice. And for it you will live and die like a Roman; you have my oath on that." While I spoke a gust of wind blew down the stone road, picking up dirt and brown, crumbled leaves and whirling them around me. The wind caught my travel cloak, pushing the hood back and lifting the fabric that hung from my shoulders so that it flapped like the wings of a raven, exposing the length of my fire-colored braid. I watched the woman's hard eyes go wide with the beginnings of fear.

"Who are—"

Before she could finish I whirled around and walked away. I'd had enough of Camulodunum. Striding around the side of the basilica, I headed toward the little cluster of trees where I hoped Cadoc and Maldwyn would soon join me. I was almost glad the Romans had defiled the statue of Brigantia. She shouldn't have to witness what her people were being forced to become within the too-tidy streets and square, anemic buildings of white stone.

I had just rounded the final curve of the building when a group of soldiers gathered before one of the wine vendors began cheering and hailing two men who were walking slowly with their heads together several paces in front of me. One was dressed in a draped white toga trimmed in red. The other wore the uniform of a Roman officer. In response to being hailed, the men stopped and turned. I felt as if a fist had struck me in my stomach. I could not breathe. I could only stand and stare.

"Toast with us, Gaius Suetonius Paulinus!" called one of the wine-swilling soldiers.

"And what of me? Do you not wish me to drink with you as well?" The high-pitched, nasal voice sliced down my spine as the skin of my back spasmed in remembrance of when last I'd heard it.

"Of course, good Procurator!" another soldier called jovially. "You are always welcome to share cups with us!"

Decianus turned his meaty face away from the group of soldiers to whisper something to Paulinus, but the governor frowned at him and shook his head. Then, without another look at the procurator, he strode with long steps, smiling warmly at the soldiers, who cheered again and handed him a mug of wine. Paulinus was tall for a Roman, though he would have been considered diminutive were he an Iceni warrior. I could not deny that he was fit and moved with athletic grace. Decianus hurried after him, his flesh wobbling with the effort. As he raised his arm to take the mug of wine another soldier offered to him, sunlight flashed off the golden torque that gripped his sagging bicep. *My torque.*

I thought I would be sick—right there in the middle of the wide Roman street surrounded by enemies and the soulless opulence of this city. That terrible day flooded back to me. I could feel the slice of the lashes on my back. I could hear my daughters' screams. I could see the spear that ended my mother's life skewer her again. I could smell the metallic scent of blood and the reek of bowls loosening in death. I swallowed bile as I realized I'd stopped and was staring at the group of soldiers, causing people to push past me with increasing irritation.

Move! I ordered my leaden feet. *Get out of the way!*

As if they belonged to someone else, someone watching outside my body, my feet led me to stagger forward to stand beside a triple-tiered fountain directly across from the group of drinking soldiers. The crystal water gurgled into a large basin, and I reached out and plunged my shaking fingers into the water as I tried to reconnect with my body.

"To the Fourteenth Legion and our general, Gaius Suetonius Paulinus!" shouted the soldier who had first called to Paulinus.

The other men echoed the toast, and the governor smiled and raised his mug with the men before drinking.

"To the Twentieth Legion and Gaius Suetonius Paulinus!" said the second soldier, raising his mug again.

They all drank. Then Paulinus lifted his mug and the men went quiet. "And we cannot forget our loyal procurator, Catus Decianus." The governor's words were little different from the soldiers', but the tone in which he said them was patronizing—as was the unenthusiastic cheer that followed them.

Decianus did not seem to notice. His lips turned up in the priggish smile I remembered. He drank and then said, "Yes, who would fund your little wars were it not for me and the taxes I collect? And I shall continue to collect them when you depart for Ynys Môn in three days to rid that isle of the Druid filth."

Paulinus frowned at the procurator. "Decianus, I've had reports that some of the native tribes have been gathering and even perhaps arming themselves. While I deal with the Druids, you would do well to call for the Ninth to support you and remain within the city until I return."

Decianus scoffed. "The centuria I used this summer to teach the Iceni queen her lesson should return from escorting our fur merchants west in a fortnight or so. But because you insist, I shall send a runner today to recall them earlier. They will be more than enough protection from the barbarians while the Druids learn their own lesson."

I heard Derwyn's voice lifting from my memory. *Ynys Môn calls to me. Last night in my dreams the oaks keened.* And like a fire in my head, my anger ignited, burning through the last of my body's numbness. I needed to act. I had to act. My hand went to the hilt of my knife and I took two strides toward the soldiers. Later I wondered at my foolishness, but then all I knew was rage.

Suddenly Cadoc was on one side of me and Maldwyn on the other. Like I was a sheep being herded by hounds, my two warriors guided me away from the soldiers. Cadoc's strong hand latched onto my elbow and he propelled me forward, but not before I heard Paulinus ask the procurator, "Did you see her? A tall Brittani woman. Held herself like a man. She seemed almost familiar."

"How can you tell one from the other?" Decianus's nasal voice answered. "Unless they are naked and lie beneath me I cannot abide . . ."

And then we were out of hearing range, though my warriors did not slow. They steered me hastily through the crowd. When I stumbled, Maldwyn's hand closed on my other arm and they almost carried me between them. We reached the corral that held our horses and Maldwyn took me directly to Tân.

"Can you stand here while Cadoc and I gather the tack?"

I nodded and then rested my forehead against Tân's warm neck. I forced myself to breathe deeply, slowly. Eventually the shock began to dissipate. By the time Maldwyn cupped his hands to boost me astride my mare, I could reason again. I dug my heels into Tân. People scattered as we clattered down the street to the Balkerne arches and sprinted through them, leaving the admonishing shouts of the Roman lookouts and the tainted city behind us.

CHAPTER XXIV

We didn't speak. We rode fast, eager to put distance between us and Camulodunum before darkness would force us to stop for the night. Pushing Ennis to the edge of the powerful stallion's strength, Maldwyn broke off from us twice and circled back to be sure no one had recognized me and sent soldiers after us. But no one followed, and eventually even Cadoc stopped looking over his shoulder. We focused on urging the horses on.

Tân was covered with the white froth of her effort to maintain such a pace when the Roman road took a westerly turn. Eagerly we left Roman stone behind us and continued north through forests that became more and more familiar.

Finally Maldwyn's voice called over the pounding of our horses' hooves. "We must slow to cool the horses and then stop for the night soon. It would be too easy to misstep in this darkness."

I pulled Tân up gently from a swift canter to a trot and finally I allowed her to walk. All of the horses were exhausted and dripped sweat. Steam rose from their sodden coats as the night went from chilly to cold. We had to move slowly through the dense forest, and when the horses were dry enough we followed the musical sound of running water until we came to a creek. I dismounted and rubbed Tân's salt-stiffened coat, murmuring to her about how much I appreciated her strength and swiftness. Then I worked beside Maldwyn and Cadoc to wipe down all six of our horses. After they drank their fill from the stream, we tied grain masks over their muzzles and gave them the last of the feed we'd brought. Maldwyn predicted they would be asleep almost before they finished eating, and he was right. As we built a fire and settled in for the rest of the night, the horses' weary sighs and the sweet smell of them soothed my nerves.

I was prepared to eat stale bannock and cold jerky, but Cadoc surprised me by unwrapping a large hunk of smoked pork, a wedge of soft herb-spiced goat cheese, and an entire loaf of bread from his packs.

He smiled as he cut the pork and began to warm it over the fire. The meat sizzled and released scents that had my mouth watering. "I felt the wind shift this afternoon and thought we'd do well with something warm in our bellies tonight."

With a shy flourish Maldwyn brought out a large bladder, which he offered to me first. I uncapped it and sniffed—and my gaze cut to his.

He shrugged. "And I thought we might as well drink their wine before we drive them from our lands."

"Ha!" Cadoc laughed and clapped his big hands. "Right you are, Maldwyn." His eyes glittered at me across the fire. "What do you think, my queen?"

I sipped the wine. I'd had wine before, of course. When Prasutagus lived he often returned from trading or raiding with barrels of it. This wine was red and potent, and its warmth felt good as it filled my belly.

"I think I am glad my two warriors had such excellent foresight today. This"—I lifted the bladder and with it gestured at the pork sizzling over the fire—"is greatly appreciated." I tossed the bladder to Cadoc, who caught it one-handed and tipped back his head to drink deeply.

We ate and drank, and did not talk much until our bellies were full and our bodies relaxed. I sensed that the two men were reluctant to bring up the events of the day, so I began.

"How did you get to me so quickly?"

They did not have to ask what I meant. Cadoc cleared his throat and then jerked his bearded chin in Maldwyn's direction. "Maldwyn and I had just met and were heading to the trees when he recognized Decianus and then saw you. We knew we had to move fast."

I looked at Maldwyn and shook my head slightly. "But you had never seen the procurator. How did you recognize him?"

Maldwyn took a long pull from the wineskin and wiped his mouth with the back of his hand. He tossed the skin to Cadoc and then stared into the fire as he answered. "It was Brigantia. She sent a ray of sun to strike Decianus's arm at the exact moment I glanced his way. It set your torque aflame. I knew then who he must be."

"I did not intend to put us in danger. I am sorry." I turned my gaze to the crackling fire. "I do not know what I thought I could do. It was such a shock—so unexpected—to see him. Decianus." My lip lifted and I sneered his name. "I was taken back to that day and I had to do something."

"You thought to kill Decianus," said Cadoc. "And you would have killed him—slit his throat like the animal he is. You probably would also have killed Paulinus, as neither man would have expected the attack."

"But then I would have been cut down. Killed," I said.

"No," said Cadoc. "Not unless you fought so fiercely you forced them to kill you to contain you."

"Which is what our queen would have done." Pride filled Maldwyn's voice as he turned his gaze from the fire to catch mine. "I know how swift and strong and brave you are. Had you attacked Decianus, you would be feasting in Annwn with Andraste this very night. And we would have joined you."

Cadoc nodded. "Aye. Gladly."

I sighed. "And then Addedomaros would have attempted to lead the Iceni and the Trinovantes against the Romans."

Cadoc shrugged his wide shoulders. "Mayhap our people would have followed him, but only long enough to burn Camulodunum to avenge you. After that they would not follow the Trinovantes chief."

"No, they would not," I said. "And burning Camulodunum is only the first step in what must be done."

"Then it is good that you chose to let us guide you out of the city," said Maldwyn. "As no one but Boudicca, queen of the Iceni, Andraste's Victory, can unite Iceni and Trinovantes."

"And others as well," added Cadoc. "We haven't spoken of what else we learned. The Catuvellauni are well and truly weary of Rome.

They have increased the taxes so that many farmers worry how they will make it through the winter. And, of course, there is the fact that farmland has been taken from the Catuvellauni and given to Roman soldiers. That has angered them even more than the taxes. Also I saw tribesmen today, slaves to the Romans, whose bodies bore the symbols of Dobunni, Atrebates, and even the western Silures tribes."

"Rome believes if they enslave enough of us we will bow to them. Instead what they do is surround themselves with their enemies," I said grimly.

Maldwyn nodded. "I heard talk from soldiers at the wine stall. The Twentieth and Fourteenth legions are leaving the city. Soon."

"Paulinus is leading them to Ynys Môn to attack the Druids," I said.

"We must warn Derwyn," said Cadoc.

"The reason Derwyn was so eager to leave Tasceni after interring our elders in the Chief's Barrow is that he'd been sent a dream wherein the sacred oaks keened," I said. "He has already been warned, but I will send a rider to the isle as soon as we reach Tasceni so he knows Paulinus is on the march."

"So Camulodunum will be left unguarded except for the old soldiers who have retired there?" asked Cadoc.

"Yes, and the centuria that attacked Tasceni." Anger warmed my body more than the food and drink. "Paulinus suspects the Trinovantes and our people are arming against Rome. He warned Decianus to call for the Ninth Legion to protect the city. Decianus, fool that he is, made it clear he would only need the centuria he used in the spring to teach me *a lesson*." I repeated the distasteful words.

"This is what Andraste planned all along," said Maldwyn.

"Yes," I said.

Cadoc stretched and yawned. "Maldwyn, take the first watch. I'll take the second."

"Done," Maldwyn said.

Cadoc rolled himself into the thick pelt he'd packed as bedding, but before he slept, his gaze found mine across the fire. "I am glad we live to bring war to the Romans, but it would have been glorious to fight to the death by your side today, my queen." His smile flashed white in the light and then he pulled the pelt over his head, yawned mightily again, and remarkably quickly his snores were echoing from within the bedroll.

I smiled at the large mound that was the old shield. "He can sleep anywhere."

Maldwyn laughed softly. "It is a gift." He sat closer to me than Cadoc, and as he leaned forward to feed more branches into the fire he glanced over his shoulder. "My queen, you should sleep. I will keep watch."

I sighed. "I don't think I can."

Maldwyn sat back, propping himself against a moss-covered boulder. "It was difficult for you to see Decianus."

"It was."

Maldwyn met my gaze. "He will never hurt you or your girls again."

"My mind knows that, but today when I heard his voice my body believed something different. I was suddenly back there on that horrible day." I shivered and pulled my own pelt up around my shoulders. "And I almost allowed that fear to kill the three of us."

"No, my queen. It wasn't fear that had you reaching for your sword and moving to slit that pig's throat. It was the warrior spirit within you. It was rage. It was confidence. It was skill. As Cadoc said, you would have killed them both. Then we would have gladly fought to our deaths by your side, and tonight instead of drinking Roman wine and eating Roman pork, we would be feasting with Andraste."

As I studied his face, I saw the savage joy behind his words and I felt a rush of gratitude for this shy, patient warrior who had spent the past many months sharpening me so that I could be the blade Andraste would wield to avenge our people.

And the last of the horror of the day fell away from me as I realized Maldwyn was right. I hadn't been afraid when I'd moved against Decianus. I'd been the arm of an avenging goddess.

I reached over and placed my hand on his shoulder. His savage expression warmed instantly to his familiar shy smile.

"Thank you," I said. "For your faith."

"Always." Maldwyn's smile sobered. "I will always have faith in Andraste and in you, my queen."

A companionable silence settled over our little camp. I liked being there beside Maldwyn. We didn't need to speak. His constancy warmed me with the fire, and soon Cadoc's rhythmic snores made my eyelids heavy. I worried when my eyes closed that I would return to that day and the field and the whip, but I only dreamed that horses surrounded me, watching over me, keeping me safe.

We entered Tasceni not long after midday. Our village was alive with warriors and excitement, and as I made my way from the stables to the lodge, my people called jubilant greetings.

"Is Addedomaros still here?" I asked Briallen as my daughters rushed to hug me at the wide front doors of the lodge. I kissed them and scratched the gangly wolves' ears.

"Yes. As is his son." Briallen frowned as she answered me, and I wondered what the Trinovantes chief or his son had done.

Enfys and Ceri hugged me again and then hurried out the doors, explaining that they were going fishing with their wolves.

"Leave the boars be today," I called after them. "Briallen is needed here."

"Oh, Mama, don't worry so!" Ceri said before the two of them disappeared from view, their wolves galloping at their sides.

"They aren't going far," said Briallen.

"Good, because I need you. First, have a rider leave immediately for Ynys Môn. Tell Derwyn that Gaius Suetonius Paulinus is marching the Fourteenth and Twentieth legions to raze the isle."

"As you ask, so will I do, my queen."

"Then send word to Abertha and Addedomaros that the war council is meeting. Cadoc and Maldwyn will join us shortly. Gather my guard. Have them wait close to the lodge. I will call for them." As I spoke I moved into the lodge and went to the chest that held the rolled sheet of beaten and smoothed hide on which Addedomaros had used a stick of charcoal to draw the rough map of Camulodunum we'd memorized before our journey there.

All during the journey home my mind had whirred with strategy. I knew what must be done and how to do it. I had the map spread out over the long central table and was adding the placement of Claudius's temple, the colonia, the basilica with the barracks that surrounded it, and Brigantia's desecrated shrine to the existing marks when Addedomaros, his son, and his shield joined me, followed closely by Rhan, Cadoc, Abertha, and Maldwyn. Briallen remained at the door, though she caught my gaze and nodded, letting me know my guard was close by.

"How did you find the city?" Addedomaros lost no time in firing the question at me.

"Infested with Romans," I said. "Sit." I motioned to the table, and the warriors took seats at the benches on either side of it while I remained standing. Wulffaed poured mead for us and I drank deeply, appreciating the sweetness of its bite more than the cloying Roman wine I'd had too much of the night before. "The Balkerne Gate was as Addedomaros described. It is wide enough for our chariots to enter." I pointed to the four arches on the map and then I drew in two square lookout stations butting up to them. "There are guards here and here."

"Though they maintain a poor watch," said Cadoc. "May I?"

I nodded and gave him the charcoal stick.

He made X marks at four spots along the rectangle drawn to represent the city boundary. "These gates are not wide enough to allow chariots to enter the city, but the ditches on either side of them are too shallow to repel our cavalry, which can enter as our warriors flood through the gates."

Maldwyn took the charcoal stick then and blackened in the barracks, explaining what we'd discovered about the retired legionnaires stationed there and that the two legions usually billeted in the city would soon be marching west across Britain to Ynys Môn.

"Decianus has recalled the centuria that attacked Tasceni," I said.

"Two hundred soldiers." Addedomaros stroked his beard. "That is still enough to block the chariots from entering. All they need do is close the Balkerne Gate. They will eventually fall, but we must move quickly. A siege would allow Paulinus time to turn back with the legions and surround us. We'd be squeezed between Camulodunum and the Fourteenth and Twentieth. Not an enviable position."

"That will not happen," I said. "We will have burned Camulodunum to the ground and moved on to Londinium before Paulinus can return to engage with us."

Adminius snorted. "Londinium?"

I met his gaze steadily. "Yes. Did you think destroying Camulodunum would be enough to force the Romans from our lands?"

"Well. No."

"Exactly." I turned my attention from the chief's son and continued. "We will take Camulodunum, Londinium, and then Verulamium—one after another—and show the Romans they cannot survive on lands held by Britons."

"But that plan hinges on taking Camulodunum quickly," said Mailcun. "I hear Cadoc. The city guards are lax, but no soldier is lax enough to overlook an army of one hundred thousand attacking his city."

Rhan, Cadoc, Maldwyn, and Abertha remained silent, confidence in their steady gazes as they watched me. My advisors and I had often spoken of the fact that we must destroy all three of the major Roman cities to have a chance at pushing them from our lands, so it was no surprise to them. They knew I had a plan, and their belief in me filled me with such keen joy that my blood pounded hot through my veins.

"Briallen, tell my guard to join us," I commanded.

With Briallen leading them, my Queen's Guard strode into the lodge. The twenty-four warriors had been handpicked, and they stood straight and proud, looking to me expectantly, eagerly. I got directly to the point.

As I used Addedomaros's map to explain my battle plan, I studied the warriors. Iceni are not mindless fighters. They are wise and masters of strategy. I knew that the warriors present there in my lodge would not blindly agree to my plan. Every one of them was more experienced than I in battle. Every one of them had been raiding and fighting since before their sixteenth nameday.

I knew their response could very easily end my reign as a warrior queen before it had really begun.

When I'd finished speaking, I looked from Cadoc to Abertha to Maldwyn and finally to Rhan. Their expressions were equally ferocious, equally expectant. Rhan nodded once, and the coiled tension within me began to loosen. Then my gaze went to Briallen, leader of my guard.

"What say you, Briallen?"

Her smile was savage. "I say on to *victory*, my queen!"

"Aye!" the guard echoed as Addedomaros, his shield, and finally even petulant Adminius stomped their feet and repeated, *"Victory!"*

Addedomaros, his son, and his shield departed Tasceni directly after the war council. I would not see the Trinovantes chief again until our armies joined in the forest west of Camulodunum.

Tasceni was teeming with warriors and the caravan carts that would follow us into battle. The Iceni do not go to war alone. In the rear of the army would be our support system—caravans driven by family and filled with weapons, healers, tents, and supplies, and followed by herds of livestock tended by shepherds and farmers. Our army would not sow destruction upon our lands as we moved across it. Farms would not be looted. Farmers' crops would not be stolen or burned. We carried with us the means to survive and thrive. We would not destroy the land and the people we loved in our attempt to rid ourselves of Rome.

The forest surrounding Tasceni thrummed with the excitement of our people. The sounds of drums and flutes and women's lilting voices drifted through the village with the chill wind. I visited many fires that evening and night, and met with the same reception at each.

My people were prepared. My people were strong. My people believed in Victory.

I was inordinately glad when I finally was able to retire to my bedchamber. Phaedra had a steaming bath filled with herbs waiting for me. I relaxed, listening to her gossip about how many warriors were vying for the attentions of Wulffaed's daughters and granddaughters. She spoke of Sunne and Mona, and how the Iceni loved that my daughters were always shadowed by their wolves. My eyelids were heavy when she finished loosely braiding my hair for the night. As Phaedra slipped out of my chamber, Rhan held the pelt curtain aside and sent me a questioning look.

"Come in, come in." I yawned and added to Phaedra, "Please bring Rhan a mug of mead, too." I climbed wearily into my bed and motioned for Rhan to sit beside me. "I'm glad you came. I thought you would want to talk about Derwyn and Ynys Môn."

Rhan sat beside me and waited until Phaedra had returned with our drinks and then left us alone before she spoke. "Derwyn was forewarned that the Romans would target the isle."

I nodded. "Yes, but it cannot be easy for you to be with me while your home is being invaded."

Her dark eyes studied me for several long breaths before she answered. "Ynys Môn is not my home, Boudicca. My home is here."

"I'm glad of that."

"Derwyn and I spoke before he left. He asked me to tell you this when the time was right, and the time is now right. He said, 'What must be will be—for us both.'"

A chill shivered across the nape of my neck. "He is going to die."

"There will be many deaths to come," said Rhan. "Our countrymen will die in the battles you have planned."

I felt a shock of hurt at her words. "Do you admonish me for that?"

She shook her head. "Not at all. We each have our destiny to face."

I sipped my mead and leaned back against the cushions Phaedra had mounded at the head of my bed. "I knew as I walked through Camulodunum that I was seeing dead men."

"And women," Rhan added.

"Yes. There are countrymen *and women* of ours who have chosen Romans and their way of life. That will also be their choice of death." I leaned forward, looking into Rhan's dark eyes. "True Britons will leave Camulodunum before our army arrives."

Rhan nodded. "Yes. I dreamed of it."

"Tell me," I said.

"Last night I dreamed a white stag left Camulodunum and behind him were does and fawns and other stags, all following him from the city to disappear into the forest."

"Brigantia!" My hands gripped the mug as I recounted for Rhan my experience at the goddess's desecrated shrine and what I'd heard from the people. I did not tell her of my words to Minerva. I do not know why, only that they clogged my throat and would not come out.

"You will fulfill Andraste's curse. Brigantia will be there, too. I thought it was because she also wants vengeance for those, like your mother, who are her children and who were slain by Romans," said Rhan. "But now I know it is even more than that. The desecration of her shrine is unforgivable. Use her fire. Make it rain the wrath of Brigantia as you bring the spear of Andraste to Camulodunum."

"Yes, I will." I yawned then and placed my empty mug on the table beside my bed. "It is good to be home, even though it will only be for five more days."

Rhan stood to leave but I reached out and took her hand.

"Would you stay with me tonight?"

Her smile softened her face, and in the dim candlelight she looked like a girl again as she curled beside me on the bed so that we faced one another.

"He will never hurt you or your girls again," Rhan said quietly.

"I know, but seeing him—hearing him." I shivered. "It is as if his shade followed me from the city and even here it shadows me with the darkness of that day."

"Tomorrow we will leave libations at Andraste's shrine. The goddess will not allow his shade to haunt you," said Rhan firmly. "And tonight I will be here."

"Thank you," I whispered to her. "It is good to be home," I said sleepily as I rested my head on her shoulder and closed my eyes. As she had when we were children whispering our dreams to each other, my friend's hand stroked my hair. I was replete and relaxed; my breath deepened. "Rhan?" At the edge of dreams I whispered the word as a question.

"I am here. I will always be here."

"You have seen the battle?" I don't think I would have asked had I not been in that mystical place between awake and asleep.

Her hand did not stop stroking my hair. "Parts of it. Yes."

"Do I die?"

"No." She spoke the word quickly, with no hesitation.

"That is good." And then I knew nothing more until dawn.

CHAPTER XXV

In the morning I walked through Tasceni again. The village was a beehive of activity. Caravans were being carefully packed. Smoking meat had the cool air redolent with savory smells. The sound of blacksmith bellows and hammers echoed throughout the camp and the surrounding forest. My daughters and their wolves walked beside me, greeting our tribesmen and -women with a poise far beyond their years. We made our way through Tasceni to the stables and corrals, filled to overflowing with horses. Maldwyn appeared to be everywhere at once—supervising the final touches on the last of the chariots to be completed, checking the soundness of one pair after another of our horses, and being sure enough feed was packed into the cavalry caravans. When he caught sight of the girls and me, he wiped his hands on his woad-blue tunic and hurried to us.

"My queen." He bowed and smiled. "And queen's daughters. I have something for the three of you."

"Oooh!" Ceri clapped her hands. "More wolf pups?"

Maldwyn laughed. "No, I'm afraid two wolf pups is my limit." Then he jogged to the nearby tack building and disappeared within. When he reappeared he carried three bronze helmets. He handed me the largest of the three. It was much like the bronze helmet I'd worn daily since spring, but this one had thick spikes of sorrel horsehair decorating the top of it, culminating in a thick red horse tail that was almost as long as my own hair.

I touched the bristles appreciatively. "This is the same color as Tân's mane and tail."

"It should be. I cut and combed it from Tân. I thought you would like her close, even though Ennis and Finley will be pulling your chariot into battle," said Maldwyn.

I met his eyes. "I would, indeed."

His cheeks flushed with pleasure and he turned to the girls, handing each of them a smaller version of my helmet, complete with Tân's magnificent red mane.

"It's beautiful," said Enfys. "Thank you, Maldwyn."

"Yes." Ceri put the helmet on her head and nodded, making it bob back and forth. "It's so perfect!"

Enfys turned her somber gaze on me. "I hope this means you will allow us to join you in battle, Mama."

"Yes, Mama. We have been practicing. We are ready," added Ceri.

My stomach clenched so tightly that for a moment I couldn't answer them.

Maldwyn smoothly covered my lack of words with a chuckle as he ruffled the closest wolf's ears. "Oh, I am quite sure our queen will want you beside her when she speaks to our army, but there isn't room on our chariot for you during the battle."

I cleared the fear from my throat and added, "Yes, of course you will be with me before the battle, and then the two of you will be joined by Briallen, protecting my rear while we bring Andraste's curse to Camulodunum."

"We will be sure no one gets past us to you, Mama," said Ceri.

Enfys's gaze was older, wiser. "I would see the centuria destroyed." Her voice was flat, emotionless, though her eyes blazed.

I nodded. "And you will." Enfys held my gaze for several long breaths before she nodded and finally looked away.

"Mama, we need to show Briallen our new helmets," said Ceri. "Enfys! Let's go find her." Ceri darted off with Mona trotting at her side and Enfys and Sunne following closely.

I breathed out a long, shaky breath. "Thank you."

Maldwyn nodded. "I was not surprised by their request. They are the daughters of Boudicca."

"Well, I was surprised." I wiped a hand across my face. "Just the thought of them going into battle fills me with fear."

"Understandably, but I have watched them over the past six months. Enfys is a strong, tenacious swordswoman. Ceri is too young to be as strong, but she is fast and fearless. And their wolves never leave their sides. They would kill to protect those girls. They will be safe with Briallen behind the battle lines, and should an enemy break through, they will protect themselves."

"My head knows that. My heart does not," I said.

"Perhaps you should speak with Andraste about it," said Maldwyn.

"Perhaps you are right." I returned the gleaming bronze helmet to him, knowing that it would join the rest of my battle armor, which I would change into just before I led the armies into Camulodunum. I started to turn away, my mind already in the forest and partway to the shrine of my goddess, but paused. "Thank you for the helmets. I will wear mine with pride."

"And I will proudly be beside you as we bring vengeance to the Romans."

I didn't take the most direct route to Andraste's shrine. Instead I cut through the pasture area that adjoined the forest. I walked among the horses, letting their presence soothe my nerves. Tân saw me and trotted to join me. I was glad I'd anticipated seeing her and brought an apple with me. She munched it and then walked slowly by my side until I gave her a final caress, and then I climbed over the fence and went into the forest.

This area would normally have been free of everyone except perhaps those Iceni foraging for mushrooms and herbs. Today it was almost as busy as the village, with neat tents and caravans dotting the forest. I pulled the hood of my cloak up and lowered my face, needing solitude to collect my thoughts before speaking to the goddess.

As I approached the area of the forest that held the shrine, I was surprised to hear a rhythmic rattle. The cool breeze brought with it a pungent scent, ripe with decay, and I moved more quickly. Andraste's shrine was close, and as I jogged down the path that led to it I saw that someone had built a large cook fire before the altar. Held suspended over the blazing fire by large rocks was an iron pot. Even from a distance I could see that the contents steamed and bubbled.

Rhan danced around the fire. She was a wild thing, spattered with blood, blond hair loose and tangled, eyes framed by black—the same black of the Ogham symbols tattooed and painted around her neck, down her arms, and across her shoulders. She shook a gourd rattle while she whirled and swayed and chanted around the fire. Every few steps she reached into a leather pouch tied to a mistletoe belt around her slim waist and brought out a handful of something that looked like ash, which she threw into the pot. I slowed to watch her, as always mesmerized by her grace and the tangible sense of magick and power that radiated from her. The browning grass under her bare feet was wet with the libations she had poured, and as I got closer I could smell the fetid scent of old blood and knew those libations had been more than ale and honey and goat's milk.

There was a long, slotted wooden spoon resting against one of the rocks that ringed her fire. Rhan paused in her dance and chant, put down the gourd rattle, and picked up the spoon. As she began stirring the bubbling concoction in the pot she said, "May the joy of the day be with you, Boudicca."

My answer was automatic. "And may the blessings of the earth be on you, Rhan."

She glanced over her shoulder at me. "I am glad you are here."

"Do I interrupt you?"

"Not at all. I have just finished my dance." She motioned for me to join her at the cook fire.

I did and looked down into the gray bubbling mess she was stirring. The water smelled of old meat. The whiteness of bone could be seen through the murk as she lifted the long spoon and nodded, speaking more to herself than to me. "Yes. Good. They can come out now." She began fishing bones out of the bubbling liquid and placing them on the hot rocks that ringed the fire.

"What is all of this?"

Rhan explained while she sifted through the liquid, pulling out more and more bones. Some of them were small, only the size of a child's little finger, and some were considerably longer, but they all had an odd, delicate look. "This is Andraste's latest gift. Ah, yes, this is done as well." Rhan lifted the wooden spoon from the bubbly liquid, and within it was the skull of a large bird. The beak was long and wickedly hooked. She placed it carefully on a flat rock, where its empty eye sockets stared sightlessly at me. Rhan smoothed her hair back from her sweaty face. "It is a golden eagle."

I blinked in surprise. "Truly?"

"Truly. I came upon it just there, beside Andraste's shrine." She jerked her chin at the wooden image of the goddess who watched over us. "It was dead and ravens were picking at it. As I approached they flew away, leaving the remains."

"That is an excellent omen," I said.

"It is. I poured the last of its sluggish blood as an offering and fed the rest of its entrails to the watching ravens. I burned the feathers and now I clean and dry the bones. I will use them to create our standard to carry into battle against the Romans." Rhan stared up at Andraste as she spoke.

I remembered the golden eagle sigil the centuria had brought into Tasceni that awful day. "You will use the bones of their sacred bird to create it?"

She scoffed. "I will use the bones of their sacred bird to *decorate* it, and that sigil will be a beacon from our battlefield in Arbred to Annwn. Then the Romans will behold the wrath of our vengeful goddesses as they follow that beacon and answer our call."

"Andraste and Brigantia."

"Yes." She turned to me. "I will not return to the lodge until I have created this sigil."

I nodded. "I understand. Will you be here?"

"I will."

"May I have Wulffaed bring you food and drink?"

"Only drink. I must fast until this is finished." She cocked her head and studied me. "What has happened?"

I blew out a long breath. "Nothing that should take you from this."

"You take me away from nothing. I can easily speak with you while I pull the rest of the bones from the cauldron. What is it, my friend?" Rhan went back to working the spoon through the boiling water to extract bone after bone.

"Enfys and Ceri want to go into battle with me."

Rhan didn't even glance up as she nodded. "I am not surprised."

"Neither was Maldwyn. Apparently their mother is the only one surprised. Enfys said she would see the centuria destroyed."

Rhan nodded. "And she should."

"Enfys is a child who has no comprehension of what she's asking. She will see men hacked in half, spitted by spears and arrows, beheaded, disemboweled, and burned alive." I closed my eyes for a moment and drew in a deep breath. "It will fill her nightmares."

Rhan straightened so she could meet my gaze. "Enfys already has nightmares. Witnessing the defeat of the centuria will free her from them."

As Rhan turned back to her cauldron I considered her words. I knew my daughters had dreams that terrified them. I'd comforted them often in the darkest part of the night. "I will not allow them to go into battle with me."

"You should not. They are not old enough. Yet. But when the battle is over and the centuria dead—*then* your daughters should join you."

I turned her words over in my mind and felt the weighty truth of them. "That is what I shall do."

"Good. Speak to Andraste about your fears. She will help you conquer them. The goddess knows your strength, your heart, your worth. She did not name you her Victory lightly," said Rhan.

I went to Andraste, stared up into her fierce, loving face, and did as my seer advised.

The morning of the fifth day dawned bright and cold and clear. Maldwyn brought Tân, her slick red coat painted boldly in Iceni blue symbols, to the lodge. He held a tall black gelding for himself, painted with symbols in white framed perfectly by his tar-colored coat. Ennis and Finley would pull no chariot nor be ridden until we entered Camulodunum. One of the many stable hands had brought two matched white mares, long legged and fleet, for my daughters.

They, too, had been painted in blue with Ogham and crescent moons. Beside him Cadoc and Abertha were mounted, holding their painted, prancing horses in place as I stepped out of the wide double doors of the lodge. Enfys and Ceri were beside me. Their wolves' eyes were luminous in the morning light. My daughters would ride at the front of the army with me until we descended on the city, when Briallen would guard them in the caravan with Wulffaed and her daughters and granddaughters. Rhan stood only a step behind me, looking lean from her days of fasting at Andraste's shrine. A bay gelding, covered in white Ogham that matched the symbols tattooed on Rhan's body, waited for her.

As I appeared, Briallen called my guard to attention and they struck their shields with their spears as they faced front, a line of blue-clad warriors eager to play their part in destiny. All around me there were the flashes of weapons catching the morning sun as my people lifted their spears and swords and bows and a great cry of *victory* echoed through Tasceni.

I stepped into Maldwyn's linked hands and he boosted me onto Tân, who tossed her head and snorted. I motioned for Enfys and Ceri to flank me. My lead warriors came next, followed by Rhan and my guard. We moved down the main road of Tasceni as the people cheered. At the stables the Tasceni cavalry spread out in waves of equine power. Each rider wore a bronze helmet decorated with horsehair dyed as white as their hair. My chin lifted with pride at their wild beauty. As one they saluted me and shouted "*Victory.*" Then they, too, fell into step.

Next came our foot soldiers, row after row of them, deep as the sea. Behind the mass of soldiers our chariots followed, and then came our caravans filled with weapons and supplies, healers and elders. Like our other villages, Tasceni would be deserted. Our harvests and livestock were either already at our winter stronghold, deep in the wild Thetford forest, or being driven there now. No Iceni would remain behind to be brutalized or captured by marauding Roman soldiers.

Because the Romans underestimated us, we had been given half a year to prepare. We had trained and sacrificed and planned. No matter the outcome of the three battles, I knew one truth—Rome would never again underestimate us.

It was a wondrous thing to lead the army. I could feel the determination of my people and their single-minded intent to finally *do something*. To move against Rome. To refuse their subjugation and the erasure of our way of life. To fight for our freedom.

We retraced the southern route I'd so recently taken with Cadoc and Maldwyn, moving through the familiar forest with surprising ease and swiftness for such a large group. We pushed hard so that we could stop to camp well before sunset. Our warriors would not go into battle exhausted.

That night the camp was subdued. As I made my way from fire to fire, speaking with the warriors and their families, it felt as if the Iceni were being blanketed by Andraste's cloak—kept calm and warm and safe by our goddess so that we would be ready for what tomorrow would bring.

When I finally returned to my tent, Enfys and Ceri were soundly asleep, nestled between their wolves like they were pups. Rhan and I sat near the fire and I peered into the basket beside her. I instantly recognized the implements within. "Who are you going to tattoo?"

"You, my queen, if you allow it." Rhan spoke formally and I felt the weight of the importance of her words. "Last night I dreamed that within a great Samhain bonfire the flames formed a mighty oak, a holy holly, and then a magickal yew before the trees shifted into a blazing raven that soared from the fire into the sky. You are that raven, Boudicca. I believe Brigantia and Andraste sent me the dream, commanding me to mark you with Ogham symbols of protection so that you may soar through battle."

A sizzle of magick bloomed across my skin, lifting the tiny hairs on the back of my neck. I hadn't been tattooed before. The permanent marking of skin was something sacred. Something that should only be done solemnly, inspired by the gods. I saw that divine inspiration reflected in the seer's dark eyes.

"Yes. Mark me, Rhan."

236 P. C. CAST

Rhan motioned for me to move even closer to the fire. I sat on the ground beside her and watched as she took from her basket a smooth whittled piece of wood, about the length of my forearm. The end of it had been carved to look like a miniature hoe, like something one of the tiny fae folk would use to tend a garden. The blade edge of the hoe had been worked thin and razor sharp. From the basket Rhan brought out clean cloths and began steeping antiseptic herbs in hot water poured from the cauldron that was always bubbling over the fire. Rhan had a pot of thick yellow salve that she placed on the ground behind me, next to the mug of steeping herbs.

Lastly, she took out a small stone mallet and then uncovered a wooden bowl filled with the blue dye for which the Iceni were so well-known. It wasn't the same woad dye we used on our clothes—that was too harsh to be carved into our skin—but the tattoo dye had been carefully crafted to perfectly match the color of woad.

I watched Rhan prepare with excited curiosity. I had, of course, seen tribesmen and -women tattooed and I found myself eager for it.

Rhan began by using the steeped herbal mixture to cleanse my chin, cheeks, and neck. Then she disappeared into the tent and returned with a rolled blanket from my bed pallet and put it behind me so that I could lean back comfortably.

"Ready?" she asked.

I nodded, feeling just a flutter of nerves.

"First, I mark you with the symbol of our mighty oak. May it give you strength in battle."

She began by dipping the blade of the small wooden tool in the dye. She placed the sharp edge under my bottom lip. Using the stone mallet, she began tapping firmly on the whittled wood at the place on the tool where the slender shaft met the hoelike blade. It was uncomfortable but far from unbearable. As Rhan continued to dip the blade into the dye and tap a solid dark blue line horizontally under my lip from one side of my mouth to the other, she sang softly, wordlessly. The power in her song skittered across my skin as she marked me, wiped away the blood that dripped from the wound, and then continued tattooing me.

I stared into the fire as Rhan finished the thick, solid line, and then from the center of it she tattooed two more lines, parallel to one another, down my chin. When she finished she applied the yellow salve.

Next she moved to my cheekbones, beginning with the one under my right eye.

"I mark you with the sign for the magickal holly trees. May it grant you courage in battle." Again, Rhan started with a solid blue line that stretched from the top of my cheekbone to my jawline. From the center of that completed line she tapped out three parallel lines moving inward, toward my nose and mouth. When she had completed the marks on both cheeks and rubbed soothing salve into them, she asked me to stretch back my neck.

"With the sacred yew I mark you thrice. May it protect you eternally."

Rhan tapped a line twice as thick as the other two from the top of my throat to my collarbones, ending just above where my torque nestled. Then, slashing horizontally through that line, she created five more bold blue lines, like spears without tips. Gently she spread salve into my final tattoo. The new marks felt hot on my skin. I was glad of their heat. It reminded me of the power imbued in the three trees and their symbols—now within me.

After Rhan finished we shared a cup of mead. We didn't speak but sat staring into the fire, not needing to fill the night with words. When my eyelids went heavy, Rhan and I went into the tent. She lay beside me on my pallet.

"May I plait your hair tomorrow?" Rhan's voice startled me awake.

I rubbed my eyes and yawned. "I'm going to wear my hair loose tomorrow."

"Yes, I agree, but I have bespelled some things and Andraste has sent me items. I would leave your hair free but use slim braids to knot these things of power into your hair. Would you agree to that?" she asked.

I nodded. "Yes. And I would ask that tomorrow you go with

Enfys, Ceri, and Briallen to the rear caravans when the time comes," I said softly.

"I will do so after I invoke the blessing of Andraste and Brigantia."

"Thank you." I took her hand. "I almost cannot believe that this time tomorrow Camulodunum will burn. It seems one of the ancient stories Arianell used to tell me at bedtime when I was even younger than Ceri."

"Your mother is proud of you," said Rhan.

Surprise jolted through me. "You have spoken with her?"

"She did not speak to me, but she appeared in my dreams each of the nights I fasted and worked on the sigil. Arianell looked young and beautiful. She watched you from a distance and she blazed with pride so fierce it was clear Brigantia stood with her." Rhan squeezed my hand. "Your mother knows you will avenge her."

"Lately I have missed her so much," I admitted.

"It is because she has been close. You feel her presence."

"Do you think she'll stay close after Camulodunum?" I asked.

Rhan moved her shoulders. "I think she will always come when you have need of her, but the peace Arianell will feel after you destroy her enemies will allow her to rest easily in Annwn. And remember, one day you will see her again and feast with her at the goddess's table."

I gave a little snort. "I look forward to that day, though I hope it will not come too soon."

Instead of answering, Rhan caressed my hair. Combing her fingers through my long fire-colored strands, she hummed a Trinovantes lullaby that I remembered hearing the women of her tribe sing, causing sleep to pull me into its waiting arms.

CHAPTER XXVI

I woke before dawn and dressed quickly. The camp was just beginning to stir when I exited the tent to find my Queen's Guard
waiting silently in a half-moon formation. Briallen stood in the center
of them, calling the warriors to attention as I emerged.

They watched me with an intensity I'd come to understand from
my months of training. They were the spearhead of our attack and I
knew their strike would be true. They had exchanged their distinctive
Queen's Guard blue tunics for bland brown. Swords were strapped to
their backs, concealed completely by worn travel cloaks. Behind the
warriors stood twenty-three of our swiftest horses. Their only tack
was the slightest of saddle blankets and slim bridles.

"Remember to blend in with them. Call no attention to yourselves." I walked along the half circle, meeting the gaze of each
warrior. "Wait for the carnyx."

"Aye, they are ready, my queen," said Briallen.

"No queen has ever had a better guard," I said. "You make me
proud. May Andraste guide your swords."

They mounted and, with the ominous sound of pounding hooves,
disappeared into the dove-colored dawn.

"I know you wish you were going with them," I said to the silent
warrior at my side.

Briallen shook her head. "There is no honor greater than being
entrusted with the lives of my queen's bairns."

I rested my hand on her shoulder. "I can fight today with a clear
mind knowing they are under your protection."

"I will keep them safe, my queen." Briallen's accent thickened
with emotion. She cleared her throat and added, "I'll be readying the

bairns' horses the now." She bowed to me and headed to the hobble line behind our tent.

I watched her stride away and from my memory lifted a vision of her that day when she had been sliced up, beaten, and violated by Rome, yet she had clawed her way back to my side, back to my girls. *Andraste, be with Briallen.* There was a movement in the boughs above me, and a raven croaked and clicked before taking wing into the lightening sky.

There were no victory shouts as we broke camp and made our way to the Roman road. The army was subdued but expectant, calm and confident. Each Iceni knew his or her role in the coming battle, and each Iceni was ready.

Tribe Trinovantes met us as we reached the Roman road. Addedomaros and his many warriors were in full battle dress and they were an awe-inspiring sight. Their red cloaks waved bloody in the breeze. They'd painted themselves in scarlet and black. Each horse was dressed with white ribbons in their elaborately braided manes and tails—honoring their patron goddess, Epona.

Addedomaros, his son, and Mailcun joined me at the head of our combined armies and we marched toward Camulodunum. We made no attempt at stealth. That would have been foolish. There was no hiding an army that swelled to almost one hundred twenty thousand. I'd sent out scouts to the west, the direction from which the Fourteenth and Twentieth legions would return should Paulinus get word of our attack. Scouts were also sent north, following the Ninth Legion's path, with orders to return to me if they caught sight of the centuria Decianus had said he would recall to protect Camulodunum. And, of course, our fleetest scouts went before us to return with movement reports.

As we drew closer to the city, we came upon groups of people fleeing Camulodunum. The majority of them wore the colors of the Catuvellauni. We allowed them to pass unmolested, though I saw fear and awe in their furtive gazes as they began to understand the strength of our army.

As dusk approached, we pulled back to halt within the cover of the last tree line before Camulodunum. The Balkerne Gate was visible in the distance, a sacrifice waiting for the knife. Addedomaros and his army, except for their chariots, melted away from us. Half of his army skirted the city to the north and the other half to the south. Tribe Trinovantes would wait within whatever cover they could find until they heard my signal. Then they would rush the city, their infantry and cavalry entering through the four gates we'd chosen because of the shallowness of the ditches that framed them.

While the chariots were brought to the front and made ready, my daughters and I went into Wulffaed's caravan, where Briallen, Rhan, and Phaedra waited. Enfys and Ceri dressed in short, brightly colored tunics that would allow them to run or ride or fight without the hindrance of skirts. Wulffaed painted them in bold swirls of woad blue while Rhan and Phaedra saw to me.

I dressed in my own short, sleeveless tunic made from cloth Wulffaed had dyed especially for battle. It was a blaze of color. Iceni blue created a strong background to strips of red and yellow, green and purple, that were woven throughout it. Onto my forearms and legs Phaedra strapped thick leather guards. Rhan braided raven feathers into my hair. Around the ends of the thin plaits she added the smallest of the eagle's bones, so that when I moved they clacked and clattered around my waist. Finally, I placed the new bronze helmet on my head. Trimmed in Tân's red mane and tail, it seemed to be an extension of my hair. My daughters donned their own helmets and I felt such pride in them that I hugged the girls tightly, whispering to them how fierce and fine they were and how much I loved them. I kept my breathing steady, refusing to allow nerves or fear to taint this moment.

"May Andraste's strength fill you," said Wulffaed.

"May the goddess keep you safe," added Phaedra.

Neither woman wept. Their eyes were bright, but with excitement, not tears.

I led us out of the tent. Maldwyn was there in the chariot. He, too, was painted for war, with Iceni moons and the outline of plunging horses on both of his muscular arms. He wore a bronze helmet decorated with the silver-white mane of the two magnificent stallions that pawed impatiently, eager for battle. There was a second chariot in which Cadoc rode. He was the god of war, Belatucadros, incarnate. From his helmet sprouted stag horns. A woad mask had been painted across his eyes, with bold Ogham marks up and down his thickly muscled arms between the tattooed Iceni crescents and stars that had been permanently marked into his skin years before I'd been born.

Abertha's chariot was beside his. Her beauty was savage. She wore only a short leather tunic that was dyed woad blue. It and her body were painted in coal-colored Ogham symbols. She'd cut her hair short and its tips were dyed blue and spiked. Her bronze helmet was trimmed the same as the rest of the cavalry, in dyed white horsehair. Around her neck she wore a collar made of raven feathers.

Briallen was also in full battle dress. She sat astride a gelding while she held two more riderless horses. I nodded to her and she saluted me.

"Lead us to the front of the army," I told Cadoc. "Rhan will ride with you. She carries the sigil until she invokes Andraste, and then Maldwyn and I will take it into battle."

Cadoc's grin was a baring of his teeth. "As you ask, so will I do, my queen."

Rhan joined him in his chariot as my girls squeezed in between Maldwyn and me. Sunne and Mona, whose silver-gray coats had been painted with my daughters' woad-colored handprints, galloped close to the chariot as Maldwyn clucked to the horses. Briallen and Abertha brought up the rear. We followed Cadoc swiftly through the caravans to the army, which parted for us as if we were sunlight spearing through clouds.

Maldwyn drove our chariot out before the army and then turned to face our tribe. Briallen and Abertha waited at the edge of the army with Cadoc, who halted his chariot so Rhan could step down. She carried the sigil she'd made. It was a magnificent sight. She'd prepared a long oak bough, working it smooth until it shined. It was twice her

height, tall and straight. From the top of it hung a large circle made
by willow branches. Within that circle was a woad-colored spider's
web of hemp twine that formed the triple Iceni moons. Dangling
from leather straps all around the willow circle were the largest of the
eagle bones. They clacked in the evening breeze with the dry voices
of wraiths. In the very center of the sigil Rhan had woven the skull
of the eagle upside down, defeated, dead, useless.

Rhan moved into the space between my chariot and the army.
She wore her ovate robe of green and brown, and as she began to
dance and chant, her cloak billowed around her. She was beautiful
and wild and glorious.

> *Hu rì o hùo ro—hu rì o hu*
> *Strike, cut, spear thrust straight, straight and true.*
> *E ho hùo hùo*
> *Brigantia's fire flow.*
> *Hu rì o hùo ro—hu rì o hu gaol i*
> *Andraste's promised vengeance fulfilled by thee.*
> *Hu rì o hùo ro—hu rì o hu*
> *Strike, cut, spear thrust straight, straight and true.*

The army beat out the rhythm of her song on their shields until
the earth shook with the force of our rage and I knew that the goddesses could not help but hear it in Annwn.

Rhan spun and leaped, swayed and stomped her bare feet. Her
hair flew around her with her cloak. She was a creature that slipped
between Annwn and Arbred. When she finally halted before my
chariot, the power of nwyfre, the life force that filled our land and
our bodies, crackled in the air like lightning.

Rhan handed me the sigil, and as I raised it, the army went
silent. Maldwyn knew what to do. He knelt down in the front of
the chariot and clucked softly to Ennis and Finley, and they trotted
back and forth across the front line of the warriors, necks bowed,
straining against their bits. Beside me Enfys and Ceri stood straight
and strong. Their hair streamed behind them, mingling with mine

like small flames joining a wildfire. Their wolves kept pace with us. I understood why I saw savage glee in the eyes of my people. We were Iceni and we were magnificent.

I drew a deep breath and spoke to my people.

"Iceni! Today we do not fight as Romans do for land or spoils or riches. We fight for life. We fight for freedom. We fight for the right to live in our land unmolested by those who do not belong here, who do not know our gods, who violate children as they call us barbarians. If fighting for my children makes me a barbarian—if refusing to submit to Rome makes me a barbarian—if honoring Andraste makes me a barbarian—*then I say I am a barbarian!*"

The army and my daughters roared, *"Aye!"*

Maldwyn wheeled the chariot around to face the center of the army. I raised the sigil high and lifted my other hand in a fist to the sky as, in a voice amplified by Andraste, I repeated the curse the goddess had promised to fulfill.

The army was completely silent as my curse echoed around us. A single raven croaked from above me. It circled us three times before it landed in the uppermost branches of the closest oak. The setting sun flashed behind it, and I knew it was time. I motioned to Briallen, who galloped to me, leading the spare horses.

"Kill them all, Mama," said Enfys.

"Yes," said Ceri. "All of them."

I kissed each daughter before lifting them onto the backs of the waiting horses. Rhan mounted her horse, Briallen bowed her head to me, and then they were gone, riding fast for the rear of the army, where they would join the caravans that would retreat into the western forest and wait for the battle to end.

Cadoc's driver maneuvered his chariot beside me. Abertha's chariot moved up so that she was positioned on my other side. "Is it now, my queen?" Cadoc asked.

"It is," I said.

Cadoc lifted the long bronze war carnyx to his lips. And from the snarling boar at its end came the sound that called the Iceni to war. It rang across the land to Camulodunum's Balkerne Gate. Over and over Cadoc blew the horn in long, eerie notes as the horses pawed and stomped and snorted impatiently.

I stared at the city, waiting. And suddenly saw hundreds of burning arrows slash the sky above Camulodunum. They flew in a beautiful arch up and up, and then as one they dipped and sped down into the city.

"Again, Cadoc," I said.

Cadoc blew the carnyx, holding the note long so that it echoed across the empty stretch of land between Camulodunum and us. Again the sky burned with Trinovantes arrows.

"Once more, Cadoc!"

The carnyx sounded and death rained from the evening sky.

I placed the sigil in the ties Maldwyn had fashioned for it at the front of the chariot, took up my first spear, raised my shield, looked over my shoulder, lifted my gaze—and waited until the sun finally kissed the trees, blinding anyone who would be looking west from the city.

"Now, Maldwyn!"

With a savage cry, he let loose Ennis and Finley. On one side of us Cadoc's chariot surged forward—on the other Abertha's team pounded the ground in time with us. Behind us the mass of Iceni chariots thundered, causing the world to vibrate with their might. My blood pulsed hot and fast. I was not afraid. I did not have time for fear. I opened my mouth and shrieked the Iceni war cry. All around me my warriors did the same. From north and south of the city I heard Trinovantes' voices joining us with their battle cry.

We were at the four arched stone entryways so soon that it shocked me. I had half a breath to worry that the iron-barred gates would slam closed, but they did not, and as we charged into the city I caught a glimpse of my Queen's Guard cutting down the last of the Roman lookouts.

And then the first Roman soldiers were upon us. As we had prepared for this day, Maldwyn, Cadoc, and Abertha had spoken to me often of what it was like to be in a battle. They described the tunnel-vision aspect of war. They talked of the confusion and the raw brutality that would seem endless, though it might only last moments. Most especially they drilled into me that I would not have time to think—that I must practice over and over and over so that my body would act when my mind was overwhelmed.

They had been right, but what they had not described to me was the unexpected intimacy of battle. As I took lives, it was as if I were alone with each man at the moment of his death. I saw his shock—his fear—his pain—his release.

I killed the first man almost immediately. A gray-bearded soldier rushed me from the side, surprisingly swift for his obvious age. Maldwyn saw him and swerved our chariot. My body moved automatically. I threw my spear and caught the soldier cleanly through his throat. It seemed to take a very long time for my spear to skewer him. Blood arched, shockingly bright red. His eyes fastened on me, wide with surprise as he took in my tunic, my hair, and the fact that a woman had just killed him. The light went out of his eyes as he fell and we thundered on.

Our chariots hurtled forward, reverberating deafeningly over the stone road as we raced toward the colonia and the heart of Roman Camulodunum. The city was already on fire and we had to dodge burning men and debris. We passed pockets of Trinovantes cavalry engaged with soldiers on our flanks, and as we reached the main barracks, red-cloaked warriors joined those in Iceni blue as they surrounded the surprised Romans, squeezing them into doomed circles that closed tighter and tighter.

"Cadoc! To Brigantia!" I shouted.

The old warrior, whose chariot was always beside mine, nodded and barked a command. A row of chariots broke off to follow us south to the Gosbecks District. As we'd planned, Abertha took command of the rest of the chariots and continued into the heart of the burning colonia.

We raced through the Gosbecks. Here the flames licked high into the darkening sky as there were more of our wooden roundhouses and less Roman stone. The heat pressed against my skin and I was glad for our speed. The district appeared deserted. We pounded up the slight hill to Brigantia's desecrated shrine, our horses' hooves tearing great hunks of turf and dirt, which lifted behind us. Though the buildings around the hill were aflame, the shrine was untouched. The only fire on the hill was the one dedicated to Brigantia. Maldwyn pulled Ennis and Finley to a halt and I leaped from the chariot with a coiled rope in my hands. I ran to the statue and wrapped the noose of the rope around the goddess's neck, where it rested beside my mother's pendant. As I looked into the goddess's face I noted that no one had washed the rust of my blood from her cheeks.

"Blessed Brigantia, now you will be free." I touched her face gently before I stepped back.

Cadoc joined me, looping another rope around the goddess's neck. "Your desecration is over, mighty Brigantia," he said.

The dozen chariots that had followed us also cast their ropes around the goddess's neck, until her face was covered. My eyes were drawn to my mother's pendant. The ever-burning fire before the shrine caught it, lighting the flames stamped in gold so that they appeared to truly burn.

We returned to our chariots and secured the ropes. I raised my hand high. "Minerva!" I lifted my voice above the sounds of battle and the roar of devouring flames. "Return to Rome. You are not wanted here." I dropped my hand. "Now!"

As one, our chariots surged from the shrine, pulling the statue of the goddess so that she fell forward with an enormous crash directly onto Brigantia's flame. There was a great *whoosh* as the iron receptacle that held the well of oil was pierced. We threw our ropes free and galloped down the hill as the shrine exploded in orange and gold flame.

Cadoc pulled up beside us as we paused to watch it burn. I wiped sweat and blood and grime from my forehead and met the warrior's gaze. "And now we do the same to the Temple of Claudius."

He bared his teeth. "Aye, my queen!"

We raced back through the burning Gosbecks and into the colonia, where the fire was spreading, but less quickly. The wide stone streets were filled with Iceni and Trinovantes cutting down pockets of Romans as the battle moved closer and closer to the huge temple that proclaimed their dead emperor a god.

Later my warriors reported how the people who had chosen to side with Rome and remain in the city had fled to Claudius's temple, but then, in the heart of the battle, I knew only what was before me. Maldwyn and I cut down soldier after soldier. I threw my spears again and again. We were a magnet for the Romans, who were drawn to us by our sigil and by the sight of me, a tall barbarian woman whose flame-colored hair lifted in the heat of the burning city and whose spear arm threw true. My arm did not weaken. My voice, which shrieked the Iceni war cry, did not falter.

When a pilum sliced across the outside of my bicep, I did not feel pain, only rage. I snarled at the Roman as Maldwyn wheeled our chariot around. The soldier tried to crouch behind his shield but I knocked it away with the blunt end of my spear. As we thundered past I pivoted, twirled the spear in an arc, and thrust it down between his neck and his shoulder. Blood gushed from his mouth, and his eyes widened at me before they rolled to show white and he fell forward onto his face.

And then we were at the temple. Roman soldiers attempted to set up a defensive line around the front of the huge building. They locked shields and were able to hold their line as people flooded into the temple behind them. As Maldwyn and I got closer, I saw Decianus. He was just ahead of a group of Iceni foot soldiers, fleeing toward the line of Roman shields with a group of women. Even from a distance I could see the terror on the procurator's face. It appeared as if he were melting. Sweat poured down his wobbling cheeks and darkened his soiled white toga.

"Catus Decianus!" I roared the name.

The procurator's head whipped around as he looked over his shoulder. His small eyes went glassy with shock as he caught sight of me. Maldwyn moved us closer.

"Through my blood and with my goddess-blessed breath, I have cursed you unto death!" I hurled the final words of my curse at him, and his florid face went the color of old milk just as his group reached the

line of Roman soldiers. They did not part quickly enough. Decianus grabbed the voluptuous woman dressed in a sheer toga who was in front of him and threw her at the soldiers. She hit the shield wall and fell, her head cracking on the stone pavement. She was the woman I'd spoken to when we'd scouted Camulodunum—the one who had chosen to live, and die, like a Roman. I stared at her as Decianus stepped on her stomach and raced through the hastily parted shields.

"My queen!" Cadoc's voice pulled my attention from the temple as Decianus ran, stumbling and falling, up the stairs and finally reached the wide doors and disappeared inside. "The city burns. We must signal to leave or risk getting trapped in the flames."

"First push anything that will burn against the temple and into this line of Romans. Have the archers shoot arrows dipped in pitch into the debris and the roof of the temple. *Then* sound the carnyx."

"We should leave, my queen," said Maldwyn.

"In a moment. I want to see it burn first."

Wooden tables from the nearby market were dragged to the temple. Our warriors used them as huge shields to press the line of Romans back and back and back until they were at the steps of the temple.

"Cadoc!" He turned to look at me and I pointed to the bronze head of Claudius that had rolled down the temple steps. "Take that vile thing. Drown it as a gift to Andraste."

"Aye!"

The old soldier shouted an order at one of the charioteers, who raced in, looped a rope around Claudius's head, and then dragged it away. Then Cadoc called another command and arrows sizzled through the air, bringing more flame and heat, and with the sound of a great exhalation the debris heaped against the temple caught fire. The Romans who had been holding the line in front of the temple were forced all the way to the wide doors, which they opened and rushed inside.

"Push the debris to the door. No one escapes. No one," I said.

Cadoc directed the foot soldiers. Using tall, curved shields taken from the bodies of fallen Romans, they ran at the burning piles of tables and furniture, bushes and wine barrels, knocking the flaming mess up the stairs and into the entryway of the temple, clogging it with death. When the screaming began within, I turned away.

"Sound the carnyx!" I called.

Cadoc lifted the great horn and blew three times, short and swift, paused, and then blew three times again. With the other chariots, Maldwyn turned our team and we raced through the burning city, followed by the cavalry and foot soldiers. It was an inferno. I smelled my singed hair. My skin was so hot that later I found blisters on my arms. But at that moment I felt nothing except savage joy. Catus Decianus was dead.

We burst through the Balkerne gates and kept racing away from the city. The heat grew so intense that our own people would be immolated if they did not keep moving. Finally, we met the line of caravans that remained to rearm us and treat the most severely wounded. Only then did Maldwyn turn the team so that we could look back at Camulodunum. He wrapped the reins around their hook and leaped from the chariot, going to Ennis and Finley and running his hands down their legs and over their bodies, checking for wounds.

I meant to join him, but I could not look away from the blazing amber jewel the city had become. To me it seemed very little time had passed between entering the gates and leaving them, but the sky was the black of deep night. I did not see stars sprinkled above. Instead there were flames and sparks and smoke the color of the gray mist called the breath of the dragon.

The army was forming up around me, stretching in its vast numbers southwest, toward the cool forests and the caravans that waited there to welcome us. Cadoc and Abertha halted on either side of me. And then Addedomaros, his son, Adminius, and his shield, Mailcun, were with us as well.

"It is a decisive victory. The city is no more!" Addedomaros wiped gore from his face and grinned. "Let us join the caravans so that we may feast and rejoice."

"The curse is not fulfilled," I said.

"What?" Adminius blurted. "The city has been destroyed. Many Romans are dead."

"The centuria that attacked Tasceni was not in Camulodunum. The curse is not fulfilled," I repeated.

"But surely—" Addedomaros began to protest, but a scout galloped up on a horse frothing with sweat, cutting off his words.

"Queen Boudicca! The Ninth comes!" He spoke quickly as he gasped for breath. "On the Roman road north of the city."

"The entire legion?" I asked.

He shook his head and sweat rained from his long hair. "No. Only a centuria from the Ninth."

It was as if my body changed then, shifting from flesh to armor, turning bronze and unfeeling except to know itself a weapon.

"Gather the chariots and the cavalry. We will destroy the centuria," I said. "Send our infantry to the caravans. We will join them afterward."

"But we should—" Addedomaros began, and my words sliced through his.

"Not you. This is Iceni business. You, your son, and your warriors may go to the caravans. Feed and rest your men. Tend to your wounded. We leave tomorrow for Londinium."

Addedomaros seemed as if he would say more but finally nodded and turned his horse, calling to the Trinovantes to follow him. Eagerly, Adminius galloped with his father from the field. I felt eyes on me and my gaze caught Mailcun's. The Trinovantes shield bowed to me and pressed his fist over his heart before he followed his chief.

Chapter XXVII

The burning city lit the night as we raced north. Once again I was framed between Cadoc and Abertha as our chariots sped forward. We were covered in sweat and soot, blood and dirt. Our horses were the things of nightmares, gore-spattered and singed but eager for more. We pounded up the Romans' road. I had time to think how ironic it was that their carefully paved stones were aiding us to bring death to them much quicker than if we'd had to traverse a dirt path at night.

Our chariots roared like wild beasts as we bore down on the two hundred Romans. When we reached them they had already formed their phalanx—a rectangle of soldiers, shoulder to shoulder, interlocking their long, curved shields. They were like a turtle, tucking up its head and legs. But, like a turtle, all one had to do to defeat it was to expose its underbelly and drive a spear between shell and flesh.

Except for their officer, the centuria were on foot, and as we encircled them I saw how unprepared they were. They had no long spears to hold steady within their turtle shell while they pierced the flesh of our brave horses. They stood their ground with only shorter pilums and swords.

Cadoc ordered the archers to fire, which they did, round after round. The phalanx became smaller, tighter, after each volley of arrows.

"Set them aflame," I told Cadoc.

He called a second command and fire was added to the deadly arrow tips, and the phalanx finally broke. I shouted the undulating Iceni war cry. Ennis and Finley galloped into the confusing mass of shields and men and fire.

I pointed at the officer, still astride his horse, fighting in the middle of the dying Romans. I recognized him as one of the men who had jeered at Briallen and dragged her away. "Take me to him."

"Aye!" Maldwyn said through gritted teeth.

Our chariot plowed through them, its spiked wheels slicing men's legs while our battle-trained horses used their teeth and the terrible force of their bodies to clear our path.

I knew the moment the officer recognized me. His expression went slack with shock and then he turned his horse and spurred it through his soldiers as he attempted to flee.

Beside me Maldwyn's laughter was dark with savage joy as we gave chase. The officer reined his horse off the road, hurtling into the darkness of the surrounding land. Maldwyn followed, and I thought for a moment we would lose him as he wove through the trees at a run, but just as he was pulling away from us, his horse went down with a terrible shriek, its leg snapped by a hole made by a hare.

I smiled, knowing Andraste's hand was in this.

The Roman leaped free of the struggling horse, drew his sword, and faced us. I hurled my spear, driving it deeply into his gut. The officer was lifted off his feet and thrown back by the force of the blow, landing with my spear pinning him to the ground.

"Care for the horse," I told Maldwyn. "While I put an end to him."

Maldwyn pulled Ennis and Finley up beside the broken animal. I jumped out of the chariot and strode to the officer. He was holding the end of the spear that protruded from his belly with both hands. Blood soaked the mossy ground around him, darkening it to black. His face was white, though scarlet rivulets dripped from his mouth to stain his cheeks and neck.

I stood over him and felt nothing but satisfaction.

"What are you? A demon?" He coughed blood and gagged before he continued. "A dark goddess?"

"Neither. You may call me Victory." I sliced through his neck with my sword, wiped my blade on the moss not tainted by his blood, and turned my back on him.

Maldwyn ended the horse's pain and then we returned to the battle. The phalanx had been completely destroyed by the time we reached it. Pockets of Romans still fought back to back, but they were swiftly being cut down. I lifted another spear, ready to rejoin the fight. To my right I heard a familiar voice scream, *"NO!"* A Roman had come at Abertha's chariot from the rear. His spear had skewered Abertha's driver, causing their team to bolt from the road in panic when he'd fallen forward, onto their traces. The chariot tilted and fell on its side, throwing Abertha to the ground with such force that she lost her sword and shield. The Roman ran toward her, his sword raised.

"Go!" I shouted to Maldwyn, but he had already cued our team. We raced toward Abertha.

The spear master got to her feet. She held one arm close to her side. The other she lifted defensively as the Roman came at her.

I raised my spear and cursed. We were still too far away for me to throw true. Helplessly, I watched as the Roman struck. Abertha pivoted and kicked at the back of his leg, knocking him off balance, so that his blade did not disembowel her but sliced across her ribs, cutting through her leather tunic. She went down on one knee. The Roman whirled around, lifting his sword for the killing blow. I shouted my fury and let loose the spear—and it pierced his ear, driving through his head so that he fell in a gush of blood and gore.

I leaped from the chariot and ran to Abertha. She was struggling to sit. Her left arm was useless. It hung at a strange angle limply from her shoulder. Blood oozed down her torso.

"You cannot die!" I shouted at her.

Her gaze found mine and she grinned. "Do not worry, my queen. I cannot be killed by one little Roman." Then her eyes rolled to show only white and she went limp, slumping against the ground.

Around us the battle was over. My warriors were wading their way through the piles of shields and men, using swords and spears to make certain every one of them was dead. And suddenly Abertha's words seemed funny and a little laugh bubbled from my lips.

Cadoc rushed up with Maldwyn. "Is she . . . ?" asked the old soldier.

I realized my laughter was edged with hysteria, so I pressed my lips together and forced myself to breathe deeply. When I opened them again to speak I was relieved only words spilled out. "She lives. The wound is not mortal. I believe it's pain from her shoulder that made her lose consciousness."

Cadoc dropped to his knees to inspect her wounds. He grunted. "Dislocated. I can fix that, but then she needs to get to the caravans so that cut can be washed and sewn. Hold her, Maldwyn."

It only took a moment, but the sound of Abertha's shoulder being forced back into place would stay with me a long time. She regained consciousness shortly thereafter, cursing the Romans, the panicked horses, and even her lost shield and spear. Cadoc helped her into his chariot. He led our warriors back while Maldwyn moved our team slowly through the centuria. I had him halt in the middle of them.

"Through my blood and with my goddess-blessed breath, I have cursed you unto death!" My words spread around us, falling among the piles of newly dead—a promise fulfilled. "Now we can go to the caravans."

"As you ask, so will I do," said Maldwyn, and we rejoined our victorious warriors.

We gave the burning city a wide berth, circling around it. Camu-lodunum lit the night. Screams and cries echoed on the fire-heated wind, riding the breath of it to us, though they faded as the fire continued to feed, devouring life as it consumed the city.

As we crossed to the first of the caravans, I saw Rhan. She stood alone as close to the burning city as she could get. I touched Mald-wyn's arm. "Let me off here. I'll join you at the healers' tent."

I walked to Rhan, who did not look at me as I approached. When I reached her side she still seemed not to see me. Her dark eyes were fixed on the city. In them I watched the golden flames dance. Gently, I touched her arm. "Rhan?"

A shiver passed through her body and she drew a gasping breath, as if she'd only just then remembered she needed to breathe. She turned her head to look at me. "You're bleeding."

I glanced down. I was filthy. I couldn't tell what was blood or dirt or sweat. I didn't think any of the blood was mine, and then the light of the blazing city made the liquid line on my arm glisten and I remembered. I touched the wound and flinched. It hadn't hurt until then, but as feeling returned to my body, so too did pain. "Most of it isn't mine," I said. "And what is isn't bad." I looked up and met her gaze. "Why are you out here?"

"I can feel them."

I was suddenly cold. "Them?"

She nodded and her gaze returned to the burning city. "The Roman shades. They speak to me."

"What do they say?" I asked.

"Many of them are lost. That is why I am here." Her eyes snapped back to mine. "You freed Brigantia?"

"Yes. And told Minerva to return to her own land—her own people."

Rhan released a long sigh. "Good. I will guide the shades to her—to Minerva. That is why I must hold vigil here tonight. We do not want the shades of Roman soldiers haunting our lands."

I shivered, not exactly from fear but more from the eerie feeling it gave me to know the spirits of men I'd killed might be hovering close by. "Would you like me to stay with you?"

"This is not something my queen nor my friend can help me with. This is a task a Druid must do alone." She cocked her head to the side in that birdlike way she had. "And you must rejoin the living while I deal with the dead."

Her words confused me. *Rejoin* the living? I was alive. What could she mean? "But, I . . ." My words faded as her sharp gaze held mine, and I saw more than I wanted to know within their depths.

"When you finally feel it, know that you will survive it. You will be changed, but you will survive."

My gaze skittered away from hers. I did not want to think too much, nor feel too much. I wanted to be Victory for a little while longer.

"Go, my queen, my friend. I have everything I need here, and soon you will have everything you need, too." Before her gaze left mine I was sure I saw a deep sadness in her eyes. Then she faced the city and raised her arms, opening them wide as if to embrace the flames. Rhan was gone from me then. This was not my childhood friend. She was not even the Iceni seer. This Rhan was a Druid ovate, powerful, magickal, wondrous, and strange.

I turned and followed a far tamer light to our caravans.

There were five caravans at the edge of the tree line facing the burning city. Fires had been lit and litters holding wounded warriors spread around the wagons, though far fewer of our people were injured than I'd expected. A large surgical tent had been erected in the center of the stretchers and I ducked within.

"Mama! Mama!" My daughters rushed to me. For an instant I almost turned away, not wanting them to see me covered in battle gore, but that was the response of a weakling and not a queen. So I hugged them tightly, ignoring the pain in my arm. Even their wolves pressed against me, licking me and wriggling with happiness.

When the girls stepped back I saw that they, too, were blood spattered. Pride filled me. They had been tending the worst of the wounded, as should the daughters of a warrior queen.

"Mama, you're bleeding." Ceri pointed at my arm.

Enfys squinted at the bloody line. "It doesn't look too serious, though."

"My queen!" Phaedra rushed up. Her overdress was as blood spattered as my daughters' tunics. I was glad to see her. She had aided my mother often in the preparation of tinctures and salves. She would be excellent help to our Druid healer, Adara. "Come, I will dress that wound."

I waved her away. "In a moment. Is Abertha here?"

Phaedra nodded toward the rear of the tent. "She's there with Adara. Cadoc and Maldwyn carried her in, then they left to care for the horses."

I nodded. Of course the old shield and my horse master would be sure our swift, brave horses were tended, even before they cared for themselves. I turned back to my girls. "Enfys, Ceri, you have made me very proud today."

"Did you kill the Roman soldiers who hurt us?" Enfys asked.

"I did," I said.

"Every one?" Ceri asked.

I nodded. "Every one."

The girls sighed out a long breath together, then Enfys added, "We still want to see them. We have to be sure." Ceri nodded in agreement with her sister.

"And you shall, but not tonight."

"In the morning."

Enfys did not frame it as a question, but I responded, "Yes. In the morning." Then I glanced around the tent. "Where is Briallen?"

"There, Mama." Enfys pointed to the far side of the tent, where I could see Briallen was bent over a stretcher. "With Eadric."

"He is mortally wounded, Mama," added Ceri, sounding much older than her ten years.

Sadness washed through me. Eadric was one of my original Queen's Guard. He had served me since the day I married Prasutagus. I touched my daughters' cheeks and kissed their foreheads before I moved across the tent to join Briallen while my brilliant, brave girls returned to tending our wounded.

Briallen knelt on the ground beside a stretcher. She held Eadric's hand in both of hers. I crouched next to her and squeezed her shoulder. From his waist down, Eadric's body had been flattened. A blood-soaked cloth covered what was left of him.

"My queen." Briallen's voice was hoarse.

"I'm glad you are here with him," I said. "I will wait with you."

Then I was amazed that Eadric's eyelids fluttered open. His gaze was bright and lucid and found me immediately.

"My queen!" He struggled to sit and I leaned forward and gently pressed his shoulders to the stretcher.

"Rest, Eadric. You must save your strength," I said.

He smiled. "I know that I will soon be feasting at Andraste's table. I go happily, eagerly, as my wife and chief are there before me."

I swallowed back my tears and returned his smile. "Greet my husband for me and raise a mug to our victory today."

"We did it? We fulfilled the curse?"

"Yes."

He seemed to deflate then. Eadric coughed and blood-flecked spittle rained from his lips into his graying beard, yet still he smiled. "It was a good battle."

"Because of you and the rest of my guard we entered Camulodunum easily. Without you stopping the Romans from closing the gates the battle would have raged for days." I leaned forward and brushed the sweat-damp hair from his eyes and touched his cheek gently, much as I'd just caressed my daughters, before I kissed his forehead. "Be at peace, mighty Iceni warrior."

"It has been my greatest honor to serve you, my queen." He paused to cough again and more blood spewed from his lips. "I—I may sleep now."

"Aye, well, you should," said Briallen. "You'll be needing all your strength for the feast to come. Tell my dunderheid brother I've been missing him."

Eadric's gaze found Briallen's. His scarlet lips lifted one last time. "We'll raise a mug to you, too . . ."

Then he breathed out a long, rattling breath and died—his lips still lifted in a smile.

I closed Eadric's eyes and smoothed his hair. "Thank you," I whispered to him.

Briallen raised the cloth so that it covered his face and said a small prayer to Andraste before we stood.

"You're bleeding," she said.

"I have to check on Abertha, then I'll let Phaedra clean it. Did we lose any more of my guard?"

Her back straightened and her chin lifted. "Not a one, my queen. And the centuria, are they truly all dead? Even Decianus?"

"Truly," I assured her. "Decianus burned cowering inside the Temple of Claudius."

"I thought so. I felt the weight of it lift and knew they must be dead," Briallen said.

"It?" I asked.

"The knowledge that those who violated us and slaughtered our people were walking free, unpunished for their dread crimes. We have been avenged. Arianell has been avenged. My brother has been avenged. Our elders have been avenged. 'Tis a great weight lifted," she said.

"Yes, it is. Next we march for Londinium, but not until we've burned our dead and I've taken the girls to witness the remains of the centuria. I would like you and the rest of my guard to join me."

Briallen bowed her head. "As you ask, so will I do." She looked up and down my body. "With your permission I'll be staying here with your bairns till the wounded have been tended, then I'll help them bathe and tuck them into their pallets. You'll need time for yourself tonight, my queen."

I nodded, though I wasn't sure what she meant. "You have my permission." Then I headed to the rear of the tent, where Adara had Abertha on a table and was bent over her. "How is she?"

"It's nothing compared to childbirth, my queen," said Abertha, though her face was colorless and her voice gravel.

"You haven't had a child," said the woman sitting on the other side of the table, clutching her hand.

I grinned at Dreda, another member of my guard, happy to see her there and unwounded. "She hasn't given birth," I said. "But I do remember she stood guard the night Ceri was born."

"Aye." Abertha sucked in a breath as Adara pierced her skin with a slim bone needle and continued to sew closed the long laceration that crossed her ribs. "I'll never forget the sounds my queen made that night, and until I growl like a wild beast as she did, I'll know my pain *isn't that bad.*" The last words she said were clipped and she closed her eyes tightly.

Dreda lifted a damp cloth and wiped the sweat from Abertha's face. "Hush, love. Adara is almost finished."

The Druid healer placed two more stitches and then straightened, rolling her shoulders. "Dreda, spread the healing salve on the wound and bandage it. Give her plenty of the tea for pain and you'll be able to move her to your tent for the night. She can travel in another day, but only in one of the carts."

Abertha scowled, but before she could protest I said, "My spear master will do as you say, Adara."

"Good. Now, let me look at your wound."

Before Adara could lead me away, Abertha spoke. "Thank you for my life, Queen Boudicca."

I wasn't sure what to say. I hadn't saved anyone's life before. So I simply spoke the truth. "I'm glad I was there."

"As am I," said Dreda. Her eyes were filled with tears that fell down her cheeks as she bowed to me.

And then I had to stifle a painful gasp as Adara poked and prodded my wound.

"It does not need to be sewn," the Druid said. "But must be cleaned thoroughly and bandaged. And you must be cleaned thoroughly as well. We are almost finished here. Phaedra can go with you to your tent and be sure the wound is cleaned and dressed after you've bathed."

"I don't want to take her from you," I said.

"Then send her back when she is done. I can make use of her as we move the wounded to join the rest of the caravans deeper within the forest."

Adara was all business, completely focused on tending the wounded. I had a new understanding of such focus, and I nodded. "That is what I will do. Thank you, Adara."

She nodded briefly, called, "Phaedra, tend to the queen in her tent," and turned to the next wounded soldier, who wore the red of Tribe Trinovantes.

Phaedra hurried up to me. She carried a basket filled with strips of clean cloth, a jar of salve, and several bundles of herbs. I said good-bye to my girls, who were already helping Adara with the wounded Trinovantes tribesman. Their wolves lay out of the way but not far from them, their yellow gazes rarely leaving my daughters.

We left the tent, and the cool of the night made me shiver. The wind blew from the east, and the scent of smoke and burning flesh almost made me gag. I was relieved when Phaedra led me to a line of fresh horses tethered behind the tent. We mounted and rode silently into the forest, winding slowly around huge oaks and mossy boulders, heading deep into the dense woodlands. I could feel my heartbeat returning to its normal rhythm, and as we reached the encampment the first wave of weariness washed over me. My wounded arm ached. My other arm felt as if it had turned to stone. My mouth tasted terrible and was gritty, like I'd eaten sand. I wanted to slouch down and let my head loll, but then I heard the first voice murmur, *"Victory."*

I sat up straighter and passed a hand across my face. A flash of something to my right drew my attention and I turned my head to see Andraste. The goddess rode Brigantia's white stag. His snow-colored coat was covered with grime and blood—as was the goddess. She carried a spear that was dark with blood, and a battered shield. Goddess and stag looked as if they'd been in battle beside us, beside me. Andraste's gaze met mine. Her face was spattered with blood but she smiled, her teeth flashing in the eerie violet light of Annwn. "Well done, my Victory," she said.

Like a loosened tide, the word crested around me as I moved through the camp.

"Victory."

"There is our Victory."

"Queen Boudicca—Victory."

I was a chant my people spoke, or rather a prayer. I looked to my right again, but the goddess had vanished back into the Otherworld. I met my people's gazes, nodding, acknowledging, honoring their tribute, their loyalty, their love, knowing our goddess was near and was receiving their praises, too.

My tent was set apart from the others. Rhan's sigil had been planted in the ground before it and the skulls clattered softly in the breeze. The tent glowed with candlelight from within. Outside was a large cook fire over which two iron cauldrons bubbled. I was so relieved to see the Mother of Twenty that I almost threw my arms around the old woman.

"Queen Boudicca, my daughters will have your bath poured immediately. I've food for you waiting within." She bowed quickly to me and then began ordering her daughters around.

When I dismounted, I had to focus on not falling to the ground, as I discovered my legs were almost as stiff as my stonelike throwing arm. Phaedra tossed one herbal bundle to Wulffaed, saying, "Brew this for our queen," and then took my elbow and guided me within my tent, where she went to a table that sat beside my bed pallet, poured a full mug of honey mead from a waiting pitcher, and gave it to me.

I drank it all without taking a breath. As Phaedra took the mug and poured me another, I tried to pull off my tunic but staggered and almost fell.

"One more. Drink it all, my queen." Phaedra handed me the full mug.

Again, I drank it down. Phaedra began untying the leather guards from my forearms and shins. I was shivering, but I felt no cold. She took off my clothes as Wulffaed's daughters began coming and going, pouring steaming water into the copper tub that they'd carried in my caravan from Tasceni.

"Phaedra, I don't want to soak in this filth." My gesture took in my body, including my hair, which was matted with grime and blood and smelled of smoke and death and scorched flesh. "Get some buckets of water. I don't care that they're cold. I want them poured over me." My voice sounded normal, calm even, but my body would not stop shaking. I felt something building within me—something dark and terrible. I had to get the blood and gore from my body soon.

"But, my queen, if you wait just a moment we can warm—"

"Now." I interrupted her and, naked, strode from the tent.

Phaedra rushed after me. Wulffaed looked up as I emerged. She took in my nakedness and nodded. Before I could say anything she gestured at her four closest daughters. "Each of you fill a bucket of fresh water. Take them to the queen and pour the water over her."

Moments later I was surrounded by women. One by one they gently poured icy water over me as Phaedra and I scrubbed my skin and my hair. I looked down and saw the filthy, rust-colored water pooling at my feet. Then I tilted back my head and they poured water over it, too.

Shivering now because of the cold, I hurried back into my tent and slowly lowered myself into the steaming tub. I was surprised to feel the sting of the water on my new tattoos. I'd forgotten about the Ogham symbols of protection Rhan had marked me with the night before. It seemed as if that had happened in another lifetime. Wordlessly, Wulffaed entered the tent and handed me a mug that smelled strongly of herbs and honey. I nodded my thanks and sipped the hot liquid carefully as Phaedra sprinkled more herbs into the water and knelt beside me, cleaning my wound. I closed my eyes against the pain and sipped the tea.

When my wound was clean, Phaedra replaced my empty tea mug with more mead before she went to work on my hair. She began unraveling the raven feathers and eagle bones from the snarled braids and then soaped and rinsed it. Gently, she used a wide-toothed wooden comb to detangle the mass of it. Her touch mixed with the tea and mead was a drug, and I allowed myself to relax. I did not think. I felt only the strokes of the comb through my hair as I listened to the lullaby she hummed. When she had worked through all of the snarls, she plaited it in one long, loose braid and helped me from the tub, drying me gently with a clean cloth. She wrapped me in the cloth and I sat on my bed pallet as she smeared salve into my wound, dressed it in long strips of cloth, and rubbed more of the salve into my fresh tattoos. Then she helped me into my soft nightdress.

"You may go now, Phaedra. Adara has need of you back at the healer tents."

Phaedra gave me a doubtful look. "But, Queen Boudicca . . ."

I shook my head wearily. "There is no need for you to stay. I will eat, then I will sleep. Tell Wulffaed she and her daughters must join you. The wounded will all need to be moved to this camp tonight."

Phaedra sighed but bowed to me. "As you ask, so will I do."

Before she opened the tent flap and ducked out I said, "Thank you, Phaedra. You have helped me greatly this night."

She looked back at me, and in the candlelight I could see the shine of unshed tears in her eyes. "I am honored to serve Victory."

Then she was gone. I heard her relaying my command to Wulffaed, followed by the rustling of women departing. I moved slowly to the table on which a plate of meat and cheese and bread waited. I poured more mead, ignoring the fact that my hand shook so hard that I spilled much of it. Feeling centuries old, I sat and ate. I tasted nothing. I focused only on chewing and swallowing, and as I ate, my body continued to awaken.

I hurt all over and I tried to keep my mind on the dull, toothache-like pain of my wound, the leaden weight of my spear arm, the incredible weariness in my legs and back and shoulders. I finished eating and went to my bed pallet. I lay back and gave in to the exhaustion that filled every particle of my body.

An odd feeling washed through me. It was as if my spirit was finding it difficult to remain attached to my body. I was dizzy. I trembled. My breath came short and fast. I panted as if I were running through the woods. My stomach heaved and I swallowed the saliva that filled my mouth, trying not to lose the food I'd just eaten. My chest felt tight.

That was when they returned to me. Each of the men I'd killed, beginning with the old soldier near the Balkerne gates. Their eyes haunted me. Their last breaths rattled through my body. Their shrieks of pain filled my ears.

I didn't realize that I sat—my arms wrapped tightly around myself as if I were trying to hold my disintegrating body together—that I was sobbing openly, wrenchingly, until the flap of my tent opened and I looked up through tears to see Maldwyn.

CHAPTER XXVIII

I should have gotten here sooner," Maldwyn said as he strode into the tent. He was dressed in clean clothes. His long moonlight colored hair was still wet. There was a slash on his cheek that I hadn't noticed before, and I wondered when he'd gotten it. He stopped just a few feet from me and crouched down so that our gazes were level. "Shhh," he spoke softly in the same tone I'd often heard him use with a frightened horse. "I know. I know how it is after a battle, especially a first battle."

I nodded and tried to stop my tears. I even wiped angrily at them with hands that trembled, but they kept coming. I was a well of misery that could not run dry. "I-I cannot seem to s-stop shaking."

"You will," he said.

"D-do you ever s-stop seeing them when you close your eyes? Do you ever s-stop hearing them?" I blurted the questions as I wrapped my arms around myself again.

"You will stop hearing and seeing them, but you will never forget them." He stood. Moving slowly, he sat beside me on the bed. "And we shouldn't. Killing should never be easy."

"I don't want easy, just bearable." I put my face in my hands. "How do I bear it? I killed so many of them. And ordered the death of even more. Andraste would be ashamed to see me right now. This is not what her Victory should look like."

"Oh, my queen, of course this is what victory looks like—human, compassionate, bittersweet. Andraste is a warrior goddess and a mother. Think you that she doesn't understand what it is to mourn the necessity of battle and death? Think you that she does not weep with you?"

I dropped my hands from my face and fisted them in my nightdress to keep them from trembling. I met Maldwyn's gaze and saw that tears were falling silently down his cheeks. "You do understand."

"I do. As do Cadoc and Abertha, Briallen, and every warrior who is not dead inside," he said.

"I wonder if being dead inside is better."

"No, my queen. It is not. The death of spirit births men like Decianus. The world does not need more spirit-dead people." His tears continued to fall as he spoke soothingly.

The cut on his cheek was weeping pink blood. I used the sleeve of my nightdress to blot it. "When did you get that?"

He smiled and then grunted as it pulled at the wound. "On the race from the city. I hardly noticed it." He glanced at my bandaged arm. "Are you well?"

"Physically, yes, though even all of the months of practice did not ready me for how my spear arm would feel tonight." Stiffly, I reached over to dip my fingers into the pot of salve on my bedside table and then began smoothing it onto his wound.

He sucked in a breath before relaxing under my touch as the salve began to numb the cut. "But all the months of practice made you strong enough to be able to get through the battle, and you did. You were magnificent."

I continued to tend to his wound and didn't meet his gaze. "I do not feel magnificent. I feel like a killer."

He caught my hand by the wrist and lowered it. The other cupped my chin and lifted my face so that I had to look into his blue eyes. "You feel like a warrior who has just survived her first battle. You are not a killer."

I turned my hand so that our palms pressed together. "Inside," I whispered, "I am raging, shrieking in horror at what I've done. There is so much darkness within me tonight that I do not think I'll ever feel anything but death and this terrible sadness."

"Boudicca, let me help you find your way through the darkness," he said. "Let me help you feel alive."

I gazed into his eyes. I saw hunger there, and a fire ignited low in my belly as my body recognized that hunger and answered it in kind.

I slid my arms up to rest on his strong shoulders and spoke one word: "Yes."

Maldwyn's lips met mine. There was no hesitation in him. He devoured me. I hadn't been kissed like this, hadn't felt the raw and beautiful strength of a man's body, in almost one year, and my passion blazed. I ignored the pain of my wound and the weariness in my limbs and let desire consume me. Maldwyn pulled my nightdress over my head and pressed me back on the bed. His lips were hot and insistent as they traveled from my neck to my breasts. I moaned and arched my back, welcoming the scratch of his day-old beard and the sharp, sweet nips of his teeth.

I pulled at his shirt, and he lifted away from me long enough to wrench it and his leather breeches from his body, and then his nakedness met mine and we blazed together. I'd forgotten the delight that could be found in a lover's touch, and when his fingers worked cleverly at my slick, hot core, I climaxed so fast that I shouted his name in surprise.

He smiled down at me, and then his smile shifted to a moan of pleasure and his eyes closed as I found the hard length of him and stroked, slowly discovering the smooth feel of his taut skin, of his heat, of his desire.

With a quick shift of my balance, I rolled him onto his back, and then *I* smiled down at *him* as I understood a new use for the close combat skills he and my other lead warriors had drilled into me. I pressed the length of my body against his, reveling in my strength. I wanted to taste him and hear him shout my name in ecstasy. I took his hardness in my mouth and licked and teased until he cried out and pulled me up to him. He tried to press me back into the bed, but I am a queen and choose to follow my own desire. I straddled him and guided his hands to the curves of my waist. We found our rhythm, and I reached another climax easily. Only then did I roll again, pulling him on top of me. His weight was delicious. As he slid in and out of me, my hands explored his arms, his chest, his shoulders. Our mouths met again and I lost myself in his heat and taste—and then I lifted my legs, urging him on harder, faster. He raised himself so he could look into my eyes and drove into me.

My body responded, coming fully alive as Maldwyn's passion chased the darkness from my spirit and tethered me to the land of the living.

He did shout my name—many times—that night.

When we were spent, Maldwyn wrapped his arms around me and covered us with one of the pelts we'd kicked from the bed. I nestled against him, warm and sated, as he whispered to me.

"Know that you will never be dead inside. You are mighty and fierce, kind and compassionate. You spirit is too strong to fade, to falter, to fail. You are Victory. You will always be Victory."

When I closed my eyes I saw no dying faces. I heard no last screams. Still, I did not think I would find sleep, but it came for me gently and took me as easily into its dreamless embrace as had my lover.

I woke and reached for Maldwyn and opened my eyes when I did not find him beside me. I sat and saw him lacing up his pants. He smiled at me—that shy smile that made his cheeks flush. "Good morning, my queen."

"Good morning, my lover," I said.

His smile widened and lost its shyness, though his cheeks remained flushed. He strode to the bed, bent, and kissed me. "I go to check Ennis and Finley and the rest of our herd." He cupped my cheek with his palm. "Are you well?"

"Very well." I glanced around the tent, not surprised to see that we were alone. "Would you tell Phaedra she can attend me?"

"Of course."

"Send word to Cadoc that I will break my fast, take my daughters to see the dead centuria, and then I will call a war council here," I said. "Have Cadoc send for Addedomaros as well."

"As you ask, so will I do." He bowed and then hesitated, cleared his throat, and spoke quickly. "Boudicca, I am glad I came to you last night. I am glad I could help lift some of the burden from you that comes from taking lives, but you should know I expect nothing from you."

I sat up straighter. My hair was a riot, falling over my shoulders and covering my nakedness. I studied him silently. Queens and chiefs often took lovers, whether they were married or not. Prasutagus and I had chosen not to, but that had been our preference. I knew many chiefs, like Addedomaros, who had multiple lovers. Queen Cartimandua openly took men and women to her bed, often at the same time. The tribes did not hide from their passions—we embraced them, acknowledged them, explored them without shame or censure. What I saw in Maldwyn's gaze was not fear of discovery as my lover but respect, concern, and the understanding that I would lead us forward in this new aspect of our relationship, but only if I so chose.

And I realized I did choose Maldwyn. I had no desire to marry again, but my bed had too long been a place devoid of passion. "You led me from a great darkness last night. For that I will always be grateful. You gave me great pleasure and helped me to feel alive again. I look forward to the next night that I welcome you to my bed."

Pleasure flashed through his eyes and the tension in his shoulders eased. "As will I." He bent and kissed me again. This time it was filled with a promise of more to come, and I met his promise with one of my own.

He was smiling this time when he bowed to me and finally turned to the tent flap, which opened just before he touched it, revealing Briallen silhouetted by the early morning light. Her gaze went from Maldwyn to me and I watched her lips twitch and then lift in a knowing smile.

"May the joy of the day be with you," Briallen told my lover.

"Aye, it already has," he said, and disappeared into the morning.

"'Tis good to embrace life after a night of so much death," said Briallen.

"I agree."

"Your bairns are breaking their fast. They and your guard are ready to view the centuria when you are, my queen."

I heard stirring outside my tent, saw the flickering outline of a newly stoked fire, and heard the murmur of women's voices. "I'll eat quickly and then be ready to ride. Have Tân brought to me and be sure my guard is mounted. I mean to make this fast, Briallen. The girls may need to see the dead centuria, but they should not spend overmuch time there."

"Aye, my queen," she said.

Phaedra pushed through the tent flap as Briallen exited. She carried a tray with fresh bread, cheese, and meat and a pitcher of mead. I ate quickly as she changed the bandage on my wound and helped me to dress in one of the sets of leather pants and tunic Wulffaed had dyed and decorated for me. She braided my hair loosely again. My muscles were sore. My back felt stiff and my arm ached, but I welcomed the sensations of my body. It was better than being dead inside.

I left the tent and stood close to the cook fire, enjoying the warmth. The day was young and clear. There was little breeze, for which I was glad. Camulodunum would burn for days, and I had not looked forward to smelling it for the time we would be here.

"Mama, we're ready." Enfys joined me by the fire. Sunne was beside her with Ceri and her Mona. Behind them Briallen held three horses. My guard was with her, all mounted.

"Mama, may we go now?" Ceri asked.

"Yes, as soon as Tân is here." I wondered what I should say to prepare them, but as I studied my daughters, I understood that they had been preparing for this moment since I declared war on the Romans. They'd seen death the day we were attacked. They'd seen death last night. They were as prepared as they could be.

Tân arrived shortly, led by a stable hand, and we mounted. Though we moved at a quick trot, it took longer than I expected to reach the tree line where the caravans had been the night before. All but one of the large covered carts and a modest tent had retreated into the forest with the rest of the army. I motioned for our group to halt and hurried inside the tent. There were many fewer pallets in this tent than in the larger one I'd entered last night, but it was obvious that the warriors in the pallets had all been mortally wounded. Several women silently tended them. They looked up at my entry and bowed. I found Adara sitting beside one of the pallets holding a dying man's hand. I was silent as the soldier rattled his last breath and she closed his eyes and covered his face with his blood-soaked cloak. Adara sighed deeply before standing to face me.

"You look much better this morning, Queen Boudicca," she said.

"You look exhausted," I said.

She nodded. "Such are the ways of war for a healer."

"You have my gratitude. How may I aid you?"

Adara looked around the tent and then motioned for me to follow her outside. She drew a deep breath of the morning air and rolled her shoulders before answering me. "Those inside the tent will die today. Then I can join the rest of the camp. I will need the tent taken down and packed. Rhan is supervising the funeral pyre." She jerked her chin out toward the cleared area beyond the tree line. I could just see the smoke that hovered above Camulodunum. Between the distant city and the tree line a pyre was being built. Beside it was an open-sided tent. I didn't need to see within it. I knew that it was where Rhan was overseeing the preparation of the dead. "She and I will light the fire and speak the prayers for the dead."

"I'll send help for you and libations to add to the pyre," I said.

"Mama," Enfys said, moving her horse closer. "When we return Ceri and I will gather the libations and bring them to the pyre."

"Then that is how it shall be," I said. My girls continued to fill me with pride, not just as their mother, but as their queen. "Adara, can the rest of the wounded be moved?"

"Do you want the truth or what a warrior queen would like to hear?" Adara's words would have been disrespectful had her gaze not been so steady, so filled with grief and weariness.

"I will always want the truth," I said.

"Four days' rest and most will be able to be moved. Those who are the most badly wounded either will die before then or will be strong enough to survive if they ride in our caravans," she said.

"Then we rest four more days." I hoped I wasn't making the mistake of remaining in the forest too long before marching on Londinium. I believed we had time. My last report of Paulinus and his legions placed them closing on Ynys Môn. It was possible that a swift rider with fresh mounts could reach the isle from Camulodunum in five days. To march two legions the return trip would take at least twice the time, and we needed that time. We were counting on that time, as I would not desert our wounded.

"Excuse me, my queen," a woman called from the entrance of the tent. "Adara, a warrior calls for you."

"Go with my gratitude," I told the old healer.

She nodded and disappeared inside the death tent. I remounted and we picked up the pace, cantering quickly past the burning city, which glowed orange even in daylight.

While it had taken longer to get from our camp to the tree line than I'd remembered, it was a much shorter distance to the site of the centuria's end.

No one had tended to the Roman dead. I realized that was one reason why Rhan had needed to guide their shades to their eternal rest, but I couldn't bring myself to order that their bodies be gathered and burned. Not after what they had done to my mother, my daughters, and our elders. They deserved to rot. As we approached I saw that they wouldn't be allowed to rot. The road was crowded with huge moving shapes. We neared and the shapes took form as feasting vultures. The birds were bold. They barely moved when we halted before the stream of death. The scent was almost as terrible as the sight of the Romans. Clotted blood and entrails darkened the stones. The carrion birds had added to the damage, starting with guts and eyes and open wounds. I swallowed my gorge and turned my gaze to my daughters. I saw them share a look. Enfys nodded and together they coaxed their reluctant mounts to the very edge of the massacre. Their wolves slunk with them, growling low in their throats. Briallen followed as my guard spread out around us.

When the girls halted their horses, they were standing among the first of the bodies. They took their time, studying the rotting flesh that had been men.

Then Enfys spoke, and her young voice was strong and steady and it caused the vultures to squawk and flap their black wings restlessly.

"You did not break us!" Enfys shouted.

Ceri added, "You could not break us! And now you are dead!"

"And we are not!" Enfys finished. Then she spat down into the bodies. Ceri did the same.

I was surprised to see Briallen spit, too. My daughters turned their horses and trotted to me.

"They are dead. Now we know it," said Enfys.

"We won't have any more nightmares," said Ceri.

As one, we cantered away, leaving the dead as a feast for the birds that rid our lands of rot.

When we neared where the pyre was being built, I commanded my guard to assist the warriors in preparation. Briallen returned to our forest camp with the girls, where she would help them load the libations for the burning. I broke from the group and went in search of Rhan. It wasn't difficult to find her. She was with our dead.

The open-sided tent was filled with bodies. They spread out around the tent as well, all covered with shrouds made from cloaks. She saw me as I dismounted, wiped her hands on a cloth, and came to me.

I expected Rhan to look like Adara, weary and worn, but she almost glowed. Her skin was so pale I could see the delicate blue of the veins in her neck and chest. Her dark eyes were huge against the white of her face. Her hair was a wild mass of moonlight caught in a thick braid that went down her back and was decorated with beads and bells, so that she made music when she moved.

We said nothing. I opened my arms and Rhan stepped into my embrace. We clung to each other. She smelled of oils perfumed with rosemary and lavender, though they didn't quite hide the putrid scent of death. When we finally parted I asked, "How are you?"

She didn't answer immediately. Instead her gaze went distant as she looked past me to the burning city. When she finally spoke, her voice was rough, as if she hadn't used it in a very long time.

"I am becoming intimate with death."

Her words sent chills along my skin. "Is that a good or a bad thing?"

"It is neither. It is a useful thing for a people at war," she said. "The girls witnessed the dead centuria?"

"They did. They are so brave."

Rhan nodded. "How could they not be? Their mother is Queen Boudicca." Her sharp gaze studied me. "Your spirit is better today."

"It is."

"Maldwyn helped with that?" she asked, though I saw in her eyes that she already knew the answer.

"He did," I said.

"I am glad."

"I saw Andraste last night after the battle. As I returned to camp she rode with me for a little way. Rhan, I think she was beside me during the fighting," I said.

"I have no doubt of it. And she will be with you in the next battle and the next—one right after another."

My heartbeat thudded in my chest. "The goddess sent you sign?"

"She did. At dawn, when I finally turned from the Roman shades as I was making my way across the field to the healer's tents, I passed this place." She gestured to the growing pyre not far from us. "Three hares leaped from the grasses before me. They ran there." Rhan pointed into the southwest. "In a line—one following the other."

"Camulodunum, Londinium, and Verulamium." I repeated the names of the three Roman cities I intended to destroy.

"Exactly. Andraste's sign says she will be with you."

I let out a long, relieved breath. I'd believed I was doing the goddess's will, but her sign meant that I could do more than believe; *I could know*. And I would be certain my war council knew as well.

"There is something else," Rhan said.

There was a strange shift to her voice. It hitched over the words and softened. "What has happened?"

"Ynys Môn is no more."

A wave of shock and grief crested over me, and I staggered. Rhan grasped my elbow, holding me steady. "No more? How can that be? How could our gods allow it?"

Rhan shook her head slowly. "I do not understand it either. Even Andraste has remained silent. Boudicca, the sacred oaks are dead— burned and dead. It was as Derwyn said. Last night as I kept vigil with the shades, I heard the oaks keening." Rhan shivered. "It was the most terrible sound I have ever heard."

"Derwyn! Do you know if he is alive?"

Rhan's hand shook as she smoothed back her sweaty hair. "Derwyn has crossed over to Annwn. Boudicca, every Druid who was on the isle is dead."

My lips felt numb and I had to force words past them. "But what do we do now?"

"We survive. We continue. We honor our goddesses and gods as always and trust that they, too, will not die."

Fear speared me, making me lightheaded. "Can they die?"

Her gaze went distant again as she stared past me to the city. "When they are no longer cherished, no longer worshipped, when their names are no longer spoken and libations are no longer poured and sacrifices no longer made, any god can die."

I drew a deep breath. "Then Andraste will live forever as the Iceni will never forget her."

Rhan's gaze snapped back to mine and her voice sharpened. "Then you must survive to be certain of that."

"I intend on it." My words were confident, though my spirit quaked.

CHAPTER XXIX

"By the gods, yes!" Addedomaros's fist pounded on the trestle table Wulffaed had materialized outside my tent. "Londinium and then Verulamium. Finally, the Trinovantes return to take back all that was ours."

"But is it wise to wait four more days before we march on Londinium?" Adminius asked from his seat beside his father.

"Paulinus and the Twentieth and Fourteenth legions are at Ynys Môn," I said. "They have just finished a battle there. Even if today they departed the isle and marched to us, we would be days gone when they arrived here, and though Londinium is larger than Camulodunum, it is because of the number of merchants rather than soldiers billeted there."

Maldwyn's sharp gaze caught mine. "There has been a battle at Ynys Môn?"

I drank from the mug of mead Wulffaed had placed before me, swallowing down the gravel that filled my throat at the thought of the death of the Druids. "The isle is no more."

Cadoc's broad shoulders jerked in shock. "Derwyn?"

I shook my head.

"Our high Druid is no more?" Addedomaros's face had gone pale.

I could have lied. Perhaps I should have, but I had no stomach for it. If I could bear it, then so too could these men. I met the chief's gaze and spoke truth. "The only Druids I know for sure are alive are the two we have with us. Your daughter, the Iceni seer, and Adara, our healer. All who were on the isle perished, including the sacred oaks."

For several heartbeats no one spoke. Wulffaed and her daughters and granddaughters froze. My war council, Cadoc, Maldwyn,

Abertha—who had been brought on a litter—Addedomaros, Mailcun, and Adminius, was silent.

Finally Adminius whispered, "Have the gods deserted us?"

"No!" My voice cut through their despair. "How can you even think such a thing after the victory we were given at Camulodunum? Last night as I returned to camp, Andraste rode at my side on the white stag of Brigantia. Addedomaros, did you not feel the presence of Epona with your cavalry?"

Addedomaros cleared his throat. He still looked stunned, but he nodded. "Aye, as always I felt the goddess near."

"Our goddesses will remain near as long as we honor them," I said. "I know the truth of this deep in my spirit. I have spoken with Andraste. The goddess will not desert the Iceni. To prove her fidelity she gave sign to Rhan at dawn. Three hares appeared, running in a row toward Londinium. Three—one each for Camulodunum, Londinium, and Verulamium. Andraste promises those cities to us. She has made that clear."

"Then in five days we burn Londinium," said Cadoc.

"And because our army will be well rested, immediately following the burning of Londinium we march directly to Verulamium and level that Roman municipium," I added.

"I still think we should march sooner. Perhaps in three days," insisted Adminius.

I met and held his gaze. "Then it is a good thing that I am in charge of this army and you are not."

His face darkened and he looked as if he would say more, but Mailcun's hand went to his shoulder, gripping it so tightly his knuckles whitened. Addedomaros stood and nodded to me.

"It will be as you say, Queen Boudicca. In five days our cavalry and Epona will enter Londinium with you and Andraste," he said. "Come, Adminius. We have horses to tend."

Adminius stood and stalked away without looking at me. Addedomaros nodded briefly and followed. Only Mailcun bowed to me with the proper respect.

At dusk the pyre was ready. It was an enormous mound of logs and brush and our dead. Like the pyre at Tasceni, it was laid out in a circular formation. Choice pieces of meat had been placed within the pyre, as well as mead, ale, honey, and milk. The bodies had been liberally anointed with oil. Rhan sent for me when all was ready, and as the sun set behind us and the burning city glowed before us, Cadoc lit my arrow as Mailcun lit Addedomaros's, and together we let loose the burning brands. They lifted into the twilight sky, arched, and returned to earth, setting the pyre ablaze.

I was surprised that Adminius hadn't joined his father at the lighting of the pyre. There was no doubt that he believed Tribe Trinovantes would be his at the death of Addedomaros. He should have been at his father's side. Rhan had been correct. Adminius was the same spoiled favorite child he had been when I fostered with them, only now he wore a man's skin. I glanced at my daughters, who stood not far from me, watching the pyre burn with their wolves beside them. I did not know which of the two would follow me as queen of the Iceni when I joined Andraste in Annwn, but I was grateful that both were maturing into honorable young women who cared deeply for their tribe.

That night the army was subdued. I moved from campfire to campfire, speaking with the warriors, telling them that they were to rest for four more days before we would march on Londinium. I promised them that they could loot the warehouses that lined the Thames before firing the wooden buildings, and that any merchandise they could carry from the city would be theirs. My words were met with pleasure. There had been almost no looting at Camulodunum. I'd been eager to defeat the Romans billeted there and fulfill the curse. But Londinium was different. In the southernmost point of traitorous Catuvellauni land, it had been swallowed whole by Rome decades before and was a major trading center. I'd traveled there several times every year since I married Prasutagus and knew it well.

It was a city filled with merchants with almost no defenses, especially once the wooden bridge over the Thames was breached. Unlike Camulodunum, the city had few Roman buildings, which meant the wooden roundhouses and warehouses would burn hot and fast—and my army was welcome to anything they could pillage before it was no more.

I was weary and returned to my tent, where I soaked in a hot bath as Phaedra combed out my hair. While I bathed, Briallen reported that Enfys and Ceri had fallen asleep almost immediately upon returning from the pyre, and that before they'd slept they had told the warrior that they would be fine without her now.

"The bairns are curled in a pile with those wolves and I cannot tell which one of them snores the loudest," she said with a wistful smile.

I understood the wistfulness of her smile. "They're growing up."

"Aye, well, it was bound to happen."

"You've cared for them well," I said. "And you'll continue to. Someday you will be Queen's Guard to one of them."

Briallen's brows lifted. "Och, well, do not make that day come too soon, my queen."

I grinned at her. "I won't."

Briallen bowed and left as Maldwyn entered. His eyes crinkled at the corners when he saw that I was naked in my tub, but he bowed formally to me and said, "Queen Boudicca, I came to report that the herd is recovering quickly, though I am glad you're giving them time to rest. It will serve us well when we drive them to Londinium and Verulamium."

"How are Ennis and Finley? Was any of that blood that covered them theirs?"

"It was, but the wounds were only minor. Because of the days you have granted us they will be ready when next you need them." He paused and his smile turned intimate. "Is there anything else you need tonight, my queen?"

I looked into those kind eyes and remembered the passion that had ignited between us the night before. I felt a flutter of desire and opened my mouth to say yes, there was something I needed from him, but the tent flap moved and Rhan stumbled in. She'd lost the glow that had carried her through the night before and this day. Now she just looked wan and weary. Dark circles bruised the delicate skin under her eyes. Her hair was a matted mess and I could smell the scent of death she carried with her, even over the sweet herbs that perfumed my bath.

"Oh, forgive me, Queen Boudicca. I did not mean to interrupt," she said quickly. "I shall ask Wulffaed to show me to the girls' tent. Tomorrow I will have my own erected and—"

"Nonsense," I interrupted as I stood and motioned for Phaedra to wrap me in a blanket. "You'll stay here." My eyes went to Maldwyn. "Thank you for your report, Maldwyn. Tonight I need nothing more from you."

"Then I wish you a good night, my queen." He bowed to me. "Good night, Rhan," he said, and nodded to her pleasantly before he slipped out of the tent.

"Phaedra, have Wulffaed's daughters empty the tub and then refill it for Rhan." I glanced up at Rhan. "Have you eaten?"

"Today? I—I do not think so," she said.

"I shall bring food," said Phaedra.

"And more honey mead," I added.

Phaedra hurried from the tent. I sat at the table beside my bed and used one end of the blanket to dry my hair.

"I do not want to be a bother," said Rhan as a line of women began emptying and then refilling my tub with steaming water.

"Was I a bother when you cared for me when I could barely hold my arm up during those long first months of training?" I asked.

Her lips quirked into a ghost of her impish smile. "Would you believe me if I said yes?"

"No. Now take off those clothes. You smell like a grave."

Phaedra gathered Rhan's filthy clothes as one of Wulffaed's daughters brought a tray of food and mead. I dismissed Phaedra when Rhan settled into the tub with a long, exhausted sigh. I pulled my nightdress on over my head and found the bowl of herbs Phaedra always sprinkled into my tub. Liberally I tossed several handfuls in as Rhan grinned up at me.

"Do I smell that bad?"

"Worse," I said. "Dunk your head down and get your hair wet. I'm going to wash it for you. I can't have grave smell in my bed."

She looked up at me. "I really can go to your daughters' tent."

"Why? I'd rather not be alone. Dunk your head." I pushed gently on her shoulder.

Before she went under, she caught my gaze. "Maldwyn would not let you be alone."

"True, and he doesn't smell like a grave, but he is also not the person I am closest to in this world, and tonight *you* should not be alone."

Rhan closed her mouth, nodded, and ducked under the water. When she came up, I handed her a mug of mead, and while she drank I worked soap into her hair. I could feel Rhan relaxing, little by little, and when I refilled her mug I handed her a hunk of cheese and bread, which she began devouring immediately.

"How bad was it with the shades?" I asked as I continued to work soap through the long strands of her slippery blond hair.

"It was odd," she said between bites.

"How so?"

"You know how Romans bray about being so superior to women?" she asked.

"Oh, indeed I do. And I have the marks on my back to prove it," I said.

She looked over her shoulder at me and flushed. "Of course. I'm sorry. I wasn't thinking. I—"

I waved away her apology. "I understand. But what does their loathing of women have to do with the oddness of their dead?"

"Their shades were like small boys searching for their mothers. So, in life they subjugated their women, but in death they cried for women to save them. It was sad," she said.

"And you showed them compassion," I said as I poured clean water from the bucketful Phaedra had left.

"Yes. Are you sorry I did?"

I thought about my answer and decided that it was different that night than it would have been before the fulfillment of my curse. "No. They paid for invading our lands with death. Vengeance was served."

"I'm glad to hear you say so. It means you've healed," she said.

"Hmm, I suppose it does. Briallen put it well. Fulfilling the curse lifted a weight from me. I am lighter knowing that those men cannot violate anyone else. And now I will move on."

Rhan ate the last of her bread and cheese and stood. I wrapped her in the blanket and she stepped from the tub. As she sat beside the table and attacked the remaining food with enthusiasm, I dried her hair, thinking how it was like the finest of embroidery threads and white as moonlight.

"Did you note my brother was not with my father at the pyre?" she asked suddenly.

"I did. I wonder how many of Tribe Trinovantes noted it as well."

She sighed and took a deep drink of mead. "Many of them. Adminius really has not grown up. Imagine his shock when Father dies and the tribe rejects him."

I stopped drying her hair and sat on the bed. "Have you seen it? Will they reject him?"

"I haven't seen it, but as I spoke those words to you I felt the truth of them. Adminius will never be chief of the Trinovantes."

"That is a good thing for the tribe," I said.

"I agree. But . . ." Her words faded as she stared into the flame of one of the candles that sat in a bronze holder on the table. She shivered.

"What is it?"

Rhan spoke softly as she continued to stare into the flame. "I feel a great darkness when I think of the next Trinovantes chief."

"Do you mean the next chief will be wrong for the tribe?"

"No," she answered quickly, then paused, her unblinking stare trapped in the flickering flame. "The next chief will be chosen by the tribe, but that choice is made because of a great darkness." Rhan's breath released in a gasp and she blinked several times.

"Are you back with me?" I touched her shoulder.

"I am. My brother is a problem that will resolve itself in a way that will be good for the tribe and bad for him. That is all I can see now, but I feel that there is more to it—something dark, something wrong." Rhan drank deeply again and speared a hunk of meat.

"Should we do something?" I asked.

"What? Work to take away more of the consequences he has earned but my father has shielded him from? No." Her voice was emotionless, and I understood why. Adminius had been a difficult, contemptuous child who had grown to be a sullen, self-indulgent man. I thought about my daughters and how much they loved and supported each other, and wished that Rhan had known that kind of love and support from her sibling.

Rhan's shoulders had bowed with weariness, so I changed the subject as I took one of my nightdresses from my chest and helped her into it. I was a head taller than her, and it made me smile to see the soft cloth swallow her and make her look like a girl again.

"Come." I patted the spot beside me on the bed. With a deep sigh, she lay back. "I've been thinking about where we should winter."

Her eyelids had been fluttering closed, but at this they opened and she propped herself up on her elbow facing me. "I assume we aren't returning to Tasceni."

"I wish we could, but I do not believe the Roman legions will simply pack their ships and leave Britain to us. We won't be safe in Tasceni. I'm afraid we won't even be safe in Thetford." Thetford was the Iceni's winter stronghold deep in the heart of the forest west of Tasceni. It was well defended by a wide ditch filled with water and cavalry stakes. Behind the ditch was a tall wall made of thick logs and topped with lookout platforms. There was only one gate into the settlement, and that was easily barricaded. Within were wells aplenty and our winter food stores. Our cattle, goats, and pigs not with the army had been driven there. When the snows came it was difficult to navigate the forest surrounding it, but the Romans did know about Thetford and I would not underestimate their siege ability, even in winter. "There is another answer. I believe I should consider something unusual."

Rhan smiled. "Something unusual. That sounds like you."

I returned her grin. "Is that a compliment or sarcasm?"

"Can it not be both?" At my raised brow she giggled, and I ceased to be worried about any darkness clinging to her spirit. Like me, Rhan would not let the dead overwhelm her life.

I relaxed back onto the bed and stretched out facing Rhan. "I have a feeling this winter is going to be long and cold."

She yawned and nodded. "It is already cold and it isn't even Samhain for another seven days."

"Only seven days until Samhain? I hadn't even thought of it, but if all goes well the fires lit that night will be Verulamium burning," I said.

"Our dead will approve," said the Iceni seer.

I spoke softly, sharing my innermost thoughts with my dearest friend. "Rhan, it makes me weary to think of the battles to come."

She moved so that she could stroke my hair. "You already have the next two battles planned, do you not?"

"I do."

"Then do not think of the battles to come. Think of the four days of peace you have before you must be a warrior again. Embrace that peace so that when the time comes you can release the warrior again and control her ferocity."

I closed my eyes. "Battle makes my spirit grieve. You lighten that grief."

Her hand stilled for a moment on my hair. "Does Maldwyn lighten it, too?"

"Yes."

"Then I am glad the queen of the Iceni has both of us." Rhan stroked my hair again and her touch worked on me like a sleeping potion.

"I love it when you do that," I whispered, half asleep.

"Then I will not stop until you sleep," Rhan whispered back.

"Thank you," I murmured.

Just before I knew no more, I heard Rhan whisper, *"Boudicca, you make the world's sadness bearable for me, too."*

CHAPTER XXX

The next four days were peaceful and passed too quickly. The wind changed direction and blew from the north, bringing with it unusual cold and making me glad for the shelter of the thick forest.

I spent the days traveling around the camp, speaking with my warriors, checking on supplies, and meeting with scouts. I'd stationed scouts along the Watling road—the path the Roman legions would retrace from Ynys Môn. So far the Romans had not been spotted, which was good and bad news. Good for us, but bad for the Druids and Tribe Ordovices, who held the mainland adjoining the isle.

The morning of the fifth day, we broke camp and began our two-day march to Londinium. The sky was gray, the clouds low, but the army was rested and eager for the spoils of the merchant city. The mood was festive. Frequently our warriors sang marching songs and battle songs, and even bawdy drinking songs—which made me smile. They'd made up a song they called "Victory." The lyrics recounted my breaking of the desecrated shrine of Brigantia, the burning of the Temple of Claudius, the impaling of the Roman who had almost killed Abertha, and ended with my daughters spitting on the dead legionnaires who had once violated them. I was particularly fond of the chorus of the song and sometimes even sang the words along with my people.

Victory spins her warrior web so well
Andraste watches, waits, and aids
Beneath her blade and torch the Romans fell
Vengeance served, they flee as shades.

We left the cover of the forest on the first day and chose to use the road the Romans had paved. There was nothing to gain in hiding. Londinium was close enough to Camulodunum that word had to have reached them of the destruction of the city. Londinium was a logical and obvious next target—even Paulinus would most likely make straight for it when he and his legions finally left Ynys Môn. Anyone who did not flee Londinium was a Catuvellauni fool or a Roman and deserved their fate.

We marched hard from dawn to dusk the first day, camping that night on the road. It was cold and windy, but our fires burned high and hot. In the morning we continued southwest. At midday when the army paused to eat I sent for my lead warriors, including Abertha, whom Adara had cleared for battle, and Addedomaros, who arrived with Adminius instead of his shield. They met me around a hastily erected cook fire and I spoke as we ate.

"By dusk we'll be within sight of the city. As we already agreed, the chariots will lead the way over the Southwark Bridge. We'll carry torches and follow the main road to the town center. We start the burning there, in the heart of Londinium. It will spread outward, and by the time it reaches the warehouses along the river, the looting must be done. At the bridge Cadoc will blow the carnyx thrice. At that signal the warriors must leave the city, as we will fire the bridge shortly thereafter. Is that clear?"

Addedomaros nodded. "Tribe Trinovantes is anxious to loot, but they will listen for the carnyx and retreat when they hear it thrice."

"Do we march on for Verulamium tonight?" Adminius asked.

I shook my head and glanced at Cadoc, who continued for me as he and I had decided every detail of this plan.

"We'll move away from the city as it burns, out of the wetlands that surround the Thames. Tend to the wounded. Fire the dead. Regroup. First light, we march without halting to Verulamium," explained Cadoc.

Adminius clapped his hands together. "More looting! The farms around Verulamium are ripe for the picking and burning."

"I'm glad you mention that," I said. "Addedomaros, make it clear to your warriors that they are free to loot and burn any farm outside Verulamium that belongs to a Roman, but they are to leave untouched the farms still owned by Britons."

"What!" Adminius sputtered. "How are we even to know the difference?"

"The Roman farms will have shrines to their gods. Roman homes are made of stone. Ours are made of wood. It is not difficult to tell the difference if one is willing to look," I said.

Adminius threw up his hands. "Those Britons you wish to spare are Catuvellauni scum. They stole the land from my father and his father. They are vermin we need to rid our lands of so we can reclaim what was ours."

My anger roiled at his ignorance. I did not even attempt to keep the disgust from my voice. "When does it stop? Has what we have accomplished thus far taught you nothing? Together we can be better, stronger, *unconquerable*. Together the tribes of Britain can stop any outsider from invading us ever again. I want more for my daughters than an unending legacy of war and hatred. Don't you?"

Adminius sneered. "So says the queen who burned a temple full of people, wiped out an entire centuria, and began a war for vengeance."

I felt my three lead warriors stir and move to stand beside me, but my rage carried me forward so that I strode to face Adminius. I was so close to him that I smelled his rancid breath. He was half a head shorter than me, a slender version of his powerful father. I looked down my nose as I spat my words at him. "*They are not Britons!* They are usurpers who want to take away our land, our gods, our way of life. Had our tribes stood together when the first Romans stepped from their ships, we would have pushed them back into the sea forever. Think of the deaths that would have saved.

"So no, Adminius, you will not loot and burn the farms of your fellow Britons." I stared into his eyes and wondered how they could look so much like Rhan's when he was so very different from his wise, compassionate sister.

Addedomaros moved up and elbowed his son so that he had to take several steps back. "I hear what you say, Queen Boudicca. But using your own reasoning, creating strife and division among us will not help our cause."

Instead of looking at Addedomaros, I held Adminius's gaze. "Then rein in your son or send him home."

Adminius sputtered as his face blazed crimson. His hand went to his dagger. Cadoc, Maldwyn, and Abertha were beside me in a breath.

Addedomaros raised his hand. "Enough, Adminius. The queen is not wrong. She is also our ally, and we do not raise weapons against our allies. Return to our camp and get ready to march."

Adminius whirled and strode away.

Addedomaros sighed. "My son is young."

"As am I," I said. "Youth is not an excuse for foolishness."

The Trinovantes chief's thick brows lifted. "Are you calling my son a fool?"

"Yes."

There was utter silence, in which I could feel the tension of my lead warriors. I could almost hear Cadoc's mind whirring with possibilities. *What do we do if the Trinovantes leave? Can we still take Londinium and Verulamium? More important, can we defeat the Fourteenth and Twentieth when they inevitably catch us?*

But instead of blustering or raging or stalking away, Addedomaros threw back his head and laughed. "Aye," he said. "Adminius can be a fool. May I live long enough to see him grow wise."

"I hope Epona hears your prayer." I hadn't realized the tension that thrummed through my body until then. I felt lightheaded as Addedomaros continued to chuckle.

"I will be sure my warriors do not touch any farms except those owned by Romans." He met my gaze. "What you said struck me true, Queen Boudicca. I do want more for my children than an unending legacy of war and hatred." He bowed respectfully to me and then followed his son.

Cadoc let out a long breath. "That was close, my queen."

"Aye, but if we are to lose their alliance it is best to know it now," said Abertha.

Maldwyn ran a hand through his hair. "We must watch Adminius. No matter what Addedomaros says, it is clear he does little to control his son and we do not need him sowing discontent among the Trinovantes."

"I agree," I said. "And if Adminius becomes even more of a problem?"

Maldwyn shrugged. "Accidents happen easily during battle."

Cadoc and Abertha muttered agreement, and I thought not for the first or last time how glad I was that I was their queen and not their enemy.

We broke camp shortly and continued our quick march. As always, I'd sent scouts ahead. As the sun sank toward the horizon before us, Briallen galloped to me with a scout on a horse flecked with foaming sweat. Cadoc, Abertha, and Maldwyn joined me as I motioned for Briallen to guide the warrior from the road. The army marched by while he bowed before me and reported, gasping beside his spent horse.

"My queen, I have news. Paulinus reached Londinium this day."

I was jolted by shock, though I steeled myself not to show it. "Paulinus and the legions?"

"No, my queen. Paulinus had only a centuria of cavalry with him."

"By all the gods, how did he get there ahead of us?" Cadoc said as he paced.

"Paulinus and the centuria took a galley from the Menai Strait to Deva and then galloped hard southeast to Londinium. The rest of the Fourteenth and Twentieth are far behind. My queen, they have burned the sacred oaks on Ynys Môn and slaughtered the Druids." His voice shook as he spoke.

"Yes, I know. Our seer felt their deaths."

The scout took a skin of mead that Briallen handed him. I nodded for him to drink and he gulped the honeyed mixture, spilling it down his beard, but when he spoke again his voice was steadier.

"Our Druids did not die easily. They fought for days. The banshees filled the Romans with such fear that Paulinus had to turn on his own men, killing hundreds of them before they decided they feared him more than our warrior women."

"So Paulinus and a centuria of cavalry guard the city. How many more soldiers are there within Londinium?" asked Cadoc.

"Paulinus did not stay," said the scout.

"Explain," I said.

"My queen, I heard it all from a merchant who was fleeing the city with many others. Paulinus thundered into Londinium to the cheers of the people, only to announce that a centuria was not enough to stop the army of barbarians closing on them." He grinned as he spoke the word *barbarians*. "The people begged him to stay and he turned from them. Those who were able to move swiftly were allowed to follow the cavalry north, as they plan to meet the legions returning from the isle—though the word that spread from the Romans through the crowd was that the Fourteenth and Twentieth had yet to leave Ynys Môn as they had to heal and regroup before traveling through the territory of Tribe Ordovices."

"Paulinus has been to Londinium and is already gone?" I could hardly believe it. I couldn't imagine abandoning my people to an invading army. What a miserable coward Paulinus must be.

"Yes, my queen."

"And he left no soldiers there to defend the city?" I asked.

"None. Some Romans remain, mostly the greediest of merchants."

"How can you be so sure of this?" Abertha asked.

The scout didn't hesitate. "The merchant is a Cantiaci potter. He couldn't follow the centuria because the carts carrying his goods were too slow and Paulinus made it clear that only those who could travel swiftly would have his protection." The scout smiled. "The merchant was quite angry at being abandoned and happy to tell me everything he knew, which was quite a lot."

"Briallen, get our scout a fresh horse and food and drink." I met the warrior's gaze. "What is your name?"

"Aiken, my queen." He bowed low.

"Aiken, you have done well. You have my gratitude."

Aiken flushed, smiled, and bowed again before he followed Briallen toward the rear of the army to the caravans.

"Romans have no honor," said Maldwyn.

Abertha snorted. "And they call *us* barbarians."

Flanked by Cadoc and Abertha and followed closely by Addedo-maros and his cavalry, we pounded across the wooden bridge and entered Londinium. I felt strangely nostalgic. I'd crossed this bridge with Prasutagus and Iceni trade caravans more times than I could count. I always looked forward to our Londinium trips. Goods from afar came by ship. Precious spices, reams of cloud-soft cloth, and an unending host of exotic items could be found in the crowded streets and stores of the city. It is where Prasutagus purchased my copper tub and commissioned one of the last brooches he gifted me with. Where Camulodunum had been filled with foreign buildings and soldiers, Londinium was a familiar stranger, turned ghostlike in its abandon-ment. The streets were empty except for a modest contingent of Roman soldiers, who attempted to flee as soon as they caught sight of our army. We ran them down and I ordered their heads severed and thrown into the Thames in sacrifice to Andraste.

The city was so deserted that I was able to grant our armies ample time to loot the warehouses before we set fire to them. Londinium exploded into flame like tinder. We didn't even need to light the bridge. It caught easily and blazed along with the newly emptied warehouses that stretched along the river.

Our warriors were forced to retreat far from Londinium as the flames spread to the holding buildings and stores outside the city proper. Had the land not been so low and marshy, we would have had to flee from a raging wildfire. Instead we marched farther than I'd expected into the cold darkness of the sparse woodland well northwest of Londinium, which put us even closer to Verulamium.

Our wounded were few, our casualties even fewer. Again Rhan refused to enter the forest with us, saying she would wait as close to the burning city as was safe, guide the Roman shades to their under-world, and join us before we broke camp to march to Verulamium at dawn.

I did not see Andraste as I rode through camp in my chariot beside Maldwyn that night. Her absence had me feeling restless. Wulffaed had just begun setting up a crude camp, little more than a tent skin angled against one of her caravans, and when Maldwyn halted before it he and I shared a knowing look. We hadn't made love since the night outside Camulodunum, and desire was clear in his gaze. Welcoming him to my bed would soothe my restlessness, but I needed more privacy than an open-sided lean-to. I wasn't modest, nor was I ashamed that Maldwyn and I were lovers. It was simply that I preferred to keep my passion a private thing.

"If you ask me to, I will return to you after I care for Ennis and Finley," Maldwyn said softly.

I touched his cheek and shook my head. "Not tonight, though it is not because of a lack of desire."

He smiled and kissed my palm. "Aye. Perhaps after Verulamium."

"Perhaps."

I watched his broad shoulders as he guided the chariot toward the enclosure of rope and lines that held our mighty herd. He'd saved my life that night. From a dim alley a Roman had hurled a spear at me. I hadn't seen it coming, but Maldwyn had turned the chariot abruptly to the side, so that the spear that would have hit me in the center of my chest passed harmlessly by us.

I whispered a prayer to my goddess. "Thank you, Andraste, for the loyalty and love of Maldwyn. Protect him as you would me."

Wulffaed had my tub unloaded from the caravan. Her daughters had begun filling it as soon as the camp halted. As I approached the crude tent, she bowed.

"Queen Boudicca, my daughters have buckets of clean water warmed to pour over you before you settle in your bath. Food and drink are ready as well."

I nodded my thanks and, with the help of Phaedra, stripped out of my shin and forearm guards and the blood-spattered clothes that reeked of war. The night was frigid, but I ignored it and stood naked before our fire as they poured buckets of water over me. I'd killed men that night, and the memory of their dying screams haunted me as I sank into the warm bathwater, ate my dinner, drank a pitcher of mead, and wrapped myself in heavy pelts to settle in to rest for what was left of the night.

I could not sleep. I needed . . . something. Maldwyn's body would have been a distraction, though I knew passion wasn't the answer I sought. Finally, sometime after Wulffaed had banked the cook fire and Phaedra snored softly on her pallet at the foot of my bed, I gave up on sleep.

Quietly, I pulled on my leather boots, wrapped my fur-lined cloak around my shoulders, and began walking through camp. My intention was to go to the horses, find Tân, and let her warm, solid presence soothe my restlessness, but my feet took me in the opposite direction, deeper into the soggy woods. The chill of the night was relentless, but my compulsion to keep moving would not leave me.

Compulsion . . .

I stopped and shook myself as if coming in from the rain. *I'm being compelled into the forest.* With new purpose, I strode forward. My goddess was calling.

The longer I walked, the thicker the woods became. The leaves of the trees made a carpet of rust and brown, saffron and orange, that swallowed the sound of my footsteps. The moon was a fat yellow sickle that cast just enough light through the naked trees for me to see. When I came to a wide creek, I followed it to a waterfall that cascaded down, disappearing into watery mist and the night so that it appeared to pour into a great, dark mouth. Willows that still held on to their leaves formed an arch before the waterfall. I drew a deep breath and strode through the arch. The night shifted.

Moonlight sharpened, changing from wan yellow to brilliant white. The white light illuminated the waterfall, turning the mist to billowing clouds that roiled up, forming shapes. I moved closer to the edge of the cascading water and stared down, mesmerized by the images of charging boars, soaring ravens, and hares, long ears twitching as they played in the mist. I knew Andraste's hand was in this. She must have been sending me sign, but all I saw were creatures frolicking within the spray. All I heard was the thundering of water hitting hidden rocks below.

"By the balls of Priapus, I hate this fucking barbaric land!"

I startled at the sound of the deep voice coming from my side of the creek and moved quickly away from the edge of the waterfall and into the concealing shadows of the willows, peering through the arch they formed.

"General, are we to camp here for the night?"

"Not unless you want to chance waking to one hundred thousand screaming Brittani. Keep the line moving, but have my guard hold where they are. I need time to think."

"Yes, sir."

I knew that Roman's voice even before he strode into sight, pulled off his helmet, and threw it to the ground, where it bumped and rolled in my direction. His brown hair was plastered to his head and his face was slick with sweat.

"Fucking barbarians! Fucking Decianus! He started all of this and left the mess for me to clean up." Gaius Suetonius Paulinus followed his helmet and kicked it so that it flew even closer to where I hid.

I did not move. It wasn't possible that I had walked far enough to catch up with Paulinus and his cavalry, but there he was, just on the other side of the entrance to Annwn.

"My fucking legions are exhausted. Their heads have been muddled by Druids and they languish on the other side of this gods-forsaken country, terrified by what they witnessed on that gods-forsaken isle, licking their wounds and utterly useless! Oh, Rome, how I miss you."

Even in death our Druids protect us as they haunt the minds of their murderers.

Paulinus wiped a hand across his damp face and sighed. Grumbling more curses under his breath, he walked to where he'd kicked his helmet, bent to pick it up, and as he stood his gaze lifted and he looked directly at me.

I did not move.

He straightened. His lips formed a slow smile that did not reach the mean glint in his eyes. "Well now, what have we here?"

My cloak had slipped down from my shoulders and I pulled it more tightly around me. I knew what I must look like with my sheer nightdress and my freshly washed hair falling around my waist. I did not speak but took one step back, wishing that I had ridden Tân into the forest.

Paulinus took a step toward me, raising one hand, palm out. "Easy there. It seems the gods have given me a gift, as you are exactly what I need to put my head right tonight." He crooked a finger and gestured for me to come to him. "You wouldn't want to anger the gods, would you?"

My lip curled. "You and your gods have no rights here."

The smile slid from his face. "If I have the power to take something, then it is mine *and* my gods'. That is a lesson you Brittani are slow to learn, but you will learn it here. Tonight. I will teach you."

I looked down my nose at him as my rage boiled and overflowed. "You are not the first blustering Roman to attempt to teach me a lesson *and fail.*"

Paulinus dropped his helmet and ran toward me. I threw aside my cloak and turned, intending to sprint back along the bank of the creek. I had no doubt that I was faster than the Roman general. I was faster than Iceni warriors who were younger and fitter than him. I also did not believe he would be allowed entrance to Annwn, but as we reached the willows, my legs tangled in the long skirt of my nightdress and I fell. Paulinus's hand snaked through the arched boughs and snagged my ankle, pulling me from Annwn and back into the dark, cold forest with him.

I did not panic. I wasn't a weak, hysterical Roman woman. I was an Iceni warrior. I went limp and his grip on my ankle loosened as his other hand went up under his skirted leather uniform to open the laces to his breeches.

My mind was clear and calm. I had plenty of time to watch this mighty general and to consider his needless brutality. *Why is the Roman answer to everything rape? They are worse than animals.*

"That's right. Just lay there. This won't take long—unless you'd like it to."

My hand fisted around a fallen branch, and with one movement I jerked my ankle from his grip, sprang to my feet, and swung the branch at him like a club.

Paulinus got his hand up in time to block the blow with his forearm, but he grunted in pain. I wanted to sprint back into Annwn, but he was too close and my skirts hindered my movements. So I circled him, holding the branch as a weapon and wishing it were a sword.

"Good." His smile was cruel. "I like it rough."

He lunged at me. I neatly sidestepped and cracked him on the back of his head with the branch. He staggered and shook his head, all amusement gone from his eyes.

"Fucking barbarian bitch!"

I didn't wait. I attacked. Using the branch, I drove him back and then circled around him so that as I continued to strike, Paulinus was being forced toward the entrance to Annwn.

He stopped hurling insults and pulled the pugio from its sheath around his waist. I could see by the expression in his eyes that he expected me to run at the sight of the knife. He was wrong. I had drilled over and over with Cadoc, a warrior twice the size of Paulinus who moved with the speed of a charging boar. I feinted in one direction and he lunged at me with the knife. I clubbed it easily from his hand, whirled past him, and hit him in the shoulder. He stumbled back, only steps from Annwn.

"Who are you?" As he asked the question his eyes went from my Ogham-marked face, to my hair, to the way I held the branch as I bounced on the balls of my feet, looking for my next strike. "I know you. I saw you in Camulodunum."

My stomach tightened with dread. I had to get around him. I had to flee to Annwn. If the Romans captured me our war was over. Addedomaros wasn't well enough liked by my Iceni—nor was Adminius. My tribe wouldn't follow either man. They would take what they'd plundered from Londinium and melt into the forest. I continued to drive him backward toward Annwn and my escape.

Suddenly Paulinus's eyes widened in recognition. "But I saw you before that day in the city—with your husband. You are Boudicca!"

"*Queen* Boudicca," I said, correcting him. "You talk too much."

I struck with all the speed and strength I had, clubbing him in his gut. His breath left him in a loud *oof* and he dropped to his knees. He gasped, drew air, and shouted, "Guards! To me! Guards!"

The pounding feet of the Roman guard running to answer their general's call drew closer and closer as I balled my skirt in my hand, sprinted around him, and raced through the willow arch.

All had changed in Annwn. There was no difference in the light on the other side of what had been a doorway between the mortal and immortal realms. Frantically I cast my gaze around and caught a glimmer of the pearlescent light. It radiated up from the billowing mist of the waterfall. I ran to the edge of the bank, trying to see where the entrance to the Otherworld had gone.

"After her!" Paulinus roared behind me. "Do not let her escape! I want her alive."

I looked over my shoulder. Paulinus had struggled to his feet, his hand pressed against his middle as Roman soldiers ran past him, spreading out in a line to cut off my escape.

"Andraste, help me!"

I am here. Leap. I shall catch you.

I gazed down at the mist. Fear knifed through me. "Jump? I cannot!"

Do you not trust me, my Victory?

I did trust Andraste. I had to. I spread my arms wide like wings, drew a deep breath, and screamed the Iceni war cry as I leaped from the top of the waterfall. The mist swallowed me and it seemed as if time was suspended.

Well done, Boudicca. Remember this. It is not the last leap of faith you will make to save yourself—to save my victory. The next time I ask it of you, do not hesitate.

I opened my mouth to shout my gratitude and adoration, to assure Andraste that I would not hesitate, but I'd begun falling again, and the air that rushed past me took my words and my breath. The mist parted and I saw the rocks and churning water below me, and I prepared to fight for my life against both.

From beside me a raven shrieked, first one, then another and another and yet another. A great wind rushed up from the white water. It caught my spread arms and my nightdress, and I was lifted up and up until I soared with the cold current. Ravens surrounded me. I could smell the strawlike scent of their feathers and feel the brush of their wings against my body, and then I hit the ground and knew no more.

I came awake slowly. My eyes opened. My vision was blurred, though I could see that dawn had lightened the sky. I could not feel my body. I only knew I was tired and wanted nothing more than to sleep. I closed my eyes.

"Boudicca! Queen Boudicca!"

My eyes opened again. *Briallen?*

"Boudicca! Boudicca!"

No, it was Maldwyn. He sounded distressed. I wondered why. Had I been gone so long?

You cannot rest yet, Victory. Answer them.

"Them? Briallen and Maldwyn?" I thought I'd spoken in a normal voice, but it was barely a whisper.

"Boudicca!" Cadoc's voice had joined Maldwyn's.

"My queen! Where are you, my queen?" Abertha shouted.

I blinked and my sight cleared along with my head. I sat, only a little dizzy, and instantly began to shiver. I was incredibly cold.

"Queen Boudicca!" Briallen sounded closer.

I drew a deep breath and through chattering teeth called, "H-here! Here!"

"Boudicca!" Maldwyn's voice was close.

"Here!" I shouted hoarsely.

When Maldwyn crashed through the underbrush on Ennis, I was struggling to stand on legs that were numb with cold.

"She's here!" Maldwyn bellowed between cupped hands as he slid from the big gray and ran to me. "I found the queen!"

He reached me in time to catch me as my legs failed to hold me. Maldwyn pulled me into his arms. "By the gods, you're freezing!" With one hand he took off his cloak and wrapped it around me. "Are you injured? What happened?"

"I'm s-so cold." I was shivering violently.

Briallen thundered up with Cadoc and Abertha close behind, dismounting before their horses stopped.

Briallen's hands were feeling along my body—my arms, my legs, and then my torso. "I cannae find the wound. Where are you injured?"

I looked down at my body. There was no blood. My nightdress was covered with dirt. The skirt was ripped, exposing my legs. They were blue with cold, but they weren't injured. My gaze went to my arms. They were dirty but whole. I stood straighter. My back wasn't broken, and as I began to thaw wrapped in Maldwyn's warm cloak, I realized my mind was clear.

A bubble of laughter escaped through my chattering teeth. "I-I'm alive!"

"Queen Boudicca, look at me," Cadoc ordered in a voice he'd never before used with me.

I frowned and turned my gaze to the shield. "Do not command me," I snapped.

Cadoc's smile was brilliant. "She is herself."

"Of c-course I am." I shivered. "I'm just c-cold."

"I'll never let Herself out of my sight again," Briallen muttered under her breath.

"We need to get her back," said Abertha.

"Can you ride?" Maldwyn asked.

I turned my frown on him and repeated, "Of c-course I can. I'm just c-cold."

Maldwyn kept his arm around me as we walked to Ennis. He mounted and then Cadoc grabbed me around the waist and tossed me up behind the horse master. I put my arms around Maldwyn, pressing into his warmth. Led by Briallen and flanked by Cadoc and

Abertha, we headed in the direction in which, I assumed, we'd find our camp. I glanced over my shoulder, expecting to see the creek and waterfall—and saw only more forest.

"How did you find me?" I asked.

"Rhan woke the four of us and told us we must find you," said Abertha. "That you were in the forest and you needed us."

"Where are we?" I asked.

"Not far from the herd," Maldwyn said.

"Truly?"

Cadoc looked at me. "Where did you think you were?"

I met his gaze. "I know exactly where I was—Annwn."

On the ride to camp I was silent, my mind replaying what had happened with Paulinus and then my leap. I shivered again and Maldwyn's strong hand reached back, as if he were afraid my body would shake apart. Cadoc and Abertha kept slanting looks at me like I might disappear. Even Briallen peered over her shoulder at me so many times she was almost knocked off her horse by a low-hanging branch.

I understood their concern. To them I'd disappeared, only to be found half dead of cold. They were right to be worried. I'd almost been . . .

"No! I was never in true danger. Not from Paulinus. Not from the leap. All I needed to do was to trust Andraste." The words burst from me, and as I spoke them my body stopped trembling and I was suffused with warmth.

But then I felt the sudden tension in Maldwyn's body. Cadoc and Abertha stared at me. Briallen pulled her horse up and reined it around to face me.

"You saw Paulinus?" Cadoc asked.

"I did. Andraste opened Annwn to me. I was near a creek and a tall waterfall. He was there, just on the other side of the gate to the Otherworld. He was alone. He saw me wearing a nightdress out in the forest alone and assumed I was a simple woman who would be easy prey for him."

Cadoc snorted. "Did you set him right about that, my queen?"

"Yes. I beat him with a stick."

Briallen barked a laugh.

"Then what happened?" asked Maldwyn.

"My damnable skirt tripped me. That gave Paulinus and his guards time to surround me on the bank of the waterfall." I paused and my warriors stared at me. I smiled. "Andraste told me to take a leap of faith, and so I jumped."

"You did what?" Maldwyn blurted.

I laughed. "I jumped from the top of the waterfall and Andraste caught me. Then I woke to the sound of my warriors calling my name, and here we are."

Abertha grinned. "My queen, you are a marvel."

"I believe it is Andraste who is the marvel. Can we get to Wulf-faed's caravans now? I'm ravenous."

"Straightaway, Queen Boudicca." Briallen turned her horse and we kicked into a smooth canter.

It was only a short distance to camp. We went immediately to Wulffaed's caravans. Pacing back and forth before the cook fire was Addedomaros. Rhan sat quietly on a weathered log. She looked up and saw me before her father noticed us approaching. My friend's face lit with a smile and she stood.

"I knew they'd find you!" she said.

Maldwyn halted Ennis near Rhan and he helped me down, though my body had warmed and my legs were strong again. Wulf-faed rushed up, clucking at the state of me, and began calling orders to her daughters to get me fed. Phaedra burst from my tent, wiping tears from her eyes.

"Oh, my queen! I was so worried!"

"I am well, Phaedra. Ready my battle clothes. We ride for Veru-lamium shortly." Then I pulled Rhan into a hug. "Thank you for sending them for me. It would have been a long, cold walk back by myself."

She returned the hug. "Just before dawn I came to check on you, and when Phaedra said you had been gone all night Andraste whispered that your warriors should go into the forest after you. I knew the goddess would return you to us but thought it would be a quicker return with your warriors."

"You were right." I squeezed her tightly again and stepped out of her arms to face Addedomaros. "I will be ready to break camp as soon as I dress and eat. I shall be quick."

His brow furrowed as his eyes scanned my body, taking in my dirty, ripped nightdress and lingering on the high slit exposing my legs, before his gaze met mine. I held his steadily, lifted one brow, and said nothing.

"What has happened, Queen Boudicca?" he finally asked.

"I crossed into Annwn," I said.

His eyes widened and then he threw back his head and laughed. "By the gods, of course you did!"

His laughter suddenly reminded me of my good-humored father and I couldn't stop myself from joining him.

Grinning widely, he said, "So you saw Andraste?"

"I did not see her, but the goddess spoke to me."

"What is it she said?" he prompted when I said no more.

"To trust her."

"Is that all?" Addedomaros asked.

"That is all she said to me, but the goddess led me to discover that Paulinus and his legions will not trouble us at Verulamium. They are licking their wounds and not yet recovered from what they did to Ynys Môn." My gaze shifted to meet Rhan's. "Our Druids care for us, even after their deaths."

Addedomaros's laughter boomed again. "Queen Boudicca, being your ally has proven to be very interesting."

"Is that good or bad?" I asked with a smile.

"Both." He chuckled, and as he turned away he shouted, "Onward to victory at Verulamium!"

CHAPTER XXXI

We marched boldly along the Roman road that stretched wide and straight from Londinium to Verulamium. The day was cold and the sky was low and gray, heavy with rain clouds that, with the frigid wind, I had no doubt could easily become ice or snow. It was the eve of Samhain. In Tasceni we would have built large bonfires surrounding the village and feasted, setting extra places at our tables for those who had crossed over into Annwn and would be hovering near as the veil between worlds thinned.

This Samhain, Roman farms and the Roman-occupied city would serve as our bonfires.

We approached the city as the afternoon sun settled into evening, though the slate sky hardly showed any change as day turned toward night. Only very sparse woods surrounded Verulamium. The fertile land had been cultivated and farmland stretched to the horizon. I nodded as we passed farms with roundhouses and shrines to Epona and Brigantia, Cernunnos, and Maponos. They remained untouched and silent, while farms built of stone with courtyards dedicated to Minerva, Apollo, Claudius, and the like were set aflame and looted. I glimpsed Adminius pulling a Roman from an outbuilding and shouting triumphantly as he ran him through with a spear.

When we reached Verulamium there were soldiers spread out between the deep ditch and bank defense system and the city proper. Roman cavalry waited behind them with foot soldiers. In front of the ditch was an army of Britons. It shook me to see them. I counted the Dobunni green and Atrebates black and silver among the earthen cloaks of the Catuvellauni, and my stomach tightened. The words I'd hurled at Adminius came back to me as I stared at tribesmen and

-women who were willing to take up arms against us as we fought to expel tyrants from our lands.

"Should I signal the archers to make ready?" asked Cadoc.

As always, my shield's chariot was poised on one side of me, with Abertha's on the other. Briallen and my guard formed a line directly behind me. Next came the rest of our chariots, hundreds strong, and then our mighty cavalry. The Britons who stood between the Romans and our army were many, but they were no match for the combined strength of Iceni and Trinovantes. I was loath to give the command that would rain arrows down on them.

Addedomaros galloped up from his place at the head of the cavalry. Mailcun was with him. I assumed Adminius was still burning and looting Roman farms and was glad of his absence.

"What is it we wait for?" asked the Trinovantes chief.

Before I could answer there was a stirring behind me and Rhan rushed up. "Queen Boudicca, do not fire on the Britons." She paused, panting as she caught her breath. "Andraste has sent sign. I was making my way to Wulffaed's caravan to be with Enfys and Ceri and I met Paice and her hounds."

I nodded. Paice was well-known to me as Tasceni's best hunter. Her pack of huge shaggy hounds was especially good at tracking and cornering boar.

"As I approached, her two largest hounds, the big mated pair with coats black like the wings of a raven, stared at me. Then, as I watched, they turned on Paice, growling and snapping."

"Those hounds are devoted to Paice," said Maldwyn. "They would never turn on her."

"And yet I watched it happen. They drove her back and then turned their gazes to me again before they dropped their heads and approached Paice, whining like puppies."

"What does that mean?" Abertha asked.

"That they"—Rhan's gesture took in the thick line of Britons facing us across the battlefield—"are not our enemies. They will turn on the Romans, and Rome will be caught completely unaware."

"Yet they're armed and facing us *with* the Romans," said Cadoc.

Do you not trust me, my Victory? I shivered at the power of Andraste's words.

"Thank you, Rhan. You may go to my daughters now." Rhan bowed her head in acknowledgment before she turned and disappeared into the army behind us. "No archers," I told the waiting warriors. "Start forward. Slowly."

Addedomaros frowned. "We are not to charge? How will we break their line?"

"The line will break," I said firmly. "I choose to trust Andraste. Forward. Slowly."

"And I choose to trust you, Queen Boudicca, though if those warriors do attack us I will not be so trusting in the future," said Addedomaros.

I lifted my chin and repeated, "Forward at a walk."

Cadoc let out a long breath but nodded. Slowly, we moved forward, and as we did the line of tribesmen and -women facing us also moved. First they walked, but soon they broke into a jog.

"Hold steady," I said when Cadoc shot me a worried look. I could see the old shield's jaw clench and unclench, but he kept moving stoically forward at a walk.

The line of warriors coming toward us began sprinting, running full speed and eating up the ground between us. I clutched my spear and shield, my knuckles white.

I trust you, Andraste. I trust you, Andraste. I trust you, Andraste.

The tension around me was so thick that I could feel it, sticky and cloying. I wanted to shriek the Iceni war cry and shout at Maldwyn to let Ennis and Finley loose, but I held strong. Andraste was asking me to take another leap.

When they were only a few chariot lengths from us, their leader, a tall man with a shock of black hair who wore a wide golden torque around his neck and the bright green colors of Tribe Dobunni, slid to a halt. He lifted his spear and shouted an undulating war cry. As he did so he turned his back to us, and every warrior with him spun around to face the city and the soldiers who waited before it. The

Britons raised their bows and let loose a flurry of arrows that fell on the shocked Romans.

The Dobunni chief whirled around so that he faced us again. He grinned triumphantly and yelled, *"Victory!"* Then his warriors re-formed their line so that they were standing in columns wide enough apart that our chariots and horses could ride through without trampling them.

"Now, Maldwyn!" I shouted, and he let Ennis and Finley loose. All around me our chariots and cavalry responded, charging forward through the parted warriors as Iceni, Trinovantes, Dobunni, and even Catuvellauni battle cries rang like a carnyx across the field.

The Roman line broke as our chariots bore down on them. They'd expected the Britons to take the brunt of our attack and hadn't readied the stakes and long spears that might have deflected our charge. We smashed through them and into the city with the screaming Catuvellauni and Dobunni foot soldiers following.

Except for the warriors who had turned on their Roman rulers, the tribes had almost completely deserted Verulamium. The city was a mixture of roundhouses and terraced Roman buildings that appeared to be shop fronts and pubs. The chariots swung through the wide city streets, empty except for pockets of Roman soldiers and a few civilians who scrambled to hide. We set it all afire.

As Maldwyn and I led our chariots on a sweep that brought us back to the entrance of the city, the tribal foot soldiers, led by the Dobunni chief, overwhelmed the Romans with the brutality and ferocity of their attack. The violence was raw. Killing wasn't enough for them—they obliterated the Romans. Entrails were spilled, limbs were severed, heads were hacked from bodies. The women who had chosen to remain behind with the Romans were dragged from homes, their breasts sliced off and stuffed into their mouths before they were eviscerated.

It was terrible—and I understood it. I saw a reflection of myself in the warriors as they glutted themselves on vengeance.

Were innocents slaughtered that day? Yes. I mourn them.

Freedom is costly.

As the day turned to night, the sky began to spit sleet. It did not douse the raging fire that was consuming Verulamium, but it soaked our clothes and chilled us. We made camp west of the city. It was hardly a forest, but at least the stands of lime, birch, and willow provided a little protection from the freezing rain. As at Camulodunum and Londinium, Rhan refused to leave the city until the Roman shades had been guided to their underworld. I did not insult my seer by asking her to forsake her duty to the dead because of the weather. Instead I commanded a tent be raised over her and a fire built to warm her so that she didn't become a shade herself. What she was doing was honorable, but it was nights like this when I wished my friend had less honor.

All I wanted to do after the battle was to bathe and then lose myself in Maldwyn's body. Instead my war council crowded around the large fire Wulffaed had burning in the center of a circle she'd made of her caravans. A leather tarp had been stretched above us in the boughs of the lime grove we'd camped in. It kept only some of the sleet from stinging us, but I was grateful for it. My council had grown. Comux, the Dobunni chief who had led the combined Catuvellauni and Dobunni soldiers, joined us with his shield, a young warrior named Seward. There was also a representative there from the Catuvellauni, a grizzled old warrior who strode into our group proudly wearing the earthen-colored cloak of his tribe and a simple golden torque around his neck. His body was heavily tattooed with the Catuvellauni symbols of barley sheaves with crescent moons and hidden faces among intricate knot work. Ignoring the dark looks shot at him by Addedomaros and Adminius, he went directly to me and dropped to one knee.

"Queen Boudicca, I am Leofric of the Catuvellauni. I pledge myself and the two hundred warriors with me to you. Togodumnus is my fool of a cousin. He has whored himself to the Romans." His eyes met mine. They were such a light blue they appeared almost gray. He grinned. "As I am not a whore, I choose a different allegiance."

"Stand, Leofric," I said. "I gladly accept your allegiance." I heard a snort and my gaze snapped to Adminius, who was sneering at the Catuvellauni warrior. "*Any* Briton who wishes to join us against Rome is welcome in our army." Addedomaros nodded once and then placed a heavy hand on his son's shoulder. Adminius wrenched away from him and stalked into the night.

"Queen Boudicca," Comux said, moving into the space in front of me. I realized that I had met the Dobunni chief briefly several Beltanes ago when he and a contingent from his tribe had come to Tasceni to breed their mares with our stallions. He took a knee before me. "The Dobunni gladly pledge allegiance to the Iceni. I have come to understand that there is no freedom to be had in a Roman Britain, only taxation and servitude. I've found that I do not make a good servant."

I smiled. "Stand, Chief Comux. I am pleased that we are allies and not enemies today."

"It was a near thing, though, man," grumbled Cadoc. "Could you not have given us some warning?"

Comux lifted one shoulder. "We couldn't take the chance the Romans would get word that we would turn on them. I chose to believe the rumors I'd heard of the Iceni queen—that she wishes to join all of our tribes against the usurpers."

"Andraste made sure your gamble was successful," I said.

"True, but it takes wisdom to trust a goddess," said Addedomaros.

I bowed my head slightly to the Trinovantes chief, glad that he seemed to be standing firmly with me, even if that meant he was at odds with his son.

"Now what, Queen Boudicca?" Comux asked. "Do we go after the Fourteenth and Twentieth?"

"The legions led by Paulinus are my next target. When they are defeated, all that will be left on our lands are pockets of Romans that can easily be exterminated," I said.

"Then let us go after them!" Leofric said, lifting his fist into the air to punctuate his words.

The group looked to me. I took my time answering. "My intention was to march to meet the legions on the Watling road as they return from slaughtering our Druids on Ynys Môn, but last night Andraste led me to discover that those legions have not yet left the isle. Yes, we could march to the isle and attack them." I turned to Cadoc and asked a question to which I already knew the answer, but every warrior in my council knew the shield had something that I did not—decades of battle experience. "How long would it take to march our army to Ynys Môn?"

Cadoc scratched his silvered beard. "Eight full days of hard marching. More if this weather continues or gets worse." He gestured at the sleet raining from the sky. "And at the end of that march our army would be spent, while Paulinus's legions would be freshly rested and restored."

All eyes turned from Cadoc to me. "I have not ruled out the march or the battle. Like each of you, I would have the Romans defeated and forced from our lands now. But it is not my will that had led us thus far and given us three resounding victories over the Romans. At dawn I will petition Andraste to show us what *she* wishes our next move to be." I met the gaze of each of my council members. "I will abide by whatever sign the goddess gives."

"Aye," they murmured before leaving my campfire and heading to their own, eager to get out of the cold wet.

As Maldwyn passed me, I reached out and stroked the side of his arm. The horse master met my gaze. "Stay?" I framed it as a question, not willing to command his affection.

His smile lit his cornflower eyes. "Gladly."

At dawn I rode Tân to the field outside Verulamium where I'd reluctantly left Rhan. Maldwyn was with me, leading a spare horse for our seer. The morning was bitterly cold. Sometime in the night, while I had been warmed and satiated by Maldwyn's passion, the sleet had changed to snow. The city looked surreal burning against a backdrop of grays and whites. The snow was a hindrance, but at least it covered the bodies strewn in front of the city.

As we rode up, Rhan stood stiffly. She'd been sitting just inside the small tent and was wrapped in a pelt, though her nose was pink with cold. Dark circles framed her eyes, making them look twice their size. She seemed fragile and fae-like, and for a moment I did not know her—and then she smiled up at me and became my Rhan again.

"The shades have gone. Verulamium will forever be free of them," she said.

"And how are you?" I asked as Maldwyn dismounted and led the spare horse to her.

"If you mean am I well enough to petition Andraste for your next move—I assure you, Queen Boudicca, that I am very well."

"Reading my mind again?"

Her musical laughter was a relief to hear. "You know I cannot." Maldwyn boosted her onto the horse.

I raised a brow at my old friend and teased, "I know you *say* you cannot."

"And I shall continue to say so because it is the truth." She grinned. "Have the Dobunni and Catuvellauni joined us?"

"The Dobunni, yes," I said.

"Two hundred of the Catuvellauni have joined us. Those led by Chief Leofric," added Maldwyn. "Out of thousands still loyal to Togodumnus."

"But it is a start," I said.

"Aye, it is that," agreed Maldwyn.

"More will join us," said Rhan.

I turned so that I could meet her gaze. "Have you seen that?"

"It is something I have known since the day you placed the torque of Prasutagus around your neck," she said.

My body jolted with surprise. "And you said nothing to me about that until now?"

"You did not ask until now."

Maldwyn tried unsuccessfully to cover his laughter with a cough.

Once again my war council gathered outside my tent under the meager tarp that attempted to keep the mixed sleet and snow from us. The camp was awake, waiting restlessly for the outcome of our petition to Andraste. I felt a great sense of anticipation that turned to trepidation as Rhan rushed to me. I expected her to be carrying one of the sacred white hares, but her arms were empty and her eyes unreadable.

"Queen Boudicca, I would ask that you and your council follow me. Andraste has given sign," she said.

My brow furrowed. "Follow you? I don't understand."

"You will, my queen. If you follow me," she insisted.

I nodded. "Lead on, Iceni seer."

We followed Rhan out into the wet, walking in a line after her, drawing the curious gazes of the Iceni as we wove through the caravans to the area of the camp that held the animal pens. It was then that I first noticed the new deference the people showed Rhan. Word of the slaughter at Ynys Môn had spread among the army. The Druids were our king and queen makers. They settled tribal grievances. They were our most talented healers, storytellers, and artists. But beyond all of that, our Druids were our link to Annwn. As Rhan walked through the camp, warriors and the families that filled the caravans left the warmth of their tents and wagons and campfires to bow to Rhan. They watched her with an intensity I understood. Without our Druids, who would translate the signs sent to us by our gods? Who would look into the future and advise us? Who would give voice to the spirits of our ancestors? Within the scope of just a few days, Rhan's already considerable power had multiplied. I did not want to believe that she and Adara were the last two Druids alive in Britain, but whether they were or not, our people would cherish them beyond gold.

I was glad of it. I was also aware that I could benefit from the veneration with which the people regarded Rhan, my dearest friend and seer of the Iceni.

The hares of Andraste had an entire wagon to themselves. Their hutches were lovingly filled with fresh bedding daily. They ate only the sweetest grasses and ripest vegetables. The women who cared for the hares loved them as they did their children.

As we came to the wagon, the caretakers of the hares clustered outside, visibly upset. My stomach tightened. If the sacred hares were dead I did not know what I would do. How would Rhan interpret a sign so terrible? I was consumed by dread that I could not allow my people to see.

Rhan halted just outside the draped end of the wagon. It was closed to keep the hares within warm. She turned to face us.

"I came here as soon as Queen Boudicca asked that I petition Andraste for our next move. I meant to select a hare and bring it to our queen so that she might speak her question for the goddess, as I have often done. But as I drew aside the curtains of their wagon it seemed the hares answered the question before the queen could ask it." Rhan looked at me. "Queen Boudicca, I am going to draw aside the curtain and enter the wagon. When I do I ask that you speak your question to Andraste, loudly, so that your people will never wonder what their queen truly asked the goddess. Then I will go to the hutches to release a hare so that we may all see the sign the goddess gives. Will you do that?"

"I will."

Rhan nodded to me, and then, with a flourish, she threw open the curtain and climbed nimbly into the wagon. She turned and faced me, folded her hands together, and waited.

The warm, familiar scent of rabbit and alfalfa drifted from within. We could see the neat hutches. They were spacious and stacked atop one another three high, strapped to the sides of the wagon so that they would not tumble over as we traveled. The hares were clearly visible. Their white coats and pink eyes were like torches in the grayness. They turned their heads and ears to the opening, curious and utterly unafraid of humans.

I gazed at them and spoke clearly, projecting my voice so that not just my council heard the petition I posed to Andraste, but many of the warriors surrounding us as well. "Mighty Andraste, I am your Boudicca—named by you, chosen by you. I ask for your guidance.

Shall I march your army to meet the Romans now? What say you, goddess of the Iceni, goddess of vengeance, goddess of war?"

Rhan moved to the closest hutch, and as she opened the door to it, the hares within became hysterical. They scurried away from the little door to cower in a group in the rear of the hutch, shivering and screaming with high, thin voices that sent shivers down my spine.

But Rhan did not stop there. She approached every hutch and opened each one—and every sacred hare behaved the same way. As soon as Rhan opened their hutch, they panicked and raced to huddle together, trembling and screaming.

Only after Rhan closed the door to the last hutch and left the wagon did the hares calm. Within moments they returned to nibbling on their food, yawning and acting as if nothing unusual had happened. It was extraordinary.

"That is exactly how the hares reacted when I tried to choose one to hear our queen's petition and our goddess's answer," said Rhan.

My warriors were speechless. They stared at the hares. Every Iceni that surrounded me knew that this behavior was unprecedented. Andraste's hares did not fear us. They had no reason to. They were pampered and adored for their entire lives. Upon death they were mourned and often burned on a sacred pyre or buried within the Chief's Barrow. They were never harmed or misused or frightened.

I was shaken, though glad that my voice remained steady. "Iceni seer, how do you interpret Andraste's sign?"

"The goddess's will is clear. We are to find a place to winter the army. And it will be a long, harsh winter. We are not to march against Rome until Andraste has given sign that it is safe."

"So the goddess has spoken, so will I do," I said solemnly. Though how I was going to safely winter over one hundred thousand people with two legions hunting us, I did not know.

CHAPTER XXXII

W e cannot winter at Thetford." Cadoc shook his head emphatically. "Even if we could march this massive army to our winter camp without the Roman legions ambushing us, Thetford is too well-known to Paulinus. They've left it alone until now because Prasutagus always paid his taxes on time. Rome had no reason to go to the trouble of attacking our winter stronghold. They do now. If we tried to winter there we would be inviting a siege or worse. Our supplies aren't safe and must be moved."

"I agree," I said.

My war council had gathered once again in the scant shelter outside my tent. Wulffaed kept pouring steaming mulled mead to keep us warm, but the snow had not stopped. It did not take an experienced warrior to understand that I had to make a decision about where we would winter immediately or risk our massive army getting stranded. That would make us easy prey to the legions. Andraste had made it clear that we were to burrow and not engage with the Romans at this time, so burrow we would—but where? I was loath to split up our army, though I was afraid the only choice I had was to send our Trinovantes, Dobunni, and Catuvellauni allies home to disperse and shelter in their own lands. Just thinking about trying to gather them again in the spring had my head pounding with dread. In the spring it would be time to work and plant the fields. How many warriors would answer my call then? Certainly not the number our army now held. I could not believe that was what Andraste would want.

Addedomaros ran a hand through his thick, graying hair. "But you overheard Paulinus saying that the legions were still recovering from Ynys Môn. Perhaps we have time to march home, scatter, and ride out the winter in hiding as best we can."

"No." I knew there was a better solution. I just couldn't quite grasp what it would be. "We will not divide our people just as we've begun to truly join together."

Rhan cleared her throat and all gazes turned to her. "There is another answer." Her eyes went to Comux. "What is your idea, chief of the Dobunni?"

Comux stood and pulled his bright green cloak more closely around him. He bowed his head to Rhan. "The Iceni seer sees truthfully. I do have an idea."

"I will be glad to hear it," I prodded, as I could see that the chief was reluctant to speak.

"I have not mentioned it because it is rather unusual," he said.

"Our army is rather unusual," I said.

He chuckled and nodded. "Queen Boudicca, are you aware that my wife's sister is married to Caratacus, chief of Tribe Ordovices?"

Cadoc spoke up before I could. "Ah, yes. We know Caratacus. Several years ago he came to Tasceni to meet with Prasutagus." My shield met my gaze and continued. "Do you remember, my queen? It wasn't long after Ceri's birth."

"I do indeed. Caratacus was born to the Catuvellauni, was he not?"

"He was." Leofric, the old warrior who had become chief of a small group of Catuvellauni, spoke up. "He and his brother Togodumnus disagreed about how to handle the Romans. Togodumnus saw it as a chance to gain riches and subdue the other tribes. Caratacus wanted nothing to do with Rome."

"Wise man," muttered Addedomaros.

"Aye," said Leofric. "Would that I had been so wise then and followed him. It took me much longer to understand the danger of allying with Rome. When Caratacus left, nearly a third of the Catuvellauni agreed and followed him into the west."

Comux nodded and continued the telling. "Caratacus and those loyal to him joined the Ordovices. He married Caraf, one of the royal daughters of the Ordovices—my wife's sister. Caratacus was chosen chief at the death of old Ougein."

"And what has the Ordovices chief to do with your idea?" I asked.

"I believe Caratacus would allow the army to winter in the Eryri Mountains."

"Ha!" Addedomaros scoffed. "That would put us only a few days south of Ynys Môn. Too near the legions that are still there."

Comux just lifted a brow at the Trinovantes chief. "The southern mountains are far enough from the Druid isle to be hidden from the legions, yet close enough that they would not think to look there."

"Hmm." Cadoc scratched his beard. "The legions would also not think to attempt a march through those mountains to search for us."

"Because the mountains will be covered by snow and impassable!" blurted Adminius.

"Which is why we must break camp and march immediately to the Eryri Mountains before the passes are closed." I turned to Comux. "*If* there is a place within the mountains that can shelter us."

"Yes, Queen Boudicca. There is a valley just within the southern boundary of the mountains. It holds a lake called Arglwyddes y Llyn, which is surrounded by impassable peaks on all sides except one— and that one pass closes early every winter."

"But is it large enough to hold the entire army? Think of the size of our combined herds," said Maldwyn.

"It is. And the peaks that surround the valley catch the brunt of the snow and ice."

"Do you think we could get our winter stores from Thetford there before the pass closes?" I asked Comux.

He moved his shoulders. "It would be close, though if they got near enough we could transport the supplies on litters pulled by horses should the wagons not make it through the pass."

"But the army will be seen," said Addedomaros. "We could split up the supply wagons and have them travel by different routes so they do not draw attention, but an army of over one hundred thousand will draw attention."

My gaze went to Rhan. "Leave that to me." I stood. "We march to the Eryri Mountains for the winter. Cadoc, send our swiftest riders to Thetford and have them move our winter stores to meet us there immediately."

"As you ask, so will I do," said my shield.

"Queen Boudicca, with your leave I will send my shield to Caratacus to alert him of our approach," said Comux.

"You have it," I said. "We break camp now. It will be a difficult march. We must move from dawn until dark each day. This weather will chill our bones, but I agree with Comux. Tucked into the valley, we will winter safely."

"If our supplies arrive in time," added Addedomaros.

"That is why we are sending our swiftest riders," I said. "Do you not have stores at your winter stronghold, Trinovantes chief?"

Addedomaros cleared his throat. "Aye, we do."

"And they are closer than Thetford, correct?" I asked.

"Aye."

I smiled. "Then it is a good thing the Trinovantes are known to have the swiftest horses of all the tribes." As the members of the war council left and camp began to break, I called, "Rhan, Maldwyn, stay for a moment." I motioned for them to join me near the fire. "I know how we can move this army to the mountains without the tribes talking of it to the Romans." The Iceni seer and horse master turned curious gazes on me but remained silent. I drew a deep breath. I believed my thinking was sound, but when dealing with magick and the gods, one could never be sure. I locked my gaze with my dearest friend's. "Rhan, they will be silent for you."

Her brows lifted and I saw confusion in her dark eyes as she squinted at me, trying to figure out what I meant. Then she blinked several times and nodded slowly. "I understand, but it is not for me that they will be silent. They will be showing their love and respect for my people, who are no more."

"Druids?" Maldwyn asked.

"Yes," Rhan said, still not looking away from my gaze. "Adara and I could very well be the last of the Druids."

I took her shoulders in my hands. "I do not believe you are the last. There must be more Druids scattered among the tribes. After we force the Romans from our lands, we will find them, gather them, and rebuild Ynys Môn. We will replant the sacred oaks and a new generation of Druids will thrive there."

"It is a lovely dream," Rhan said softly.

"It is a dream that can be made real," I said. "Will you do it, Rhan? Will you lead us to the mountains and use your powers to keep us secret and safe?"

"I will."

"Harness Ennis and Finley," I told Maldwyn. "They will lead the army with Rhan riding beside me in the chariot."

"As you ask, so will I do."

When he left to prepare the chariot, I ordered one of Wulffaed's daughters to call for Briallen, who came quickly as she'd been close by at my daughters' tent.

"Briallen, gather my guard. Have them dress in their best and be mounted. They will lead the army with me."

"Yes, my queen!"

While the camp broke around us, Rhan and I went into my tent to prepare. We didn't speak but took our time painting our faces and dressing our hair. I did not wear my battle uniform. Instead I chose the Beltane dress that had been my mother's last gift to me and a thick fur cloak that had been dyed Iceni blue.

Rhan painted her face as I'd seen Derwyn do before major rituals in bold strips of white and black. As I watched her ready herself, I realized that she was now the senior-ranking Druid alive. Adara was older but gifted in healing more than in the Sight. Rhan was the new high Druid. The thought humbled me.

Rhan outlined the Ogham symbols tattooed on her face and neck in white so that their black lines seemed to glow, inky and powerful. She wore her ovate colors of greens and browns woven together. Around her slim waist she wrapped a rope of sacred mistletoe. She placed a wide necklace of bones and feathers, beads and shells, around her neck. It clacked and clanked whenever she moved. Lastly, from its place outside my tent, Rhan lifted the sigil that I'd taken into all three battles and carried it with us as my queen's guard escorted us to the waiting chariots.

I drove Ennis and Finley to the head of our army. Maldwyn rode on one side of me. Cadoc and Abertha were in their familiar positions on my other side, only this time I was the only one of us driving a chariot. Behind us my guard stretched across the road, looking fierce. And after them came my people in what seemed an unending sea of tribal colors.

As we started forward, the sleet shifted to snow. Large flakes caught on our clothes as they fell lazily from a sky so low and gray it seemed if I stretched my arms up high enough I could touch it.

We passed the first farm that had not been burned to the ground, and I saw a group of people peering at us from behind a hedgerow. Rhan and I wore our hair long and unbound. The winter wind lifted it so that my thick, flame-colored mane tangled with Rhan's smooth moonlight mass—fire and ice.

With graceful hands and rounded arms, Rhan traced patterns in the air before her, and as her dark gaze slid to look at the curious faces of the farmers, she pressed a finger against her lips and said one word that the wind picked up and carried around us.

"Silence!"

All that day I drove the chariot and watched my friend weave symbols of power in the air around us and invoke the protection of the gods. Every farm we passed, every small settlement, every merchant we overtook who had fled from Verulamium or Londinium, stopped and stared at Rhan, entranced by the Druid. Britons began coming out to watch us pass. I heard their whispers. *"She is the last of the Druids . . . Blessed by the gods . . . High Druid . . . seer of the Iceni . . ."* On and on we marched, surrounded by the magick Rhan wove, ancient and powerful. It and the respect of our people held us in a web of safety.

As the days passed and the army trudged through snow and ice, people were drawn to us. We entered Dobunni territory. I was not surprised when more warriors from Comux's tribe joined us, but what did surprise me was when Cadoc began announcing daily that other tribes had found us. The Atrebates sent several hundred foot soldiers. The Silures joined us with a thousand cavalry and caravans filled with their families and winter stores to sustain them. More Catuvellauni followed Leofric, pledging loyalty to him and allegiance to me.

By the time we crossed into the territory of Tribe Ordovices, our army had swelled to almost two hundred thousand. We were cold and tired, but morale was high. Drummers had taken to beating out the rhythm of Rhan's hand movements, and the Iceni seer often added her voice to the invocation, playing with the rhythmic drumbeats. My guard sang with her, mimicking her sounds and swaying in time to the sacred dance.

The power of Rhan's magick was awe inspiring. Though we were cold and wet and weary, we moved with the gods. Ravens flew over us. Stags often crossed our path. Boars grunted and snorted and followed us. And there were hares everywhere! Though we had to wade through snow and ice, the horses did not tire—the wagons did not become mired. Each night we camped, gathering around bonfires sharing drink and food and song. The hearts of the people were so warm and strong that the cold did not bite. Many times during those five long days and nights, I felt as if we were not traveling through the mortal world of Arbred but had instead crossed into Annwn. Nwyfre, the life force that fills us all, flowed freely from Rhan, seer of the Iceni and high Druid. It washed over our people, binding us together as we moved with one sacred purpose. We would winter safely. We would survive. And in the spring we would be reborn with the land and force the Romans forever from Britain.

"There." Comux pointed at a narrow pass where two jagged, rocky mountains almost met. It was just before dusk and we'd spent the entire day on a muddy path too rough to be called a proper road. We'd halted after it seemed to run into the mountains before us. As I followed Comux's finger and peered through the pass, I could just glimpse the wan winter daylight reflecting off a lake that appeared as gray as the sky above us. "That is the pass, and within is Arglwyddes y Llyn and our sanctuary for the winter."

"Looks very narrow," said Cadoc.

"That is one of its charms." Comux grinned. "It is only just wide enough to allow one wagon at a time to enter and will close with snow and ice soon." He shrugged. "Though even if the pass remains open for weeks, it is easily defended."

"It is perfect," I said. "Let's get inside and begin setting up corrals for the horses and sectioning off areas for shelters."

"Queen Boudicca, I do believe that the mountain there, near the far end of the lake"—Comux directed my gaze—"has cavelike openings around the base of much of it. They should be able to be made into shelters."

"A real shelter would be a braw thing to have this winter," said Briallen from her lead position in front of my guard.

"It does sound lovely," I said a little wistfully. Yes, morale was excellent. Yes, the nights had been filled with comradeship and the days had been productive. The army had surpassed even Cadoc's estimates of how quickly so many people and horses and caravans could be moved north. Still, I longed for shelter and the warmth and safety it brought.

"Well then, let us enter this valley and create a winter sanctuary for our queen!" said Maldwyn as everyone within hearing cheered.

The days that followed were satisfying. Though the size of our army was intimidating, especially to me, as I was the person ultimately responsible for feeding, housing, and caring for them all winter, I soon saw the benefits in having two hundred thousand Britons under my charge. My people were canny and talented. Even before our seemingly endless stream of wagons rumbled slowly one by one through the pass, builders came forward. They discussed the best ways to create winter-worthy shelters. I put the capable shields Cadoc and Mailcun in charge of supervising the cutting down of trees and the building of shelters.

Comux's young shield, Seward, returned with the blessing of Caratacus and several packhorses loaded down with cakes and mounds of exquisite furs the chief sent as gifts to me. The shield also reported that the Roman legions had broken camp several days before he'd arrived and that they had last been seen heading southeast, out of Ordovices territory.

As winter drew closer and closer, we waited for the Iceni and Trinovantes supply wagons while we foraged outside the sparse valley and cut trees for shelters. Our farmers took wagons and scouted peat bogs, harvesting the precious fuel daily.

The valley was large, easily big enough for a city, which was good because our numbers could have filled Londinium twice over. Comux had been right. The mountain that backed the far side of the lake was riddled with indentations in its rocky face. Abertha quickly dubbed it Graybeard as its peaks were always covered with mist that clung to it, looking much like an old man's beard.

It was in the largest of the cavelike indentations that my winter lodge was built. The opening and single chamber within were easily roomy enough to hold council meetings, and that was where Wulf-faed and her daughters worked their magick. I hadn't realized that they'd rolled up the tapestries from the royal lodge at Tasceni and packed them into their group of wagons, and I'm glad I hadn't known as I would have told them to leave such things behind. A warrior queen doesn't need luxuries.

I'd have been wrong. Once the tapestries were hung over the rock walls and my bedchamber was sectioned off by more tapestries and thick blankets, they built a large fire pit cunningly placed beneath several honeycomb-like openings in the rocky roof. The openings provided enough of an escape for the smoke that a fire could blaze constant and hot without choking us with smoke. The builders created crude trestle tables made of wooden logs topped by sheets of the unusual crimson and violet slate that proliferated in the valley. I was as pleased as I was surprised by the level of comfort the cave afforded me—and I was grateful for the luxury of beauty and warmth within it.

Flanking the central cavelike opening were several smaller indentations that also reminded me of honeycombs, though they were much more sizable than the pocked holes over the fire pit. My girls snuggled into one of them and Rhan chose a cave beside them. On the other side of my shelter, Wulffaed commandeered a nearby opening, in front of which the caravans filled with her daughters and granddaughters circled, creating a warm, homey area that was always alive with the sounds of women's laughter and scents of baking bread.

Addedomaros, his son, and his household servants claimed the largest of the other spaces. Comux and his shield took another. And Leofric claimed another as his own. I offered the remaining caves to my lead warriors. Cadoc accepted, grumbling about his old bones needing thick walls to keep out the winter, but Abertha and Maldwyn declined. Abertha chose to lodge with her longtime lover, Dreda, in the sprawling shelter my Queen's Guard erected. I wondered if Maldwyn would choose one of the caves so he could be near me, but his sense of duty to our herd had him sheltering in the circle of caravans that carried the tack and feed. Instead of feeling slighted, I was glad of his dedication to our horses. Briallen chose one of the little caves as her own. I'd expected her to lodge with the rest of my guard, but she'd become accustomed to being close to the girls and to me, and I was glad to have her near.

The caravans were prepared for a long winter. They were covered wagons, but the tent tarps that enclosed them would not be warm enough for the hard freezes that were to come, so the tribesmen and -women worked diligently on cutting and slicing logs into flat boards that were attached to the wagons and then adding mud daub to form walls where only tarp had been. The caravans were positioned around large fire pits, where they butted up to one another so that they looked like oddly skinny roundhouses that were open in the center. Tents blossomed against the wagons, using their wooden backs and the blankets and tapestries they'd plundered from Londinium and Verulamium to provide warmth and shelter.

Lean-tos were erected along the base of the mountains, under which scores of fire pits blossomed with light and warmth. Large holding pens were built around the lean-tos so that our precious horses were protected from the worst of the cold.

We'd traveled with sizable herds of goats and cattle, as well as a drove of fat Iceni pigs. Their pens were adjacent to the horses, also tucked against the broad mountainsides—and chickens were everywhere, which made egg gathering a daily exercise in foraging.

Arglwyddes y Llyn proved to be a marvel. Filled with carp and brown trout, the lake was too deep to freeze. From the fireside in my cave lodge, I could gaze across the lake, watching the hovering mist move lazily and our fishers casting nets and setting lines. The water was clear and cold and often so still that it seemed the reflection of the surrounding mountains had actually taken shape within its surface and was another realm.

The weather provided a reprieve shortly after we arrived, and for five straight days there was no more snow. Sunlight filled the valley, deceptively making the days appear warm, but its distant light was too wan to take the bite from the air. We were all very aware that when it began snowing again it would not end until spring, and lookouts anxiously kept watch for our supply wagons.

CHAPTER XXXIII

"There is snow on the horizon!" Addedomaros said as he entered my cave on the tenth morning after we'd come to the valley.

I looked up from Sunne, whose ears I had been caressing. My daughters took their meals with me, and their wolves were their constant shadows. The big creatures intrigued me. I liked spending time observing their intelligence and loyalty. "May the joy of the day be with you, Addedomaros," I said, gesturing for him to join me at the long table.

He cleared his throat and muttered, "And may the blessings of the earth be on you."

"Have you broken your fast?" I asked as Rhan joined me at the table.

"Yes, earlier. Though I would not refuse a mug of the Mother of Twenty's mulled mead."

"Wulffaed?" I called.

The woman appeared as she always did—already prepared. She placed mugs before the three of us.

Addedomaros flashed a charming smile at Wulffaed as he lifted the mug to toast her. "Ah, Wulffaed, what can I do to lure you away from Queen Boudicca?"

Wulffaed snorted and fluttered her fingers at him in a *begone with you* gesture, though she also smiled and tossed back her silver hair. Addedomaros definitely had a charm about him. He was an imposing figure who enjoyed the company of women. I frequently overheard Wulffaed's daughters gossiping about the endless stream of lovers going to and from the Trinovantes chief's bed. Addedomaros reminded me too much of my father for me to view him in a sexual way, but there was no denying his charisma or power.

"So, what do we do?" Addedomaros asked as Cadoc and Abertha entered the cave. Since the spring, my lead warriors had made a habit of breaking their fasts with me—it was a habit I enjoyed.

I was watching for Maldwyn when Abertha sat beside Cadoc and said, "What do we do about what?"

Addedomaros sighed heavily. "About the snow on the horizon and the fact that our supply wagons have not yet arrived, of course."

"What is it you would like to do?" I asked as Wulffaed reappeared with a pitcher of mead and a platter of grilled fish and freshly baked bread.

"Something! The snow is coming. What will we do if the pass closes before the supplies arrive and we're trapped here for the winter?"

"We will tighten our rationing. We have stock we can slaughter, and the lake is filled with fish. I've already spoken with Maldwyn and he has begun to supplement the herd's feed with heather and tree moss." I shrugged, not sure why Addedomaros was so worried when the answer to his question was obvious. "We won't be fat when we emerge in the spring, but we'll be well rested and alive."

Addedomaros took a long drink of mead and wiped his mouth with the back of his hand. "Being trapped in this valley all winter feels like a prison."

"Being *trapped* in this valley means safety and survival." I stared down my nose at him. "But, mighty Trinovantes chief, you are welcome to leave this *prison* and spend the winter fleeing from the Romans as you freeze and starve."

His eyes narrowed at me, and then he snorted and his laughter boomed. "I like your directness, Queen Boudicca."

"That is fortunate, as I do not know any other way to be," I said, which made him laugh some more.

"My queen!" Maldwyn rushed into the cave. "Wagons have been spotted!"

Even though I'd spoken with complete confidence to Addedomaros, I was flooded with relief. "That is excellent news, Maldwyn. I—"

Addedomaros stood, gulped the rest of his mead, and slammed the empty mug down on the stone-topped table. "Now, that is news to brighten a miserable winter's day! Let us go and greet them!" He nodded a quick bow to me and then strode from the cave, bellowing for Mailcun.

"Mama, he makes a lot of noise," said Ceri.

"Aye, like the rooster who pecks around outside my cave and wakes me at dawn with his nonsense," muttered Cadoc.

Abertha and Maldwyn chuckled as Rhan tried to cover her laughter. I touched Ceri's cheek. "Yes, he does. But let's not say that in front of him."

"Oh, I know that, Mama. But I can say it in front of *us*."

"Always, my little dove." I grinned at her. Then I turned my attention to my warriors. "Go ahead and greet the wagons. I will join you after I look more presentable. Our people just traveled the width of our country to reach us and they shouldn't be greeted by a bedraggled queen."

My lead warriors grabbed hunks of bread and wrapped the fish in them and then hurried from the cave, eager to get the wagons settled and our precious supplies stored properly.

I called for Phaedra to attend me and then motioned for Rhan to follow us into my bedchamber. While Phaedra undid my sleep-tousled braid and began working her way through my hair, I asked Rhan a question that had been weighting on my mind.

"Rhan, I am trying to understand your father, because it is to our benefit if the Trinovantes chief and I are of one mind, but it is difficult," I said. "Do you have any advice on how to handle him?"

Rhan, sounding very much like her father, barked a laugh. "'Difficult' is an understatement. Do you not remember how he blustered and bellowed when we were girls?"

"I do, but we were rarely the recipients of his bellows and blusters."

Rhan nodded. "Yes, they were usually reserved for his warriors and my half brothers. Though had he bellowed at Adminius occasionally, he might have grown into a more bearable man."

"I'm just grateful your brother dislikes me enough to stay well away."

"It is a blessing," Phaedra muttered under her breath.

I turned to look at her. "Has Adminius bothered you?"

"No, but only because I belong to you." Phaedra glanced at Rhan. "Forgive me for speaking so about your brother, but he is not liked."

"There is no forgiveness required, Phaedra. Adminius has been tiresome and demanding his entire spoiled, cossetted life."

"What has he done?" I asked Phaedra.

"He bullies the servants, and unhappy is the woman who catches his eye," said Phaedra.

I turned around in my seat so that I could face Phaedra. "If he is abusing women, I want to know about it immediately."

Phaedra sighed. "He stops short of physically forcing women to his bed, though often they do not feel as if they have any choice. He is the son of the Trinovantes chief."

My face heated with anger. "I do not care whose son he is. Phaedra, spread the word. Queen Boudicca will protect anyone Adminius targets. All they need do is get word to me. If Addedomaros does not rein in that petulant man-child, I most certainly will."

"As you ask, so will I do," Phaedra said with a smile.

I turned around so she could finish dressing my hair and asked Rhan, "Why does your father bicker and bait me, and then seem pleased when I silence him?"

"Well, it has been a long time since I've lived with him, but I've observed two things. First, my father desires you."

"What? No!"

Her lips quirked at the corners and mischief danced in her dark eyes. "Oh, I am sure of it. Add to his desire for you the fact that *no one* speaks to him the way you do, and it is little wonder he is obsessed. He loved my mother and was devastated by her death, but she was a timid woman whose soft voice soothed him rather than challenged him. You challenge him, and apparently he enjoys that."

"Rhan, he reminds me of *my father*. I do not desire him. I will never desire him."

Rhan nodded. "I believe everyone sees and understands that— everyone except my father."

My mind was reeling. I was not an innocent maid, but I definitely had not expected to hear that the gruff Trinovantes chief who was often a thorn in my shoe *desired me*. "What do you advise?"

She shrugged. "Continue being yourself. If he is wise he will keep his desire to himself."

I met her gaze and lifted a brow sardonically. "And how often is he wise about the women he desires?"

"Not often, but you are a powerful queen and his closest ally—not a young servant or the pretty daughter of a farmer. He is more old bull than rutting stag, and he is not stupid. He would have to be very sure of your response were he to approach you," said Rhan.

I chewed my lip. I would be very sure not to do anything Addedomaros could interpret as an invitation or even an inclination to open my bed to him. Even so, I had done nothing to warrant his desire. It seemed that too often men who held power showed poor judgment when it came to their lust.

I sighed and spoke the truth. "I've given Addedomaros no reason to desire me—no reason to believe I want any relationship with him other than that of an allied queen and friend. What he fabricates in his mind is not my responsibility."

"When he is embarrassed he becomes mean," said Rhan.

"Don't they all?" said Phaedra.

"Then Addedomaros should not put himself in an embarrassing position. I will not tread carefully around him. It is he who must manage his own emotions." I dismissed the subject of Addedomaros's lust with a wave of my hand. Phaedra finished braiding my hair and wrapped a fur-lined cloak around my shoulders. "Now, let us go meet our brave caravans and not worry overmuch about the desires of men."

The line of caravans that stretched from the narrow entrance to our valley all the way to the last rise before it was a beautiful sight. Our people hovered about, anxious to greet family and friends. There was much laughter and many shouts of welcome. I was glad that most of the ground that surrounded the lake was gravelly. It helped considerably with the mud. I stood at the entrance to the valley and waved to each wagon, smiling and calling out personal greetings to familiar faces—until I caught sight of my lead farmer, Winifred, and her grim expression. Maldwyn and Cadoc escorted her to me.

Winifred's knowledge of plants was vast. The Iceni depended upon her knowledge of crops. She set harvesting and planting dates and had a preternatural ability to make crops thrive. Farmers from neighboring tribes sought her out. I'd often come upon her in Tasceni surrounded by a group of men and women as she explained how to cure black spot or blight, and how to smoke insects from their fields.

She had no daughters but five grown sons, who approached with her. Winifred and her sons bowed respectfully to me.

"Queen Boudicca, it is good to be at the end of our journey."

"Welcome!" I smiled. "We are well pleased that you beat the snow here."

"My queen, the news I bring is not all good. Cadoc and Maldwyn tell me Comux, the Dobunni chief, is here in the valley," she said.

"He is."

"He should hear the news," said Winifred.

"Maldwyn, find Comux and bring him to my chamber. Cadoc, bring Addedomaros and Leofric as well. All the chiefs should hear the news. Rhan, I'd like you to join us, too. Come with me, Winifred," I said.

"Yes, my queen," said Winifred before she turned to her eldest son. "Royston, you and the rest of the boys stay here and help settle the caravans. I'll join you after."

As we made our way to the shelter that served as my lodge, I asked, "Did I see Trinovantes colors on some of the more distant caravans?"

"Aye, Queen Boudicca. We met the Trinovantes caravans at the base of the Eryri Mountains."

"I'm surprised by that. I expected the Trinovantes to beat you here."

She shook her head. "The reason they did not is news the Dobunni chief will need to hear. Shall I tell you now?"

"No. Wait for Comux and the other chiefs." I didn't usually avoid bad news, but I wanted a few moments more to feel only joy.

Wulffaed greeted Winifred warmly and immediately brought mead and fresh bread for her. We didn't have long to wait. Maldwyn and Comux hurried into the cave. Worry creased the chief's broad forehead. Addedomaros, Leofric, and Cadoc followed them. "Comux, Dobunni chief; Addedomaros, Trinovantes chief; and Leofric of the Catuvellauni, this is the lead farmer of the Iceni, Winifred. She has news."

Winifred bowed her head to the three chiefs, cleared her throat, and began. "As the queen already noticed, we arrived with the Trinovantes caravan."

"Yes!" Addedomaros frowned and nodded. "I haven't spoken to my lead farmer yet, but I too am puzzled that it took them so long to get here. Did they not use the Roman road as we did for a good part of the way?"

"Chief Addedomaros, your caravans had to leave the road south of Corinium and travel deep within the forest to avoid the Romans." She paused there and her gaze went to Comux. The Dobunni chief had gone very still at the mention of Corinium, the royal city of the Dobunni. "Chief Comux, the Romans have taken your city. General Paulinus arrived there first with his cavalry. Then the Fourteenth and Twentieth began straggling in. I am sorry."

Comux abruptly stood. "And my people? Is there word of them?"

"The Romans have enslaved them," said Winifred.

Comux faced me. "I must take my cavalry and go to them. I must . . ." The chief's words faded and his gaze went to the floor as he understood the reality of the situation.

I had to speak truth to the grief-stricken chief. "Comux, you cannot. Your cavalry will not be enough to take two legions that have fortified themselves within the walls of your city. It would take our army to rout them, and there is not time to reach Corinium before winter closes the passes. I am sorry. Your people are brave and resourceful. They will survive the winter with the Romans, and in the spring we will force them from our lands and free your people. You will reclaim what is rightfully yours."

Comux lifted his gaze to meet mine. "I hear you, Queen Boudicca, and I know you speak truth, but . . ." He had to look away and take deep breaths before he could continue. "My daughter and her husband remained in Corinium. She is heavy with her first child, so my wife chose to stay with her. I—" His voice broke and he had to swallow several times before he could continue. "I must go find my sons. They should hear this news from me." He bowed and hurried from the chamber.

Leofric stood. "With your permission, Queen Boudicca, I will go with Comux to speak with his sons. The Dobunni chief and I have become friends as well as allies—and I believe he needs a friend right now."

"Go with my blessing," I said.

"So the Romans will winter in Corinium," said Cadoc after the Catuvellauni chief had left the chamber. "Bastards."

"They wish to usurp all that is ours," said Addedomaros harshly.

I didn't give voice to what I saw in the eyes of everyone in that room. None of us were surprised. Our army had burned the three major cities Rome had occupied. Their choice was either to launch ships on a winter channel and return to the mainland to lick their wounds, or to occupy another city—one large enough and well enough appointed to shelter two legions. The Dobunni's winter stores would be completely depleted by the Romans. If someone was going to starve, it would not be the legions. My heart ached for Comux's wife and daughter and his daughter's newborn.

Rhan stood, and all eyes went to the Druid. "We must defeat them in the spring. If we do not, we will share the fate of the Dobunni and be made slaves in our own lands."

I stood. "I will either defeat the Romans or die trying. I will not be a slave."

Addedomaros stood and shouted, "Aye!"

"Aye!" Cadoc and Maldwyn joined him.

They made me proud, these warriors. I knew each of them was prepared to die beside me. I only hoped that wouldn't be necessary.

CHAPTER XXXIV

The snow began two days after the last caravan entered the valley. It fell with a steadiness that proclaimed winter had arrived in the mountains and would not be departing until spring—so we settled in for the long, dark months ahead of us.

I was used to wintering deep in the Thetford forest, where we would get snow, but it was nothing like the steady stream of white that fell from the low, gray sky that engulfed the Eryri Mountains. I was glad we were shielded from the worst of the storms so that, snug in our valley, I was able to appreciate the stark beauty of the snow. It had a muffling effect I'd never before experienced. Mornings when I rose with the sun, I was awed by the quiet and the way dawn's light touched the newly fallen snow, turning it to faceted jewels.

The army got to work immediately. The blacksmiths and farmers collaborated on how to adapt plow designs to the snow so that not only were we able to keep a slim trail cleared from our valley out to the peat bogs, but we were able to maintain winding paths through our huge camp and create a large training field where our warriors practiced daily. As Cadoc often said, it would not do for our army to emerge fat and lazy from a winter of inaction. I agreed with him, but more because I knew bored warriors would become troublesome rather than because I worried that they would be too portly to face down the Romans.

In a combined effort to combat boredom and fatigue, Addedo-maros, Comux, Leofric, and I joined our warriors in their training. It was nostalgic for me. I'd thrived the spring and summer before as I trained for war, and it felt good to continue building muscle and balance and skill. Within a fortnight the huge camp had settled into habits that helped us thrive.

We trained during the middle of the day, taking advantage of the slim hours of light. It mattered not at all whether the sky was clear and brilliant cerulean or slate-colored and pregnant with snow. As the wan sun sank into the mountains that protected our valley, we cared for our precious herds until it was time for dinner and the telling of tales that followed—a tradition Rhan had started when she'd asked me to share with the large group I'd chosen to eat with the story of Andraste riding beside me after the battle of Camulodunum. I'd only been partway into the tale when I noticed the crowd around the campfire had doubled. Bright eyes glistened in the firelight as they watched me recount how Andraste had ridden Brigantia's white stag, escorting me from the burning city to our camp. They'd cheered as I finished the telling, and Rhan had whispered, "Stories are precious to your people. They will collect them and hold them close during this long winter, and in the spring will repeat them proudly as we emerge and face the Romans once again."

After that night it became tradition for the chiefs and lead warriors to move from hearthfire to hearthfire, sharing tales and listening to others tell them as we encouraged our people to remember why we had become an army—so that Rome could not dilute our beliefs, our pride, our very spirits.

The long winter nights allowed time for love. I watched my people with knowing smiles as passion warmed their beds. Maldwyn proved to be an unexpected joy. I'd wondered about what might happen between us as the valley closed and the cold months stretched before us. I would never marry again. Not because I wasn't interested in loving, but rather because I had no interest in dividing my rule. I had been queen for almost one full year. I'd gained my people's trust and loyalty. I was more than simply comfortable being queen of the Iceni; I ruled wisely. I'd established a council that was rich with experience and wisdom. My people knew that even though I depended upon the advice of that council, ultimately the decisions made for them were mine. If I married, it would instantly bring into question who was ruling the Iceni.

I would listen to my council. I would consult Andraste. But I would not bow my will to any man's.

Though Maldwyn and I did not speak of it, by his actions it was clear he understood. Above all else, I was his queen. He deferred to me, not with subservience but with respect. He was always eager to come to my bed, or welcome me to his, though he never instigated our nights together. We shared long, intimate looks and smiles, and were of one mind as we trained together in our chariot, but Maldwyn never attempted to use our intimacy to advance his own desires. If the herd needed something, he brought that need to me during our council meetings. The only words we whispered to one another in the dark of night were those of passion. I felt safe with him.

I did not hide the fact that he and I were lovers. The Iceni and the other tribes had no foolish taboos about desire. We loved freely, easily, and openly. When Maldwyn and I walked to the training grounds together, I often saw my people smile knowingly at us. Passion was nothing more than another aspect of our lives. Chiefs and queens who did not display their passions were often looked upon as lacking. While I have never been one to flaunt my desires publicly, there was less privacy in our valley than in Tasceni, and my people were well aware that their queen did not lack passion.

As the nights lengthened and the days became short and frigid, I thought of my mother often, especially when I watched Wulffaed in the candlelight guiding my daughters as they practiced their needlework. The Mother of Twenty and her brood of daughters and granddaughters filled my makeshift lodge with the happy sounds of women's laughter, evoking memories of other long winters when my mother reigned over the matriarchs of our tribe. Our lodge had always been a meeting place for women to talk and share ideas, trade goods and support each other. For the first time since Arianell's death, I felt feminine comradeship and support again and realized how desperately I'd missed it.

"Wulffaed!" I called as I sat straighter and pulled my thoughts from the past.

"My queen?"

"I wish to reclaim one of my mother's favorite traditions and would like your help in doing so." My daughters turned their bright, eager gazes to me, and I smiled.

"Of course, Queen Boudicca. How may I help?"

I noticed Rhan and Briallen had also paused in what they were doing to watch me. "Spread word that the matriarchs of each tribe will gather there"—I jerked my chin toward the dark body of water outside the cave—"at the bank of the lake tomorrow before I go to train with the warriors."

"As you ask, so will I do," said Wulffaed.

The next day was clear and cold. I shouldn't have been surprised by the number of elders who waited at the bank of the lake. They stretched like a colorful frame around the rocky shore, elder matriarchs who proudly wore the colors of their tribes and who laughed and spoke easily to one another. They went silent when I appeared, curious faces upturned as I climbed atop a boulder so that I could be more easily heard.

"I have been thinking of my mother recently." I paused as gray heads nodded in agreement and understanding. "The day she was murdered by the Romans, I thought I would never feel content and safe in my own lodge again. I could not imagine a future without her wise presence." Again, the women nodded. "But surrounded by my tribe, and now the elders of our allies, I have found contentment, even joy, again."

"Aye." The word rippled through the women.

"We understand the value of our matriarchs—our elders. It is just one of the many beliefs that separate us from the Romans and the stunted way they live. A people cannot thrive if they do not esteem those who are life bringers."

"Aye!" Eyes flashed as the matrons responded.

"My mother had a weekly tradition I would like to continue.

Once every seven days the women of Tasceni would gather—some in my lodge and some in the homes of the other matriarchs of our tribe—and we would wash our hair and then spend the afternoon before our hearthfires, drying and then dressing each other's hair as we shared wisdom and laughter, food and drink. Did any of you have this tradition in your villages?"

"We did!" Wulffaed spoke up immediately.

"Aye, as did the Dobunni!" called a woman whose long silver hair waved around her waist.

The voices of women echoed across the lake, raised in excitement. Their eyes glistened with remembrance and hope. It was the hope that I held close to me. It was the hope we all needed to hold close.

"Tomorrow, instead of training, the women of the army will unite. Elders, speak with the maidens and mothers of your villages. Have them prepare." I smiled. "And by 'prepare' I mean open the special winter mead."

"Aye, that we can do!" Wulffaed called, followed by women's laughter.

"Every seventh day shall be Arianell's Day, in honor of my mother and all of the mothers we miss," I said.

The first Arianell's Day was filled with joy that was so familiar I could easily imagine my mother close by, approving as Dafina grumbled about needing a bigger space for so many women. We began at the bank of Arglwyddes y Llyn, where Wulffaed had supervised the building of many fires, over which cauldrons of water scented by herbs warmed. The women of the army flocked to the lake, bringing mugs of mead, which they drank deeply of as they waited in turn to wash their hair in the cold lake, and then to rinse it in steaming herb-scented water. Women's voices rang across the lake, as sweet as the scent of herbs. Then, heads wrapped in drying cloths, the women made their way to the caves and caravans and tents that housed their elder matriarchs.

My cave lodge was filled with women, young and old. Wulffaed and her daughters took turns with women I did not know serving food and mulled mead, and by the end of the day I knew the name of each of them—and I, too, had taken a turn serving the strong, beautiful women of my tribe.

"Rhan!" I finally caught sight of my friend through the crowd of women. I'd looked for her at the bank of the lake but had lost her in the milling mass.

"Queen Boudicca," she said after she'd pushed her way to where I was seated before the central hearthfire.

"There you are. Come, sit before me. I have a surprise for you." Phaedra was behind me, working a wide-toothed comb through my damp hair, and I turned to her. "You know the pebbles on the table in my bedchamber?"

"I do, my queen."

"Get them for me, please." Phaedra nodded and went to do my bidding. I motioned to a short stool before me on which I'd been resting my feet. "Sit, Rhan." The seer gave me a slanted look that was a clear question, but I simply smiled and pointed to the stool. Rhan sighed and sat before me.

"Enfys, Ceri—did you bathe your wolves?" Rhan asked with laughter in her voice.

My daughters sat on either side of me. Their wolves, now almost fully grown, lay in front of them, as close as they could get to the fire, their muzzles in their paws, looking waterlogged and miserable.

"We did!" Ceri chirped. "Mona and Sunne rolled in something very stinky and we decided it would be perfect for them to join us on Arianell's Day."

"Yes," Enfys added. "Especially as Nain would not approve of our wolves making our bed pallets stinky."

I laughed. "She certainly would not." Phaedra returned and passed me a handful of pebbles. I leaned forward, showing them to Rhan. They were all tiny but of varying shapes. They were as black as Rhan's eyes, and each had a hole through its center. I'd been gathering them daily when I walked along the bank of the lake and had been waiting for the right time to gift them to Rhan.

Rhan peered into my palm. "They look like miniature seer stones."

"That's what I thought, too." Druids sometimes used much larger versions of the pebbles in my hand to focus and look beyond into Annwn. I was glad Rhan saw the similarities. "Turn around. I'll braid them into your hair."

Rhan's cheeks flushed bright pink. She lowered her voice. "Oh, no. That wouldn't be appropriate."

"Of course it would." And then I realized that she had never spent cold winter days with the women of her tribe dressing each other's hair. Her mother had died when she was just a child. Addedomaros had not remarried, and then at fifteen Rhan had been sent to Ynys Môn to train with the Druids—I did not imagine they had this particularly homey tradition on their isle. "Rhan, my mother often dressed the hair of other women."

"Yes, Rhan," Ceri said, nodding. "Nain even braided Dafina's hair."

"When Dafina let her," added Enfys.

"It's appropriate. Today I'm not a queen. I am an Iceni woman."

"Then I thank you, my qu—" Rhan caught herself and grinned. "Boudicca."

Rhan's blond hair was almost silver when it was wet. It dried quickly, smelling of rosemary as I combed it out and began braiding the pebbles into the ends of it so that as she walked they would clink musically together.

I was so content and warmed by the fire and the mulled mead in my constantly refilled mug that I didn't notice how late it was until my daughters stood, yawned, and kissed me good night.

I blinked and looked around me as I finished placing the final pebble in Rhan's hair. "When did the sun set?"

Wulffaed laughed as she walked past me carrying a tray laden with dirty dishes. "Some time ago, my queen. It is well past the dinner hour."

"But none of the warriors came for a meal," I said.

"Naw, they took one look at this lodge packed with women and decided to find another hearthfire for the evening," said Briallen as she bowed to me. "'Twas a bonny day."

"Yes, it was," I said, smiling.

"On the morrow, then," Briallen said. "I'll see the bairns to their beds." She followed the girls and their newly dry wolves from the cave.

"It was a lovely day," said Rhan as she stood.

I snagged her wrist before she could leave. "Stay. Please. I wanted to talk with you about something." I yawned and then laughed. "Though it is later than I thought."

"Or you've had more mead than you thought," mumbled Wulf-faed. She winked at me, bowed, and then took the final tray of dirty dishes from the cave, followed by the last of her daughters. "'Tis snowing. Again. Get the fire in my chamber built up, Ravenna. The chill is . . ." Her voice trailed away as the muffling snow swallowed her.

"She's not wrong," I said, grinning at Rhan. Then I turned to Phaedra, who had just ducked out of my bedchamber. "It's been a busy day, Phaedra. I can manage to put myself to bed."

"Yes, my queen. There is more mead and some fresh bread and the herbed goat cheese you like so much in your chamber. Good night." Phaedra bowed and then retreated to the little room I'd had sectioned off for her, as her habit of sleeping at the foot of my bed had become rather awkward the nights Maldwyn joined me there.

"Phaedra thinks of everything," Rhan said as she followed me into my bedchamber and motioned to the pitcher of mead, two mugs, and bread and cheese placed thoughtfully beside it. "Would you like some more mead?"

"Why not?"

"Why not indeed?" Rhan grinned and poured our mead, and then unlaced the back of my dress.

I sighed in pleasure as I stepped out of it, pulled off the heavy winter chemise, and replaced it with one of my soft sleep shifts. Then I tossed a second sleep shift to Rhan, and clutching the mug of mead, I hurried into my bed and pulled the pelts up around me. "You should put that on and stay with me tonight. Unless you want to go out in that snow."

Rhan grimaced. "I'd much rather not." Her dark eyes sparkled. "I think I've had more mead than usual, too."

"Here, turn around. I'll untie your laces." Rhan did so and was soon out of her Druid's robes. She pulled on my borrowed shift and curled beside me under the pelt, shivering as she sipped mead and regained the warmth we'd lost when we'd left the hearthfire.

I felt no rush to talk. Rhan and I were used to sharing companionable silences. I thought about how nice it was to have her in my life again. I know it was selfish, but I was glad of the long winter. I would lose her after spring thawed the mountains and we defeated the Romans. I would keep my word. The sacred oaks on Ynys Môn would be replanted. The Druids' island would thrive again under Rhan's leadership—and she would no longer be at my side.

I shook off the sadness that followed that thought. Perhaps Rhan's destiny would allow her to return to Tasceni. I hoped so, but I also knew even a queen must bow to the will of the gods.

"I've been thinking of the gods." My voice seemed loud in the silence between us, but Rhan only nodded, leaned past me to put her empty mug on the little table beside my bed pallet, and then lay on her side facing me. When she said nothing, I continued. "I miss Andraste's shrine and our trips to care for her and leave offerings. Do you think the goddess would approve if we created a new shrine to her here in the valley?"

Rhan's fair brows lifted. "I believe she would. But I also believe the other tribes should be allowed to erect shrines to their patron deities as well."

I drained the last of my mead and placed the mug beside Rhan's before I lay on my side to face her. "That would be lovely, wouldn't it? If our artists carved images of our patron goddesses and gods all around the valley."

"Yes." Rhan reached out and brushed the length of hair that had fallen across my eyes from my face. "That is a beautiful idea, Boudicca."

I closed my eyes as she continued to caress my hair. "I'm glad you think so. We'll have to consider the best time to gather our artists so they can begin the carvings." I opened my eyes. Her face was very near mine. "I don't think I tell you often enough how very glad I am that you are here with me."

"You don't have to say it. I know."

I gazed into her beautiful dark eyes. She was my oldest, dearest friend. Since I'd lost my mother, Rhan was the only person left in this world who had been my companion in childhood. Love for her filled me with such intensity that I covered her hand with mine, stilling it against my cheek. I felt her draw in a breath and hold it as my gaze moved from her eyes to her lips. Had I noticed before how perfect they were? I did not think; I only felt. I leaned into Rhan and kissed her.

Rhan's lips were like the petals on a flower—soft and sweet. Her body had gone very still and I almost pulled away, almost apologized, but then she released her breath with a trembling sigh and parted her lips, deepening our kiss.

I explored her mouth, loving the warmth of her silky tongue and the pleasure that shivered through my body to pool deep within me as we kissed. I wanted more. My hand found the curve of her waist and I pulled her closer to me so that our bodies pressed together. She was smaller than me, delicate in my arms, but there was nothing delicate about her passion. She moaned against my lips, whispering, "Yes . . . yes . . . yes . . ." Her nipples were taut against the soft shift and my mouth teased them through the gauzy fabric. Rhan arched, gasping with pleasure.

I pulled back, just far enough so that I could watch her face as my hand moved to the hem of her shift and began sliding it up. "Tell me to stop and I will," I whispered as I caressed the smoothness of her thighs.

"Don't ever stop," she begged breathlessly.

The feel of her naked body against mine brought me such a wave of pleasure that it was my turn to gasp. She was hot and slick and we fitted together perfectly. I had never made love to a woman before that night, and the depth of my desire for her was an unexpected gift. I delighted in her body—in the scent and taste of her. It was so different from the pleasure I'd taken from Prasutagus or Maldwyn. Rhan's pleasure seemed infinite, and because hers had no end, neither did mine. We brought each other to climax over and over, discovering secrets we had never shared before then. And as dawn crept into the lodge we finally slept, wrapped together as if our bodies had become one.

CHAPTER XXXV

Phaedra seemed completely unsurprised when she entered my bedchamber and found Rhan and me naked and entwined.

"My queen, the lead warriors have begun to arrive. Shall I tell them you are indisposed this morning?" Phaedra asked as she began tidying our discarded nightdresses and gathering the empty mugs.

"No, have Wulffaed begin serving breakfast, then return to help me dress." Phaedra bowed and hurried from the chamber, and I turned to see Rhan watching me with inscrutable dark eyes. "Good morning," I told her before I kissed her.

Her eyes changed then, softening with her smile. "Good morning."

I was already standing and stepping into one of my heavy winter underdresses when Rhan sat. The pelt slipped from her shoulders to expose the plump beauty of her breasts. I went to her then and kissed each mound, lingering when she arched to meet me. A wave of desire crested over me, heavy and alluring, and I reveled in the pleasure it promised.

"Ahem."

Rhan startled at the sound of Phaedra behind me, but I did not release her. Instead my lips moved from her breast to her lips and I kissed her lingeringly. "Later," I whispered as she shivered.

I dressed quickly and Phaedra hastily combed my tousled hair and braided it into a single thick plait. Then, while she helped Rhan dress, I joined my lead warriors, who were already in the middle of a lively discussion about some kind of contest.

"Contest?" I asked as I sat at my usual place across from Maldwyn. I smiled and nodded to him, finding it interesting that the night I'd spent with Rhan had not diminished the attraction I felt for him.

Actually, my body was extra sensitive and it was easy to imagine his rough hands on my naked hips as he slid into me.

"Aye!" Cadoc boomed. "And it is an excellent idea, my queen."

"Aye," agreed Abertha and Maldwyn together, though Maldwyn's gaze on mine sparkled with more than just amusement over a contest.

Wulffaed filled my mug with rich winter beer, which I decided was a better choice than more of her heady mulled mead. I was ravenous and spooned several fried fish and a hunk of warm bread onto the wooden plate waiting for me. Around a mouthful, I said, "What is this contest you're discussing?"

"One between the chiefs *and queen*." Cadoc waggled his bushy gray brows. "We know who will win such a contest."

I swallowed quickly. "Me?"

"Of course you!" Briallen said as she reached for another fish.

I looked at each of my lead warriors. "I still don't know what you're talking about."

"Adminius started it with his boasting," said Wulffaed as she placed a full pitcher of beer on the table.

"Does everyone in camp know about this except me?" I asked.

"And me," Rhan said as she sat in the space beside me, the decorative pebbles I'd braided into her hair clicking musically.

"Tribe Trinovantes has issued a challenge," said Maldwyn. "They boast that no other chief can best Addedomaros in a contest of speed."

"Speed? Like a horse race?" I frowned at my warriors. "The Trinovantes have the fastest horses. What makes you think I can beat him?"

Cadoc snorted a laugh. "Because young Adminius was brash enough to be baited into more than just a horse race. The challenge is now a test of battle skills as well as a footrace that *concludes* with a horse race, and the Trinovantes' pup has wagered one of their prime broodmares, heavy with a foal out of Addedomaros's own stallion, as a prize."

I sat up straighter and grinned. "I can beat all three chiefs in a footrace."

"As well we know," said Abertha happily.

"You will accept the challenge?" asked Briallen.

"Of course she will!" said Cadoc. "Our queen will accept *and* win."

"I'll accept." That morning I felt as if I could do anything. "I want that mare and her foal."

"Aye!" Looking like an excited boy, Maldwyn rubbed his hands together gleefully at just the thought of such spectacular horseflesh.

"What prize are we wagering?" I asked.

"Does it matter? You will not lose," said Cadoc.

"Your faith in me is appreciated, but it does matter," I said.

"What if you wager a length of Wulffaed's finest cloth? She is revered in all the tribes for her dye work," said Rhan.

My gaze went to the Mother of Twenty, who seemed to swell with pride. "Wager it, my queen, though I do not plan on losing it."

"Have Comux and Leofric accepted the challenge yet?" I asked.

"Leofric has," said Abertha. "He has wagered one of their prize Catuvellauni bulls."

"Comux has not answered the challenge yet," said Cadoc, the amusement draining from his voice. "He mourns his wife and daughter."

"When the Dobunni chief hears that Boudicca has accepted the challenge, he will, too," said Briallen. "And that will be a good thing."

Cadoc nodded soberly. "Comux's camp feels heavy with sadness. Not even Arianell's Day lifted the pall of gloom that hangs over them."

"Though it helped," Abertha said with a smile. "It helped the whole camp. I've missed those days with your mother and the other elders."

"Yesterday was special." As I spoke, my gaze went to Rhan and we shared an intimate smile. When I looked from her to Maldwyn I saw that he was watching us, his cheeks pink and his expression guarded. I met his gaze steadily and included him in the warmth of my smile, and saw the worry lines that creased his eyes smooth as he relaxed. "So, explain to me exactly what I must do to win this contest."

❖

The training field was a huge oblong area. It needed to be huge to accommodate our thousands of warriors. It was situated in the middle of the valley, the area that was least protected against the elements by the giants that framed our home. By now, the middle of winter, it took daily effort to keep the enormous field free enough of snow that the army could train, which was good. An idle army was a dangerous thing, but between plowing the training field, drilling, gathering peat, and caring for the extensive herds we'd brought with us, our warriors were being kept active and engaged.

"There is where you will begin." Maldwyn pointed to the distant end of the field that was closest to the snow-packed entrance to the valley.

"See how they're already building the tournament course?" Cadoc gestured to the warriors who were setting four rows of straw targets about midway in the field.

"Oh, now it's not simply a race or a contest but a tournament?" I raised a brow at my shield.

The old warrior grinned at me. "Aye, my queen! When the Catu-vellauni chief accepted the challenge, it became a tournament."

I put my fists on my hips. "Well, one of you better explain what you've gotten me into."

"Here's what has come from Adminius and his boasting," said Maldwyn. "The beginning is a footrace to there." He pointed to a spot about a third of the way up the field, where the warriors were setting four rows of straw targets. "Where your chariot will be waiting. You'll weave your chariot around six targets, striking each."

"And you will be driving my chariot?" I asked Maldwyn.

Cadoc snorted. "No. Adminius boasted that his father was the best chariot driver of all the tribes, so each chief—"

"And our queen," Maldwyn added.

"Of course," Cadoc said, nodding. "Each will have to drive their own chariot *and* strike the six targets."

I shrugged. "I can do that."

"With more accuracy than Addedomaros," added Maldwyn.

"Aye!" Cadoc agreed.

"It was foolish of Adminius to boast about something so easily disproven," I said. "Maldwyn is by far the best chariot driver in all the tribes."

"He is indeed," said Cadoc.

Maldwyn's cheeks flushed, but he nodded. My horse master's skills were no secret.

"So we conclude the contest with a chariot race?" I asked.

"No," said Cadoc. "After you strike all of the targets, you'll leave your team at the end of the row and race on foot again to there, where your horse will be waiting." He pointed at the other end of the field. "You'll mount, and it's a horse race all the way back across the field to the starting line, which will also be the finish."

I grinned. "Two footraces. That is very good for me." I shook my head. "I can't imagine what Adminius was thinking. Does he really not know how fast I am and how much older and slower his father is?"

"I do not believe Adminius pays attention to anything except himself," said Maldwyn.

"When his boasting became offensive, Mailcun tried to quiet Adminius," said Cadoc. "But the foolish pup wouldn't listen to his father's shield. Instead he kept blustering and making outlandish claims."

"Like Addedomaros being the best chariot driver in all the tribes," I said sardonically.

"Exactly," said Cadoc.

"You were there, weren't you?" I asked my shield.

The old warrior didn't even attempt to hide his grin. "I was indeed. Which is why the Iceni was the first tribe to accept the Trinovantes challenge."

"Oh, so I accepted before I accepted?"

Cadoc did manage to look a little chagrined. "Would you really have stood by and let that spoiled boy spout lies?"

"No, I don't suppose I would have. I am surprised his father didn't step in and put an end to it, though."

"Addedomaros wasn't present," explained Cadoc. "By the time Mailcun had fetched him, Leofric had accepted the challenge as well."

"And Addedomaros couldn't back out without looking cowardly," I said.

"Aye," said Maldwyn. Then he shrugged and smiled. "The tournament will be good for the army. It will give each tribe something to cheer about."

"And all will cheer when the queen who leads the army wins," said Cadoc firmly.

Abertha jogged up to us, her face flushed. "Comux has just accepted the challenge!"

Maldwyn and Cadoc shouted and clapped each other on their backs like youths.

"What is he wagering?" I asked.

"A barrel of Roman wine he pillaged from Verulamium," said Abertha.

I was unable to hide my smile. "I look forward to toasting my victory with Roman wine."

"Yes!" Abertha's fist shot skyward.

"I prefer Wulffaed's mulled mead, but I will make an exception," said Cadoc, his eyes sparkling mischievously.

"When is the tournament?" I asked.

"Tomorrow," said Cadoc. He glanced at the low gray sky. "Though I'm afraid the weather is going to be miserable."

With a sly grin I said, "Then it is good that I am the only chief who's young enough that my joints won't be affected by the cold and wet." I turned to Maldwyn. "Walk the course with me and let's discuss horses."

"Always a pleasure, my queen," said Maldwyn.

"And I'll go be sure no Trinovantes bastard sets your targets incorrectly," said Cadoc.

"I'll get the queen's armor ready," said Abertha. "Queen Boudicca, will you be using your spear or bow for the targets?"

"My spear," I said. "It would be too awkward to drive the chariot and shoot a bow."

"Aye," said Maldwyn. "Good choice."

As my shield and spear master hurried off muttering to themselves,

Maldwyn said, "Perhaps seeing his father thoroughly beaten will temper Adminius and his boasting."

Sounding much like my shield, I snorted.

"You're sure I can't talk you into changing mounts?" Maldwyn asked for the third time.

We'd walked the racecourse and then circled around to our herd. Ennis and Finley were in fine flesh. Maldwyn proclaimed them ready for the tournament. Then I'd called Tân to me. I noted that she, too, looked ready to run, which is when Maldwyn objected. It wasn't that my mare wasn't fit, but that stallions are larger and usually swifter than mares. The other chiefs would almost certainly be riding stallions, and Maldwyn thought I should be, too.

"I'm sure." I caressed Tân's flank. Her winter coat was thick and a lighter red than her sleek summer coat. She reminded me of a fox, and I laughed when she nuzzled me. "Stallions *are* bigger and faster, and they need to be if they're going to carry the weight of the other chiefs. Maldwyn, I'm tall, but I'm also lean. I weight several stones less than even Comux, who is the smallest of the three chiefs."

Maldwyn sighed and nodded. "You do have a point. The weight of the chiefs will be an equalizer."

"It's about more than just weight and speed. You saw the icy patches and the roughness of the training field. Racing over that ground will be treacherous and I'll need a horse I trust completely." I patted Tân's soft muzzle. "That is Tân. She'll keep me safe and bring me across the finish line victorious."

"I cannot argue with one who knows victory so well," said Maldwyn.

I smiled up into his eyes and took his hand. I knew I needed to talk with him, and the sooner the better. The last thing I wanted was for jealousy to fester between us. "Maldwyn, Rhan and I have become lovers."

He did not look away as he nodded. "Yes. I thought so. What does that mean for us?"

I answered him with the honesty he deserved. "My heart is big enough to love the both of you, so my preference is that it change nothing between us, but that is not up to me. A queen who tries to command love is doomed to fail. It is your decision whether you continue to welcome me to your bed—and I mean me, Boudicca, and not your queen."

Maldwyn cupped my cheek with his hand. "I could never turn from you, not the queen and not the woman. I am yours completely any way you will have me."

I stepped into his arms and let my kiss be my reply.

Maldwyn remained with the herd, insisting he check and recheck the chariot and harnesses for tomorrow's race, so I walked alone through camp back to my cave lodge.

"The goddess be with you tomorrow, Queen Boudicca!"

"Aye, we'll be cheering you on."

"Show those chiefs what a warrior queen can do!"

My people waved and shouted encouragement to me as I passed campfires burning brightly. I paused frequently, accepting a cup of mead at one fire, a steaming chicken thigh at another, and a hunk of roasted pork at yet another. By the time I made it to my lodge, it was dark and I was sated and warmed by the enthusiasm of the Iceni.

Rhan was seated before the central fire, working black raven feathers into an elaborate silver necklace. She looked up as I entered, and her smile lit the room.

"There you are!" said Wulffaed. "Your girls have already eaten and just took themselves and their wolves off to bed. Shall I bring you a plate of stew and bread?"

"No, I ate with the army. You may retire for the night, Wulffaed."

The older woman bowed. Before she left the room she looked over her shoulder and grinned at me. "Teach those chiefs a thing or two tomorrow, my queen."

"I shall." Then I called, "Phaedra?"

Phaedra's head popped out of the blanket that curtained her small room from the rest of the lodge. "My queen?"

354 P. C. CAST

"I'd like a bath."

"Of course, my queen." Phaedra bustled around the lodge collecting cauldrons before she called for several of Wulffaed's daughters to help her fetch water to warm. While I waited, I sat beside Rhan, content to watch her long, slender fingers expertly wrap the raven feathers with silver.

"Are you nervous about the race tomorrow?" she asked without looking up from her work.

"No. I'm looking forward to it."

"You're riding Tân." She didn't frame it as a question, but I answered.

"Yes." I paused and added, "How did you know?"

"It's the right choice. You trust her. She trusts you."

"Exactly," I said.

"My queen, your bath is ready," called Phaedra from my bedchamber.

I stood and held my hand out to Rhan. She looked up from her work then, smiled, and placed it on the stool beside her chair before she took my hand. Fingers entwined like silver and feathers, we retired to my bedchamber and the copper tub that was just big enough for two.

CHAPTER XXXVI

The next morning the low gray sky spit a stinging mixture of snow and ice, but the crowd that framed the training field was in such high spirits that they brightened the gloomy day.

Though I chose to go into battle with my hair unbound, I'd taken one look at the sky and had Phaedra braid the mass of it back away from my face. I'd awakened to an empty bed. After I'd dressed in the beautifully dyed leathers Wulffaed had made for me, I understood why Rhan had not slept beside me. When I joined her in the main room of the lodge to break my fast, she presented me with the exquisite silver necklace dressed in feathers she'd spent the night completing. It rested just above my collarbone under the thick golden torque I never removed. The silver caught even the wan light of the winter morning, and the feathers rustled like they were living things—and whenever I touched them I felt the presence of my goddess.

"Ah, Boudicca! I thought for a moment you might choose not to leave the warmth of your bed today," shouted Addedomaros as I joined him and the other two chiefs at the starting line of our race.

I smiled at the Trinovantes chief, pleased that he was in good humor, even though it was his son's bragging that had gotten him into a race that he must have known he would be hard-pressed to win.

"How are those old joints today, Addedomaros?" I asked with exaggerated concern.

"Do you insult my father?" Adminius thrust out his chest and glared at me.

Addedomaros cuffed the back of his son's head. "Enough! Make yourself useful and go hold Black. Try to keep him calm so he doesn't work himself into a lather before his part of the race begins."

Adminius threw me a narrow-eyed look but stalked away toward the far end of the course, where our mounts would be held until the last leg of the contest.

"Well, I don't know about Addedomaros, but I'm not ashamed to admit that my old bones are feeling the damp and chill today," said Leofric, who was stretching and jogging in place, as if to keep his muscles limber.

"What about you, Comux?" I asked the Dobunni chief, who was closest to my age of the three men.

Comux barked a laugh, which sounded gravelly. He was pale, and the dark circles under his eyes were puffy and bruised, but his smile was authentic. "The Dobunni are used to the chill of winter. This is but a refreshing morning to me."

We all chuckled at that, and then Rhan, who had been chosen to open the race, lifted her arm, motioning for us to take our places at the starting line. Earlier, we'd drawn lots for our positions. Addedomaros was in the first lane. I was next, with Comux beside me and then Leofric to his right. As I took my position, I had time to stretch, shake out my legs, and ready myself. Maldwyn was holding Ennis and Finley just before the man-sized straw targets about one-third of the way up the big practice field. Beyond them I could just make out Tân's red coat where she waited for me, held by Cadoc.

"Chiefs and queen, ready yourselves!" Rhan called. "When I drop my arm, the contest begins."

Rhan met my gaze, grinned, and then, with a dramatic flourish, dropped her arm.

I sprinted forward as the army cheered, but I shut them out, concentrating only on the field directly before me, which was rough with frozen ruts, black ice, and hunks of dirty snow. Within just a few feet I relaxed my upper body as my stride lengthened. I'd been training regularly, but it had been a long time since I'd felt the freedom of pushing my speed to the limit. In an instant I was transported to my familiar forest. The frozen ruts became roots of ancient oaks, and mounds of dirty snow turned to rocks and fallen limbs. I seemed to fly and was a little disappointed when I reached Maldwyn and the chariot.

"You are in the lead," Maldwyn said quickly as I leaped into the cart, wrapped the reins around my left hand and forearm, and lifted the first spear. "Comux is a chariot length behind you. Leofric and Addedomaros are another two lengths behind him, but do not underestimate them—especially Addedomaros—and do not look back. Go, my queen!"

I didn't look back.

"Hup!" I called to the familiar team of horses, and they surged forward. I controlled them, but only just. Ennis and Finley were eager to run and I wished I could give them their heads, but if I did so I would not be able to weave them through the six targets—and crossing the finish line without following the rules of the tournament would not be a true win. I also had to consider the rough ground. There was an especially deep rut of frozen dirt that ran the width of the space between our first two targets. Had I charged the team over that rut at full speed, the chariot could have been thrown into the air. So I held the eager team in check and threw my first and second spears before I noticed the other teams.

As I reached for my third spear, I saw Comux on my right, now less than a chariot length behind me. I threw the spear, hit the target, and as I lifted the fourth spear I caught a glimpse of Leofric on my far right. He had not caught Comux or me, but he also had not lost any ground.

When I lifted my fifth spear, Addedomaros suddenly flashed into my peripheral vision on my left. I could tell that he was closer than Leofric, and as I threw my sixth spear and then pulled Ennis and Finley to a halt beside Abertha, the Trinovantes chief caught up to and passed Comux.

"Run, my queen!" shouted Abertha with a feral grin.

I jumped from the cart and sprinted forward, breathing deeply and quickly and sending every bit of strength I had into my legs. Ahead of me I could hear the huge Trinovantes stallion snorting, more dragon than horse, though I kept my gaze shifting between the rough ground over which I ran and Tân, who waited quietly beside Cadoc, ears pricked toward me as I raced to her.

I reached her ahead of the chiefs. Cadoc's hands formed a basket into which I placed my left foot and he easily boosted me atop Tân.

"For the Iceni!" Cadoc shouted.

As the other chiefs raced up to their mounts, I leaned forward, dug my heels into Tân's flanks, and screamed the Iceni war cry as my brilliant mare exploded into motion. Unlike with the chariot team, I did not even attempt to hold Tân back. I knew my mare. She would not foolishly endanger us by ignoring the rough footing, and as we raced back along the path I'd so recently come down, she proved my confidence in her by jumping over blackened mounds of snow and avoiding spots of black ice.

I had time to look over my left shoulder to see that Comux and Leofric were neck and neck several lengths behind me. They didn't seem to be gaining ground. I did not have to glance over my right shoulder. Even above the roar of the army and the sting of the sleet, I could hear the pounding hooves of Black. His dark muzzle came into view, then the rest of his head and neck.

I grabbed a fist of Tân's mane and leaned closer to her neck. Her ears were flattened against her head as I encouraged her to give more. From deep within, my mare found a reservoir of speed, and Black stopped gaining ground. I heard Addedomaros shout and from the corner of my eye saw that he, too, was low over his stallion's neck as the massive horse's stride lengthened.

We'd passed the majority of the straw targets. I could see the finish line where Rhan stood, arm lifted again, ready to drop it when the winner raced past. *Just a little more! We're almost there!* I shouted the Iceni war cry but realized Tân had slowed as Black's muzzle came into view to my right again. He was definitely not slowing.

I almost dug my heels into Tân to insist she give me more speed, and then I remembered the roughness of the trenchlike width of the frozen, broken ground and did not ask my mare for more. As I understood why Tân slowed, I heard a horrible sound, and suddenly Black was no longer in my peripheral vision.

Instantly I pulled Tân up as I turned to see Black fall. I'd watched horses go down in battle—we all had. It is terrible and tragic. The unearthly shriek Black made as his front left hoof hit the ridge of the broken ground echoed throughout the valley. The tremendous speed at which he was going caused his cannon bone to snap like a piece of kindling. Black crumpled, head over rear end, throwing Addedomaros onto the unforgiving ground. The massive stallion rolled over the Trinovantes chief before the horse slid to a stop several feet away.

A great silence fell over the watching army as I vaulted from Tân's back and ran to the fallen chief.

Blood trickled from Addedomaros's mouth. He lay on his back. His thick, muscular body was flattened. Blood had begun to seep through his clothes, staining the snow around him bright scarlet. I went to my knees beside him and his eyes immediately met mine. I was surprised by the clarity in them.

His bloody lips twitched as he tried to smile. He coughed, spewing reddened froth down his chin. "Did I win?" He whispered the words.

I used the sleeve of my tunic to wipe the bloody sputum from his face and smiled. "Of course you won. No one can beat you and that stallion."

"Yes, Black and I . . ." He smiled, exhaled a rattling breath, and did not take another.

Gently, I closed his eyelids and bowed my head as I rested my hand on his broken chest. "May you feast with your ancestors and know only eternal joy."

"Father! Father!" Adminius shouted as he ran to us.

I stood and moved aside so he could kneel by his father's body. Dazed, I looked up to see that Leofric was with Black. The stallion had somehow managed to stand. It was a terrible thing to see, as his front leg was useless, snapped completely in two. Only skin held it together. The Catuvellauni chief met my gaze and shook his head. He turned back to the stallion, attempting to calm him.

Comux joined me beside Addedomaros's body. "Stay here with Adminius. I must get Maldwyn to deal with the stallion." I hurried toward where Tân stood as Maldwyn, driving our chariot, thundered up. He looked at Addedomaros and Adminius, who was shaking his father's shoulder as he called his name over and over. His gaze went to me. I shook my head. Grimly, he jogged to where Leofric was still struggling with the wounded stallion.

Maldwyn went to the big horse's head. He took it between his hands. I couldn't hear what he said, though I saw his lips move and watched as the stallion stopped fighting and stood, trembling, on three legs. Maldwyn continued to speak softly to the stallion and stroke him as he draped an arm around the horse's neck. He pulled a dagger from a sheath at his waist and in one swift motion slit Black's throat. With a grunt and a sigh, the stallion dropped to the ground and lay still in an expanding pool of steaming scarlet.

Rhan was suddenly there with Cadoc and Mailcun. She came to me before she approached her brother and father.

"Is he dead?" she asked.

I nodded and rested my hand on her shoulder. "I'm so sorry. It was fast. He did not suffer."

She blew out a long breath and then went to crouch beside her brother, who was still shaking his father, as if trying to wake him.

"Adminius, Father is gone," said Rhan.

Her brother turned his face to her. "No. He can't be. This—this was just supposed to be a friendly competition. Something to show everyone the greatness of Tribe Trinovantes and the might of our chief. No one was going to die."

"It was an accident." Rhan spoke slowly.

"No," insisted Adminius, who went back to shaking his father's slack shoulder. "Father, you must get up. Now!"

Mailcun moved around Rhan to Adminius's other side, where he crouched so he could look into his face. "Adminius, he is gone. The Chief's Guard is bringing a litter so that Addedomaros can be readied for his journey to Annwn."

"No!" Adminius flung himself on his father's bloody body. "He cannot be burned! He's going to wake!"

Mailcun looked up at me. His eyes were filled with tears. Rhan stood and backed away from her brother, shaking her head. I could see that Addedomaros's Chief's Guard had entered the field and carried a litter between them. My guard had spread out across the field and had been joined by the lead warriors of the Dobunni and Catuvel-launi, ready to keep us from being overwhelmed if the Trinovantes tried rushing to their fallen chief, though the crowd remained sub-dued, watching silently. I knelt beside Adminius and wrapped my arm around his shoulder.

"Adminius, your father is gone. Tribe Trinovantes will look to you for stability. You must be strong for them."

He turned his tear-and-blood-streaked face to me. "This is my fault."

I shook my head. "No one is to blame for what happened today. It was a terrible accident. Your father spoke to me before he died. He asked if he'd won the contest and I told him he had."

Adminius laughed, though it was a sad, broken sound. "He be-lieved he'd won?"

I smiled and tightened my grip on his shoulders. "He did, which began his journey to Annwn with a smile."

"That is good. That is good," he murmured.

The Trinovantes Chief's Guard arrived and stood quietly waiting. I wiped Adminius's face as I'd so recently cleaned his father's. He seemed very childlike, suddenly reminding me of how grief-stricken my daughters had been by the death of their father. "Come, Adminius." Gently I guided him to his feet. "I will escort you and your father to his chamber." My gaze went to Rhan. "Your sister will join us. She and I will help you prepare Addedomaros for his pyre."

"Y-yes." Adminius nodded shakily. "Stay with me. Please?"

"Of course."

The crowd parted as our somber procession moved slowly from the field to the cave Addedomaros had made his lodge. It wasn't as spacious as mine but every bit as well appointed. The guard carefully placed the litter holding their dead chief on the table. We had only been there long enough to begin heating herbed water to cleanse the chief's body when Wulffaed and half a dozen of her daughters poured into the chamber, bringing oils and clean strips of cloth. Adara, our healer, was with them. One look at Adminius, who was slumped in his father's thronelike chair with silent tears slipping down his cheeks, and she began brewing a tea. Its scent told me that it was a sleeping potion and I breathed a sigh of relief when Adminius gulped it down. As his head began to bob and his eyes close, I again put my arm around his shoulders and guided him to his father's sumptuous bed pallet in the rear of the chamber. Before I could walk away from him, he grabbed my wrist.

"You are very kind," Adminius rasped.

I patted his hand. "Sleep. Your tribe needs you clearheaded and strong."

CHAPTER XXXVII

I hadn't realized how much time had passed while I helped Rhan, Wulffaed, and her skilled daughters prepare Addedomaros until Cadoc and Mailcun joined us, proclaiming that the pyre had been built in the center of the field.

I nodded wearily. "Thank you, Cadoc and Mailcun. Has the stallion been added to the pyre?"

Cadoc's nod was tight. "Yes. Maldwyn readied the stallion."

Mailcun ran a hand through his graying hair. "Your horse master even painted Black's coat with our tribal symbols and braided his mane and tail."

"That is as it should be. Black will join Addedomaros in Annwn." It was then that I rolled my aching shoulders, glanced toward the mouth of the cave, and realized it was fully dark. "I will have our fattest boar slaughtered and the choice cuts added to the pyre, which we will light tomorrow at dusk." I looked to the Trinovantes shield. With Adminius drugged into a deep sleep, he was the ranking tribal member. "It would be my honor to host the feast after the lighting of the pyre, if that is acceptable to you."

"It is." Mailcun nodded. "Addedomaros would appreciate the fact that his feast meal was prepared by his favorite cook, the Mother of Twenty."

Wulffaed's face flushed with pleasure. "And a grand feast it will be," she said.

"Wulffaed, if Queen Boudicca agrees, you and your daughters may go begin preparing for the feast," said Rhan from her place at the head of the chief's body. "All that is left to do here is to paint my father's body and braid his hair. I can tend to that."

"Yes, of course," I said. "Wulffaed, you and your daughters may go, and thank you."

As the women filed out, Mailcun cleared his throat. "Rhan, I would like to stay and aid in the last of the preparations for my chief." His gaze went to Addedomaros's still body. "I have spent more years by his side than not. I will miss him greatly."

"My father would approve," Rhan said.

Mailcun breathed out a long sigh of relief and joined Rhan, helping her mix the wooden bowls of body paint.

"Queen Boudicca." Cadoc spoke my name softly. I wiped the herbal oils from my hands and went to my shield. "It is Maldwyn. I worry for him. Ending Black's pain was difficult but the right thing to do."

"Of course it was. Had Maldwyn not done it, the Trinovantes horse master would have. It was fortunate Maldwyn was there so swiftly. His touch calmed Black and allowed the killing blow to be gentle," I said.

Cadoc nodded. "I agree, but Maldwyn is young. Outside of battle injuries, this is the first healthy stallion he has had to put down. He is not taking it well, my queen."

"Thank you for telling me." I touched my shield's arm. "I will see to Maldwyn."

Cadoc bowed to me before the icy darkness outside the cave swallowed him. As I turned to rejoin Rhan and Mailcun, my best friend and lover was there beside me.

"Go to Maldwyn. You should be with him tonight. He needs you," said Rhan.

"And you?" I asked.

"I will finish preparing my father and then sit vigil with his body. I do not feel his spirit strongly. It is as if he has already begun his journey to Annwn, but I will be here to guide him if he loses his way."

I lowered my voice for Rhan's ears alone. "I do not wish to cause you any more pain today."

She looked steadily at me. "You going to Maldwyn's bed does not cause me pain. He is a good man and an honorable warrior. There is a vast kindness about him. And Maldwyn makes you happy. I wish for you to be happy. What we have together will not be diluted by your love for him."

"No, it will not be." I touched her cheek gently. "I am not sure I would be so generous if you were to choose another lover."

"There is no other lover for me, nor will there ever be," she said.

I pulled Rhan into my arms and held her close.

While I bathed, Wulffaed prepared a basket of food and winter beer, and as soon as I was dressed I hurried to Maldwyn's caravan, which butted up to the side of the mountain closest to our herd. I'd gone to his caravan before—I'd even spent the night in his bed there and was used to the soothing sounds of the nearby horses and the usually raucous stable workers, who shared a big central campfire with Maldwyn and liked to sing battle songs and drink well into the night.

Tonight the camp was subdued, most especially Tribe Trinovantes, the bulk of whom sheltered near the herds. The sleet had changed to an unending blanket of falling white. The hood of my heavy, fur-lined cloak was pulled up over my head to shield me from the weather. It and the snow also made it difficult to tell that I wasn't just another warrior making her way to her campfire on this somber night. I was glad for my temporary anonymity. Not because I had any desire to hide the fact that Maldwyn and I were lovers—I'd never hidden that, nor would I. That night I was weighed down by sadness and I needed solitude to gather my thoughts. Addedomaros and I hadn't always been in agreement, but his death was a shock. I would miss the cantankerous old chief.

When I reached Maldwyn's caravan, he did not notice me. He was sitting alone on a log near the big community campfire, sheltered from the majority of the snow by animal hides stretched from one caravan to another. His head was bowed and he stared into the fire. He looked defeated and far older than he had that morning. I tossed back my hood and strode to him. He finally looked up. I saw the surprise in his eyes, which were red and swollen. When he started to stand I pressed his shoulder down and sat beside him instead, and began unwrapping food from my basket.

"Wulffaed packed this for us," I said.

He cleared his throat and then said, "You have not eaten?"

"Not since this morning. I've been with Rhan preparing Adde-domaros."

Maldwyn grunted and nodded. We ate silently, staring into the fire and sitting so close together that our thighs touched. I hadn't realized how hungry I'd been until I'd taken the first bite, and Maldwyn must have felt the same, as we ate quickly and ravenously. I pulled out the bladder filled with beer and we passed it back and forth. After we'd finished the food, I felt better, more grounded, and continued to sip the beer when it was my turn.

"Cadoc tells me you made sure Black was properly prepared and part of the pyre," I said. "I'm glad of it."

"Killing that stallion was . . ." His voice faded as a shiver passed through his body.

"It was a great mercy," I said. "You soothed Black and stopped him from panicking and causing himself more pain."

Maldwyn looked at me then. His eyes were tortured. "That stallion made it through three major battles with little more than scratches. He should have had years left, siring magnificent offspring and proudly carrying his chief." His breath hitched on a sob then, and he buried his face in his hands. "I-I don't know why this has broken me. You and I have seen much worse on the battlefield."

"Maldwyn, you're responding to the tragedy of it. The accident shouldn't have happened at all. In battle we're prepared to die and to lose the warriors with us, which includes the warriors that carry us into the fight." I slid my arm around his broad shoulders and he leaned into me. "Today was supposed to have been a contest among friends. It should have ended in a feast where one of us celebrated and the other three conceded defeat graciously, not in the loss of a great chief and his most cherished stallion." I held him tightly. "None of us was prepared for that."

He nodded, sighed, and wiped his face. "How is Adminius?"

"Adara drugged him. He's been asleep since we began preparing his father's body."

"And what of Rhan? He was her father, too," said Maldwyn.

"She and Mailcun are still with Addedomaros. She will sit vigil with him tonight. I do not think she has had time to consider the true impact of her loss yet." I sighed. "That will come later, after the Trinovantes choose Adminius as their chief."

"If they do," said Maldwyn.

"What have you heard?"

"That Adminius is not respected by his tribe," said Maldwyn.

I shook my head, not surprised by Maldwyn's words. "A tribe will never choose a chief they do not respect."

"I did not hear one Trinovantes warrior speak the words *chief* and *Adminius* together today."

"Do they blame Adminius for his father's death?" I asked.

"Yes and no. They acknowledge that it was an accident, but the whole army knows the accident only happened because Adminius's boasting goaded Addedomaros into the contest." Maldwyn shook his head in disgust. "What a waste of life."

I nodded. "We light the pyre tomorrow at dusk. I'm hosting the funeral feast."

"That would make the old chief smile. He liked you," said Maldwyn.

I sighed. "He often reminded me of my father. I will miss verbally jousting with him."

Maldwyn almost smiled. "Is it true he thought he won the contest?"

I did smile. "Just before he died, he asked me if he'd won and I told him yes."

"You would have won," said Maldwyn.

"I know." I stood and held out my hand to him. "Come." I led Maldwyn to his caravan and the bed pallet there that was piled thick with pelts and blankets.

That night Maldwyn made love to me with a tenderness I shall never forget. I shall also never forget how he woke from a nightmare before dawn, weeping and whispering the stallion's name. I held him until, utterly spent, he finally slept deeply and dreamlessly.

I thought the lighting of Addedomaros's pyre would flood me with memories of saying goodbye to my mother, but it did not. Though both were tragic, the chief's death was so different from what had happened in Tasceni that I had no difficulty keeping the two separate. The pyre was just large enough to hold the bodies of Addedomaros and his stallion and the rich offerings his tribe sent with him to Annwn.

Rhan led the funeral, embracing her role as high Druid. The pyre was small enough that Adminius had only to step to it and light it with a torch, instead of shooting a fiery arrow into it, but he was still so filled with grief and, I suspected, guilt that he almost dropped the torch. I was standing close by and quickly steadied him. As the pyre lit, Adminius wept so brokenly that I began wishing I hadn't offered to host the funeral feast. I was relieved when he, his lead warriors, and his father's guard entered my cave lodge clear-eyed, with Adminius seemingly in control of his emotions.

As my temporary lodge wasn't nearly as spacious as the Iceni royal home at Tasceni, there were considerably fewer warriors in attendance than there would normally be at a funeral feast for a chief. I had made sure several fat Iceni boars and goats had been slaughtered and gifted to the Trinovantes camp. It was still snowing, but cook fires lit the valley like giant glowworms, and the cold breeze was scented with roasting meat.

As I had no table long enough to accommodate Adminius and his warriors as well as my people, I'd had Wulffaed position four tables in a large square. I sat in the middle of one table, with Cadoc on my left and Maldwyn and Abertha beside him. To my right Rhan took the position of honor that was rightfully hers as high Druid. Beside her sat Adara, our only other Druid, and then Briallen. The two other tables that made up the square were populated by Comux, Leofric, and their lead warriors.

Wulffaed and her daughters served us. The group was mostly silent, which was unusual for a funeral feast. Even after the lighting of the pyre that held my mother and so many of our elders, the feast had been punctuated by stories of those who had journeyed to Annwn and laughter mixed with tears.

I cleared my throat and stood with my cup of Wulffaed's mulled mead in my hand. "Addedomaros often vexed me with his stubbornness and his belief that he was never wrong." I grinned to take any bite from my words and was glad when Mailcun smiled and nodded. "But I will miss our verbal sparring. I will also miss his big, booming laugh, which reminded me of my father. I can easily imagine Addedomaros, as young as he was when I fostered in his household all those years ago, sitting beside his beloved wife at Epona's table, drinking and making merry in Annwn this very night. To Addedomaros, who was well loved and will be well missed!" When I raised my mug, shouts of *"Aye, to Addedomaros!"* echoed from the cave's walls.

As I sat, Mailcun stood. The shield looked pale. His eyes, usually clear and expressive, were red and weary, but his smile was genuine when he lifted his mug. "I do not know if everyone here has heard, but our chief's last words were . . ." Mailcun met my gaze and lifted his brows.

"'Did I win?'" I said.

Mailcun waited until the laughter had faded before he finished. "And Queen Boudicca told our chief that he had, indeed, won the contest, sending him to the arms of Epona joyous with victory. To Addedomaros, who truly believed he could never be bested in any kind of race that included Trinovantes horseflesh!" As he drank, the room exploded in ayes and fists pounding tables.

That lightened the mood—until Adminius stood. The young man looked terrible. His face had aged decades in one day. His skin was sallow and loose. His eyes were puffy. He was, of course, wearing his best finery, and his hair had been combed and carefully pulled back and braided, but somehow he still was bedraggled and small. Carefully, I kept my eyes from Adminius's neck, which was bare of the torque that would have proclaimed him chief of Tribe Trinovantes.

Beside me I felt Rhan stiffen.

Adminius raised his mug to me. "First, I would like to thank

Queen Boudicca for her hospitality. She has proven herself not just ally but friend."

I bowed my head slightly in acknowledgment as the room echoed his toast and drank.

"Next, I want to make it official that I will not change the lead warrior choices my father made." Adminius glanced at the men who sat on either side of him, nodding at each of them, though they made no response. Adminius, who seemed oblivious to their silence, continued. "Especially you, shield of the Trinovantes." He nodded to Mailcun. "Your place should always be at the right hand of the chief, thus you will remain there when I wear the torque." Adminius raised his mug again. "To my father, who was victorious in life as in death!"

There was a subdued response to Adminius's toast, and Rhan released a long breath as her brother sat and then leaned close to me to whisper, "I'd hoped he would not force the issue tonight, but as he has, I must speak."

A chill fingered down my spine as Rhan stood, and the room instantly went silent. I knew what was happening. I'd experienced it. Twice. Though the first time differed dramatically from the second. When Prasutagus died, Derwyn presented me with my queen's torque during his funeral feast, *after* Prasutagus's shield and senior warriors had consulted with the high Druid and all had been in agreement that I was to lead the Iceni.

The second time had been unusual, but I had not initiated my naming as a wartime queen. The goddess Andraste had gifted me with Prasutagus's torque. The wearing of a torque is always the decision of the tribe and the high Druid—or of the tribe's patron goddess or god—and never of the prospective chief or queen. I knew why Rhan had stood and what she would say, though the knowing did not make it any easier.

"Adminius, son of Addedomaros, as high Druid it falls to me to tell you that your lead warriors and I have not yet decided who will wear the Trinovantes torque."

Absolute silence followed her words. I felt Cadoc stir beside me to put his hand on the dagger he always wore sheathed around his waist.

The chiefs of the Dobunni and Catuvellauni tensed, as did Mailcun and the other Trinovantes warriors.

My gaze went to Adminius as I, too, readied myself for one of the explosions of temper for which he was so well known.

"Of course! Of course, good sister." Adminius's smile appeared guileless. "Forgive me for speaking of such things too soon. You are correct. Tonight we remember my father. We can discuss the torque and who should wear it later. Wulffaed! I'd like more of your excellent mulled mead. Tonight, I drink not just for myself but for my father—and that is certainly a mighty task."

Wulffaed hurried to fill his mug as the room released a collective sigh of relief. Losing a chief unexpectedly was difficult enough on a tribe, but to lose him and then have to deal with infighting over his torque would be doubly tragic.

The Dobunni chief stood next, telling a story about when he'd traded with Addedomaros for several unbroken yearlings, and now those yearlings had proven to be the swiftest, though most headstrong, horses in their herd—obviously reflecting the attributes of the Trinovantes chief.

Surreptitiously, I watched Adminius as the warriors drank more and more and told story after story about his father. He appeared to be increasingly drunk, slouching and slurring his words, but *he drank almost nothing*. Oh, he seemed to be drinking, and Wulffaed refilled his mug often. Only I noticed that Adminius spilled more mead than he drank, and when he thought no one watched he would tip his mug, pouring it under the table.

I leaned close to Rhan and lowered my voice. "Your brother's drunkenness is a ruse."

Rhan said nothing, but she, too, snuck glances at her brother until she whispered to me, "Beware and be ready."

I nodded, and next time the warriors all laughed at a story Mailcun had told about his chief, I bumped Cadoc's thick leg, drawing the old shield's attention. "Adminius is pretending to be drunk."

Cadoc narrowed his eyes, watching Adminius, before he whispered to me, "Aye, he's up to something."

But nothing happened. The warriors continued to tell stories. Adminius laughed with them, sloshing mead from his mug and pretending to drink.

As the night grew old, the Trinovantes warriors were slurring their words. Some were even snoring with their heads on the tables. I began to relax. They would all leave soon. It could be that Adminius was so grief-stricken that he had no stomach for drink that night and the only ruse he'd planned was to pretend otherwise so that he didn't appear weak to his warriors.

So when Adminius stood for a second time that night, I smiled at him, expecting that he would thank me again and then call the feast to a close.

"Queen Boudicca, again I thank you for the generosity you have shown me," said Adminius.

"Tribe Trinovantes is the Iceni's closest ally. It has been my honor to host the funeral feast of their chief," I said.

"In return I would gift you—gift us all—with something."

I began to assure Adminius no gift was necessary, but he spoke over me.

"Join with me as more than allies. Marry me, Queen Boudicca, and unite Tribe Trinovantes and Tribe Iceni forever."

Again, his words brought stunned silence to the lodge. I felt the shock in the pit of my stomach—along with anger. This was why Adminius needed to appear drunk but actually be clear minded.

I met his gaze and spoke slowly and distinctly. "Adminius, son of Addedomaros, I will never marry again." I stood. "And now I will wish you and your good warriors a peaceful night."

Adminius chuckled and slurred his words. "Of course! Of course! Prasutagus was quite a man—quite a chief. And you are quite a queen. Good night, all!" Adminius staggered and almost fell. Mailcun caught his arm and steadied him, leading him from my lodge. The rest of the Trinovantes warriors bowed respectfully to me as they silently departed, followed by the Dobunni and Catuvellauni.

CHAPTER XXXVIII

When everyone except my lead warriors and Rhan had left the lodge, Cadoc broke the silence. "That Trinovantes pup needs to be muzzled."

Briallen's lip lifted in disgust. "The mead. Adminius was mad with it, but 'tis no excuse for his behavior."

"He wasn't drunk," I said.

"Boudicca is correct," said Rhan.

"Aye," agreed Cadoc. "I watched him, too. He drank almost nothing." The shield went to where Adminius had been sitting and squatted, touching the ground beneath the table. He snorted. "This is where his drink went." He stood and pointed to the slick surface of the table. "And here."

"He pretended to be drunk in case Boudicca turned his proposal down," said Maldwyn, his voice tight with anger. "Tomorrow he can say it was the drink that caused him to speak out."

"How could he have believed that there was any chance that I would accept him?" I said.

"You were kind to him yesterday." Rhan sounded weary. "Today you showed him compassion and respect."

"I didn't show *him* respect! I showed Addedomaros and Tribe Trinovantes respect!" Anger lifted my voice. "And I was kind to him because I know what it is to lose a father."

"To a man like Adminius, everything is always about him," said Briallen, who still sat beside Rhan. "He would believe any woman who showed him kindness also lusted for him."

"Then he is a fool," I said.

"Yes," said his sister. "Which is why only one of the tribe's lead warriors put forward his name for the torque."

"Mailcun," said Briallen.

Rhan raised one brow. "Yes."

I looked at the leader of my Queen's Guard. "Why would Mailcun want Adminius to wear the torque?"

"Because it is what Addedomaros wanted, and Mailcun is loyal to his chief even after his death," said Briallen.

"The others will not choose him," said Maldwyn. "There was more talk today. No one trusts Adminius."

"He has proven himself unfit to lead over and over, beginning when he was just a boy," said Rhan. "Tomorrow after we break our fast I will join the lead warriors of the Trinovantes as they choose another for their chief."

"Will it be you?" I asked. My stomach tightened at the thought and I reminded myself that I would lose Rhan eventually. Should we be victorious against the Romans, she would return to Ynys Môn to rebuild the isle of the Druids. But were she queen of the Trinovantes, Rhan would be closer to Tasceni, and that would actually make seeing her easier.

"No," Rhan said firmly. "I have made it clear to the Trinovantes lead warriors that my life's path has already been chosen. I am a Druid—now high Druid; I cannot also be a queen."

"How much of a problem will Adminius be when another wears the Trinovantes torque?" I asked, more thinking aloud than looking for an answer.

Abertha shook her head. "We cannot know for sure what he will do. What we do know is that he will not be able to fracture Tribe Trinovantes as the Catuvellauni did when royal brothers disagreed over how to deal with the Romans."

"True," said Maldwyn. "Adminius doesn't have enough support to split the tribe."

Cadoc snorted. "That pup has no support. Once the new chief is chosen, Mailcun will swear fealty to him."

"So we watch Adminius and be sure we limit whatever damage he tries to do," I said. "Briallen, tomorrow have my guard take turns shadowing him, but do not make it obvious."

"Aye, my queen," said the warrior, who bowed before she left the lodge.

"We will all be watchful," said Cadoc. "Though there is little he can do except to continue to make a fool of himself. Good night, Queen Boudicca."

"Rest well, my queen," said Abertha.

"May the blessings of the earth be on you," said Maldwyn. He paused, and when I only smiled and wished him a good night, he nodded to Rhan and left.

"I should go, too," said Rhan as she stood.

I took her hand in mine. "Please stay."

I sent Phaedra to bed. Rhan and I helped each other undress and then we snuggled together under the thick pelts, sharing our body heat against the frigid night. As had been her habit when we were girls, Rhan smoothed my hair while we talked, and the stress of the evening was washed away by her touch.

"I still do not understand how Adminius thought making such a public offer of marriage to me would help him," I said. "He is arrogant and foolish, but he had to have at least considered that I might turn him down."

"He is arrogant and foolish, but Adminius is not stupid," said Rhan. "Had your refusal not been so emphatic, he could have dangled the possibility of joining the Iceni and Trinovantes as incentive for his lead warriors to offer him the torque. It is probable that several of them would look favorably on joining the tribes."

"Which means they would look favorably on Adminius." I sighed. "But I said no. Emphatically. And now he can say he was drunk and grieving and not himself."

"Exactly. Though he may try to coax you into a union again."

"No. He will not wear the torque. That means he is simply a young Trinovantes warrior who will not be invited to any war council. After tomorrow there will be no reason for him to have access to me." I touched her face. "It is you who must be careful. He cannot take out his anger on me and he is no match for any lead warrior. He may target you."

"Do not fret, Boudicca. I am the high Druid and well protected." Rhan leaned into me. The stones clattered as her hair formed a curtain around us while she took her time exploring my mouth.

I loved her taste and touch. The passion I felt for Rhan began deep within my spirit, and when I thought of it I realized that it had always been there, first in the form of friendship, and now so much more. Soon we were glad of the cold night as the heat between us slicked our naked bodies and we laughed as we kicked the thick pelts from us. Her softness and heat had me gasping as waves of pleasure built and crested, and then built again.

"You sly whore! Now I know why you rejected me!"

Shock jolted through me at the sound of Adminius's voice. I turned to shield Rhan's naked body as I faced him. "Get out of my lodge. Now."

Though the only light in my bedchamber was from a single candle, I could see Adminius clearly. His face was scarlet and his lips were drawn back, exposing his teeth in a snarl. "Everyone will know that you fuck my sister and the two of you conspire to steal the torque from me! But you won't get away with it!" He moved more quickly than I expected, closing the short distance to my bed. He grabbed my arm, jerking me toward him.

I used the momentum to fly into him. Unbalanced, he stumbled backward, and I easily broke his grip. I lunged past him to the wooden chest that sat at the foot of my bed, wrenched it open, and pulled out the Roman dagger I kept there—the dagger with which I had already ended one traitor's life. My rage boiled over and I was on him. He lurched away from me and drew a dagger from the sheath he wore around his waist. Adminius jabbed it at me, but he was no Cadoc or Maldwyn or Abertha or Briallen. I easily sidestepped and sliced his bicep. He let out a shriek and dropped the dagger. Naked, I drove him from my bedchamber out into the lodge, where the fire burned low, sending ghostly shadows against the tapestries that covered the curved walls.

"You bitch! You cut me!"

With a well-practiced motion I tossed my dagger from my right hand to my left. From a nearby table I grabbed a heavy iron candleholder and hit him across the face with it. He cried out and fell to his knees, pressing a hand against the bloody gash in his cheek. I fisted his hair, pulled back his head, and placed the sharp point of my dagger against his throat.

"Do. Not. Speak," I commanded. "Phaedra!"

Phaedra was rubbing sleep from her eyes as she parted the blanket that served as door to her small bedchamber. And then she froze in shock.

"Get Cadoc."

"Yes, my queen!" Phaedra ran from the lodge.

"Cadoc is not my chief," sneered Adminius.

I pressed the dagger against his neck until it wept a single drop of blood. "I told you not to speak."

A cloak was placed around my bare shoulders and Rhan, fully dressed, moved to stand beside me. She looked down at her brother, who glared up at her with narrowed, hate-filled eyes.

"You would do well to remember that you no longer have Father to hide behind." Rhan's voice was devoid of emotion.

Adminius started to speak, but the pressure from my knife silenced him.

Cadoc burst into the cave lodge, his sword drawn, and skidded to a halt to stare. "What in all the gods is this?" he sputtered.

"I need your sword," I told Cadoc.

My shield did not hesitate. He strode to me and gave me his sword, which I rested in the center of Adminius's chest before taking the dagger from his throat.

I straightened and tossed back my hair. "There. Now I don't have to bend over. Wake Mailcun and the Trinovantes lead warriors. Get them here. Call for Comux and Leofric, as well as my lead warriors. What happens next will be witnessed by all."

"As you ask, so will I do, my queen," said Cadoc. But before he left he jerked his chin at Adminius and added, "Shall I bind him first?"

"No," I said without looking at Adminius. "If he tries to run I will hamstring him."

"She already cut my arm and my face," Adminius squeaked, trying not to move his throat as his eyes beseeched Cadoc.

"Be glad I haven't slit your throat," I told him. "Yet."

Cadoc bowed to me before he jogged from the lodge.

When he was gone, Adminius seemed to deflate. "What now?" he asked me.

"Now you wait. Silently," I said. Phaedra reentered the lodge. "Phaedra, Rhan and I would like mugs of Wulffaed's mead."

"Yes, my queen. Shall I bring you your clothes, too?"

Though the night was frigid, rage warmed me. Naked, I'd bested this warrior easily, and that is something my army would know, would sing of proudly. I met her eyes and smiled fiercely. "No."

It didn't take long for the lead warriors and chiefs to arrive. They poured into the lodge, silent and wide-eyed. I stood in the center of the room. With one hand I held Cadoc's sword against Adminius's chest. With the other I held a mug of mead, which I drained before I tossed the cup to Phaedra. Rhan sat at the table, which wasn't far from me.

Mailcun stepped forward and was instantly shadowed by Cadoc and Maldwyn, whose blue eyes were bright with rage. Briallen and Abertha followed closely behind. No one else approached me.

Mailcun stopped before the still-kneeling Adminius and me. He bowed to me. "Queen Boudicca, what has happened here?"

I lifted my chin and met the loyal shield's gaze steadily. "Adminius broke into my bedchamber. He threatened me. He threatened the high Druid. He put his hands on me and meant me harm. As you can see, he was not successful."

"Mailcun! They are lovers. My sister and the queen. I caught them. They've been plotting all along to take the torque from me so *my sister*"—he spoke the words like they tasted foul—"will be named chief in my place!"

Mailcun blew out a long breath before he lifted his gaze from Adminius to me. "Are you wounded, Queen Boudicca?"

"He does not have the skill to best me," I said.

"You bitch! I should—" Adminius began to hiss at me, but Mailcun struck him across the mouth with the back of his hand, causing blood to well on his bottom lip.

"Enough." Mailcun did not raise his voice, but the command carried the weight of decades of leadership. "You have long been a fool, Adminius. Who the queen takes to her bed is no concern of yours. And the high Druid, your sister, has refused to even be considered for the torque—though I can tell you if she agreed to wear it I would gladly follow her."

"But I—"

"Be silent!" Mailcun said before looking to me again. "What would you do with him, Queen of the Iceni?"

"I would like to know what the chief of the Trinovantes would do with him," I said.

"We have no chief. Not yet," said Mailcun.

I looked past him to the Trinovantes lead warriors, who stood silently, frowning at Adminius. "What say you? Who will wear your torque?"

Ackley, spear master of Tribe Trinovantes, stepped forward. "I say Mailcun should wear the torque."

Mailcun's body jerked, and he turned so that he could face the warriors. He opened his mouth, no doubt to protest, but I placed a hand on his arm and he pressed his lips together.

Next Miburga, the brilliant horse master of the Trinovantes, stepped up beside Ackley. Miburga's mane of sliver-streaked auburn hair hung wild and long to her waist. She was a tall, lean woman who had for two decades led the breeding program that created the swiftest horses in Britain. Her choice was as important as the high Druid's to her tribe. She spoke without even glancing at Adminius.

"I say Mailcun should wear the torque."

Adminius made a sputtering sound, but I pressed the tip of the sword more firmly to his chest and turned my gaze to Rhan. "What say you, high Druid? Do you support the choice of Tribe Trinovantes in naming Mailcun their chief?"

Rhan stood. She walked to Mailcun, opened her hands, palms up, and closed her eyes. Immediately from somewhere outside came the piercing call of a stallion. It echoed against the curved, tapestry-covered walls around us so that it seemed the horse stood beside Mailcun.

Rhan opened her eyes and smiled. "I do, as does Epona."

"The goddess has spoken!" said Miburga. "Mailcun will forever be known as chief of Tribe Trinovantes!"

"Aye!" shouted the warriors.

"What is it you would do with your tribesman?" I asked Mailcun.

Mailcun stared down at Adminius and blew out another long breath before he spoke. "Because of my love for your father, I will not kill you. Nor can I pass that task to any of our people."

Adminius's shoulders sagged in relief.

"Miburga, ready one horse. Fill its packs with supplies."

"As you ask, so will I do," said the Trinovantes horse master.

"Adminius, you are sentenced to banishment," continued Mailcun. "From this day forth you may not enter any lands held by Tribe Trino-vantes. If you do I will not allow the love I had for your father to stay my hand. I will kill you myself."

"But it's the middle of winter. Being sent out there means death!" Adminius sounded like a child arguing with his elders.

"Then that will be the will of the gods." Mailcun turned to me. "I shall take him from you now, Queen Boudicca."

I nodded and stepped back. Mailcun grabbed Adminius's arm and jerked him to his feet. The newly made chief bowed his head to me. "I apologize for the insult a Trinovantes tribesman committed against you this night."

I bowed my head in return. "The insult was not of your making. You have nothing to apologize for."

His voice deepened with sadness. "I do, though it is far too late to fix a lifetime of looking the other way." Mailcun shook his head as if to rid himself of the past. "Will you join me in seeing the banishment fulfilled, queen of the Iceni?"

"When?" I asked.

Mailcun's gaze went to the opening of the cave. The sky was just beginning to lighten with the gray of morning. "As soon as Miburga can ready a horse."

"Then yes, I will join you," I said.

The sun had just lifted above the snowy tree line when the solemn group of Trinovantes warriors approached the one entrance to our valley. Rhan and I, with my shield and lead warriors, had already arrived. We waited by the valley pass, which through a lot of daily work from all of the tribes had been kept clear enough of the seemingly never-ending snow that one horse could fit through it at a time. The only cleared path from our valley swept around the forest edge and then wound down to the peat bog, so that our supply of wood and peat would not be cut off. Past that, the world was a wall of white.

There was one horse in the Trinovantes procession. It was loaded with packs and was led by a stony-faced Miburga.

"I feel sorry for the horse," muttered Cadoc. Maldwyn grunted in agreement.

Mailcun, whose new torque glittered around his thick neck in the weak morning light, walked between the horse and Adminius, followed by his Chief's Guard. Adminius wore layers of woolen clothes and had a thick fur-lined cloak fastened tightly around his shoulders. The cut on his cheek blazed scarlet against the sallowness of his face. I'd expected him to beg, or at the very least argue angrily with Mailcun, but Adminius had set his jaw. His lips were pressed together and his eyes were bright with rage. As they approached, every member of Tribe Trinovantes turned his or her back to Adminius, silently showing that he was dead to them and they supported their new chief.

The group reached us and halted. Adminius mounted without help.

"Adminius, son of Addedomaros, you are hereby banished from Tribe Trinovantes. Should you be found in our lands, your life will be forfeit." Mailcun's deep voice rang with authority.

Adminius didn't so much as look at him. He clucked to the horse, who sloughed through the snowy pass. We watched him follow the cleared path. I wondered what would happen to him and thought what a waste it was that his life should come to this. He had just reached the spot in the cleared path where it dipped down and out of sight when he pulled the horse to a halt and then reined it to face us. He glared back at us, meeting my gaze.

"You will be sorry!" Adminius shouted. He spat into the snow, whirled the horse around, and dug his heels into its flanks so that it galloped off.

"A petulant child to the end," said Cadoc.

"Aye," agreed Maldwyn.

My sword master shook her head as she turned away. "The winter will end him, and I say good riddance."

Rhan said nothing. She stared out at the path long after her brother had disappeared from sight, her expression stony and dry-eyed.

CHAPTER XXXIX

The winter solstice came and went during a blinding snowstorm. Yule logs were decorated, added to hearthfires and watched all that longest night of the year so that their flames did not extinguish until the sun was reborn at dawn. Addedomaros's death had left a pall over the army, though all were in agreement that Mailcun was an excellent choice as the new chief and his banishment of Adminius was just. But before the accident the camp had felt lighter, joyful—and now the joy seemed to have fled with the sun.

Imbolc approached, the beginning of lambing, which heralded lengthening days and the much anticipated spring thaw. But I worried that my army had lost its heart, which held a special irony for me as that winter I found my heart.

I hadn't been so content since I was a child in Isurium, running wild through the forests surrounding the royal home of Tribe Brigantes, dearly loved by my mother and father.

My daughters thrived. When the weather allowed, Cadoc took them with him on quick hunting expeditions into the forest near the valley. They always returned with cheeks pink with cold, smiles stretching their faces, and stories about how their wolves had aided them in hunting whatever they'd tracked and killed. The girls and their wolves had grown tall and strong—and continued to train with the warriors. I, too, trained almost daily. I loved the strength of my muscles and my speed and balance, and my lead warriors continued to push the limits of my abilities so that I consistently got stronger and faster.

I enjoyed the weekly Arianell's Day, bonding even more completely with the women of my tribe as we celebrated Andraste, our elders, and the power of our matriarchy. Wulffaed continued to make my cave lodge not just comfortable but cheerful—no matter the sobriety of the rest of the camp, my lodge was often filled with the sounds of happy women and healthy children.

And then there was the joy Rhan and Maldwyn brought me. Their love warmed that long, cold winter so much that as the days slowly began to lengthen, I secretly wished for a late spring. The two of them contented me. I took both to my bed. Not both at once—though I silently admitted to myself I would enjoy that. I did not broach the subject with either of my lovers. Not because they were jealous or possessive. On the contrary, Rhan and Maldwyn honestly liked one another. The three of us spent many late nights happily drinking fireside and telling stories. The full truth was that I did not want to do anything to threaten the balance between us and our happiness.

That winter would have been perfect had the somber mood of the rest of the army been lifted. I worried about morale and wished all of my people could know the contentment I had found.

It was a night just about a fortnight before Imbolc, when Cadoc joined Rhan, Maldwyn, and me under the guise of wanting to taste Wulffaed's new batch of mead, that the solution came to me.

Cadoc took a long drink from his mug, wiped his beard with the back of his hand, and grinned at Wulffaed. "Aye, well, you have out-done yourself again, Mother of Twenty."

Wulffaed huffed, though her eyes sparkled with pleasure. "You say that every time you drink my mead."

"Because it is true!" bellowed the shield.

"Well, I'd better get you some bread and cheese to soak it up, as you're drinking enough for several old shields," groused Wulffaed, though her smile softened her words.

As Wulffaed hurried off, Cadoc's expression sobered. He cleared his throat, pulling my attention from the tunic I was embroidering with deep-blue ravens. "Queen Boudicca, it might be a good idea to invite Mailcun and perhaps the other chiefs to your lodge to share in some of these evenings with you."

My brow furrowed. "But they break their fasts with me—with all of us, in addition to Abertha and Briallen—almost every morning."

"Aye." He nodded contemplatively. "But that is more of a formal thing. A holdover from our morning war councils. This"—he gestured around us at the snug, warm cave, the friendly hearthfire, and the comradery that made the evenings so enjoyable—"is much more than a war council. It is a tribe, a family." He blew out a long breath. "It's peaceful, and I do not think the other chiefs are enjoying such peace."

I put down my embroidery. "I have felt the gloom in the rest of the camp."

"Aye," said Maldwyn. He sat across the fire from me on a large stump that had been carved into a wide-backed chair. He liked to drape his fur cloak along the back of the chair so that he seemed to sink into its softness. "We've spoken of it, the queen, Rhan, and I. It began with the death of Addedomaros."

Rhan was beside me. She preferred to sit on a thick woolen blanket, folded and placed on the floor so she could rest her back against the side of my chair. "Cadoc, has Tribe Trinovantes not accepted Mailcun as their chief?"

"Oh, they have. It is odd that there is such a sense of gloom over their camp as the inner workings of the tribe run so much more smoothly under Mailcun's leadership," said Cadoc.

"Much of that is because Adminius is no longer constantly causing problems with the other tribes," said Maldwyn.

"Yes, and one would think that his absence alone would lighten the mood of the camp," continued Cadoc, "but it has not. Instead the gloom seems to be deepening. Comux is restless and worried for his family, which does not help the morale of the Dobunni."

"What of Leofric?" I asked.

Cadoc shrugged. "His tribe is rather isolated. Even though the Catuvellauni he leads rejected Rome, there are still too many in the other tribes who have lost friends and family to his brother for them to fully embrace Leofric and his people."

"I have noted the same," said Rhan. "It is as if the other tribes have lost their spirit."

"That's it!" I sat up straighter and smiled. "I know how to heal their spirits. Cadoc, I'm going to need four large logs—so big they can be carved into life-sized images. Can you get them for me?"

Cadoc lifted a shoulder. "It hasn't snowed for several days. I should be able to go far enough into the forest to drag out some old logs."

"How soon could you do that?" I asked.

"When do you need them?" the old shield countered.

I grinned at him. "Yesterday."

"Aye, well, as you ask, so will I do, my queen." He sounded long-suffering, but his smile was warm and generous.

It only took Cadoc two days to find and haul back to camp four large logs from the huge trees felled in the last ice storm. The evening he brought the last of them to camp, I had him set up the logs just outside my cave entrance. The next morning, when the chiefs and my lead warriors joined me to break their fast, I had Wulffaed hold serving the food until after I spoke.

"I ask that you join me outside before we eat," I told the warriors, glad that the morning was sunny, though clouds threatened over the western mountains. Sending me curious glances, they followed me out of the entrance of the cave. "I have come to understand what it is that is missing in our camp this winter."

Mailcun's brows went up. Leofric's gaze went from the logs to me, where it stayed as he watched me with open curiosity. Comux was, as had become usual for him, silent.

"As an Imbolc gift, I give each chief one of these logs, as well as talented artists from among the Iceni who will carve the logs into images of each tribe's sacred goddess or god." I motioned to Rhan, who joined me. "And then I will ask that each idol be blessed and each shrine dedicated to . . ."

Rhan continued, turning to Mailcun first. "Epona, horse goddess and patroness of Tribe Trinovantes." Her gaze shifted to Comux. "Sulis, goddess of waters and patroness of Tribe Dobunni." She looked from Comux to Leofric. "Brân, god and guardian of the land, patron of Tribe Catuvellauni." Finally her eyes found me. "And Andraste, goddess of war and the patroness of Tribe Iceni."

Silence greeted Rhan's proclamation and my stomach began to

sink—and then Mailcun stepped forward and stroked one of the wide old logs. "I can see the face of Epona within this wood." When his gaze went to me, his eyes were bright. "Though I would like to carve our goddess's image myself."

I felt a huge rush of relief. I knew well that Mailcun was a gifted sculptor. He'd often carved little trinkets for my mother. I had hoped my gift would intrigue him.

Mailcun's interest was like a dam break, and the other chiefs surged forward, studying the logs and making their choices.

"Queen Boudicca," said Comux, "I choose this log and accept your gift gratefully, though I feel certain my Dobunni artists will insist that only they can bring alive the image of Sulis properly."

"Of course, Chief Comux," I said graciously.

Leofric cleared his throat. He stood beside the thickest of the logs. "And the Catuvellauni will gladly accept this log. I, too, would prefer one of my artists carve the image of our god."

"That is understandable," I agreed, careful not to smile victoriously.

That left the tallest log to be carved into Andraste's image. I was glad of it. I was also glad of the lively conversation about the idols and where they should be placed that dominated our mornings for the next several days.

The atmosphere of the camp began to change as soon as the four artists, one from each tribe, began working the wood to expose the goddess or god within. Rhan had suggested that we place the logs equidistant around the practice field, so that our patron goddesses and god would watch over our warriors as they trained. I agreed and knew very soon that her idea had been brilliant. Crowds formed every day to observe as the idols took shape. It became a type of competition, but it had a much different feel than the one that had led to the death of one of our chiefs. This competition was permeated with a sense of wonder and magick as the goddesses and god began to emerge from the weathered wood.

At Imbolc, a holy day on the wheel of the year when we celebrate new life and the reawakening of the earth after its long winter slumber, all four idols were completed enough that they were included in the festivities. Candles were lit around the base of each statue. Honey cakes and bowls of sheep and goat milk were left out as offerings, as well as crystals, beads, and feathers. Thereafter the sense of melancholy lifted, and as the army honored its gods, it once again found its spirit.

It was then that I noticed I was ill. The illness began as exhaustion and nausea. My daily training was a struggle. I said nothing, but my lead warriors began watching me closely, which made me redouble my efforts to appear well.

I could not shake the lethargy that snuck upon me at unexpected times. One day I would get through training just fine, with only the usual well-earned tiredness. The next day I would have to end early and retire to my bedchamber for the rest of the day.

Food tasted odd. Sometimes I was ravenous and others I couldn't bear anything except sipping a little bone broth. My body ached and was overly sensitive.

I was irritable. I refused to speak of my illness to Rhan or Maldwyn, but as February came to a close, I was still not well. I'd thought I'd mostly kept my infirmity secret, but when our healer Adara joined my lodge during the next Arianell's Day I knew I had not been as good at hiding my illness as I had hoped.

That day I was annoyed that I felt especially sick. Wulffaed had taken one look at my sallow face and begun boiling bones for broth. I tried to laugh with the women but found I wasn't able to do much more than sit still while Phaedra brushed and braided my hair. As the women left my lodge, smiling and replete with mead and comradery, Adara remained behind with Rhan.

I took a deep breath and readied myself as the two women approached me together.

"Boudicca, I asked Adara to attend you today," said Rhan almost shyly. "I have been worried. You have lost weight. You are often exhausted. I—I am concerned you have a wasting sickness."

Adara chuckled.

Rhan and I turned our twin frowns on her. "Is my illness amusing?" I snapped at the healer. I had felt increasingly unwell as the day progressed and had little patience for foolishness.

"Of course not, my queen," said Adara with a smile. "Tell me, when did you last have your moon days?"

Rhan gasped, and I suddenly felt numb—and foolish. I'd borne two children, and though it had been many years, I certainly should have remembered what it had felt like to be with child. Hastily, I counted back. I'd not bled for well over one month.

I had to swallow several times before I could speak. "I'm with child."

"Aye, that is my guess," Adara said, nodding. "Though if you allow it I will examine you to be sure."

Adara's examination supported what I had already realized. When the Druid healer left and Rhan and I were alone, my lover came to me and took me tenderly into her arms.

"A child. It is such a blessing," Rhan said. Then she laughed. "I didn't even consider it! I was worried you had a wasting sickness."

"Well, Ceri has known ten namedays. When Prasutagus and I conceived no more children, I believed I would not bear another child." I relaxed in her embrace and allowed myself to be filled with relief that I wasn't deathly ill, as well as joy at the knowledge of the new life within me. "Maldwyn will be pleased," I said softly.

"Yes he will," Rhan said. "As will all of the Iceni. This is wonderful news, proving the Iceni are fertile and strong and well blessed by Andraste."

"Well, if this pregnancy is anything like my other two, I will only feel ill for just a couple more full cycles of the moon, and then I will be filled with energy until just before I give birth. That should give us time to defeat the Romans before we celebrate a new member of the royal Iceni family."

"Yes," Rhan said softly. "Yes."

I sent word to Cadoc that I wished to entertain the chiefs for dinner that evening, and that I would also like Abertha and Briallen to join us. As Wulffaed prepared a special meal of fat chickens glazed with honey and precious baked apples, I went to our herd, where I knew I would find Maldwyn.

"My queen!" He grinned when he saw me feeding one of the apples Wulffaed hoarded to Tân. "Does the Mother of Twenty know that you have absconded with that? I tried to sneak one for Ennis not long ago and she rapped my knuckles with a stick!"

I laughed. "Oh, she knows. And as I'm celebrating, she didn't seem to mind overly much."

He joined me at Tân's side and stroked her neck. "Celebrating? Has there been news?"

"Yes." I kissed Tân's soft muzzle and then hooked my arm through his. "Walk with me to the pass. I'd like to watch the sunset."

"As you ask, so will I do."

We didn't speak as we made our way through the camp to the opening to our valley. Dinner was quickly approaching, and the scent of roasting meat that wafted with the breeze had my stomach roiling. I hoped I would be able to eat the honeyed chicken, which was usually one of my favorite dishes. Maldwyn shot me a surprised look when I led him through the pass, which was becoming increasingly muddy as the days lengthened and warmed. We followed the cleared path to where it dipped down, and I stopped. The sun was just dropping beneath the western forest, setting the sky ablaze before it slept beneath the horizon. Its reddish-orange color reminded me of the wildflowers that blanketed Tasceni in the spring, and I felt a sudden deep yearning for home.

Maldwyn placed his hand over mine where it rested on his arm. "Boudicca, what is it?"

I looked at him, surprised to realize my eyes had filled with tears. "I am with child."

His body went very still. He blinked several times and his gaze slid from my eyes down to my stomach.

"You can't tell yet," I said with a breathless laugh.

His gaze shot back to mine. "That's why you've been ill!"

I nodded. "Yes."

"A child?" He spoke the words as he would a prayer. "Truly?"

"Truly," I said.

Laughing joyously, he pulled me into his arms, lifted me, and spun me around. "A child!"

I was laughing, too, but when he put me down I staggered a little and almost vomited.

"Oh! Oh, no! Forgive me! I—I didn't mean to—"

I pressed a finger to his lips. "I am well but should probably not be spun around."

"Yes, of course! Yes." Hesitantly, he placed his big hand on my stomach. When he looked up at me again, tears tracked down his cheeks. "I have never known such joy. She will be the finest equestrian in our tribe."

"She?" I asked with a smile.

"Oh, aye. *She*," he said firmly, and I saw no need to argue with him.

The reaction to the news of my pregnancy ignited the army, chasing away any leftover melancholy lingering after the death of Addedomaros. Unlike Romans, who consider women property to subjugate and control, our people cared for the sacredness of a new life and not whether it was conceived in a marriage or in the freedom of a lover's bed. As would any Iceni woman, I continued with my daily routine. The only difference was that I now understood my temporary weariness, and when it came over me I listened to my body and rested.

My daughters were perhaps the only Iceni happier than Maldwyn about the child, though they told me they would prefer a baby brother to a sister. Wulffaed immediately began working special reams of cloth for the infant. I received gifts from all of the tribes within camp—mostly choice cuts of meat and precious fruits and vegetables they had hoarded throughout the winter.

A sennight after my announcement, it began to rain, and for the first time since we entered our valley it did not change to sleet or snow, but instead finally heralded the end of our long winter isolation and the beginning of spring—and the freedom we would claim as our own.

PART III

SPRING 61 CE

chapter xl

The spring sun was high in an unusually cloudless sky and I was sweating on the practice field as I attempted to take on Cadoc and Abertha at the same time, mostly unsuccessfully, which the bruises from their wooden swords would bear witness to tomorrow. Except for when I first woke in the morning, I'd stopped feeling sick, but had found that the weeks I'd spent not eating had taken a toll on my strength and speed—a toll I was now paying.

"A rider comes!" One of the sentries always stationed at the narrow mouth of our valley raced up to me. The other chiefs, who were practicing much more successfully not far from me, stopped what they were doing and joined me.

"Roman?" I asked. My voice sounded calm, but my heartbeat pulsed fast and hard through my body.

"No, my queen. He wears the colors of Tribe Brigantes and carries their sigil."

I hid the flood of relief that almost made me feel dizzy. "Just one rider?" I asked.

"Yes, my queen. He stopped outside the pass and called to us that he has a message for Queen Boudicca from Queen Cartimandua."

"Escort the rider here. Care for his horse as you would any guest," I said.

"As you ask, so will I do!"

When the sentry jogged away, I faced the chiefs and their lead warriors.

"Will you join me to greet this messenger from the Brigantes?" I asked.

"Cartimandua is a traitorous bitch," said Leofric. "She has whored her tribe to Rome."

"I am aware of that," I said.

Comux shook his head. "I don't like it. If she knows we're here, does that mean the Fourteenth and Twentieth legions are just beyond the forest?"

"That is one reason we need to hear what her messenger has to say," I said.

Mailcun nodded. "We need more information. I would hear this messenger."

"Aye," agreed the others, but reluctantly.

Cadoc looked grim. "I will escort the messenger here." I nodded and my shield strode off toward the one entrance to our valley.

It didn't take long. I was still wiping sweat from my face when Cadoc returned with a travel-weary man. He was tall, with dark hair that had just begun to be streaked with gray, and was wearing a cloak dyed the familiar Tribe Brigantes colors of bright flame yellow and black. He stopped before me and bowed deeply.

"Queen Boudicca, I bring you greetings from Queen Cartiman-dua." He reached into a leather satchel slung across his shoulder. Cadoc stiffened but relaxed when he pulled forth a long golden chain from which was suspended a pendant stamped with the flames of the goddess Brigantia. It was almost identical to my mother's pendant—the one I'd placed around the goddess's neck at her desecrated shrine in Camulodunum. "She sends her kinswoman this token of her affection."

I accepted the necklace. "Your queen is generous, though I know you did not come all this way only to gift me." My eyes widened as I saw through the dirt and weariness and recognized him. "Deorwine?"

"Yes, Queen Boudicca!" His smile youthened him and I easily saw the man I'd known when I was a girl living in Isurium, the royal home of Tribe Brigantes. He'd been a stable hand then, and as I spent much of my youth on horseback, I'd known him rather well. "My queen hoped you would remember me."

"I do." I returned his smile. "How could I not? I grew up in the Isurium stables."

"Aye, and now I am horse master for my queen."

"I am not surprised," I said. "So, what word do you have for me from your queen?"

"Queen Cartimandua would like to meet with you. She asks if she may have safe passage into your valley."

Instead of answering I said, "I doubt that I will be in this valley by the time your queen travels from Brigantes territory here."

"Queen Cartimandua is only half a day's ride from here," he said. "She is eager to speak with you and left Isurium the day the roads began to clear enough to travel, hoping that your mountain pass, and you, would allow her entrance."

I nodded. The tribe into which I'd been born commanded a large area north and east of the Eryri Mountains, and it was also mountainous enough that Cartimandua would have been able to gauge a spring thaw. But how did she know our location? And what did she want?

"Who marches with your queen?" I asked, and heard the chiefs shift restlessly at the question.

"Only her Queen's Guard," said Deorwine.

Leofric spat on the ground. "Her guard *and* a Roman legion?"

"No." Deorwine's gaze never left mine as he answered the Catuvellauni chief. "My queen is weary of Roman rule."

Cadoc snorted. "Since when?"

I held up my hand, cutting off Deorwine's reply. The air around me sizzled with the chiefs' barely controlled rage. "Return to Queen Cartimandua. Tell her I will happily receive her and her guard as my guests. Will you rest the night before you ride out?"

"No, Queen Boudicca. My queen eagerly awaits your answer. I would leave immediately."

"Cadoc, be sure Deorwine eats and then bring him a fresh horse." I smiled at the Brigantes' horse master. "Your mount will be well cared for until you return."

Deorwine bowed low again. "Thank you, Queen Boudicca. Expect Cartimandua tomorrow at midday."

"Indeed I shall," I said.

When Deorwine was out of hearing range, Abertha said, "Do we follow him, my queen? If he speaks truthfully we can easily end Cartimandua and her guard, and rid the Brigantes of a traitor."

"Not here," I said. "My lodge. All of you."

The chiefs and Abertha followed me to my cave lodge. Rhan joined us, having seen the Brigantes messenger with Cadoc. As Wulffaed was pouring mead, Cadoc returned with Maldwyn, who had been with the herd when a fresh horse had been chosen for Deorwine.

"Do we follow him?" Cadoc repeated Abertha's question with no preamble.

"Yes," I said. "But stealthily. I want Cartimandua to think I believe her message to be genuine." I drank deeply, clearing the dust from my throat. "Mailcun, we need the fleetest of the Trinovantes horses to follow Deorwine. See if he spoke the truth about with whom the queen travels, and then return here ahead of Cartimandua and report to us."

"Aye," Mailcun said. "That can be easily done."

I motioned for one of Wulffaed's daughters to take Mailcun's order to the Trinovantes camp.

"I still believe it would be wise to kill her. Now," said Leofric.

I nodded. "I understand that desire. Cartimandua has proven to be self-serving. I know that better than anyone here. My father was kinsman to her husband, Venutius. He disagreed with her about allying with the Romans and she divorced him, then commanded her guard to execute several members of his family."

"Why even meet with her?" asked Comux.

"Because we need to know not just what she wants of us but how she knows we wintered here," I said. "If she is the tip of the spear for the Roman legions, it will not matter whether I turn her away or not. *The Romans already know our location.* If I turn her away or kill her, it will not change what the Romans know, but it will ensure we have no more knowledge about them than we do at this moment."

"I do not think we can trust her," said Maldwyn.

"Aye," the chiefs muttered.

"We aren't trusting her. We're listening to what she has to say.

But we shall do more than that. Tomorrow at midday the practice field will be filled with our warriors training. Spread the word. We wear our battle finery." My smile was filled with confidence. "Queen Cartimandua will witness for herself the might of our army."

The warrior sent to follow Deorwine returned at first light after having ridden all night. He reported that Cartimandua was, indeed, only escorted by two dozen Queen's Guard and her horse master. He even backtracked the queen's trail and saw no sign of Rome or any other warriors.

When the sun was high overhead, the crowded training field rang with the sounds of blows and the thunder of chariots. Goats and pigs and cattle had been slaughtered and spitted so that enticing aromas wafted throughout the camp. Iceni, Dobunni, Trinovantes, and Catu-vellauni wore their colors proudly when Queen Cartimandua, in an ornate chariot pulled by matching black stallions and driven by Deorwine, entered our valley with Cadoc escorting them within. Her Queen's Guard followed, all mounted on black horses, as was tradition for Tribe Brigantes. They were a magnificent sight.

I waited at the mouth of my cave lodge wearing the Beltane dress my mother had embroidered for me. My hair was free and my torque was my only jewelry. Rhan stood beside me wearing the white robes Wulffaed had meticulously dyed and fashioned for her, proclaiming her station as high Druid for all to see. Under my direction, Wulffaed had staged the interior of the lodge carefully. My chair had been draped with fox pelts and elevated to become a throne. On either side of me, chairs had been situated. Mailcun, Leofric, and Comux sat to one side. On the other were chairs for Rhan, Cadoc, Maldwyn, and Abertha. Briallen would stand guard at my throne. The long table had been placed before my throne, so that Cartimandua, her horse master, and the leader of her guard could sit. The rest of her guard would remain outside.

As Cartimandua came into view, I was reminded of her beauty. Though she was far from young, the queen of the Brigantes was a striking woman. She wasn't tall, but what she lacked in height she made up for in presence. I remembered her as foxlike. Her chin was pointed and her nose straight and strong. Her eyes were an unusual amber color. Her hair had been a unique mixture of blond and auburn but was now completely silver gray—a mane that spread out around her in a mass of thick curls held back by a gold coronet. Her face was painted in bold lines of black and white and brilliant yellow that met the black tattoos adorning her neck and chest. She wore a flame-colored dress. Its bodice was covered with a huge stag embroidered with white thread. Her torque was familiar. She'd been wearing it since I was a child—twisted gold that ended in antlers. Her arms were covered with gold bangles, and around her shapely waist there was a slender golden chain from which dangled a large pendant of a golden stag.

Deorwine helped her from the chariot. The leader of her Queen's Guard dismounted and went to her side as she and Deorwine followed Cadoc to where I waited.

Cartimandua paused before me and bowed her head. "Queen Boudicca, it has been far too long since last we met." Her distinctive voice, low and husky, evoked my childhood, when the queen would often come to our lodge for drinks and discussions about which horses my father would keep and which stallions would be bred to that season's mares. I steeled myself against an unexpected wave of longing for my dead father.

I bowed in return. "Welcome to my winter lodge, Queen Cartimandua. Enter as an honored guest."

But instead of coming into the lodge, Cartimandua's sharp fox-colored gaze went to Rhan. "I see you have a Druid. I envy you. They are rare."

"I am Rhan, *the* high Druid, Queen Cartimandua," Rhan said, correcting her immediately.

The queen's gaze traveled down Rhan's white robes. "Yes, I can see that. It saddens me that Derwyn did not escape the massacre at Ynys Môn."

Cadoc, who had already walked past me to take his seat, snorted, and I heard the low, disgruntled mutters of the chiefs who were already inside.

"Will you join me within?" I asked Cartimandua. "You must be hungry and thirsty after your long journey."

"Indeed I am. But first, I brought you a gift." She motioned over her shoulder at one of her guards. "Two barrels of fine Roman wine." The guard led forward a black gelding who had barrels strapped on either side of his wide back.

"A generous gift," I said as she followed me inside. Her Queen's Guard also tried to enter, but Briallen stepped before them, spear blocking their way. When Cartimandua's warriors began to protest, the queen looked back at them and smiled.

"Remain outside. There are thousands of Iceni all around us. If Queen Boudicca means me harm, the dozen of you will not stop them." Still smiling, she returned her sharp gaze to me. "Shall we?"

I led her to the table and motioned for her to take the center seat. Deorwine and the leader of her Queen's Guard sat on either side of her as I called to Wulffaed. "Queen Cartimandua has gifted us with two barrels of Roman wine. Have one brought within and served, and the other opened and served to her guard."

Wulffaed frowned but did as I asked. I knew the wine had been a test. If I'd refused it, I would have insulted Cartimandua. If I'd accepted it but not served it, I would have appeared at best selfish and at worst needy. By serving it, especially to her guard, I demonstrated not just my generosity but also that I did not *need* her wine.

"Queen Cartimandua, beside me are Iceni allies, the chiefs of the Trinovantes, Dobunni, and Catuvellauni." Before I could introduce each man separately, Cartimandua spoke.

"Yes, I recognize you, Comux." She nodded to him and he jerked his head in response. "And you as well, Leofric, though I did not know you called yourself chief of the Catuvellauni. I had not heard of the death of Togodumnus."

At his cousin's name, Leofric clenched his jaw. Through his teeth he said, "I am chief of the Catuvellauni who have not whored themselves to Rome. My brother is no chief. He is a traitor."

"Ah, I see." Cartimandua was completely unruffled by his anger. She simply turned her gaze to Mailcun. A frown creased her forehead. "But you, chief of the Trinovantes, I do not recognize."

"Addedomaros died midwinter. I am Mailcun, named chief by the tribe and sanctified by the high Druid."

"Ah, yes. Addedomaros's shield. I do recognize you now. I am sorry for the loss of Addedomaros. He was a mighty warrior," said Cartimandua.

Wulffaed and her daughters began serving wine as I took control of the conversation. "Queen Cartimandua, why have you journeyed so far to speak with me?"

"So we'll get right to it." She nodded in approval. "Good. I abhor useless chatter. I propose an alliance between Tribe Brigantes and the Iceni."

The room was utterly silent.

I sipped my wine before answering with a question of my own. "How did you know where to find me?"

The queen smiled. "Oh, I have eyes and ears everywhere."

"Roman eyes and ears?" I asked.

She blew out a short derisive breath. "Romans rarely know what is happening beneath their own noses. No, Queen Boudicca, Rome did not hear the whispers of our people that spoke of a great army wintering in the safety of Tribe Ordovices's mighty mountains."

"And by 'our people,' exactly who do you mean?" asked Leofric.

"Britons!" Cartimandua brought her fist down on the table.

"For many years Tribe Brigantes has embraced Rome—not Britain." Leofric almost spat the words.

Cartimandua's eyes met mine. "I did what allowed me to survive, as would any wise queen."

"And there is my problem." I spoke conversationally, with none of the anger Leofric showed. "How do I trust an alliance with a queen who is willing to do anything so *she* will survive? You did not say you did what you had to for your *tribe's* survival, only your own."

Cartimandua lifted her chin. "When you have been queen for as long as I have been, you will understand that what is good for you is also good for your people—and what is good for your people is good for you. I cannot be separated from the Brigantes. *I am the Brigantes.*"

Rhan tilted her head and studied Cartimandua as she asked, "Why have you suddenly decided to change your allegiance from Rome to the Iceni?"

"It was not a sudden decision, High Druid," said Cartimandua. "It has been brewing since the Romans attacked Boudicca at Tasceni. Until then I'd believed what was best for the Brigantes was to ally with Rome—weather their storm so that when they finally tired of attempting to subjugate Britain, my tribe would be whole, thriving and prosperous, and ready to rule in their absence." She laughed at the outrage on the faces of the chiefs beside me. "Oh, don't pretend shock. Which one of you wouldn't want to rule all of Britain?" Her fox gaze returned to me. "You understand. You've united more tribes than have ever allied before. At this moment, were there to be a queen of Britain named, it would be Boudicca."

"I would not sell myself to the Romans for any title," I said. "And, once again, you make it difficult to trust you knowing that your ultimate wish is to rule us all."

"It is because I am open about my desire to rule that it should be easy for you to trust me. I don't hide anything. You know me. You know my motives."

"I know you divorced your husband and had his family, my kinsmen and -women, killed." I shot the words at her.

Her brows lifted. "Yes, I did. Tell me, how do *you* handle traitors?"

"There are no traitors to Queen Boudicca in this camp." Cadoc's deep voice rumbled.

"Then your queen is fortunate, but she has only been queen for one year. I have ruled for two decades. I choose to kill traitors. Venutius knew that and fled when I discovered his betrayal, so I was left with no choice but to flush out the traitors he left behind and end them. Judge me after you have been betrayed, Queen Boudicca, and not before."

"And by 'betrayed' you mean your husband's refusal to ally with Rome," I said.

"Yes." She nodded. "I am queen of the Brigantes. I made the decision for my tribe, much like Prasutagus chose to sign a co-regent treaty with Rome shortly before his death. Did you agree with that, Boudicca?"

"That was the chief of the Iceni's decision," I prevaricated. I had agreed with Prasutagus, but only because he'd purposely misinterpreted the signs from Andraste to make it seem the goddess's will.

"Exactly," said Cartimandua. "What would the mighty Prasutagus have done had you betrayed him by inciting his warriors to rise against him?" She shrugged. "I cannot imagine he would have ignored such a slight."

"Prasutagus was trustworthy and honorable," said Cadoc. "You are neither."

"Enough!" The room bristled at her tone. Cartimandua then continued as if they were cheering her on instead of wishing they could skewer her with their spears. "Yes, I have been close to the Romans for many years. Yes, I am ruthless. You should be grateful for both! Do any of you know how to lure the Fourteenth and Twentieth into a trap?" She leaned forward and pounded her fist on the table again. "No, I think not! But I do. I can serve you the two remaining Roman legions as if on a platter for Britain to feast."

"If we destroy the Fourteenth and Twentieth, we end the Roman hold on us," I said into the silence that met her words.

"Exactly! And after we have our country back, you and I can *decide* who rules Britain." Cartimandua's eyes glinted as she smiled. "What say you, queen of the Iceni? Shall we ally and defeat Rome together?"

"What is it you propose?" I asked.

Cartimandua outlined her plan while we ate and drank well into the evening, and then Cadoc escorted the queen and her company to an opulent tent hastily erected by the lake. After she was tucked away for the night, my war council gathered in my lodge.

"Her plan is sound," said Cadoc.

Leofric stood, knocking back his chair. He paced in front of my throne in agitation. "She cannot be trusted!"

"Not completely true," said Mailcun. "I would not trust a rutting stag, but I know what he wants and how he plans to get it, and I can use that knowledge to track and kill him."

I tried unsuccessfully to suppress a bubble of laughter. "Are you comparing Cartimandua to a rutting stag?"

"Aye, he is!" said Leofric, who'd stopped pacing to stare at Mailcun.

"He isn't wrong," said Cadoc. "We know what Cartimandua wants, and what we can trust is that she will do anything to get it."

Maldwyn nodded. "We don't need to trust her, at least not beyond luring the Romans into our trap. After that we part ways and she will, once again, be our enemy."

"And she will not have the backing of Rome." Leofric's reddened face was slowly returning to a normal hue. "Which means the Catuvellauni will defeat her."

Mailcun spoke up. "Aye, with the aid of Tribe Trinovantes. And we will retake our royal home of Camulodunum."

"Aye," Leofric said.

"So it is decided. Cartimandua expects my answer tomorrow when we break our fast." I turned to Rhan, who was seated at my side. "I am inclined to agree to her plan, but not without the approval of Andraste."

"At dawn Andraste will hear your petition," said Rhan.

Rhan had spoken little during the evening, but had watched and listened. "What say you of Cartimandua's plan, High Druid?"

"I agree that it is sound," answered Rhan. "What she proposes is logical. But being allied with Queen Cartimandua is like being in bed with a viper. She will eventually strike, and her bite will be deadly."

"That is exactly why Andraste will decide whether we ally with her or not," I said.

It wasn't that I trusted Cartimandua. I did not. What I trusted was her need to survive and thrive. Rome had proven too difficult for her to manipulate. She couldn't control them, which meant allying with them no longer added to her power. When they no longer served her, she would turn on them without a moment's hesitation, as she had done with her husband's family. Rome no longer served Queen Cartimandua, and that should benefit us all.

The morning dawned cold as winter, but the sky was cloudless and the sun promised warmth. I tucked my fur-lined cloak more closely around me as Cadoc and my lead warriors followed me from my lodge. Rhan had left my bed while it was still dark, saying that she would cleanse herself and leave offerings to Andraste before she chose a hare.

It was so early that the camp was just beginning to stir and I was surprised to see Cartimandua, her shield, and her Queen's Guard standing outside their tent. The queen approached me, followed by her people.

"I assumed you would petition Andraste early," said Cartimandua. "May my escort and I join you?"

"Yes," I said without hesitation. "I always petition Andraste publicly. Anyone in my camp may join me."

"Anyone?" Cartimandua sucked air through her teeth. "That is most *generous*."

She spoke the word as if it was an insult. I glanced at her as we continued toward the practice field. I knew exactly what she meant. She, like Prasutagus, chose to control how much her tribe knew of her divine petitions.

I understood all too well what a spectacular mistake that could be.

"It isn't generous," I said. "It's honest."

Cartimandua made a derisive sound in her throat but said no more.

As we approached the practice field, Mailcun, Leofric, and Comux joined us, looking grim as they slanted glances at Cartimandua.

Rhan waited in the center of the field. At her feet was a small hutch. In the crisp dawn I could easily see the white fur of the sacred hare, marred only by the blue crescent painted on its chest to mark it as chosen. This creature looked especially large. Not surprising, as it had been fattened and pampered all winter. Rhan wore the robes of the high Druid, which matched the snow color of the hare. She'd painted her face with Ogham symbols in Iceni blue. Her light hair was a halo around her head and shoulders. She was strong and magickal, looking as if she'd just stepped from the heart of Annwn.

"Queen Cartimandua, I would ask that you and your escort stand there." Rhan pointed to a spot several yards in front of her and the hare.

Cartimandua nodded and took her place. Deorwine stood beside her, and her guard stretched behind them in a two-by-two column.

"Cadoc, you, the Iceni lead warriors, and the chiefs may encircle me," said Rhan.

Cadoc and the chiefs did so, leaving plenty of room between each of them but including Cartimandua and Deorwine in their circle.

"Queen Boudicca, your place is beside me."

I went to Rhan and nodded that I was ready. The high Druid of Britain lifted the sacred hare from her hutch and held her aloft. "Speak your petition to Andraste, goddess of war and patroness of the Iceni!"

Warriors had come out of their shelters and stood watching us at the edge of the field. I was glad of it. My people deserved to hear my question and witness the response of their goddess.

In a clear, loud voice I said, "Mighty Andraste, your Victory asks whether the Iceni and our army should ally with Cartimandua of the Brigantes and lure the Romans into battle. As always, I shall abide by your divine will."

Rhan placed the hare at my feet. Immediately it darted off directly toward Cartimandua and her guard. The queen held very still as the hare circled her three times before streaking back toward Rhan and me. It ran between us and kept going out of the practice field. Rhan and I jogged after it, with our group following.

The hare raced through the camp in a direct line to the narrow entrance. The warriors stationed there froze when they saw the sacred creature. It darted through the entrance, paused outside, and then turned to the southeast and streaked off, disappearing into the rising sun.

"What say you, High Druid?" I spoke formally, being sure my voice carried.

"Andraste has given sign. We are to ally with the Brigantes in a final battle with Rome!"

Cartimandua's people cheered, but my lead warriors and the chief did not join them until I raised my fist and shouted the Iceni war cry.

CHAPTER XLI

Cartimandua left that morning. I'd told her it would take us five days to break camp and then another five days to march to our preplanned rendezvous site. She would need all ten days to accomplish her part in luring the Romans into our trap. The first five days passed in a busy blur, and then it hardly seemed real to be mounted on Tân and leading the army from the valley that had sheltered us for months. I stopped at the tree line and reined Tân around, feeling oddly melancholy.

Rhan trotted her horse to me. Her smile was warm and knowing. "It saddens you?"

"It's silly. Must be the babe." I rested my hand over my stomach, which was just beginning to round with my growing child.

"It isn't silly." Rhan reached out and took my hand, squeezing before releasing it. "We have been safe here. It has been a respite of peace in a time of war. I will miss it, too."

I looked back through the narrow entrance to our valley and could just make out the four large carved idols that framed our practice field.

"Maybe we should take them with us," I said. "No one will know they're here. No one will bring offerings to them and care for them."

"They belong here." Rhan's voice remained soft, but it was filled with the surety of a high Druid. "And the next people who shelter in this valley will happily discover them, sacrifice to them, love and care for them—and so it will continue for generations."

I wiped unexpected tears from my cheeks. "I like that."

I gave the valley one last look and then with Rhan by my side galloped to my place at the head of our army.

The trip from the valley was drastically different from the trip to it, and not just because the weather was clear and beautiful with the earth awakening and bursting into bloom around us. When we'd entered the Eryri Mountains we'd longed for sanctuary and respite. After sheltering safely all winter we emerged revitalized and eager. We made no attempt to hide. Cartimandua's plan required us to act boldly, as if we had no doubt that we could defeat the two legions remaining in Britain. Our arrogance was necessary for Rome to be lured into our trap.

Joyously we marched east from our valley, moving ever forward on a tide of will and spirit and hope. We crossed into the territory of Tribe Cornovii as we headed to the Midlands and Watling Street, the long Roman road that bisected our country. Viroco, the Cornovii chief, welcomed us with an elaborate feast as we camped on our second night near Viroconium, the tribe's royal city, located not far from Watling Street. From there we chose to stay off the Roman road and not chance an encounter with a stray centuria, though we did travel parallel to it in the forest, working our way southeast to where the Romans believed we could be trapped.

Each day, Rhan would break her fast with my lead warriors, the chiefs, and me—and then she would melt into the forest. Each night she would return to our campfire, ravenous and smelling of rosemary and mint, pine and apple blossoms, grasses, decay, and fertile earth— the scents of dreams and nightmares, Annwn and nwyfre.

After we'd feasted with the chief of Tribe Cornovii, Rhan lay beside me, stroking my hair. It was a night to ask quiet things and receive whispered answers. Sleepily I asked, "Can you tell me what it is you do, where it is you go, when you're gone all day?"

Her hand stilled, but only for a moment. When Rhan answered, her voice was as soft as her caress. "I prepare."

My eyes had been half-lidded and I'd been drowsy, but those two words had me coming fully awake. "You prepare for what?"

She sighed. "The future."

"Should I be worried?"

"Worry serves no purpose. Your decision has been made. We head to battle the Roman legions. Doubt and worry are unproductive," said Rhan firmly.

I couldn't stop myself from asking, "But do you prepare for victory or defeat?"

"Both and neither. I weave between Annwn and Arbred, calling on our ancestors and Andraste to guide us, remain close to us, help us to strike true and to carry ourselves with honor—to make them proud." She kissed me gently. "Andraste is near. So is Brigantia. Just this afternoon I saw her white stag."

"That seems like a good omen," I said.

Rhan kissed me again, this time more insistent than gentle, and we spoke no more that night.

As we continued on our march, more tribesmen and -women joined us. Cornovii, Corieltauvi, Demetae, Silures, and even warriors from as far north as Tribe Parisi added to our numbers, so that by day four Cadoc reported that as close as he could tell we had more than two hundred fifty thousand warriors and family members—all willing to fight for Britain's freedom.

My army vastly outnumbered the Roman legions. The Fourteenth and the Twentieth would each have about five to six thousand men. Logically, what was left of the Ninth would join them, equaling another five thousand or so men. It seemed that we could not lose, but I was restless. I did not like that Queen Cartimandua was the key to our plan. Often, I reminded myself that at this moment Cartimandua and I wanted the same thing—the Romans driven from Britain. After the battle was won and the Romans were gone, *then* Cartimandua would be an enemy to anyone who did not bow to her as queen of Britain. Until then it served her to fight beside us.

It was early afternoon on the fourth day when Maldwyn galloped to me with one of our Iceni scouts beside him. I was riding at the head of the army between Cadoc and Rhan, and we halted immediately. The scout's horse was dark with sweat, but the warrior's eyes were bright and his smile was eager.

"Queen Boudicca!" Still astride, the scout bowed to me. "Tribe Brigantes is in position. Queen Cartimandua's shield reports that the Fourteenth and Twentieth legions have taken the bait and are two days' march from the Midlands valley."

"Did you see Cartimandua's army?" asked Cadoc.

"I did." The scout nodded and ran a hand through his sweaty hair. "They wait to the east of the valley and will be well within sight of the legions when they arrive. When we reach the valley Deorwine said he will show us exactly where our warriors and caravans should be positioned so that all will be ready for the trap."

"You have done well," I told the scout. "Care for your horse and yourself."

"Thank you, my queen."

"All seems to be going as Cartimandua planned," said Maldwyn.

Cadoc snorted. "It would *appear* so."

"You have doubts?" asked Rhan.

"Always," Cadoc said. "It is uncomfortable to be bait."

I smiled at the gruff old shield I'd come to care for deeply over the past year. "I would not worry overmuch, Iceni shield. Our *bait* is stronger by thousands of warriors than the Romans. Two legions cannot overcome us." Absently, I placed my hand over my abdomen. "I believe the child I carry has made you worry more than Wulffaed."

"Oh, aye," said Cadoc. "The babe makes me worry."

"The babe makes us all worry," added Maldwyn.

I frowned at them. "I will not stay out of the battle."

"We would not ask you to," Cadoc said hastily.

"No, of course not," said Maldwyn. His eyes had taken on the faraway look they got whenever we spoke of the child growing within me.

"But babes cause worry—oftentimes needless worry," said Rhan.

And then we all smiled as Enfys and Ceri galloped past us, their two grown wolves running at their horses' sides.

"I'm going after those two," said Cadoc. "We're getting too close to the Romans for them to be dashing ahead of the army."

I nodded, and Cadoc kicked his horse into a gallop, chasing after my daughters.

"I wonder how they escaped Briallen," I said.

"I saw her not long ago." Rhan jerked her chin back behind us and to the right. "By your leave I'll go to her and let her know her charges are being corralled by Cadoc."

I smiled. "You definitely have my leave."

As Rhan galloped away, I could feel Maldwyn's eyes on me. "I've been too busy with the scouts and the herd today and haven't seen you since this morning, my queen," said Maldwyn as he kneed his horse around so that we rode so close together that our legs almost touched. Some nights Rhan warmed my bed, others Maldwyn did—and some nights I did not care to share my bed at all. There was no jealousy between Maldwyn and Rhan. A deep friendship had developed between the two of them that brought peace and laughter as well as passion to my campfire. It was because of the two of them that I wasn't simply content but was truly happy. "You didn't get sick this morning." Maldwyn's deep voice broke into my pleasant thoughts.

I smiled at him. "No, I didn't. It was the same with Enfys and Ceri. As my stomach swelled I stopped being sick and was filled with energy until very close to the end. It was only when I was heavy with child that I became awkward. I was grateful then for the ease with which I carry my babes. I am doubly grateful for it now, though I cannot help but long for the comforts of Tasceni."

Maldwyn took my hand. "We will vanquish the Romans and be home long before harvest. You'll give birth to our daughter in your lodge surrounded by your women."

Just the thought had my shoulders relaxing. "Home . . ." I sighed happily. "It will be a wondrous thing to return to Tasceni."

"Indeed." His smile was slow and intimate. "You look like yourself again." His gaze slid down my body from my breasts to my abdomen. "Well, except for some small changes."

I laughed. "Which won't remain small."

"And you still believe she'll be born near Samhain in the fall?"

Maldwyn had asked me versions of this question over and over, though I did not tire of answering. I enjoyed seeing the light in his cornflower eyes as he spoke of the babe. "Yes, though I'm not as sure as you that the child is a girl."

Maldwyn deepened his voice and scratched his chin like an elder dispensing wisdom. "Fathers know such things."

I laughed. "Well, Enfys and Ceri say daughters know such things, too, and they insist I carry their baby brother."

"When they are disappointed by *her* birth, we shall simply have to try again for that brother for which they long." He cleared his throat and added, "I do not say it enough, but the thought of being a father fills me with joy." Maldwyn's face flushed, which reminded me of our early days together.

I reached out and stroked his cheek. "You will be a wonderful father."

His eyes trapped mine. "When you first loved me I did not think anything could make me happier, but now this." Maldwyn paused and his gaze flicked down to the little mound under my hand. He looked away then, blinking rapidly. "This babe has completed my life." Maldwyn met my eyes again. "You and she are my world."

I pulled Tân up then, raising my arm and signaling for the army to halt. "Dreda!" I called to the tall Queen's Guard member who rode not far behind me at the head of my guard.

She clucked to her horse and joined us. "Yes, my queen?"

"We'll take a short break here before marching to tonight's camp-site," I said.

"As you ask, so will I do."

As Dreda began calling down the wide, thick line of warriors to halt for a break, I raised a brow and grinned at Maldwyn. "I need an escort, Horse Master." I didn't wait for his response but kicked Tân into a gallop and turned her toward a distant cluster of willows.

I arrived at the trees ahead of Maldwyn—something that wouldn't have happened had he been riding Ennis. As I expected, the willows' long, tight line framed the bank of a lazy little stream. When Maldwyn joined me I smiled at him. "Help me down?"

His eyes widened with happy surprise at my request. As a warrior queen I rarely asked for help dismounting, but my horse master was more than willing to assist me. I dropped from Tân's back, allowing my body to slide intimately against his. When my feet touched ground

I did not move away. Instead I wrapped my arms around his broad shoulders and kissed him. My tongue teased his and Maldwyn responded enthusiastically, breaking our embrace only long enough to take off his travel cloak and lay it across the mossy ground under the willows. While he watched, I slowly, seductively took off my clothes. On his knees, he kissed the swell of my belly and whispered words of love to his child, and then those words were mine as I straddled him, bringing us to an intense climax so quickly that we collapsed together, sweaty, breathing hard, and laughing softly.

I was tucked against his shoulder and smiling happily when Maldwyn said, "What will you name her?"

I decided to indulge his insistence that the babe was a girl. "I shall call her Arianell."

He propped himself up on his elbow so he could gaze down at me. "Yes. That is perfect." His lips trailed down my neck and over my breasts to my not-so-flat stomach. Maldwyn kissed the slight mound gently and whispered, "My Arianell, my beloved."

The babe chose that moment to flutter a kick against her father's cheek.

His eyes met mine. They were filled with wonder. "She heard me!"

"She'll be as wise as my mother. She has to be. She already knows her father's voice," I said.

He rested his cheek on my belly again and whispered more endearments to our child as my fingers combed through his soft blond hair.

It was self-indulgent that I commanded the army to wait while Maldwyn and I loved one another. I know that. But I will always remember and be grateful for that slight moment in time and how Maldwyn rested his cheek against my body, laughing whenever the babe kicked him. We talked of nothing and everything—of how life would be when we returned to Tasceni. How the royal lodge would, once again, be filled with the sounds of an infant—and how the Mother of Twenty would hover and cluck and take charge, as she had already announced that she would be remaining with her queen even after the Romans were only a bad memory. But mostly I will never forget how love and joy and hope filled Maldwyn's blue eyes and how it seemed forever stretched before us, beckoning with the promise of new life and fulfilled dreams.

If only it had been in my power to make that moment last.

We reached the valley as the sun was high above us the next day. It was as Cartimandua had described. In this part of the Midlands the land was fertile, and many fields were cleared and the dark, fecund earth was newly planted. But it was also hilly, with creeks flowing from tree-covered slopes too steep and rocky to farm. The valley was situated green and lush between craggy, densely forested hills. There was only one easy way into the valley. It was like a mouth that opened, beckoning with the softness of the grassy stretch within. It was large— big enough to hold our warriors and the legions—and the hills that framed three sides of it were steep. The chiefs and my lead warriors and I were at the entrance to the valley when Deorwine joined us.

"Greetings, Queen Boudicca!" He bowed his head first to me. "Chiefs and warriors." Deorwine greeted each of them, and I thought that Cartimandua had made an excellent choice in her horse master. He was intelligent and articulate. It was obvious the chiefs liked him considerably more than his queen—not that I blamed them.

"Will Queen Cartimandua join us today?" I asked.

"My queen wishes she could, but she and her guard have traveled down Watling Street to meet Paulinus and assure him you have, indeed, been lured into his trap," said Deorwine with a grin. "But it is my honor to show you the details. Come, let me begin by guiding you to where your caravans should make camp during the battle."

I nodded, and as a group we followed Deorwine. I was not bothered that Cartimandua wasn't there. Her greeting us had never been part of our plan, and I did like hearing she was continuing to follow the plot we had created in a different valley just ten days before, though at that moment it seemed as if I'd left the Eryri Mountains behind so much longer ago.

I was surprised to see that the back side of the hills that framed the valley dropped steeply down and then joined rows of hillocks crisscrossed with streams. Trees, rocks, and dense brambly underbrush ruled their slopes, and as we surveyed the area my stomach tightened. It was, indeed, a trap. Any army that was caught within the valley would not be able to easily escape—the forest was too tightly packed with ancient trees and underbrush to allow chariots to pass, even if they could traverse the steep rear slopes. A cavalry wouldn't fare much better. A few horses could pick their way through the forest, but an entire army? Absolutely not. Foot soldiers could scramble to flee, but if well-trained bowmen stood their ground and sent arrows into the woods, most of those slow-moving soldiers would be cut down.

Yes, it was a perfect place for a trap.

"And here is where your caravans will be safe to camp." Deorwine gestured to the slope of the western hill framing the valley. "They can hug the side of the hill here. The legion will come from Watling Street in the southeast. If the caravans are tucked into this part of the slope, the hill and valley will be between them and the Romans, and the Romans will be focused on the valley where you will wait within." His smile was open and warm. "Some of your people might want to climb the hill so they can look down and watch the destruction of the last Romans in Britain."

"The last Romans in Britain!" Mailcun shouted. "Those words fall on my ears like rain after drought."

"Aye!" the chiefs agreed.

"And where is your army?" I asked Deorwine.

"Ah, well, if you climb the eastern hill and look out to the southeast, you will see Watling Street. The warriors of Tribe Brigantes are camped under cover of the forest there." Deorwine gestured as he spoke. "There we await Queen Cartimandua's signal."

"She still plans to ride to the valley with the Romans?" I asked.

"Yes, of course. She and her guard. Paulinus believes he knows our queen well, so when she says she prefers to watch the battle from the northern hill, he will not be surprised. Cartimandua has convinced Paulinus that she does not wish to dirty her hands in battle."

Deorwine scoffed. "He believes her because Roman women are so weak. My queen has told him that from there"—the Brigantes horse master pointed up to the northern hill—"she will signal her warriors to close the trap on you, when in truth that signal will be the end of the legions."

"When will the Romans arrive?" asked Leofric.

"As the mouth of the valley points to the east, Paulinus will march his legions into it tomorrow as the sun rises at his back," said Deorwine.

Cadoc grunted. "As would I. We will hear the mighty sound of legions approaching but be unable to see all of them. It is a sound tactic."

"As is our trap, once sprung," Deorwine said, grinning. "Queen Cartimandua has told the Romans that you are so arrogant and sure of their defeat that you will camp within the valley."

I nodded. "Some of the caravans will have to enter the valley so it appears as if we are actually camping there."

"Yes," said Deorwine.

"Not many of them, though," said Comux. The Dobunni chief was always quick to consider the families following our army. I understood. His family was still under Rome's thumb, waiting for this battle to be won so he could free them.

"I agree," I said. "We need only move a few wagons into the rear of the valley, where they'll be glimpsed by the Romans. By the time the legions are within the valley and realize the caravan has been staged, it will be too late."

"Exactly!" said Deorwine. "And now I must return to my queen. May the gods be with you tomorrow."

"May they be with us all, and may Britain be forever free," I said.

"Aye!" the chiefs shouted.

chapter xlii

We spent the rest of the day preparing. We tucked the majority of the caravans into the western slope of the hill, only bringing a dozen wagons within the valley and situating them well to the rear, positioned so that they could just be seen from the entrance. Among those dozen caravans, the chiefs and I, with our lead warriors and guards, would spend the night before the battle. But we did not retreat to our campfires until after we'd walked among our warriors. Morale was high. Army camps become a living thing, with personalities and emotions. Our camp was restless and eager—a young stallion straining to race the wind. Of course there were nerves, but Camulodunum, Londinium, and Verulamium had seasoned the bulk of our warriors. They knew what would be expected of them and were eager for dawn and another victory.

Offering bowls filled with sweets and mead dotted the camp. Bundles of dried herbs were burned and richly scented smoke drifted with the night breeze. I'd just begun wondering after Rhan when she seemed to materialize from the herb-laden smoke. I smiled and hooked my arm through hers. She smelled of the forest and of the rosemary smoke through which she'd come. We walked together slowly without speaking.

Maldwyn had already bid me good night and gone to sleep with Ennis and Finley, as he was wont to do the night before a battle. I suspected that he got little sleep but spent most of the night checking and rechecking their harnesses, the chariot, and our weapons.

As usual, Rhan knew the slant of my thoughts. "Maldwyn has gone to be with the horses already?"

"Yes. The chiefs and I are sleeping within the valley. Would you join me?"

Rhan pressed her shoulder into mine. "Always."

We'd come to the mouth of the valley and turned within. "Enfys and Ceri are insisting on staying in the valley as well," I said.

Rhan nodded. "It is only right that they do. I assume they will join you when you speak to the army before the battle tomorrow?"

"Yes, I'll drive the chariot. The girls will be with me, and their wolves will run beside the chariot," I added with a smile.

Rhan laughed softly. "You will be quite the sight. The mighty Queen Boudicca, Andraste's Victory, her daughters, and the wolves who watch over them."

"The warriors do love those wolves," I said. "Not that they can actually touch them without being in danger of having their arms taken off."

Rhan shrugged. "Briallen can touch them. You can. I can. Oh, and Maldwyn, of course, can. No one else needs to."

"Exactly what I think." We approached the wagons where my guard, my daughters, and my lead warriors congregated around a large central fire. Three of Wulffaed's daughters were singing an old planting song that spoke of new life being sown. Their voices sounded like home and evoked memories of the fertile fields that surrounded Tasceni.

As Rhan and I approached, Cadoc stood, bowed to me, and motioned for me to take his seat on a rough log. I thanked him and sat, with Rhan close beside me. Wulffaed's daughters had begun an Ostara song that celebrated the awakening of the earth as the goddess arises from her winter sleep when Enfys and Ceri joined me. My daughters sat on the ground in front of me, leaning back on my legs. Their wolves curled on either side of them, snouts on paws, appearing sleepy, but in truth the firelight reflected yellow in their ever-watchful eyes. My fingers combed through first Enfys's and then Ceri's long hair. My girls relaxed back against me, filling me with determination.

Tomorrow would not be just another battle. It would decide whether the war would be won or lost. We must win.

❖

I fell asleep in Rhan's arms while she caressed my hair. It seemed I had hardly closed my eyes when Rhan, fully dressed, was standing beside my pallet gently shaking me awake.

I woke instantly and sat up. "Is it time?"

"It is. Briallen is readying the girls. I have your things here but would ask that you follow me to cleanse yourself," said Rhan as she lifted a pile of my battle leathers and a basket from which I caught the sharp scent of body paint.

Wearing only a cloak to cover my nakedness, I followed Rhan outside my tent. It was far enough from dawn that the sky had just begun to change from black to gray, but our small camp was already humming with activity.

"Take this with you, my queen." Wulffaed handed Rhan and me meat, hot from the fire, wrapped in fresh bread with a thick slab of cheese. She bowed deeply to me, which was unusual. Wulffaed usually behaved like an overbearing grandmother, but in the predawn lightening I could see the somber look in her eyes. I only had two daughters and one more child growing within me. Wulffaed was the Mother of Twenty, grandmother of uncounted more. In her gaze I saw hope laced with worry. I understood that look too well.

Impulsively, I pulled the old woman into my arms, hugging her tightly. "Thank you. You brought contentment back to my lodge. That is a gift I can never repay."

I released her and she cupped my face between her gnarled hands. "Just live past this battle. That will be payment enough."

"She will," Rhan said firmly.

Wulffaed's whole body relaxed. "Aye, well, if our high Druid says it, then it will be so."

I slanted a look at Rhan, but she said no more as we chewed our food and walked from the far end of the valley and into the woods. The incline began with the trees and climbed almost straight up. I followed Rhan as she took a serpentine path that slithered up the hill, leading us to a fast-moving stream that cascaded down from above.

Rhan placed the basket she'd been carrying near the bank and then turned to me. "I did not sleep. Instead Andraste compelled me to this stream. Annwn is close here." She gestured across the narrow stream to where two rowan trees stood. They were covered in delicate cream-colored flowers and were so close that their branches wove together to create a living arch.

"Did Andraste mean for me to visit her before the battle?" I asked.

"Has the goddess called you?"

I shook my head. "No. I would still be sleeping had you not awakened me."

"Then no. But Andraste did compel me to bring you here." Rhan moved her shoulders restlessly. "I believe she wants you to cleanse yourself in the stream because it is so near to Annwn. Then I will paint your body and ready you within sight of an entrance to the Otherworld. But I also feel that there is another reason the goddess wanted you to know this place. She just hasn't made that reason known yet."

I shrugged off my cloak, drew a deep breath, and then stepped into the frigid stream. I ignored the cold and focused on the rowan arch and the closeness of Annwn as I washed. *I want to be worthy of your belief, Andraste. I ask for strength. Not for myself, but for my people. I ask for wisdom, not for myself, but to lead my people.*

I finished cleansing and was about to leave the stream when the gray of predawn changed to a lighter shade of slate, that of a dove's feathers, and my gaze was caught by a spot of white on the other side of the stream not far from the rowan arch. As if of their own volition, my legs carried me out of the stream and up the slight bank. I walked the few feet to the living arch that was farther up the steep slope. When I reached it a wave of dread washed over me, choking my breath, making me dizzy, causing me to stumble back as I gasped in horror.

I heard Rhan wade quickly through the stream behind me, but I could not look at her. All I could do was stare at the dead thing.

"Oh, goddess." Rhan's voice was hushed.

"It's a sacred hare, isn't it?" I spoke through numbed lips.

Rhan took my cold hand in hers. "Yes, but more than that. It is the sacred hare I loosed in the valley five days ago. See, there. She has the crescent moon I painted on her chest."

I nodded and continued to stare. The hare was on its side. The one eye I could see was open and opaque, sightless. Her mouth was open, too, as if frozen midscream. Blood darkened and matted the soft fur around her mouth. But that wasn't the most horrible thing about the little broken body. Her stomach had been torn open. Her entrails spilled onto the forest floor, and within those entrails was a glistening chain of three small, white things wrapped in scarlet—like a necklace of freshwater pearls that had been dipped in blood.

I clutched Rhan's hand and swallowed several times before I could speak. "The hare was pregnant." I somehow choked the words out.

"Yes," Rhan said softly.

I finally tore my gaze from the dead hare to look at my best friend, my lover, my high Druid. "This is a very bad omen."

"It is a dire warning."

A shudder rocked my body and I turned to face Rhan. "The Romans are too close. Our warriors might be able to scatter into the forest and escape, but the caravans cannot possibly get away."

Rhan nodded. "And if the warriors flee the caravans filled with the families of our people will fall to the Romans."

"Even should I ask them to our warriors would not abandon their families. There is nothing I can do." As I spoke those words the weight of them pressed down on me so heavily that I felt rooted to the floor of the forest.

"That is not entirely true," said Rhan slowly. "Boudicca, I told you I have been preparing."

"Yes."

"I have seen that you survive this battle—you, your girls, and the child you carry. But you must be willing to do as I say when the time comes." Rhan's voice had taken on the quality of strength and command it held when she spoke as the high Druid.

"But what does that mean?"

"I do not know yet. Not entirely. Just know I have prepared. I will be by your side. And you and your children will survive," Rhan said.

My reluctant gaze went back to the hare. "We cannot make this portent known."

"Agreed. It would devastate the army." Her hand cupped my chin and she turned my face from the body so that I saw only her. "Go back into the stream. Do not look at the hare again. Cleanse yourself again. I will care for the creature. Then I will paint you with protective symbols and help you dress. We will return to camp with your head held high, confident and strong."

"Because that is how it must be." I nodded shakily. "That is how they must see me."

"No, my queen." The high Druid corrected me sharply. "Because that is how it *is*. You *are* confident and strong. That is how they *do* see you, because your people see you truly."

"Yes," I whispered as she loosed my hand and I turned my back to the goddess's dead messenger. "Yes . . . yes . . . yes . . . ," I continued to whisper as I cleansed myself again. I heard Rhan moving through the underbrush, but I did not look up.

Finally she joined me in the stream, bending to wash her hands and arms thoroughly. We left the water together. I stood silently as she dried me with my cloak and then Rhan painted my body, naked except for my torque, with Iceni blue, outlining the Ogham symbols she'd tattooed so many months ago and adding the sickled moons with star points that proclaimed me a warrior of Tribe Iceni to my arms. As Rhan worked, she hummed a sonorous melody that increased in tempo until it reflected my heartbeat. It was cold that morning, but I did not notice it. I'd shut myself off from feeling anything. I was no longer Boudicca, daughter of Arianell, mother to Enfys and Ceri. I was only Boudicca, queen of the Iceni, who prepared to lead her mighty army into battle.

I dressed in the dyed woad leathers Wulffaed had spent so much time and talent and love creating. They fit like a second skin and blazed blue, trimmed in silver thread that formed ravens within knots. When I was dressed, we retraced the steep path back to the camp.

The valley was alive with activity. Our chariots and cavalry had already entered and were spreading out across the wide, flat space, facing the entrance. Behind them the foot soldiers began to stream into the valley, rivers of Iceni blue, Trinovantes red, Catuvellauni brown, and

Dobunni green, all mixed with bright splashes of the colors of the many other tribes that had joined us. I let my pride in them fill me, drowning out my dread. I would be their warrior queen to the end.

Phaedra waited within my tent. She combed out my long hair until it crackled and curled below my waist. Then she and Rhan strapped on my arm and shin guards and my breastplate. My helmet had been polished and looked striking in the flickering candlelight; the shining bronze complemented the spikes of Tân's mane and the long red length of her tail that would flow down my back and mix with my own hair on the battlefield.

Phaedra bowed deeply to me. "My queen."

I took her elbow so that she straightened and then I kissed her forehead. "Thank you, Phaedra."

Blinking back tears, Phaedra hurried from the tent, leaving Rhan and me alone. She stepped into my arms and we held each other silently. Then I looked into her dark, bottomless eyes, which were more familiar to me, more dear to me, than my own.

"I love you," I said. "I shall always love you."

"And I you, my friend, my love, my queen."

We kissed. Tenderly. I buried my face in her hair and breathed in her scent one last time before I straightened, put my helmet under my arm, lifted my chin, and left the tent.

My daughters waited beside the chariot, which gleamed in the soft pink light of dawn. The sigil Rhan had created before our first battle was strapped in its place at the front of the chariot, the eagle bones clanking in the morning breeze. Ennis and Finley thrummed with energy, even as Maldwyn soothed them. Enfys and Ceri looked fierce and beautiful. Wulffaed had dyed their leathers to match mine. Briallen had painted their faces, necks, and arms. Their hair cascaded free, haloing them in fire. Someone, probably the girls, had painted Ogham symbols in blue across the flanks of their wolves.

My lead warriors and the other chiefs would already have taken their places at the front of the cavalry and chariots, waiting for me to take the field. Briallen and my Queen's Guard stood beside the chariot. They would not enter the field without me.

I went to Wulffaed first. She and ten of her daughters bowed deeply. I lifted Wulffaed and kissed her forehead.

"I command that you and your daughters leave these wagons and this valley. Join the caravans outside."

"As you ask, so shall I do," echoed Wulffaed. "But first I have something for you, my queen." One of her daughters came forward, smiled shyly at me, and then gave her mother a large folded piece of cloth, which the Mother of Twenty shook out to reveal a cloak. It was a rainbow of colors woven together so that even in the soft light of dawn it flashed with brightness and beauty. It was not thick or wide, but a light length of fabric that would fasten around my shoulders and stream behind me without being so long that it would get in my way during the battle. "It has all the colors of the tribes in it, my queen," said Wulffaed, her eyes bright with unshed tears. "All the colors of your people."

"It is lovely. I shall wear it proudly." Then I turned and motioned for her to put it on me. It was so light I hardly knew it was there. "Now go and wait outside the valley," I said gently. "Be safe. Be well." Wulffaed and her daughters bowed again before they hurried away.

I moved to stand before Briallen and my guard. They were dressed and painted for battle. They were glorious. My guard bowed low. When they straightened, I stood before Briallen.

"Leader of my Queen's Guard, I task you with protecting my daughters. After I speak to the army, see them safely outside the valley and remain with them." I could hear the disappointed sighs of my daughters, but of course I would not be swayed. Their disappointment I could bear. Their deaths I could not.

"As you ask, so shall I do," said Briallen. "I have mounts for the bairns waiting on the field. I'll take them out of the valley after you speak to the army."

I put my hands on her strong shoulders. "I know they will be safe with you." I kissed her forehead.

Maldwyn had two horses ready in addition to Ennis and Finley, who pawed restlessly, more than ready to take to the field and defeat another enemy. He was magnificent in his battle gear. His light blond hair was pulled back and had raven feathers braided into it. His leathers were dyed to match mine, but his had been painted in bold black with our sickled moons and stars pattern. His arms were bare except for his forearm guards and the knotted tattoos that ringed his biceps. Maldwyn's cornflower eyes shined with the anticipation I recognized from our other battles, which helped to settle my nerves.

He started to bow to me, but I stepped into his arms, pulled him close, and kissed him thoroughly. When I loosed Maldwyn, his eyes were still shining and his lips lifted in a smile. I didn't speak. I couldn't. I went to the chariot cart and took my place as Maldwyn helped my girls up to stand on either side of me. Then he stepped back.

"Ennis and Finley are anxious for battle. Hold them tightly. I will join you on the field, my queen." He bowed.

I nodded. "I shall meet you there." Then my gaze found Rhan. She'd led her horse to the two Maldwyn had brought with the chariot for my daughters. I was surprised to realize it was Tân, and then relieved that Rhan would have such a reliable mount. I tried to tell Rhan with my eyes how much I loved her, though she knew. She had always known. "High Druid, I shall see you on the field, too," I said.

Rhan dipped her head. "Yes, Queen Boudicca."

Suddenly Abertha galloped into camp, pulling her horse up sharply beside the chariot. Instead of the white-horsehair-trimmed helmet she usually wore, I was surprised to see that she'd dyed her horsehair bright Iceni blue. She was in full battle regalia and looked ferocious and ready to take on the world.

"My queen! The Romans have left Watling Street. They march on the valley!"

"Good," I said. "Return to the front lines. I will follow."

Abertha dug her heels into her horse's flanks and raced away.

I said nothing more. All I could do was keep moving forward and keep hoping the battle was not truly lost.

"Hold tight, girls." I clucked and snapped the reins. My girls' wolves ran beside us as Ennis and Finley surged forward with Rhan, Maldwyn, and my guard following.

I drove the chariot through the rear lines of the army and my soldiers parted before me, beginning a chant that spread like a rippling wave on a quiet pool.

"*Bou-dic-ca! Bou-dic-ca! Bou-dic-ca!*"

Their belief in me made me stand tall. Whatever was to come, I would face it with my people. I drove through my army, buoyed by their cheers, until I was in front of them on the flat valley that opened to the death marching toward us. I turned my back to the approaching Romans and faced my people.

Cadoc was there, waiting in his chariot, looking like a wrathful god of war in his stag-horn helmet. His smile was a baring of teeth. His driver held the Iceni carnyx at the ready. Abertha had moved from her mount to another chariot. I knew she and Cadoc would frame me during the battle. It comforted me.

Stretching out along the first row of warriors were the other three chiefs and their shields. Comux, Leofric, and Mailcun bowed to me and then took up the cheer with the rest of the army.

"*Bou-dic-ca! Bou-dic-ca! Bou-dic-ca!*"

I drove Ennis and Finley back and forth along the front line of the army as my girls raised their fists and shouted with the warriors before I chose a spot in the center of the valley and halted my team. I caught sight of Maldwyn. He was standing beside Rhan. They'd dismounted and I could see that their heads were tilted together.

"Mama." Ceri tugged on my cape so that I glanced down at her. She did not sound frightened. All she said was, "Behind us I can see the sun shining on the Romans' shields."

"Don't look at them, little dove. They are nothing." I bent and kissed her and Enfys. Then I straightened and raised my hand. The army went silent. Above me a dozen ravens swooped low, gliding over my chariot and over the army to take up perches in the trees surrounding the valley. My people cheered. I raised my hand again and they went silent. I drew a deep breath and pitched my voice so it would carry.

"Britons, though we are of different tribes, we are one people, fighting for one reason, with a combined spirit the Romans have never understood, nor will ever understand! They are a people driven by an insatiable need for more, more, more! They do not come to this valley to fight for their freedom or to save their homeland or even to protect their daughters." I spread my arms to encircle Enfys and Ceri. "Romans prefer to rape daughters, slaughter elders, and enslave warriors.

"We know better! We are here for one reason—*to reclaim our freedom*! Rome has given us no choice in this war. If we do not fight they will erase us, obliterate our customs, thieve our gods, and subjugate us, making us slaves in our own lands.

"I will not be enslaved! I will not be erased! Will you?"

"NO!" the army roared.

Rhan stepped out from the front line. She held a long spear and danced toward my chariot, whirling and spinning, stomping and leaping, as she twirled the spear. Her white-blond hair lifted around her with her high Druid robes. When she reached my chariot, she faced the army and began pounding the spear rhythmically against the ground. The army echoed her with their own spears until the whole valley shook with the heartbeat of our people.

"Today we fight!" I spoke in time with the heartbeat. *"Today we shall be free—either in death or in victory!"*

As the army chanted my name, I bent to my daughters. "Go with Briallen now. Be brave. Do as she says. I love you." I kissed both girls.

Briallen raced up on a horse, leading two more, but before Enfys followed Ceri from the chariot, she looked up at me with eyes far older than her years and said, "Mama, you won't let anything happen to the babe, will you?"

Her words almost broke me. "You need not worry about the babe or me, my darling. All will be well."

Enfys nodded somberly before she jumped from the chariot to scramble aboard her mount. My gaze followed my girls until they were lost in the crowd.

Then Rhan said, "Remember. I have prepared." She mounted Tân, whom Maldwyn had led to us, and galloped out of sight.

Maldwyn jumped nimbly into the cart beside me. Cadoc and Abertha took their places on either side of us. Finally, we turned the chariots to face the mouth of the valley. The Roman legions were there. The rising sun glistened off their golden sigils and shields and armor. They seemed to stretch on endlessly, a dangerous tide of crimson and gold and bronze. I let my gaze scan the steep slopes of the hills that trapped us. Above us, exactly where Deorwine had said she would be, was Cartimandua. She was caught in a ray of sunlight that illuminated her so well that I could see the lift of her strong jaw and the steel in her eyes as she stared out at the Romans. She sat on a huge black horse and held the familiar sigil of Tribe Brigantes, a black banner with Brigantia's flame emblazoned in gold across it. The butt of the pole that held it rested against her thigh, waiting to be raised. Her words echoed from my memory. *I will allow the Romans to enter the valley. They will believe it is your arrogance that has trapped you. I will raise and wave the Brigantes sigil, which will signal my army to attack. Then it will be the Romans whose arrogance has trapped them.*

The Romans called out a command, pulling my attention from the Brigantes queen. I expected the legions to march forward, shields locked, but instead they remained outside the valley, waiting and watching.

"What are they doing?" Cadoc asked. "Shall we take them by the hand and lead them into battle?"

I had no answer except for the terrible chill crawling along my spine and up my neck, causing my skin to prickle. Suddenly panicked shouts and screams came to us before we heard the pounding of hooves and the distinctive creaking of wagons. And then our family-filled caravans, which had been hidden, tucked along the far slope of the hills, where they should have been safe, poured into our valley— driven by Roman legions.

"Oh, goddess!" Maldwyn choked the words out.

My stomach tightened with rage and dread as our terrified families joined us in our trap.

"Sound the carnyx!" I told Cadoc. Screaming the Iceni war cry, we thundered forward.

CHAPTER XLIII

All was chaos. The entrance to the valley was wide and flat, which made it easy to see Roman legionnaires overrunning every caravan except for the few that had already made it to us and slipped behind our chariots and cavalry to head for the rear of the valley. The Romans cut down our wagons like wheat before a scythe. We heard the screams of our families even above the thunder of our chariots and the clash of swords and shields.

We tried to reach them, tried to slip around or push beyond our caravans and put ourselves between them and the Romans, but there were too many of us—an explosion of people. The wagons clogged the mouth of the valley. The Romans waded through them, slaughtering elders and children, farmers and weavers, shepherds and cooks.

And then the Roman soldiers pushed wagons and bodies aside just enough for them to march into the valley in formation, shields locked, weapons ready. But they did not remain in strict, immutable formation. The legions had learned and adapted. Their locked-shield phalanx broke into smaller, movable sections. Like deadly serpents, they undulated across the valley, bringing death with every strike as they encircled pockets of wagons and groups of our warriors—closing on them, absorbing them, obliterating them. Their long spears kept our chariots from breaking through their lines. Their shields kept our arrows from reaching them.

Maldwyn whipped our chariot around, heading toward a wagon and the dozen Romans who had formed a movable phalanx to attack it. On horseback, Comux, with his shield beside him and his Chief's Guard following, thundered past us, making it to the wagons ahead of us. Maldwyn pulled Ennis and Finley up hard when a centuria of

Romans closed a circle around the wagons and Comux—and cut every one of them down.

As Maldwyn drove our team back and away from that slaughter, I had time to look up at Cartimandua. *Now!* I wished I could shout above the cacophony of battle around me. *Now is the time for you to signal your attack!*

For a moment I felt a rush of relief as the sigil was caught in the same ray of sunlight that had illuminated Cartimandua earlier. But she didn't raise it. She just sat there staring down at the bloody valley. And then a second horse and rider joined her. I could tell that it was a man and that he wore a cloak of Trinovantes scarlet. *Trinovantes scarlet?* My racing mind was having difficulty processing what I saw.

Cartimandua passed the sigil to the man, who moved his horse closer so that he could take it. As he did so sunlight flashed on him and everything within me recoiled. Adminius, wearing the torque of a Brigantes chief, glared down at the valley in which his people, *his tribe,* were being massacred. Adminius lifted the sigil and waved it over his head before he deliberately threw it to the ground. Then he and Cartimandua turned as one and disappeared down the far side of the hill.

Cartimandua's voice swirled in my mind. *Tell me, how do you handle traitors? . . . I choose to kill traitors.*

No Brigantes joined the battle. Not one warrior pressed the Romans from outside the valley to trap them between our armies. I understood then what I later learned to be truth. The signal given to Cartimandua's army was not to join us. It was their sign to leave us to our deaths. The Brigantes queen hadn't tired of the Romans. The Romans had lost interest in dealing with a woman and had decided to usurp her throne and replace her with a man they could control. When banished Adminius fled to Cartimandua, the queen seized the opportunity to maintain her rule by pretending to make him chief of the Brigantes—and then together the two of them betrayed us and solidified their allegiance with Rome.

"To your right!" Maldwyn's warning tore my attention back to the battle. A large group of Roman soldiers was bearing down on us, clearly attempting to cut us off from the rest of the army. I threw three spears quickly, one after another, striking only one man lethally. Locked shields repelled the rest. If not for the speed of Ennis and Finley, my battle would have ended there.

We raced back to the main group of chariots, now surrounded by our cavalry. Foot soldiers ran from the rear of the valley, roaring tribal battle cries as they threw themselves over and over against the walls of scarlet-painted shields.

"What has happened?" Cadoc shouted as he and Abertha pulled to a halt beside us.

"Cartimandua betrayed us. Adminius was with her." I jerked my chin up in the direction of where the traitors had been.

"Adminius!" Cadoc spat over the side of his chariot. "May he receive the death he deserves."

"What now?" Abertha showed no sign of panic. Her steady gaze was filled with confidence in her queen. She simply waited for me to answer the question.

Before I could respond, a wolf raced up to us—and then a second wolf joined him, followed by Briallen and my white-faced daughters.

"We could not get out of the valley," Briallen said quickly.

"Go to the rear of the valley. Climb the hill! Even if you have to leave the horses, you must get the girls to safety." I was amazed my voice was steady. Seeing my daughters there within the killing field had me utterly terrified.

"We tried," said Briallen. "Romans are on the ridges cutting down all who try to pass."

"W-we'll fight with you, Mama," Enfys stuttered through lips blue with fear.

"Yes." Ceri nodded. Her face was the color of old milk.

"Move! We must move!" Maldwyn shouted. "They're targeting us, my queen!"

My gaze snapped back to the battlefield, where a large group of Roman cavalry charged toward us. Cadoc blew the carnyx and Iceni warriors shrieked our battle cry in response, rushing to stand between the Romans and me. With Cadoc and Abertha flanking me, and Briallen following with my girls and their wolves, our little group retreated.

"Follow me! Now!" Rhan's voice, filled with authority, blasted at us. She sat astride Tân, who pranced in place, beckoning us with a raised arm. Maldwyn responded immediately, turning our chariot toward the Druid. She wheeled Tân around and galloped deeper into the rear of the field, heading to the dozen wagons that had sheltered us the night before.

The camp was deserted. I could only hope that Phaedra, Wulffaed, and her daughters had managed to escape. Rhan pulled Tân up and slid off her before the mare had fully halted. She turned to face us and I saw nothing of my lover before me—only the high Druid, though she no longer wore her distinctive white robes.

She wore a pair of my battle leathers. She'd rolled them up and belted them, as she was slight and slender and I was not. And then with a jolt of shock I realized that she'd painted her arms to match mine. She'd tied on my spare set of shin and forearm guards and even wore one of my older breastplates.

"Why are you dressed like this?" Even as the words slipped from me I already felt her answer deep within my battered spirit.

"I have prepared." The high Druid repeated the familiar words to me. She strode to us. "We have little time. The battle is lost. Cartimandua's army has departed. We are betrayed. Queen Boudicca, if you remain here either you will be killed or you will be captured, taken to Rome, and paraded through their streets before they execute you."

"No, I—"

Rhan interrupted. "But they will not kill you until your child is born. Then the babe you carry will be torn from your arms and dashed against a wall as you watch or allowed to live as a Roman pawn. Enfys and Ceri will be killed or imprisoned. They might be sold into slavery after Rome has made a spectacle of them and murdered their mother."

I tried to speak but my girls had moved their horses to me.

"Mama, we can never be taken by the Romans again," said Enfys. She reached out and grasped Ceri's hand. My youngest daughter had her lips pressed tightly together so that she made no sound as tears dripped down her pale cheeks. "We have decided. We would rather die."

"Y-yes, Mama." Ceri's voice shook but her gaze never wavered. "W-we would r-rather die."

I went to them and reached up, grasping their joined hands. "I will not allow a Roman to touch you. On that you have my oath." *But am I capable of killing my own daughters, my babies?* Unbidden, their screams lifted from my memory and it felt as if my heart suddenly pumped only ice for blood. *I must prevent them from being brutalized again, but kill them? With my own hand?*

"None of those things can be allowed to happen." Maldwyn took my shoulders in his hands and turned me from my girls to face him. "Listen to me. You must not be taken. Your children must not be taken. As long as you survive, hope survives."

"Aye," said Cadoc.

"Aye," agreed Abertha.

"What must we do to save the bairns and Herself?" asked Briallen.

"We will give the Romans what they want—a battle against Queen Boudicca," said Rhan as she strode to my chariot. "I must have your cloak and your helmet, my queen. For this one day I shall be you."

"And in doing so you mean to allow our queen to escape," said Cadoc. "But how?"

"Queen Boudicca knows," said Rhan as she met my gaze.

"Annwn." I whispered the word.

There was shouting behind us. "The Romans are breaking through our lines. They've followed you," said Abertha.

"We have no more time!" Maldwyn unclasped the cloak from around my shoulders. I noticed his hands shook, but his voice and gaze were steady. "You must flee. Your helmet. Rhan needs your helmet."

I understood. Rhan wanted me to go to the stream and escape through Annwn. The preparations she'd been making had been days and days of offerings so that my children and I would be allowed to slip into the realm of the gods and granted our lives.

"No! Briallen, Abertha, Cadoc—take the girls," I said. I felt as if I would explode with fear and anger and desperation. "Rhan will show you the entrance to Annwn. Maldwyn and I will return to the battle. I will not leave my people to die alone."

"You will not change their fate by dying with them!" shouted Rhan.

"And it will not only be your death. It will also be the death of our child." As Maldwyn spoke, tears streaked his blood-spattered cheeks.

"You must come, Mama! You must!" Enfys stared at me with my mother's eyes.

Ceri's little-girl voice was steady. "Mama, if you come, we live. If you stay, we all die." Then Andraste's voice came from her mouth, echoing the words she'd spoken to me once before so long ago. *"You must choose."*

Cadoc jumped from his chariot and strode to me, kneeling when he reached me. "Queen Boudicca," he said formally, his head bowed. "As your shield it is my duty to advise and protect you. I advise you to follow the high Druid's plan. And I shall protect your retreat with my life."

Abertha leaped from her chariot and knelt beside my shield. She bowed her head, so that the newly dyed woad horsetail on her helmet swayed against her back. "You must live, my queen."

Gently, Maldwyn took the helmet from my head. "As long as I draw breath, they will not get past me to you."

"Aye, me as well!" Briallen added.

"No, no, no." I shook my head. "You must all escape with me."

"What we must do is distract the Romans," said Rhan as Maldwyn fastened my cloak around her shoulders. She clasped my helmet under her arm, and my two lovers approached me.

"Queen Boudicca, I ask you to live so that hope lives," said the high Druid.

And then Maldwyn's words broke me. "Boudicca, my queen and my only love. I ask you to live so that part of me survives."

As if responding to Maldwyn's voice, the child within me moved.

Could I sentence my unborn babe to death? Chills bloomed across my skin. No. I could not, just as I could not cut my daughters' throats, even to keep them from being violated.

"One of you must accompany me," I said.

"Briallen," said Cadoc with no hesitation. "She should go with you and the girls."

"Aye," said Abertha. Maldwyn and Rhan nodded.

I took Rhan and Maldwyn in my arms. I wanted to speak, to say something these two people I loved so deeply would take with them as they faced their deaths, but my throat closed. I was afraid if I spoke, I would scream and scream and scream and never stop. The three of us clung to one another. I tried to imprint their scents, their touch, on my mind and my body. When I released them, I kissed one and then the other before I stared at each beloved face, memorizing . . . memorizing.

A roar came from behind us. Cadoc and Abertha jumped into their chariots. Maldwyn climbed into the cart, *our* cart, while Ennis and Finley snorted and stomped in anticipation. Rhan went to Tân, took her reins, and handed them to me.

"Ride fast. Ride far. Be free, my queen, my love." She turned to Maldwyn, who took her hand and helped her into the cart beside him. Her eyes remained on mine as Rhan strapped on my helmet.

As Maldwyn clucked to Ennis and Finley and wheeled the chariot around to go with Cadoc and Abertha back into the battle, the air around them rippled, like steam lifting from a boiling cauldron. The illusion was strong. I watched myself race away. Spear lifted and ready to strike, Queen Boudicca stood straight and proud beside her horse master and lover, drawing the attention of every Roman in sight. The fighting shifted—followed them—moving away from us toward the other end of the field.

Briallen's voice came from beside me. "Now, my queen. We have little time."

Woodenly, I mounted Tân and dug my heels into her flanks. She shot forward, galloping past the deserted caravans. Sunne and Mona were blurs beside me. I could hear the pounding of hooves as Briallen and my daughters raced after me. We ran until the forest forced us to pull the horses down to a walk. It was too steep, too carpeted with brambles and underbrush. I began to despair of finding the little path Rhan and I had taken, and then Tân shifted to the left, climbed through a patch of sticky brambles, and came out of them onto the trail. I pulled her up and then nudged her off the path. Enfys was behind me, followed by Ceri. Briallen guarded our rear.

"Keep following this little trail," I told Enfys. My elder daughter nodded and kneed her horse around me.

As Ceri passed she said, "You must come, Mama."

"I will, little dove. Keep going. Follow Enfys." Briallen reached me. "The trail takes us to a stream," I explained. "From there a rowan arch marks the entry to Annwn."

My warrior nodded. Her face was so expressionless it seemed made of stone. "Do not make their sacrifice be for naught," she said.

"I will be right behind you. Stay with the girls."

As Tân followed Briallen, I allowed myself to look back at the battlefield. Through the trees I could catch glimpses of the fight, like how lightning illuminates only slivers of the night as it strikes.

My gaze couldn't choose a place to settle. The battlefield had gone black with gore and rust with blood, soaking what had been thick green grasses. I couldn't make out individuals, only shapes. The sounds that drifted to us were terrible. Shrieking horses. Screaming people. Cries for the goddess. Cries for mothers. My vision blurred with tears, and then a flash of color lit the dreadful tableau.

My cloak.

The red of my horsetail helmet.

The flash of light off Maldwyn's chariot.

The chariot seemed to freeze in time as a spear sliced into the scene, the only thing moving with normal speed. It skewered Maldwyn through his neck, knocking him backward and out of the chariot.

Time sped up again. I saw Rhan reach for the reins and then she was swallowed by the chaos.

I opened my mouth to scream my grief, but no sound came from me.

Another color flashed across my gaze—another horsetail helmet, this one dyed woad blue. Abertha! I followed that proud slash of woad as she wove through the battlefield, throwing spear after spear, trying to reach the fighting into which Rhan's chariot had disappeared. When the spears were gone, Abertha lifted her sword and sliced the enemy surrounding her.

The enemy that slowly, methodically closed the noose of soldiers around her.

The enemy that pulled her from the chariot, trampling the proud blue until it was no more.

I looked for Cadoc's stag-horned helmet but did not see it. Was my shield already dead?

Pain tore my spirit, opening a crevice within me. Agony flowed with the blood of my people, soaking into this land I'd loved so well and fought so hard to keep free. It poured into me, flooding my body, attempting to fill the yawning crevice. It could not. My wound was too deep. No matter if I lived one day or many, I would carry the anguish of this battle, this loss, forever.

Tân turned one of the serpentine corners in the slender path, and the forest closed around me so that I could see no more of the death of my people.

"Mama!" Ceri's voice carried back to me. "We found the stream!"

CHAPTER XLIV

My girls and Briallen had halted their horses by the stream. Their wolves had already waded through it and were sniffing the ground before the rowan arch. *Where Rhan and I found the dead hare. Rhan . . .*

"Is this the entrance, my queen?" asked Briallen.

I began to nod but froze as the clanking of armor, the crackling of brush, and the voices of Roman soldiers filled the forest around us. Ceri gasped but pressed her trembling hand over her mouth. Mona padded to her horse's side, where she stood with her ears pricked, growling at the forest.

Quickly, I kneed Tân around the girls. I pressed my finger to my lips and then motioned for them to follow me. I waded through the stream and went to the archway. Peering through it, I saw movement in the underbrush all across the steep slope above us. Thick as lice, Roman soldiers canvassed the area, moving from the top of the hill down through the forest. A woman shrieked. Soldiers laughed and shouted. There were more screams that echoed through the forest around us, more sounds of death and brutality. They were moving ever closer to us. Desperately I urged Tân to the arched trees, looking for some evidence, *any* sign, that this truly was an entryway to Annwn, but I saw no opalescence of the sky, no welcoming mist, and did not hear the voice of my goddess.

The Romans would discover us.

I cupped my hands around my mouth and called, "Andraste! Help me! Help us!"

"This way! Someone called on one of their gods!" a Roman shouted.

I am here. Leap. I shall catch you. Andraste's voice soothed my heated mind as I recalled the rest of what she had said to me the last time I'd entered Annwn and called upon her. *It is not the last leap of faith you will make to save yourself—to save my victory. The next time I ask it of you, do not hesitate.*

I turned to look at my girls. "Follow me into Annwn. We must—"

"Mama, look!" Ceri pointed.

My gaze returned to the archway. Through it stood the white stag watching us with wise green eyes.

"We follow the stag." I amended what I had been going to say, hope fluttering weakly within my chest, as broken as my heart. "We go silently single file."

I guided Tân through the archway. Instantly my vision changed. It seemed we'd entered a strange tunnel. I could still hear the soldiers as they combed the hill for my people. I could even see them, though indistinctly.

Soundlessly, we rode on, slipping from shadow to shadow. Like long, elegant fingers on a dark hand, they reached for us, closed around us, and hid us as we were passed on to the next reaching shadow. The stag's white coat was dappled with the grasping darkness. The horses labored as we climbed the steep slope, ever upward, surrounded by death.

"Over here!" The Roman soldier sounded as if he was only feet away from us. The stag halted. I pulled Tân up and turned, pressing my finger to my lips again as I looked into the pale faces of my terrified daughters. "There's something strange there. Do you see it? Something in the shadows."

"Yes! Probably women trying to hide from us," said a second soldier.

"Come on out, little chick, chick, chicks," clucked a third soldier, his voice even closer.

I could see them now. Six legionnaires, heavily armed, approaching us. With a whisper of metal, Briallen drew her sword. I reached behind me to where my own blade rested strapped to my back, but before I could draw it Sunne and Mona pushed their heads through the dark barrier within which we traveled. Side by side they faced the

Romans. Their ears were flat against their heads, and pointed teeth bared, they growled deeply and threateningly.

The Romans stopped as if they'd walked into a wall.

"Romulus and Remus." One soldier spoke the names as if they were a prayer, bowing low as he backed away.

Together Sunne and Mona advanced a step.

One soldier held up both hands, palms out. He spoke softly to the wolves. "Brothers, we see you and we leave you to sacrifice whomever you've marked as yours." Each soldier continued bowing low as they backed away from the wolves and disappeared into the underbrush.

Sunne and Mona padded to us, tongues lolling.

"Good girl, Mona," Ceri whispered to her wolf.

"Well done, Sunne, my boy," Enfys said softly.

The stag started forward again. Silent once more, we followed. As we climbed the slope, we passed within a hand's length of many legionnaires. None of them so much as glanced our way. Bodies were crumpled mounds among the dense underbrush and thickets of brambles. I looked to see if any of them moved.

They did not.

I looked to see if I recognized any of them.

My spirit shuddered. Wulffaed was there, in the center of a circle made of the bodies of her daughters and Phaedra. They were dead. They were all dead.

Time lost meaning. It seemed the climb would never end. Tân's coat was dark with sweat. There was no sky or sun visible above us. All I could truly see was the stag before me, my daughters and their wolves, Briallen behind them, and the shadows cloaking us.

I'd begun to believe we might wander this slope of death eternally when Tân surged up and then over the lip of the hill. I pulled her to a halt, trying to see through the reaching shadows. The stag was still there—still ahead of me—but now he was picking his way down the slope, haunches almost touching the ground because of the steepness of the decline. The voices of soldiers had faded. There were no more screams. No more shouts. I turned and whispered to Enfys, "We made it up the hill. Keep going, but slowly. Watch the stag. Tell Ceri."

Enfys nodded and turned to whisper to her sister. I waited until the stag paused and looked back at me before I urged Tân forward. *Thank you, Rhan, for bringing Tân to me. Most horses would balk or refuse what I've asked of her today, but she is ever trustworthy, and because of that the other three horses follow her without fear.*

My thighs ached and Tân was breathing hard when the ground finally leveled under us. The stag broke into a trot, and our horses valiantly kept pace behind him. We trotted on and on. The stag led us through several streams, halting only long enough for our horses to drink, and then he would start forward at a trot again. Wearily, we followed until we came to a stream that was wider than the others before it. All along the bank were sacred white willows moving in a breeze that did not touch us. The stag waded through the stream and then turned and watched as we did the same. This time instead of trotting on, the mighty creature dipped his heavily antlered head, and then as he lifted it his body rippled, elongated, and blazed with light.

When I'd blinked my vision clear, in the stag's place stood a tall woman who wore a scarlet gown stitched with a silver stag across the bodice and a cloak of white deer hide over her shoulders. She tossed back her long, flame-colored hair. Antlers grew from her head. She looked steadily at me with eyes the color of emeralds.

I slid from Tân's back and went to my knees before her. Behind me I heard my daughters and Briallen dismount. Then they were beside me, also on their knees. Even the two wolves went to their bellies.

With my head bowed I said, "Blessed Brigantia, I greet you and thank you for guiding us through Annwn."

"You may rise, children," said the goddess. Her voice was the forest—rustling leaves and birdsong.

We stood and stared at the goddess. She was magnificent and wild—a blazing brand, a proud stag, a musical stream cascading to a waterfall crescendo.

"Andraste's Boudicca, daughter of my beloved Arianell, you did me a kindness in Camulodunum. For that I thank you."

"I was glad to end Rome's desecration of your shrine," I said.

She nodded, her massive antlers casting pointed shadows around her like dark blades. "Yes, would that all of my children were as faithful. Cartimandua, queen of my Brigantes, will pay for today's betrayal."

I had no words and could only bow my head.

"Now you must leave the protection of Annwn. Go north to Caledonia. There you will be out of reach of your enemies."

Shock jolted through me. Caledonia? The Highlands were days, *weeks,* away, and the route passed through almost a dozen different tribal territories. A wave of nausea washed over me and I staggered.

The goddess's strong hand caught my elbow, steadying me. "Your Queen's Guard knows the way to the realm of Beira, winter queen and mother of gods. Mighty Beira will succor you. You can do this, Andraste's Victory. And you will not be unprotected along the way. Seek the sign of the stag. There you will be safe. Seek the sign of Andraste's raven or hare. There you will be safe."

"But what of Andraste?" I blurted, feeling the absence of my goddess deep in my spirit. "Is she not here? Will she not speak to me?" *Or is she too disappointed in me to show herself?*

Brigantia touched my cheek gently. Her smile was so like my mother's that it made my breath catch. "I am here in Andraste's stead. She is with the Iceni in that valley of death, embracing each of her children as their spirit leaves their body. She is their comfort and their guide. They will feast with her this very night."

A ragged breath escaped me and I had to clench my hands into fists, digging my fingernails into my palms, to keep from keening my despair.

"Boudicca." The goddess took my face between her hands. "Know that you are being watched, and that goddesses never forget those they have chosen as their own." Brigantia kissed my forehead.

There was another blaze of light and the goddess was replaced by the white stag. He met my gaze, dipped his velvet muzzle, and then raced away. The air around us rippled, and with the sound of a sigh Annwn closed the veil between worlds, leaving us to peer around in confusion. It was late in the evening and I had no idea where we were, but as I studied the empty countryside I knew we were nowhere near the valley of death.

"We have to keep moving," I told my exhausted daughters.

Ceri nodded and patted her wolf's head. "To Caledonia, like the goddess said."

"Yes, little dove. North to Caledonia." I met Briallen's gaze. "We'll ride until there is no more light."

Briallen nodded. "We will because we must." My Queen's Guard met my gaze as she eerily echoed the words we'd spoken to each other that terrible day in Tasceni when our world had forever changed.

"Yes," I whispered brokenly. "We will because we must."

"Do not worry. As the goddess said, I know the way, my queen," added Briallen.

My hands shook as I pulled the torque from my neck. "Don't call me that. It isn't safe. When the Romans don't find my body they will come looking. And I am queen no more as my people are no more."

Ceri's hand slipped into mine. "You are my queen, Mama."

Enfys nodded. "And mine."

Briallen said, "As long as I breathe you will be my queen." She bowed low to me. "But to keep us safe I'll be calling you Herself."

Again, I had no words. I could only nod as I went to the full saddlebags Rhan had packed and strapped on Tân, opened a bulging bag, and slipped the torque within before closing it securely. We remounted. My last warrior took the lead and turned us north, urging our weary horses into a ground-eating trot as my daughters and I followed.

chapter xlv

Just before twilight we approached a wide, murky river and I knew where we were. I'd crossed the river Mersey during my wedding procession from Isurium to Tasceni and easily recognized the river as the boundary between the Cornovii and Brigantes tribes. This time my crossing was so different from the first that it didn't feel real. In truth, since we had left the valley behind nothing felt real. We did not ferry the wide river. We avoided all settlements, and as the sun sank toward the horizon to our left, we held tightly to our horses and swam the river, grateful that the bank was neither steep nor so muddy that our horses were bogged down.

Shivering, we continued northward. Briallen and I were searching for a spot to camp—somewhere within a sheltering grove where we could huddle for warmth, as lighting a fire in the territory of the queen who had betrayed us would not be wise—when Ceri called to me.

"Mama, is that a stag?"

My youngest daughter pointed to a modest roundhouse situated in the middle of a cleared area we'd been skirting. There was just enough light left to illuminate a tall standing stone before the home, on which was carved the head of a proud stag.

"It is," I said as Briallen and I exchanged a glance.

"Brigantia told us to look for signs. The goddess would not misspeak," said Briallen.

"Agreed." I turned to the girls. "We will be safe here for the night. Come, girls. Keep Sunne and Mona close. All is well." If I spoke the words perhaps I would believe them, though the weight of the sword strapped to my back reassured me as we headed to the roundhouse.

As we reached the standing stone, a middle-aged man and woman emerged. I lifted my hands, palms out, showing that I held no violent intent. "I see blessed Brigantia is the patron goddess of your home," I said.

"She is, indeed," said the man. He was tall and round with a sunlight-colored beard that was so long it rested on his barrel chest. "As she is the goddess of Tribe Brigantes."

I attempted a smile, but it felt more like a grimace. "Then in the goddess's name I ask succor for my daughters, our companion, and me for the night." I paused, and then, hoping I was correct in believing that the saddlebags Rhan had packed contained coin, added, "We can pay for a meal and a pallet. Have you a barn? That will do nicely."

The woman moved from the man's side. Staring up at me, she approached, stopping only when she reached Tân's head. Her eyes widened. "I know you," she whispered. Abruptly, she turned to her husband. "Ecgbert, be a love and scatter fresh bedding in the barn. I will feed them while their clothes dry by our hearthfire." Her husband muttered but headed toward the rear of their modest settlement. "Stay outside, mind!" she shouted after him. "Until I tell you they're dried and dressed."

"Well, what am I supposed to do out here in the dark?" Ecgbert grumbled.

"Build a fire outside the barn and it won't be dark." She sighed and added, "Get the last of the spring beer from the stream. That'll keep you happy while I tend to these poor travelers."

"Oh, aye." Ecgbert's voice lifted with his quickened steps, and with much greater enthusiasm he hurried away.

"Come, come. You are welcome in my home." The wife smiled up at me. "I'm Romilly." As we slid stiffly from our horses, she bowed. "And you are Queen Boudicca."

My gaze snapped to hers, but before I could speak she added, "My husband is Parisi. He will not recognize you. But I am Brigantes and would know the Iceni queen born in our royal city anywhere. You led an army against Rome, and that is all I know except that you are safe here. On that you have my oath in the name of the goddess Brigantia."

"May the goddess bless you for your kindness," I said.

"I'll tend to the horses and then join you," said Briallen.

The girls and I followed Romilly into her roundhouse where she cared for us, helping us out of our soaked clothes, wrapping us in blankets, and sitting us before the hearthfire as she heated slabs of pork and sliced fresh bread and cheese for us. She even fed Sunne and Mona. Briallen joined us, carrying the heavy saddlebags, within which rested a purse of coins. And then, while we ate, Romilly talked. She told us it was safest to stay west, as close to the coast as possible, while we slipped through my old tribe's territory. She spoke of the stories being told about me. How I'd united thousands of Britons against the scourge of Rome. How I'd brought hope even to tribes allied with Rome, like the Brigantes. Enfys and Ceri listened with sparkling eyes as Romilly spoke of my greatness.

I said nothing.

As the girls dressed in their warm, dry clothes, their eyelids went heavy. Briallen took Romilly to the side. I heard some of their whispered conversation—enough to know my warrior told of our defeat through treachery. When Romilly turned to me, tears streaked her cheeks.

Romilly led us to their barn, calling to her husband that he could return to the roundhouse. He staggered past us, too far into his cups to truly see us. The barn was small and tidy. Two plow horses shared one large stall. Our four horses shared the other two. Goats made nests in the straw and bleated softly as we entered but then settled quickly. Ecgbert had scattered fresh straw for us in the only section of the barn not inhabited by goats or chickens.

"Queen Boudicca, I'm sorry that this . . ." She gestured around her at the barn.

"This is perfect," I assured her. "Thank you."

"I can keep my Ecgbert in bed until the sun is above the horizon," Romilly said.

"We will be gone at dawn." I went to the saddlebags Briallen had brought from the house. "There is coin here to pay you." I reached into the heavy purse to extract payment.

Romilly was at my side in an instant. She touched my arm hesitantly and said, "No, Queen Boudicca. I cannot take your payment. My home is blessed to have been chosen to succor you the day you need it the most. That is payment enough, as Brigantia's memory is long and she rewards her own."

I bowed my head to her. "You have my gratitude, as well as the goddess's."

"And may blessed Brigantia guide you and keep you safe, great queen." Romilly bowed deeply before she left the barn.

The girls were asleep almost immediately. I curled on one side of them. Briallen took first watch and would wake me when the moon was high in the sky. She stood by the opening to the barn. Just outside, the fire Ecgbert had lit cast flickering shadows over her, illuminating the strong line of her jaw and the stubborn set of her shoulders.

"Briallen?"

She turned to look at me.

"I am glad you are here with us," I said.

She nodded, and I watched her blink rapidly as she struggled against tears before saying, "I'll always be here, my queen."

I didn't correct her, just as I hadn't corrected Romilly. Nothing felt real. It seemed I moved through a living dream—and unending nightmare. My mind was as numb as my body. My spirit was broken. The babe within me kicked and I curled around her, or him. Suddenly I wished very much that the child would be the girl her father had wanted so badly.

The image of Maldwyn skewered by a spear and falling from the chariot almost blinded me, and I realized that I could not see because my eyes were filled with unshed tears.

I hope they are laughing and feasting with Andraste—Maldwyn, Rhan, Cadoc, Abertha, Phaedra, Wulffaed and all of her daughters and granddaughters. Let them be together. Let them be free of fear and longing and pain. And let them save a place at the goddess's feast table for me.

I did not think I would sleep. Truth be told, I was afraid to close my eyes. Afraid that the images of this terrible day would play over and over across my closed lids. Afraid I would dream their deaths. I'd witnessed Maldwyn's death. I'd watched Abertha fall. I did not want to see Cadoc breathe his last. *I could not bear to watch Rhan die.*

But weariness ruled my body and I could not keep my eyes open. As darkness closed around me, I whispered a prayer to Andraste. *Please don't let me dream.* Whether the goddess heard my prayer or not, I did not dream.

We left before dawn, fortified by sleep and the dried meat and bread Romilly had packed for us the night before, and a pattern was set. Heading northwest, we avoided settlements, riding all day and only stopping to give the horses a break until twilight, when, every night, just as the sun sank into the horizon, we would come upon a round-house or a small camp or a group of hunters or traders returning from market. Each home or group was always marked by the goddesses with either a stag, a raven, or a hare. Each welcomed us. Each recognized me.

At first that worried me, but soon it was obvious the goddesses had touched everyone with whom we came in contact. Maldwyn had been correct. Just by surviving, I gave them hope, though with the dark news the people relayed to us it was difficult for me to understand that hope.

My army had been destroyed.

Out of the three chiefs, only Mailcun lived.

The devastation of my people had ended the revolution. The monster that was Rome had swallowed my world and now ruled Britain.

The night I learned that Rome had declared their victory, I waited until my daughters slept before taking out the Roman pugio Rhan had packed in my saddlebag—the same dagger the procurator Catus Decianus had used to cut my bloody bonds that day so long ago in Tasceni.

I walked to the hearthfire that crackled in the center of the small roundhouse, decorated with carvings of hares, that succored us that night. Slowly, methodically, I lifted fistful after fistful of my waist-length hair and cut it, whispering through sobs each name as I dropped a hunk into the fire. *Rhan, Maldwyn, Cadoc, Abertha, Wulffaed, Comux, Leofric, Addedomaros, Derwyn, Bryn, Arianell, Dafina, Phaedra* . . . The names went on and on.

Briallen tried to stop me. I commanded her to leave me be. She did not. She could not. Instead she pried the dagger from my fist and continued for me, cutting and cutting as I spoke a new name with each slice until my hair was so short it haloed my head in fire and I finally ran out of names.

The word officially spoken by Paulinus was that I had poisoned first my daughters and then myself, effectively stopping him from taking us to Rome to be paraded through the streets like slaves. But that was only the official word. Roman soldiers had been commanded to find me and capture me alive. Any Briton who aided in my capture would be granted fertile lands and riches. Any Roman who captured me would be rewarded with a villa in Rome. So under the guise of choking out the last of the Iceni, Roman soldiers raided, sacked, and razed our lands, when in truth they were hunting me.

During the long days and weary nights, we traveled ever northward, passing through territory held by tribes whose names I recognized but I had never known. Carvetii, Novantae, Damnonii, Caledonii, Cerones, and Carnonacae—all welcomed me. All knew me. All kept us safe.

After traveling for a fortnight, I woke one clear early morning with my throat feeling as if I'd swallowed coals and my head pounding. My skin was flushed and hot, but I shivered with cold.

"We are close," said Briallen, guiding her horse beside Tân. "Can you continue?"

"The Romans could not stop me," I said with an attempted smile. "A little illness will not."

Briallen narrowed her eyes at me but said nothing.

At midday we came to a huge stone, white as snow, decorated

with carvings of shaggy horned kine, massive swine, and curled-horned rams. Briallen kneed her horse to the stone and placed her palm against it. She bowed her head and whispered a prayer before looking at me.

"'Tis Beira's Stone. It marks the edge of the Caereni tribal lands—the lands on which I was born. We made it, my queen."

The girls squealed happily and began firing questions at Briallen, which she answered enthusiastically, though she kept glancing sideways at me.

"I am well," I assured her. "I just need rest."

She grunted but said no more. I knew it wasn't just the illness that worried her. I'd become a stranger. To her. To myself. To the world through which I had to continue to move. I wanted to find myself again, but I'd lost my mooring. My land was inhabited by the enemy. My people were either dead or scattered and in hiding. As I drifted north, I was unable to navigate my life. I'd lost my present and future and could not live in the past. So I ceased living; I only existed.

The sun was sinking into the ocean as we entered Ulapul, the royal village of Tribe Caereni. Briallen and I rode next to one another with the girls and their wolves trailing us. Even though I shivered with chills and my head ached, the excited chatter of my daughters' voices soothed me, as did the increasingly strong and constant movements of the babe I carried. When we'd stopped to rest and water the horses, Briallen had told us we would come to her birth village that evening. I'd forced myself to keep moving. I'd braided the girls' hair and brushed dirt and stains from our travel-weary clothes, trying to make us look more than we were—outcasts fleeing for our lives. As we entered Ulapul I was dizzy with fever, though not so ill that I didn't realize I needn't have worried about how Tribe Caereni would perceive us. As soon as they caught sight of Briallen, she was the focus.

"Briallen! She returns!"

The shout went up as we approached the roundhouse in the center of the village. From the open entrance a tall man with a shock of orange hair that matched his massive beard hurried from the lodge. He wore a thick golden torque decorated with the same horned kine image we'd seen on Beira's Stone. Close behind him was a man I easily recognized as Briallen's father, as he looked like an older version of her twin brother, Bryn.

Briallen and I dismounted and the girls followed us, though they didn't approach the chief but remained by the horses with their wolves. We'd learned during our fortnight-long trip that the wolves made almost everyone nervous.

Briallen bowed to the chief. "Calgacus, chief of Tribe Caereni, and his shield—"

"Come here, you bonny wee thing!" Briallen's father, shield to the chief, interrupted her. Stepping up beside his smiling chief, he opened his arms to his daughter. As she flung herself into his embrace he added, "Where is that dunderheid brother of yours? Late, as usual?"

Briallen squeezed her father and then stepped back. "Bryn is dead, Father. He died protecting the Iceni queen against the Romans."

Her father's face drained of color and his shoulders slumped. His chief rested a hand on his shoulder, saying, "Och, Colin, it hurts my heart to hear of it."

Colin nodded and swallowed. "We'll tell your mum together."

Then both men looked to me. I moved forward so that I stood beside Briallen. She cleared her throat and wiped her eyes and continued with her interrupted introductions. "Calgacus, chief of Tribe Caereni, and his shield, my father, Colin, 'tis my honor to introduce to you Herself—"

This time it was the chief who interrupted Briallen. "Boudicca, queen of the Iceni, Andraste's Victory, and the woman who united the southern tribes against the plague of Romans infesting those lands." Calgacus moved to stand before me. He bowed his head. "You are most welcome here, mighty queen."

I met his eyes. They were a gray blue that matched the ocean. In a voice rough with illness I said, "I am queen no more. I am but a woman asking for succor for herself and her two"—I paused and placed my hand over my rounding belly—"and soon three children."

His reply came with no hesitation. "Then know that Boudicca the woman and mother is as welcome in Caledonia as would be the queen of Britain. You are safe now. You may rest."

Relief added to my fevered dizziness. I bowed in turn and intended to speak eloquently about my love for his shield's daughter, my despair at the death of her brother, and my appreciation for the sanctuary he offered, but I could not catch my breath. My vision went black and then I fell.

CHAPTER XLVI

They thought I would lose the babe. I knew that but not much more for many days. Between fever dreams where Maldwyn died over and over followed by Rhan leaping into his funeral pyre, I heard, as if from far away, women's voices discussing whether my child would live or die. *She will live!* I wanted to shout, but the dreams trapped me again and I could not speak. When my fever finally broke, my first words were, "The babe? Is she . . ."

Briallen was at my side, bending over me. "The babe is well."

"Enfys? Ceri?" I croaked.

"Och, the bairns are teaching their wolves to fish. All is well, my queen."

I cleared my throat. "Don't call me that."

She raised a brow but said nothing and instead helped me gulp a cup of cool water. As I drank, my babe fluttered and then kicked. Hard. Causing me to grimace.

"How long?" I asked.

"Three days. But you're mending now, so all is truly well," she said.

And as usual Briallen was right. I recovered quickly. Ulapul was situated on the coast, a thriving port village that was the gateway to the northwest and the rest of the coastal Caereni lands. Their hearty fish stew strengthened me, and soon I was able to join Calgacus and Colin on the practice field with the rest of the Caereni warriors. Though my babe continued to swell my stomach, I was determined to be useful. I refused to be treated like a deposed queen. At first Calgacus argued with me, but I easily found his weakness and prevailed. The Caereni bred garrons, small but sturdy horses they farmed with and rode into battle, but the tribe lacked chariots. When Calgacus and Colin understood that I could teach their blacksmiths how to make chariots that could be used over the rough Highlands *and* train their warriors as drivers, the chief relented, becoming more and more excited as the first chariots took shape and warriors clamored to learn the skill of driving.

So I was useful. My babe grew steadily, moving strongly within me. My daughters thrived, and did teach their wolves how to fish, much to the amusement and wonder of Tribe Caereni.

And still I was unmoored.

The tribe built a roundhouse for me near their herd of garrons. I enjoyed training the intelligent little horses, though I often thought of Ennis and Finley. Almost as often as I thought of Maldwyn. I could not help it. Not with his child growing within me. I thought of how much he would love working with the garrons and imagined his cornflower eyes shining as he spoke soft words enticing them to trust him, love him. And they would. He had been easy to love.

I tried not to think of Rhan.

The Caereni had no Druid, though their healer had trained on Ynys Môn. I questioned Calgacus about other Druids in his tribal territory and he answered with great sadness that he knew of not one in Caledonia.

I tried and failed not to think of Rhan.

The people of Tribe Caereni were strong and honest. Like Briallen and Bryn, they laughed easily and often. Famous for their fishing skills and the intricate knot work created by their artists, the tribe was well respected and prosperous. The women of the tribe welcomed me warmly. They even adopted the tradition of Arianell's Day. I would never be Caereni, but I could easily appreciate their tribal pride. It made me miss Tasceni deeply.

Ulapul was framed by rolling mountains, beautiful and craggy, covered with heather. I liked to explore them, finding some peace as I walked ancient sheep paths. It was on a ridge overlooking the village that I found a large rock shaped like a raven. As the babe grew and the days became shorter and colder, I took to daily walking the path to what I thought of as Andraste's rock. I would leave offerings there to my goddess—brightly colored shells, feathers, bowls of milk and honey, choice pieces of succulent fried fish. I spoke to Andraste there, telling her the things I could not say to anyone else. How much I missed my life, my people, my home, my loves. How unmoored I continued to be. And how very much I wanted to know that she forgave me.

Andraste did not answer. She gave no sign. It was as if I'd never been her Victory.

I understood. Truly I did. I'd lost. The Romans had defeated me, and through me all of Britain. Only Caledonia was out of their grasp, but every tribesman and -woman in the Highlands prepared. Rome would come. They always did. Perhaps Caledonia would fall, too. I'd opened the door to their invasion when I'd failed Andraste. I could easily imagine the goddess's disappointment in me. It could not have been greater than the disappointment I felt in myself.

Samhain neared. Harvest was complete. Snow was in the air and whitening the mountains. I awakened early from a dream I could not remember, but from which I woke speaking Andraste's name. By now the babe was so large I could not get comfortable. Restlessly I paced the roundhouse I shared with my daughters and Briallen. Then, not wanting to awaken them, I draped a heavy fur-lined cloak around me, poured mead in a wooden bowl, and went out into a world turned gray. Fog had wafted in from the port, thick and blanketing. I was glad I'd walked the path to Andraste's rock so many times that I did not worry about finding my way, even in the breath of the dragon.

The breath of the dragon . . .

I wished for my sword as a chill fingered down my spine and pain tightened my belly. I grimaced and rubbed where the babe kicked against my rib. *They're just practice contractions, preparing me for the birth, and the fog is just fog—not the breath of a dragon, not sent by Andraste—and there are no Romans hiding within it.*

I took several long breaths and kept walking. It felt good to move, though I had to pause often as my stomach tightened. By the time I reached Andraste's rock I could not deny that the pains were well beyond practice. The babe was coming. I didn't fear the birth. Enfys and Ceri had been born with no problems. There was no reason for me to worry that this babe would not be the same.

Another wave of pain gripped me. I leaned against Andraste's rock and forced myself to breathe deeply, steadily.

My mother isn't here. She will not be here to comfort me during the birth. She will not be here to greet her newest grandchild. This birth will not be the same as my other two.

Still I did not start back for the village. I leaned against Andraste's rock, yearning for my mother and wishing for my goddess. As the sun lifted over the horizon it burned off the fog and I was mesmerized by the colors that painted the sky. It was as if I'd never seen such vibrant pinks and blues, yellows and oranges.

Then with a jolt I realized that I *had* seen those colors before—the last time I'd seen the breath of the dragon—in Annwn. My heartbeat thundered in my ears and my hand found the part of the boulder that formed the raven's beak. I caressed it as if it were alive. *Had I been compelled here today?*

Between contractions, I poured the bowl of mead around the boulder and then leaned against it again as another wave of pain crested and broke over me. I wiped the damp hair from my face. Over the past several months it had grown, and now the ends dusted my shoulders. I shook it back, wishing I'd thought to tie it up before I'd left. No matter. I should return and have Briallen go for the healer.

I pushed off the rock, took a step, and liquid gushed from between my legs, followed by pain that clawed at me and took me to my knees. Panting, I rode the wave and then tried to struggle to my feet, slipped in the bloody wetness that soaked the ground beneath me, and fell hard on my knees, gasping at the jolt.

Another contraction threatened to drown me in pain, and my body bowed as I struggled to breathe. When it released me I was too weak to stand. All I could do was shiver and pant with my face pressed against the wet ground.

A sob escaped my throat. And then another. And another. Before the next contraction pulled me under, I cried a single, beseeching word: *"Andraste!"*

Pain tunneled my vision. I made a guttural sound, more animal than human, as the contraction tore through my body.

I have to move. I have to get back to the village.

I tried to stand again and made it to my feet in time to hear wings flutter behind me. I turned to see a raven had perched on Andraste's rock. If I dared I could reach out and stroke its ebony beak as I had the rock moments before. Another contraction engulfed me, and the strength in my legs dissolved. I fell to my knees again. Staring up at the raven, I panted through the pain. When it released me I sobbed my agony to the creature.

"Tell Andraste I'm sorry! I ask that she forgive me. I know I failed her. I'm sorry. I'm so sorry." My tears mixed with snot and sweat. I rested my forehead against the rock, glad of its coolness.

"There is nothing to forgive, my Victory."

With a gasp I looked up. Standing on the rock was the goddess. She wore a woad-blue dress embroidered with silver knots that interlinked to form ravens. Her cloak was made of black feathers that glistened in the rising sun.

"Andraste!" I sobbed. "I'm so sorry. They're dead. The Iceni. Our people. Because of me. They're dead."

"No, child. They are not dead because of you. They are dead because of betrayal and the greed of Rome. Neither was caused by you, my Victory."

"How can you call me that? I failed you. I wasn't victorious. I lost. We lost. Britain is ruled by Rome."

Andraste bent and brushed my sweat-soaked hair back from my face. "Oh, my darling, my Victory, you have not failed me. You planted a seed that will root and grow until it becomes mightier than the tallest sacred oak and spreads farther than even the grasses surrounding our Tasceni. And when finally that seed is harvested, it will sustain a nation, our nation. Britain will throw off the yoke of

Rome and become mighty." The goddess spread wide her arms so that the raven-wing cloak became a veil. "Behold!"

Through Andraste's cloak, I saw the future. I witnessed how my country, my people, changed but survived and thrived. Generation after generation stretched out before me, so different, and yet their spirit remained—strong and free.

When the vision faded I looked through tears up at Andraste. "But they will have forgotten you."

The goddess smiled. "No. Every time they stand together, they remember me and embody you, my beloved Victory." The goddess bent and took my face between her hands. She kissed me as she had on that first day, like a mother, on my forehead, on each cheek, and finally on my lips. Then she said, "To show my love for you, I shall gift you with the same—love." Then the goddess straightened, raised her arms to the sky, and with a wild cry became a raven that circled me three times before disappearing into the eastern horizon.

I squinted as she seemed to fly into the rising sun, and then my eyes closed as I was engulfed in another tide of pain. When it finally released me, I was dazed. Andraste had left me here, alone, to birth my child. I drew several long breaths, in and out, trying to calm the panic that clawed at me along with the pain I knew would come again and again and again.

My gaze returned to the eastern horizon and I blinked. Wiped my eyes with my cloak and blinked again. Was it Andraste returned?

No.

It was a figure on a horse racing toward me. I realized two things at once. The horse was too large to be a garron, and it seemed familiar.

It could not be. I was delirious with pain, and as I thought it another contraction flooded me, and this time I wanted to push. I had to push.

"No!" I sobbed, fighting against the overwhelming need. "Not here!" I was struggling to stand again when the sound of the horse's pounding hooves returned my gaze to it.

I did know the horse. I couldn't, but I did. The big gray stallion slid to a halt just feet from where I slumped against Andraste's rock as his rider dropped from his back and closed the small space between us—and then I was in her embrace.

"Rhan!" My hands touched her face, her arms, her hands. She was there, and even though she had a pink scar that ran from her cheekbone down to her neck, she was alive and whole.

"My beloved! How are you—"

Another contraction took control of my body. "The babe comes." I managed to rasp the words before I could do nothing but bear down and pant for breath.

"I'm here. I'm here." Rhan shifted my body so that my back was pressed against the goddess's rock for support again. She pulled up the skirts of my dress and knelt between my legs. "I can see the head! The babe's hair is red like yours! Push, Boudicca!"

I braced myself against the rock, stared down at my best friend, my love, and pushed. In a rush of wet, the babe was born, sliding into Rhan's hands as if they were what she had been waiting for.

"A girl! Maldwyn was right." Rhan's voice trembled with joy. "You and he have a daughter!"

"Arianell." I spoke her name like a prayer as Rhan placed her on my chest. "Her name is Arianell."

A shadow fell on us. Rhan glanced up and her face lit with wonder. "Look!"

My gaze lifted. Circling us, ravens darkened the sky, too many to count. As we watched them, Rhan took me and Arianell in her arms and held us close, and through the ravens' calling voices I heard my goddess speak.

"In blessed Arianell my Victory lives on . . ."

FROM THE AUTHOR

I can't remember when I first heard Boudicca's story. I suspect it was in my childhood and had something to do with my father. Dad was a voracious reader, and because I always wanted to do everything he did, I too became a voracious reader. He and I shared books from the time I was a preteen, so I'm pretty sure he's responsible for my knowledge of the Iceni queen as he and I went on several historical reading binges.

I do remember when I decided I wanted to tell the story of the queen of the Iceni. It was in 2007 when I was researching a time-travel romance set in Iron Age Britain. Though Boudicca was a briefly mentioned secondary character in that book, I became obsessed with her.

Fast-forward to 2019, when I began writing the first incarnation of what this book would eventually become. As I researched and worked on the manuscript, I decided that I wanted to be as historically accurate as possible while including culturally appropriate paranormal elements. I had no idea when I began this journey how difficult the "historically accurate" part would prove to be.

The first problem with being historically accurate is the fact that the Iron Age Britons (we call them Celts now, though they called themselves Britons) didn't have a written language. The Druids used Ogham symbols to communicate, warn, foretell, protect, etc., but the general populace had no written language.

I turned to Roman and Greek historians, who most definitely had a written language and who were fascinated (perhaps obsessed) with Boudicca. But there is a massive problem with their historical accounts. They were so mired in patriarchy and the belief that their societies were superior to the "barbaric Celts" that their accounts are heavily biased and much of their writing borders on salacious and even nonsensical. They seemed almost as fascinated by Boudicca as they were baffled by and frightened of her. A *woman* leading an army of 250,000-plus warriors? Surely not! Surely she was superhuman, a goddess come to earth, or perhaps a pawn . . .

So I used the Greek and Roman historians' accounts as a blueprint for the events that were a springboard to Boudicca's rise as a warrior queen and looked to the archaeological record to fill in cultural details. This, too, was problematic, as women have long been excluded from and/or not taken seriously in archaeology. And by that I don't just mean women were/are discounted as modern archaeologists. I mean that the male account of archaeological findings has always been slanted toward their point of view, which is male centered and discounts or purposefully misinterprets findings that include women of the ancient world. *Again* too much of what was written and reported was through the overbearing and often inaccurate lens of the patriarchy.

I hired an excellent research assistant, a brilliant woman who is a published author and whose educational background is in science, and we began wading through the research, determined to remove the lens of patriarchy. Please know that I am not a historian. I am a storyteller. I have done my best to remain as close to historically accurate as possible while fictionalizing a version of Boudicca's life.

Specific notes about names, languages, Annwn, and the timeline:

NAMES—I had to depend upon the Roman and Greek historians for the names of tribal chiefs, queens, their children, and their lead warriors. Those records were exasperatingly incomplete. If the Romans didn't consider them important, they weren't included in their records/reports. For instance, the queen of the Brigantes tribe was an ally to Rome and unusual because she was another warrior woman, so Queen Cartimandua's name, along with the names of her husbands, was easy to find. But the name of the chief that led Tribe Trinovantes in 60 CE is not definitively mentioned. Nor is the name of his son or daughter. Nor were the names of Boudicca's daughters, her advisors, or her high Druid. In naming my characters I decided to choose historically adjacent names. I attempted to stay in the correct century and the correct tribe, but when that failed I chose the names of Iron Age Britons.

LANGUAGES—There were three languages spoken during the Roman-invasion era—Latin, Greek, and common Brittonic (which eventually became the accepted language). My research showed that many of the Romans, especially the officers and administrators, already knew Brittonic as it's similar to the language the Gauls spoke, and they'd just come from invading the Gauls. It makes sense to me that the royal families of the tribes and their lead warriors would have learned Latin during the invasion so they could communicate with the people taxing and enslaving them.

THE OTHERWORLD OF ANNWN—The Iron Age Britons were heavily influenced by Druids. Druids weren't just spiritual leaders. They were king and queen makers. They interpreted omens. They served as judges, peacemakers, teachers, magicians, and advisors. They were leaders who were revered and who held and passed on the stories and histories of the tribes. They and the tribes believed that there were dimensions of reality that butted up to one another. The mortal realm was called Arbred. The realm of the afterlife, of goddesses and gods, where magick was commonplace, was called Annwn. Both realms were filled with nwyfre, the energy of life.

The Iron Age Britons believed that their deities frequently sent them signs and omens from Annwn. They also believed there were openings to the realm of magick through which mortals could slip or be called by their deities. These openings were usually marked by streams or archways made of trees. They also believed the veil between worlds thinned at certain times of the year (Samhain and Beltane in particular) and that ancestors who had died and crossed over to Annwn could go through the veil between worlds and visit their loved ones.

When Boudicca slips into Annwn, she is crossing a magickal bridge to her goddess. Boudicca's people would have absolutely believed their queen could access the realm of the gods. Think of her journeys to or through Annwn as traveling through an alternative reality where time flows differently and magick is the norm.

BOUDICCA'S TIMELINE—Historically Boudicca's four battles took place one right after another. I followed this for the first three battles but added a winter break before the final altercation that decided the war.

I hope you enjoyed my version of Boudicca's story. My wish is that I have brought alive the ancient Britons, their daily lives, their beliefs, their loves and losses. Above all I hope that you loved getting to know this amazing queen as much as I have.

Wishing you happy reading,
P. C. Cast

ACKNOWLEDGMENTS

Thank you to my amazing editor, Rachel Kahan, who got *Boudicca* (and me!) immediately. Rachel, you are my dream editor!

Thank you, Rebecca Scherer, for cheerleading *Boudicca* and for believing in me. You're the best.

Thanks, Dad, for conveniently fostering two wolf cubs and becoming part of their pack so that I could pick your brain for all things wolf.

I want to show my vast appreciation for the entire Morrow team! Thank you for the care and enthusiasm you've shown *Boudicca*.

ABOUT THE AUTHOR

P. C. CAST was born in the Midwest, and, after her tour in the USAF, she taught high school for fifteen years before retiring to write full time. P. C. is a member of the Oklahoma Writers Hall of Fame. Her novels have been awarded the prestigious Oklahoma Book Award, YALSA Quick Pick for Reluctant Readers, Romantic Times Reviewers' Choice Award, Booksellers' Best, and many, many more. Ms. Cast is an experienced teacher and talented speaker who lives in Oregon near her fabulous daughter, her adorable pack of dogs, her crazy Maine Coon, and a bunch of horses.

For help or simply an understanding ear, the National Domestic Violence Hotline is 800-799-7233, and the National Sexual Assault Hotline is 800-656-4673. I also recommend RAINN as a good online resource: rainn.org.